The

Walkers

of Legend

To Stacey

Best Wishs

(signature)

Book One

in

The Walkers of Legend

Series

By

MILES ALLEN

REDBAK Publishing

www.thewalkersoflegend.co.uk

The Walkers of Legend
Second Edition

A REDBAK Publishing Book: ISBN 978-0-9568320-2-3

First published in Great Britain by REDBAK Publishing.

REDBAK Publishing
PO Box 1299
Penenden Heath,
Maidstone. ME14 9PU

Printed in Great Britain by
imprintdigital.net, Devon.

Cover Illustration by
Think Tank Inc Ltd

This first book is dedicated to my family, because the long journey by the Walkers of Legend is not only shared by the author, but his loved ones too.

With sincere thanks to:
Richard and Richard, Claire, Betty and Matt
for test reading, and who gave such an enthusiastic
appeal for the book's publication.

To Editor Ben for his insight.

And yet another Richard
for the series title.

Also Matt for allowing the use of the name
Garamon and the town of Tiburn.

And extra thanks to test reader Richard for liking it
so much that he invested in the project.

The Walkers of Legend

He worked his head between the cogs and pulleys, pressing his ear against the surface of the egg-shaped pod. It was large enough to hold a single person, and he could just hear their muffled screams. The mechanism stopped, and the screaming died away. There was the brief sound of a pump on the back of the casing, a tube stiffened and bright red liquid spiralled away into a container. He sighed. It was all very efficient, necessary to maintain the increasing demands for Yan. It just wasn't the same as watching a skilled Officer of Correction getting his instruments 'dirty' first hand. After all, where was the satisfaction if you couldn't see the knife being turned, and the smell of fresh blood as it spilled out across the blade to the cries of the receiver?

He sniffed the air, wrinkling his nose. The place smelled now of metal and oil.

'Excuse me, Master.'

He untangled his head from the device, irritated that even this minor enjoyment was interrupted.

'Well?'

'I must adjust this ACU, Master.'

Lathashal looked down upon the individual. Covered in the various tools of his trade, strapped to jacket and belt, it was almost impossible to distinguish his shape. They were ordinary citizens, rising rapidly in importance at the Emperor's command after inventing their *machines*. Engineers they were. They gave their creations long obscure names, then to be shortened to three letters: 'ACU' stood for Automated Correction Unit. Idiots. The Empire had been ruled for centuries and grown powerful using magic. Now

1

these Masters of Metal had begun replacing the need for the magii's craft.

He thought about blasting the life from the wretch. *Got a machine to do that yet?* But they were protected by imperial decree, for not enough of them existed to build and maintain the increasing demand for new chambers.

He lifted his gaze and looked over the rows of identical devices fading into the gloom. The other three dungeons in the city's palace were identical to this one. There were hundreds of palaces across the Empire. More chambers were being added, and all would be occupied. The process continued day and night.

He remembered that it was time to check on the day's main event, and he turned and headed for the two stairways reserved for special visitors. The left went to the highest of the royal Elite levels, twenty-six floors above the dungeons. The right-hand stairway was a direct route to the middle of the Emperor's suites, spanning the twenty floors above the Elite. Unless you were the Emperor or in his entourage, using the right-hand stairway was punishable by torture and death.

He was neither. Today he entered the right-hand stairway.

The familiar tingling danced across his hand as he gripped the thrinium plates of his staff. With the merest exertion of will, he began to glide over the engraved stairs, passing the elaborate decorations and carvings on the walls and ceiling. He picked up speed until the images blurred into a mess of colour. With centuries of experience, he timed his deceleration perfectly to land gently on the final step and walk to the opening.

There were no doors to prevent access to the shortcut. There didn't need to be, for discipline within the Empire was absolute. The ever-increasing need for dungeon occupants saw to that.

He entered the main hallway and joined the bustling errand-fillers doing the work of the Empire in the Emperor's name. Doors opened and closed on both sides as if part of a ballet, absorbing and ejecting occupants to and from the main stream. Almost all of them were wearing the same basic white linen uniform of the servant class, moving with the same monolithic precision; eyes downcast, expressions blank. Alcoves at regular intervals held more. In contrast to those given jobs, they were still, like figurines.

One of the non-servants snapped his fingers making one of them come to life. No words were spoken as servants were not permitted to speak or listen. The non-servant moved his hands in an intricate sign-language, his arms kept low as servants were not allowed to raise their eyes. When completed, the servant silently moved off.

He swept along the wide corridor which led to the main banquet hall. The diamonds on his gold and thrinium-trimmed night-black cloak looked like stars against a moonless sky. The breadth and extended high collar gave his modest frame both width and height over everyone. It flapped gently as if in a breeze, taking only the smallest concentration to offset the weight of the garment and create the visually impressive effect. He stood out like a god amongst insects.

The corridor turned many times before he reached his destination. The main banquet hall doors stood ahead of him like monuments of art. Solid gold and etched with deep carvings, they depicted the Emperor overseeing the wonders of the Empire. At almost four times the height of an ordinary person, each was beyond conventional mechanics to move.

As he approached, six journeymen magiis began to focus, three on each door. The doors resisted for a moment before cracking open. He picked up his pace a little to test them. If he was forced to pause because the doors were not open far enough, the magiis would be subjected to correction. Their stances changed as they realised their duty needed to be completed sooner than expected. The weight of the doors briefly resisted the increased magical influence before widening more rapidly.

He reached the threshold to see veins standing out on the necks and foreheads of the journeymen. He walked through, narrowly missing the doors on either side.

He slowed his pace to allow them ample time to close them. He needed privacy for what was about to happen.

The semi-circular room represented half of the floor level. Finished in white marble, it boasted a hundred servant alcoves spaced around the edges, separated by tall windows. The Emperor's floors were higher than any other building in the capital, providing tantalising views of the city when the long white drapes parted in the breeze.

He stopped at the head table opposite the figure on the other side. It was the Grand Regent Estatoulie, next in line to the ultimate power in the land. Lathashal considered the man's clothing as bright and garish as his own robe was dark and imposing.

'My dear Lathashal,' said the Regent. 'There seems to have been a problem with your gift to the Emperor.' He then peered down upon the smouldering remains of the Emperor, and smiled. 'Hail me,' he said, raising the finest of Ashnorian crystal to toast his success. He then picked up the priceless decanter and poured the two-hundred year-old wine over the bones to extinguish the fading embers. 'There, you see?' he said to the hissing skeleton, 'I'm not *completely* heartless.'

Lathashal chuckled. Not that he found the Regent amusing, but a measure of sucking up was prudent in the presence of the next Emperor. He watched as the Regent looked to the irreplaceable decanter for a moment, shrug, and drop it onto his victim's spine.

Both shattered.

Lathashal raised a hand and the lid from one of the food platters drifted over and covered the remains of the box that contained his magical firetrap.

'You're sure it was a painful death?' Estatoulie asked.

Lathashal knew this to be rhetorical. Even though the screams of the Emperor were contained within a bubble of silence as part of the trap, his movements and expressions would have removed any doubt as to his excruciating final seconds. Even so the magii knew the Regent well enough to know that he needed to be indulged in his triumph.

'Utterly, Grand Regent.'

'And you are sure that he cannot be recovered?'

Again the question bordered on the ridiculous; so little remained.

'Not even I could revive him, Regent.'

'There are more powerful magiis than you in the realm.'

Lathashal bowed his head at the retort to his conceit. 'A few perhaps, but I am certain that not even they could recover his eminence this time.'

The Regent nodded with satisfaction. 'Fine workmanship too,' he conceded. 'I particularly enjoyed the moment when he pulled his hand away from the trap and it remained attached to the handle. He looked to the stump of his arm with such fascinated revulsion. Was that part of the design?'

'Merely a fortunate side effect, Grand Regent. Such violent energies can never be fully predictable where mere flesh is concerned.' He watched Estatoulie nod as if understanding. He knew the man had as much chance of comprehending magic as a hawk knowing why it can fly.

'Call the guard on your way out,' said Estatoulie absently, still studying the corpse.

'Grand Regent,' replied the magii, bowing just enough to meet the demands of etiquette.

He turned and walked back to the main doors. The internal servant gave warning to the six magiis on the other side. The doors began to open well in advance of Lathashal's arrival.

As he exited, he beckoned to the Guard Captain whose job it was to protect the occupants whilst within the hall.

'The Grand Regent asks for you.'

The Captain froze.

Lathashal was not surprised at the reaction. His duty was, in any practical sense, ceremonial. The banquet hall resided in the centre of the Emperor's palace, which itself was in the centre of the greatest city. Nothing requiring the presence of a guard should ever happen here. Security was assured.

'If you keep the Regent waiting another heartbeat, I shall rip the organ from your body and keep you alive to watch it pump its final beats.'

The Captain snapped out of his inactivity. 'Yes, Master Lathashal!' He set off, adjusting his red, white and gold uniform. A pointless exercise for it would be immaculate. The penalty for having anything less than perfect presentation was gradia five correction.

Lathashal moved without hurry into a nearby room that he arranged to be empty. He concentrated and pictured the inside of the Banquet Hall around the Regent. The vision came alive in his mind.

Estatoulie was pointing to the small throne beside him. Two servants left their recesses and began energetically cleaning the blackened markings made by the previous occupant. As he sat, the chair was pushed under him with exact precision. He pointed to some nearby grapes. These were passed to him. He sat back, picking at each one of the perfectly selected fruits, popping them into his mouth.

'Regent Estatoulie, you summoned me?'

The voice came from out of the vision's view and Lathashal slewed the angle to encompass the guard Captain too.

Estatoulie replied after a measured delay and without looking up.

'The Emperor has been assassinated, Captain. I want a thorough investigation. No stone shall remain unturned. Do you understand?'

'Yes Regent,' said the soldier, his face draining of colour. The most heinous and unthinkable of all crimes had been committed on his watch.

'And Captain ...'

'Yes, Regent?' stammered the doomed man.

'All evidence shall point to your superior officer, who I shall ensure is executed for his treason, and you shall replace. Understood?'

'Yes, Regent!'

'Choose one of your men to replace your current position. Oh, and have two of the others executed as conspirators,' Estatoulie added with a casual wave of his hand. 'Congratulations on your promotion. Dismissed.'

'Yes, yes, thank you, Regent,' said the soldier as he backed away, bowing several times more than was demanded.

Lathashal broke the magical connection. So the Regent had kept his word and not implicated him in the killing. Obviously the new Emperor considered him more use alive.

He was pleased. In exchange for his magical services in dealing with the Emperor, Estatoulie had agreed that the magiis of the major northern city of Straslin would come under Lathashal's command. Then he was to assist the Attack-General Zanthak and cross the Hammerhead Mountains and conquer Mlendria, the last of the free lands. The increasing need for Yan was again creating a restless population who were being subjected to greater torture for lesser and lesser crimes. A fresh influx of imperial subjects was required. The invasion would be from Straslin, beginning in nine months.

He relished the thought of attacking the mages of other races, as they were puny in comparison to their Ashnorian counterparts. The reason for that imbalance was still the most closely guarded secret in the Empire.

He briefly looked up at the mirrored silver-golden surface of the sphere atop his staff. With the briefest concentration, wisps of blue energy formed on its surface to disappear into tiny holes like water spiralling down a drain.

His thin lips pulled into a self-satisfied smile.

Chapter 1 – Nobody's home

Such was the emotional high brought about by the winter thaw that it was all Garamon could do to refrain from singing. He restricted himself to jogging and springing over the scattered logs and stumps that covered the wood. The cool wind in his face felt exhilarating and he lengthened his stride, his young legs soaking up the pace with ease.

He decided today was the day he would visit his friend deep in the forest. Chayne's cabin was isolated during the winter months and this was the first chance to get through.

Chayne aspired to be a mage, an ambition that did not come without hazards. The frequent mishaps that accompanied his magical experimentation did not stem his inexhaustible thirst for knowledge. Garamon recalled the time when his axe blade was the subject of an experiment with magical oil that was supposed to make the blade shine. It instead stained it with a mix of blue and yellow hues. No matter what they did they couldn't remove it. Garamon hid the axe from his father for weeks before the colour faded.

He recalled the first day they met…

It was just after his fourteenth birthday, an age eagerly awaited. Fourteen meant freedom. He was allowed to travel on his own beyond the Stumpies: the name used by locals for the clearing made by the town's woodsmen, a natural playground of tree stumps. More importantly, he was allowed to take his grandfather's axe out without supervision. It was such an honour, and one of the proudest moments of his life.

He leapt out into the yard and raced off away with uncontained joy.

'Don't be late back,' he heard his father call after him, 'or you'll not hold it for another year!'

Garamon waved a hand into the air without breaking his sprint.

Even with the heavy axe he ran like a mountain hare to the far side of the Stumpies. He stood on what felt to him like the edge of a new world, waiting to be conquered. He'd been out here many times with his father and brother of course, hunting or exploring, but never alone. It was a very different feeling.

The wood beyond the clearing went on for miles. The maps in the library showed a vast lake there and he'd often pleaded with his parents to take him. They'd said it was too far and wolves roamed those parts.

He decided instead to head for one of the paths that lead deeper into the wood. He went as far as the evil Mage's cabin.

As he reached the centre of a clearing, he enacted a scene in his mind.

'Take that!' A swipe to the left.

'Ah ha! come up behind me would you!' A swipe to the right.

As always, the axe felt lighter and faster than it should have done for its size. His father said it was magical. Garamon suspected that this was an exaggeration, just to add a little spice to the boys' lives.

He continued his dance of death, fighting unseen foes in the dappled sunlight. His imagination seemed matched only by his enthusiasm.

After fifteen minutes of this exhausting play, he stopped. There was a noise behind him and he swung around to see a Draguer, a humanoid swamp creature normally found far to the north. It was well known for its deadly attacks on people with its vicious teeth and claws. He sprang at it, swinging the axe straight at its neck. He tumbled past, losing his balance and ended face down in the mix of twigs and leaves.

9

He rolled, jumping to his feet for the counter attack. To his surprise it just stood there facing him. He ran at the creature again, this time bringing the axe down squarely on its head. The blade passed straight through its body without resistance, narrowly missing Garamon's foot. The apparition still hadn't moved. He reached out his hand. It went straight through.

He dropped into a fighting stance.

'Where are you old man? Your ruses do not fool me!'

The illusion dissipated.

'I am here,' came a voice from behind.

He span around. The speaker was dressed in a dark plain blue robe and wore simple cheap sandals that could be obtained in town. His face was pale and unthreatening. His hair, pure white, was striking though. His sister would no doubt have considered him handsome. He was around Garamon's age.

'Come no closer! I could have killed that creature if it were real and many more if they dared to enter this land.' He proudly stuck out his chest, placing his axe between his two hands in a gesture of defiance.

'I think your pride is misplaced for one who only has knowledge of defeating trees. It would not carry you far against the foe I have just placed before you.'

'You know nothing. I could best it, and your parlour tricks.'

'But my comments were to help, for they were the truth.'

'I will never trust you. You are evil.'

'I hope you will come to learn that is not the case,' he replied calmly. 'In fact, as a measure of good will, I will show you a little of what the wider world has to offer.'

He began a short incantation which appeared to test him to the full. Garamon held his ground, not wishing to show the mage any weakness. After a few seconds the spell completed and a harsh ring emanated from his axe accompanied by a short flurry of magical light upon the blade's edge.

Nearly dropping the weapon he jumped back holding the axe at arm's length as if it were to bite him.

'What have you done!' he shouted. 'If you've damaged my father's axe I will make you pay in blood!'

The mage replied with a smile. 'Swing it,' he instructed.

After a few seconds and a confirming nod from the mage, he gently did so.

'It's lighter, I can swing it faster!' He gave it a few wider swings, as if he was in combat.

'This is great! Can you do more?'

'I can, but not today. I am a novice and the magic drains me. It will last only a short while I'm afraid. However come back tomorrow at the same time and maybe we can experiment with one or two others I've been working on.'

Garamon swung his axe again and looked up at the smiling mage's face. He smiled back and came to a decision. 'My name is Garamon of Tiburn.'

'I am Chayne,' replied the enigmatic figure, dipping his head slightly.

'Of where?'

The young mage thought about this for a moment before looking behind him to where his cabin could just been seen. He shrugged. 'Just up the hill a bit ...'

Garamon laughed.

Since that day they had become strong friends and Garamon spent most of his free time of the following eight years with him...

He came back to the present, his thoughts interrupted by a glimpse of the cabin through the trees. He slowed and continued to the edge of the clearing he created the previous spring. He was met with disappointment, there was no smoke coming from the stone chimney. This was unusual at this time of year, for even if Chayne was visiting town, he left the fire on for his pet.

Garamon flinched at the thought of the cat. Not only was it the fattest he'd seen, it had striking colouring and a definite psychopathic nature. He'd even seen it see off a panther that dared to enter the vicinity.

He walked out into the clearing to look for clues to his friend's absence. The door was partially open and the lock splintered. He moved across the clearing quickly, taking care to avoid the deeper snow to reduce the noise of his footfalls.

He considered the options. It wasn't an animal. No beast could make such a clean entry. He considered thieves, the most likely possibility from the evidence. From the depth of snow in the gap of the door, it happened some time ago. He readied his axe anyway. He'd never used it in anger, but having been a woodcutter since he could lift a blade, he at least knew how to swing one.

He reached the door and listened, hearing nothing. Seeing little through the gap he pushed the door. The swollen wood resisted and it made a crack as it gave up and opened. He stood shocked at the scene. The place was ransacked and covered in light snow. He moved into the room, stepping over items that were strewn across the floor. He headed for the bedroom, visualising his friend having being murdered while he slept. The mattress was upturned against the wall and the furniture had signs of being searched. There was no sign of his friend.

He moved to the remaining room. Chayne called it The Lab. It was barely large enough to fit his worktable and stool.

The door was mostly open, exposing the usual charred walls and surfaces of this beleaguered area. Standing in the doorway, the room looked as surreal as ever, except for the thin layer of snow on everything.

'Chayne?' he said weakly, barely able to stop his voice from breaking.

He opened the door until it pushed on something behind. Bile rose into his mouth as he thought that it might be the body of his friend. He stepped around the door.

Something leapt at him out of the shadow.

He reactively pulled his axe in front of him, deflecting the thing away and stumbling back out of the room to land on his back.

Chayne's cat walked out of the room. It gave an *eeeow* and nudged at his boot with its head, purring.

'Hello, *Fireball*,' Garamon said with distaste.

He felt a warm trickle down his cheek and wiped away some blood where the cat had scratched him.

The animal made another *eeeow*.

'Well you haven't lost any weight. Either your master's not been gone as long as I think, or you've been looking after yourself well enough.'

He stood back up and stepped over the cat into the lab. He checked behind the door and saw it was Chayne's heavy lab stool. He studied the room. It smelled foul. Under the snow, every surface was blackened and felt greasy.

'Nothing unusual here at least,' he said absently.

He began studying for clues to the mage's whereabouts. He noticed small drops of dark red, only just visible, splattered around the surfaces of the room. He bent down and examined the spots on the bench more closely.

A drop of blood fell from his face wound. As it landed, apart from its fresh appearance, it looked identical to the dried version. He looked towards Fireball again.

'Too little for a sword or knife wound,' he pondered aloud to the cat accusingly. 'I think somebody disturbed you from your sleep and paid the price.' Fireball *eeeowed* indifferently, licking a paw and ignoring the allegation.

Garamon decided that whatever happened here was long over, and went about what repairs he could make to the cabin. He moved back to the outside door. After a few bangs of his axe head, he straightened the lock enough to secure it. He then worked on restoring the fire and clearing up the worst of the mess.

An hour later, and although still damp from the melted layer of snow, the place was at least warm and a little more like a home.

He looked outside and cursed. The light was almost gone. He would never make it home before dark. While his father would consider these special circumstances, his mother would be sick with worry. His older brother fell during a climbing accident four years ago. His parents had surmised he was holed up with one of the many friendly families in the region. He was found dead the next day. The life priest told them that he died in the night from the fall, and that if they found him sooner he could have been saved. Mother was inconsolable, blaming father and herself for the decision not to search. Since then neither he nor his sister came back later than dusk.

He melted snow to provide Fireball with drinking water and placed more logs on the fire for the night. Locking the cabin as best he could, he left.

He made slow progress in the dark and was relieved at last to see the lights of the farm. Vaulting over the perimeter fence he ran through the vegetable field. In the lantern light of the porch he could see his mother weeping in his sister's arms, looking out across the field for any sign of him.

'It's okay, I'm fine!' His sister snapped her head up in his direction. Squinting to locate him, she threw an arm up in his direction, speaking to their mother who ran the remaining steps to meet him. They embraced and she sobbed uncontrollably.

'Dad's called the Rangers you know, he's out with them looking for you. I've been here for an hour with mom upset like this. I should have been out with Jarrow Mackelson this evening. He was taking me to a dance.'

'Sorry sis. Something's up. It's good the Rangers are out.'

'What is it?'

'Not now. Let's take Mum inside and get her some warm milk.'

14

His sister nodded and headed off toward the kitchen.

Holding his mother in his arms, he guided her back into the house.

It was midnight before his father returned with three Rangers. Garamon's mother leapt up and ran into her husband's arms and started weeping again. He held her tight whilst looking over her to Garamon. He looked half-puzzled and half-annoyed, but did nothing in front of his distraught wife. The Rangers didn't look too pleased either.

'Annie, I need to talk to the boy, I'll do it in the kitchen, okay?' She pulled away.

'No arguing Renous, not tonight. I couldn't bear it.'

'I promise. Now go sit down and rest.' A glance to his daughter and she took her mother's arm, leading her to her bedroom. He then gestured Garamon towards the kitchen. Garamon walked under his glare. His father followed and shut the door behind them.

'I hope there is a mighty good explanation for your lateness, half the town's Rangers are now out looking for you.'

'It's Chayne, Father,' replied Garamon. 'I think he's been taken, maybe killed.'

His father looked to the Rangers and exchanged what Garamon thought was a knowing look. 'Tell us what you know.'

'I took my first run out there to see him today. I found his cabin broken into, the fire was out and he was nowhere to be seen. There was even some dried blood on the floor. What do we do?'

'The Rangers will handle it from here,' his father replied. He then bade the Rangers goodbye and they left.

Garamon knew the Rangers to be meticulous with such things. Their lack of questioning was telling.

'Father, what's going on?'

'Nothing son. Leave it to the Rangers, they will sort it out.'

'You know something, don't you?' His voice was rising and his father put his hand up, gesturing to remind him of his mother in the other room.

Garamon dropped his voice to a harsh whisper. 'You *do* know something! What is it, what's going on? Please tell me, he's my friend!'

His father seemed to consider the wisdom of his next words.

'There have been kidnappings in the area.'

'Kidnappings!' blurted Garamon, and raised his hand quickly over his mouth. His father frowned and waited until his son was back under control.

'Five over the last few months. All young mages.'

Garamon's eyes opened wide in horror. 'No! Where were they taken, who has them? We must organise a party and rescue them!' He was getting louder again.

'Sit *down* Gar,' said his father in a hushed voice.

Garamon did and attempted to calm down again. He wanted to run out and search the whole wood.

His father continued. 'None of the victims have been found. They were all taken from their homes at night, clearly to look like a common robbery.' Garamon was bursting with a hundred questions. His father raised a finger to put off interruption.

'We have tried everything we can. We even asked Arch-Mage Thrane for help. He agreed to locate them with a powerful spell of finding. They were either a great distance away or being shielded from his magic. We have been at a loss to locate them or uncover any clues.'

Garamon knew his father well enough. 'What are you not telling me?'

His father looked reluctant to release the next piece of information to him.

'There was one, barely detectable and inconclusive reading.'

Another pause.

'*Please* father, he's my friend, what did the spell find?'

His father looked into his eyes, as if consoling him for the news he was about to receive.

'The reading came from over the mountains to the South, across the border into Ashnoria. We checked the maps in the great library. If correct, your friend has been taken to the old city of Rulimbar.

The Ashnorians now call it Straslin.'

Chapter 2 - Breaking trust

Garamon woke from a fitful sleep in which he had dreamt about his friend in the hands of Ashnorian torturers. He heard talking from below in the house. It sounded like his father speaking to the Rangers.

He leapt out of bed and rushed out onto the landing. Three men in the green and black leather armour of the Rangers stood just inside the front door talking to his father. He grabbed his trousers and starting pulling them on, hopping his way to the top of the stairs. He stopped to complete the job and then bounded down the stairs four at a time, taking a leap out from the fifth stair as he neared the bottom. He crossed to the men just as his father bade them farewell and closed the door.

'What news, Father?'

Renous turned and held a finger up to his lips and beckoned his son to the study. Once both inside, he closed the door. 'Your mother is sleeping, let's keep it that way.'

Garamon nodded eagerly.

'The Rangers have scouted the area around Chayne's cabin. They discovered tracks buried beneath several months of snowfall. Two men dragged another between them to three horses. They believe your friend was tied to the third horse and taken south across the mountains.'

Garamon stood expectantly, waiting for words of the rescue plan. None came.

'When do we leave?'

His father shook his head. 'We do not.'

'But we must, while the Rangers can still track the trail.'

'Your friend's cabin is remote. Traces of what happened were preserved. No tracks on the southern trail would have survived.'

'I will not abandon my friend.'

'There is nothing we can do.'

'I will go after him.'

His father looked on sympathetically. 'I regret the decision, son, but some things cannot be. We will never find him now and it is still too dangerous to cross the mountains until the season's snowstorms have ended.'

'And *that's* a good enough reason to abandon him to torture or death!'

'You know well that there is much to do in preparation for the spring season. We must look after your mother and sister and the farm.'

'And who will look after Chayne?' Garamon replied bitterly. He spun around, leaving his father to stand alone.

The busy days went by as Garamon worked to complete his chores for the spring. Every waking minute, his thoughts were overflowing with the dangers that his friend could be facing. The nights were worse. Nightmares filled his restless sleep and he woke time and time again soaked in sweat from seeing visions of his friend subjected to the torturer's blade.

On the tenth night, he could endure no more. He tried to reason with his father again the next morning, but he would not relent.

Later that morning he returned home when he knew his father would be out. With his sister at school and his mother shopping for supplies in town, he prepared for his journey. He was not experienced in mountain travel, but felt that he was sensible enough to stay out of serious trouble if he was careful.

He collected up various provisions for the venture, including as much food as he could carry and his brother's old skinning knife. With his backpack full, he pulled out a note and placed it on the kitchen table. It explained that he was to visit the Spru Wealer in the next valley for a few days to take his mind from Chayne. It would buy him enough time to get to the mountains and evade the Rangers that would come after him.

He stared around the kitchen. There was a sense of unreality for what he was about to do. It struck him that he would not be back here for some time. In fact he may never return here again. His eyes returned to the note. How inadequate the words were to cover for such an eventuality. He shook his head. This was no time for doubts. He thought back to Chayne and his plight, and left the kitchen.

Crossing the main room he headed for the final thing. He stopped at the fireplace and reached up to take the axe and its scabbard.

'I hope you approve, Grandfather.'

He strapped it to his back, and with one last look around, left the house.

He jogged out across their farm stopping at the edge of the trees which marked the end of his family's land. He took a last look back. Closing his mind to his conflicting emotions, he made his way into the woods.

An hour later he was once again in sight of Chayne's cottage. He approached, ensuring that no one was nearby to ask questions. He reached the door and found it heavily barred. No doubt by the Rangers.

He felt something push against his leg, he leapt back.

'Oh you fat cat. You made me jump!'

Fireball continued to rub his legs, purring loudly.

Garamon shook his head and knelt down to the bizarre creature. In the safety of his winter gloves, he put his hand forward experimentally to stroke the creature. Fireball complied by rolling over onto its back. Garamon laughed, enjoying the unusual rapport with the animal, and began rubbing the fur on its ample belly. It responded by trapping his hand and raking it with its back claws and biting viciously. Garamon tried to pull his hand away, but the cat held on. In the end, his hand came out of the glove. He kicked out angrily in revenge for the damage to the garment and missed. He didn't know how such a ponderous-looking creature could be so agile. It at least let go of the glove. He picked it up.

'I needed this!' he shouted, waving the glove towards the animal. He tried on the glove. It had several large tears in the leather and one of the fingers was half-severed.

'I swear cat, if I don't find your master I will come back and make you into a replacement for these.' He wasted no more time on the sadistic creature and searched for signs of where the Rangers said Chayne had been loaded onto horseback. He located the spot a short distance from the cabin, with tracks heading off in the direction of the south road. He set off at an easy jog.

An hour later and his route intersected with the wide north-south trade route. He came to a halt and spied for Rangers. The way was clear.

The road led into the mountains that separated him from Ashnoria and his goal. The tall peaks had made him feel safe throughout his life, lording over the landscape as immutable protectors. Now, laden with snow and lying under dark clouds, he felt that they were watching him, mocking his resolve. He thought of Chayne again and what he was going through. He took a deep breath and set off.

He immediately tripped, landing face down in a blend of mud and trodden snow. He grunted as the air was pushed from his lungs. He turned around to scowl at the rock that caused his stumble. His eyes widened in disbelief. There, sitting on its haunches cleaning itself, was Fireball. Garamon knew next to nothing about cats, but he thought that they were inclined to be lazy animals that slept all day, exerting themselves only to get food or catch a mouse. The notion that this fat, slumbering feline could have kept up with him running for several miles seemed absurd.

He got up and brushed the snow from his clothes.

21

'Well, you'd better give up now as you won't be able to survive the mountains, and I'm not going to look after you.'

It looked up into his face and gave another eeeyow.

'Look, go away. Shoo!' he said, flicking his hands toward it.

It had no effect.

He decided there was nothing for it but to pick up his pace and outrun the creature.

He sprinted off. After a few minutes of his fastest pace, he glanced back to find no sign of the animal. He slowed back down to a normal stride and continued on.

A few hours later and he made it into the foot of the mountains. The wind was against him and this added to the problem of packed snow sticking to the tread of his boots. Fresh snow was falling and drifting onto the front of his body too. The gradient of the slope was increasing which made for even harder progress and slowed him to a walk. He decided to take short rest. They were becoming more frequent and he was starting to worry. It was nearly dark and he needed to find shelter soon.

As if to confirm his anxiety, the wind gusted and he took a step back to maintain his balance. The wagon tracks he had followed had now disappeared and he could only hope that he was still on the trail. Every direction started to look the same under the white blankct, and visibility was diminishing. A stronger gust of wind found its way into the gaps in his clothing, catching the sweat on his body and making him shiver. He gave a shrug to hoist his backpack into a more comfortable position and started to hum a tune to encourage himself. He continued his trudge through the mounting snow once more.

Another half an hour passed with no sign of shelter. Darkness fell and with it the wind increased. His pace reduced to little more than a staggering shuffle. It was no longer snowing, but the wind was picking up the icy covering on the ground, whipping it into his face. He was exhausted and unable to think beyond placing one foot in front of the other. He stumbled and fell to his knees. Immediate relief flooded through his body at the rest and he struggled to get the will to stand again. He looked down. Through the stinging blasts of icy snow he could see his clothing covered in a sheet of ice. Guessing the danger that it represented, he hauled himself to his feet again, and tried to take another step. The wind gusted strongly and he toppled backwards, causing his backpack to lodge into the snow. He fought to rise, but the packs were stuck. He rocked from side to side until they freed and hauled himself to his feet with his back to the wind this time. Another blast struck him and he fell face-first into the snow. He lay there for few moments. Thoughts of his family came unbidden to his mind. He saw them sitting in the main room at home in front of the fire. His mother was knitting. He realised that he'd never paid attention to his father's activities in the evenings and he found that curious now.

His body suddenly jerked. Had he fallen asleep? His exhausted mind tried to alert him to the danger. He felt strangely cosy. Did he find the cave after all? He tried to focus his thoughts.

Chapter 3 - Warriors shadow

Opening her eyes she saw Kinfular her mate. His smooth, lean frame, blurry through her still-awakening vision, was moving swiftly and with purpose around their tepee. He was the *Hlenshar*, the tribe's warrior-champion.

'Good morning my love,' she said in a sleepy tone, stretching out her long and lithe body. The use of the word, and the sight of his brown, indistinct form, took her thoughts back to the previous night of wonderful passion. Kin was the finest lover she had bed. To her knowledge he had taken no other since they had joined that first time two years ago. She wondered if he loved her. She smiled despite herself. Of course not, he is a male, a warrior especially so.

She cocked her head to one side as her vision cleared. His body came into focus. Her smile broadened.

'Come to bed, it is cold.'

Ignoring her he thrust his spare leather tunic into his rucksack.

She sat up, the animal skin cover she made falling smoothly from her olive-tanned skin to the bed.

'You can be quick,' she giggled seductively, eyes sparkling.

Kinfular looked up, his eyes falling upon her naked form. He shook his head and continued to pack with even more vigour.

'What is wrong?' Shinlay threw back the cover and leapt forward to grab his arm as packed another item. He reacted swiftly, shrugging his elbow and making a sharp guttural sound. The force threw her back onto the bed.

He stopped.

His gaze came up to meet her crumpled expression, tears welling in her eyes. He dropped the clothing and climbed onto the bed, kneeling beside her and taking her hands in his.

'A Ranger came. Their bandits attack early this year.'

'No,' she replied, her voice unsteady, 'It should be another month yet.'

He stroked her face.

She turned from him, leaping from the bed.

'I will come with you.'

'No. You are the First Daughter. Ultal is old and yet to sire a son.'

She spun around, restraining her voice to prevent others from hearing her through the skin walls of their home and humiliating him.

'I will not stay while you face death. If you were to die, I will be beside you to travel to the Mystics. I will not wait here hoping that each day is the day you return to me.'

'Your father will refuse.'

'My father need not know until it was too late. I could slip out in the night and catch you up.'

Kinfular's face went stern once again. 'You would bring such shame upon him? He lives as the finest example to our people, and you would set this to the winds so easily?'

'You are right my love,' Shinlay replied in soft tones and stroking his face in return. 'Such thoughts are wrong.'

Kinfular wasn't fooled by her sudden change. He lifted her head to set his eyes intently with hers. 'I mean it. I would bring you back here myself if you disobeyed.'

She stared back for a moment, as if trying to see some crack in his resolve. Eventually, her eyes dropped and she nodded her head in defeat.

Kinfular lifted her from her feet and hugged her. 'I will be back,' he whispered.

The group assembled as the sun was at its deepest red, dropping below the mountain skyline. Eighteen warriors in all, including two Elites acting as Kinfular's personal guard, as befitting the tribe's Hlenshar. Although a small team, they were exceptional mountain fighters. Their lack of the heavier armour possessed by the armies in the North gave them the advantage of speed and agility. But most of all, they were feared for their uncanny night-time vision. This last skill made them terrifying opponents. Their enemies were forced to maintain extra guards at night. They had a short life expectancy, meaning those in camp could never sleep soundly. This, over time, stole their resolve and strength in a fight.

The warriors stood in a line in front of the chieftain, identical but for the shield-less ThreeSwords, the huge Sholster and his massive wooden shield and club, and Kinfular with his unique buckler. Round and smaller than the normal tribal shields it was mounted with strangely-shaped hooks that, in the hands of the skilled Hlenshar, could trap a sword and even snap thinner blades.

The formalities of the day gave some comfort to warriors and loved ones alike. Blessings and good luck charms were given as was their custom. Kinfular was given a Dintoose tail by Shinlay. It was a tiny mammal whose fur was fine and soft to touch, but difficult to work with. It was an example of her skills that she platted the tail into a sword crossing a heart. It represented a block against a fatal strike. It was exquisite. He tied it around his neck and rested his hand over it, whispering a short prayer to his war god, Rolk.

As the orange rays left the tops of the mountains, the group assembled in front of the Chieftain. Kneeling, each warrior kissed the hand of their tribal leader, and in turn received his personal blessing and gift of two Locan leaves. The leaves grew in the most inaccessible cracks, high up on the exposed faces of the mountains. Collecting them was dangerous. Their ability to prevent infections forming in wounds made the leaves invaluable in battle. They had saved many limbs and lives of warriors.

When the last warrior was blessed, the Chieftain completed the final travelling prayer and said his personal goodbyes.

With his fighters, Kinfular headed from the camp, their dark night-clothing soon fading them into the shadows of the low light. They headed east for a route that would bring them down to the Sinserti plain; an open landscape that took a day's hard run to cross. On the far side were the Hammerheads, the vast and treacherous mountain range that separated the Mlendrians from the rest of the land.

They moved into an open section of ground and he could see all of his men. First was the lean frame of Rainen. The least powerful of the group, his value came from his acute senses and cunning. He was always Kinfular's first choice as scout.

Next was Sholster. Almost seven feet tall, he looked impossibly clumsy in comparison to the nimble Rainen. He wielded a huge shield and a massive club. The sight of these alone was terrifying to his enemies.

Then there was ThreeSwords, the first of his personal guard. He was a jet-black-skinned Heslarian from the land of the so-called Black Devils, far to the South. He was an exemplary swordsman, second only to Kinfular himself. With a real name that was difficult to pronounce for Kinfular's people, he soon adopted a fighting name based on his choice of carrying three swords into combat. They were strapped to his back in a specially crafted triple scabbard. No one had ever seen him draw the one in the centre scabbard.

Kinfular slowed his paced to drop back level with the veteran Grast, the other of his personal elite guard. His best friend since childhood and fifteen years his senior, all of Kinfular's battle tactics were passed through him.

'Your thoughts?' he asked his friend. The strong lungs and lean muscles that blessed his race made running almost as natural a state as walking for others.

'I was thinking of Juenni,' replied Grast in his usual warm voice.

'You have been with her twice as long as I with Shinlay. Do you not crave a younger woman?

'She is little burden to me. And my physical desire for a younger woman is less nowadays. She also nags me less each year, which I have come to find a more valuable blessing.'

Kinfular smiled and nodded his understanding. In truth it disturbed him, for it forced a realisation that his friend was getting to the point of retirement. The prospect of fighting without his long-time friend by his side was not a pleasant one. Even so he considered leaving Grast behind this time. In the faint starlight he noted the sheen of sweat covering Grast's face already.

'You are staring.'

Kinfular couldn't reply.

'It is my age.'

'You are still the finest veteran in the mountains,' rebuked Kinfular.

'That's a lie and we both know it. I'm slowing and my stamina is failing. This run is already making my lungs burn. We used to run for a day without resting. I want this to be my last time.'

Kinfular couldn't bear to hear the words, although he could not deny that the man had earned it.

'Then we shall make sure it is one to remember.'

They briefly gripped each other's forearm before Kinfular moved ahead again.

The remainder of the team trailed behind Grast, well-trained and trustworthy fighters.

Back in the camp a figure moved through the dancing shadows of the camp fires, slipping silently passed the outer sentries and heading out into the night, turning in the direction of the departed warriors.

Chapter 4 - A new life

Chayne regained consciousness with a sharp intake of breath and spluttering, water dripping from his head. It took him a few moments to gather his senses and see the man in front of him holding an empty pail.

The man's clothing was torn at the edges, the shades dull with various stains. But the look was false. His entire garb was created to look the part of a dungeon jailor. Even the dirt was imprinted as part of the fabric.

'Ling cho, Kan dor!' he shouted, staring menacingly into Chayne's eyes. The words were spoken in an educated tone, attempting to be intimidating.

Chayne brought his hand up to the pain in his nose and found that it was broken. He looked around to see that he was in a small, stone-walled room with nothing more than a low bed and a covered bucket. It *seemed* like a cell, except that everything was pristine. The floor and walls, while plain, were spotless. Most surprising was the metal bucket, which was polished. Even the wooden cover was varnished and shining.

His jailor pulled him roughly to his feet. A longer sentence was spoken in the same manner.

Chayne shook his head to remove the sluggishness in his brain, which only made his head spin and his nose ache more.

'I need to talk to somebody in authority. There has been a mistake.'

The brute gave a snarl, pulling him by the front of his tunic. Chayne heard the sound of stitching tearing. He was thrown towards the door and stumbled on the three stone stairs leading up out of the cell. The brute hauled him close to his face. More shouting followed, concluding with an attempt at an evil smile. The normal black and broken teeth expected of one of his profession were replaced with an array of perfect white and gold ones. Chayne couldn't help but jump back at the sight.

He was pushed up the stairs out of the cell into a much larger area, and then again, propelling him forward towards the centre of the room. A red robed figure sat amidst piles of parchments stacked in neat bundles. A queue of people stood before him, their clothing in a variety of colours and materials far richer than Chayne had seen before. Each held a parchment identical to the ones stacked on the desk.

The walls of the room were lined with dozens of other doors just like the one to his own cell. Few doors were open. As with his cell, this area was clean and polished. Two red and gold tapestries hang on the far wall, displaying a coat of arms he did not recognise. In between the tapestries was a set of double doors, flanked by two guards wearing red leather and chainmail armour with the same livery.

He was brought to a halt at the side of the table opposite to the queue. The jailor stood to attention before the seated man, who was writing. The leaden mood of the individuals in the queue did nothing to quell Chayne's anxiety.

He turned his attention to the desk man who was dressed in a heavily patterned full robe, again of red and gold. As he finished writing, he placed the parchment on one of the stacks, and turned to the jailer. Without exchanging words, the jailer passed a parchment of his own to the seated man, whose fingers were full of bejewelled, heavy gold rings. He studied the parchment before dipping his quill in a polished gold ink well, and writing in a language Chayne didn't recognise.

When finished he passed it back to the jailor who pushed his hand once more into Chayne's back to propel him forward, this time towards the two large doors.

Both doors remained open as visitors were constantly checked in and out of the room.

When it was his turn, the jailor handed over the parchment to the guard. The guard checked it and called out. Two more guards appeared from behind the doorway and sandwiched Chayne, front and back. They began to march, Chayne quickly got into step. They led him up a dimly lit stairway, easily wide enough to accommodate those passing in the opposite direction, none of whom needing escort into the cells, which he thought odd.

They reached the top of the stairs and another set of double doors. Once again the parchment was checked by the new door guards. Chayne raised a hand to protect his eyes from the bright light beyond. Pain shot through his forearm arm as his hand was smacked back down. The guard at the rear shouted something to him which he didn't understand.

'I'm sorry, I did not mea -' The guard struck him equally hard around the back of the head and spouted another unintelligible rebuke.

Chayne nodded. He got the idea.

At the top of the stairs he was assigned two different guards. These were dressed in polished plate mail armour, adorned and complemented with various red silks and a crest that Chayne recognised: Ashnorian.

By the size and grandeur of the corridor that stretched before him, he guessed he was in an important building, most likely in a city. There was a city not far from the mountains bordering Ashnoria. He struggled to remember its name or how far it was from the mountains.

One of the new guards turned and spoke in passable Mlendrian. 'You will not speak, and you will stay at all times between us unless you are ordered otherwise. If you try to escape, you will be caught and corrected.'

It was said with a calm certainty.

As he walked this new corridor he was struck by the beauty of the design and decoration. The bright light came from many windows that extended from the floor to the high ceiling, covering both sides of the hallway and only interrupted at ten-pace intervals by recesses. Within each recess stood incredibly lifelike statues of men and woman in cream-coloured clothing that blended in with the colour of the alcove. The eyes of the statues were downcast and the faces expressionless. He expected grander figures in such an impressive place. A breeze puffed out fine cotton hangings of alternate white, blue, green, purple and red colour. It was like being in a dream. He looked down to see his reflection in the polished dark marble floor. Embedded flecks of white made it look to him like tiny petals floating on water.

He tried to get a view of the outside, but could only manage a glimpse through occasional gaps, making out a surrounding cityscape of gold and cream-domed architecture against a backdrop of distant snow-capped mountains. It confirmed his suspicions about his location. If correct, then his home was in that direction. He then realised that no matter what happened, he would not be seeing home for some time. It was the start of the winter and the mountains would not be passable until the spring at best.

He pushed such gloomy thoughts away and returned to his observations. Everywhere was evidence of organisation and rigid bureaucracy. Magnificently attired guards, like those accompanying him, marched in pairs. Many civilians were also moving around purposely, carrying parchments, scrolls and boxes. They were dressed in beautiful coloured silks adorned with fine gold and silver ornaments.

A civilian ahead of them stopped and snapped their fingers. One of the statues came to life. Chayne jumped in surprise and caught his heel with the foot of the guard behind. He blanched. It did little to lessen the painful strike to his already sore arm. He sprang back into line.

The statue person walked over to the caller. Some kind of hand gesture was made by the caller, the statue person moved off. Whoever the statue people were, they were utterly subservient.

As he was taken up more levels through the building his surroundings became ever more impressive with ornate ceilings and fine furniture on display. The windows were always tall, elegant and sparkling, covered by fine coloured drapes.

With occasional stops to get permission to continue into the next area, they reached the most impressive set of doors so far. They were over fifteen feet tall, and to Chayne's taste, obscenely ornate. Two more guards were stationed outside. These were more heavily armoured, standing with huge, shining double-headed axes which they stood on their handles. Glittering chainmail gloved hands rested, one atop the other, keeping the weapon perfectly upright by its head.

The key guard said something formally in Ashnorian, looking directly ahead and therefore to the door itself. He then thrust out the piece of paper used at various checkpoints along the route. The right-hand door guard responded sharply by flicking his axe upward and caught it mid-handle. He then spun it over to have its head face downwards, bringing the weapon back down to rest on the floor. He then let it go to remain balanced on his wide head. In formal movements he turned and moved forward to take the document and read it. He then folded the document and passed it back. Looking out into the corridor and addressing no one in particular, he spoke as if making an announcement.

Both door guards then arranged themselves in front of the doors and opened them in unison.

Even the splendour of the corridors did nothing to prepare Chayne for the sight now before him. It was the longest room he'd ever seen, awash with marble, silver and gold, and a velvet carpet as wide as the corridor he was in, reaching from the doors to the far end. There was a table off to the left side of the carpet, roughly halfway into the room. It was surrounded by officials and more guards.

Distracted, he hesitated as the guards walked on again, earning himself a thump in the back that almost knocked him to his knees. The front guard did not stop and it was all Chayne could do to keep on his feet and catch up while being shouted at by the guard behind.

He was starting to feel light-headed. He wasn't sure if it was the brisk walk in his weakened condition, having not eaten in days, or the drugs they may have given him to keep him asleep during his abduction.

As they continued, a scuffle broke out ahead. A man started shouting and struggled against his two escorts. He looked to be pleading with the officials. One of his guards raised a gauntleted hand and brought it down onto the man's face. The man slumped.

Orders were given by a man unseen within the ring of officials.

As Chayne was led level with the desk, the man subjected to the punishment was dragged past him on his back. His head hung back displaying a gash from his right eye to the left side of his mouth. His nose looked broken and there was blood flowing from several of the deeper cuts. Chayne's stomach knotted and he was beginning to feel like he might faint.

His own guards drew level with the desk and stopped, manoeuvring a turn to the left to face Chayne towards the person at the desk. He was wearing a long robe of office even more grand than that of the man in the cell room.

Chayne waited as the seated man wrote on a piece of parchment and rolled it up. He then reached across his desk and picked up a lit maroon-coloured candle and dripped hot wax onto the edge of the parchment to create a seal. He pushed a large gold ring on his finger into the hot wax before handing the paper to one of the officials, who then bowed and left.

Chayne was next. He was trembling. The seated man looked up at the front guard. The guard held out the parchment to nobody in particular. If the guard's back was any stiffer, Chayne felt it might snap. He heard the word 'Tiburn' in the middle of the Ashnorian's sentence.

A clerical type took the note - they were easily identified in any culture, Chayne thought - and handed it to the seated man who briefly checked it.

He looked at Chayne.

'*Name*?' he said in perfect Mlendrian.

Chayne felt like he was going to vomit and his head started to swim.

'Chayne,' he managed. The word sounded distant to him.

The right-hand guard jerked into life. 'You will address the Administrator as "*Administrator*", or you will be corrected!'

The room began to swirl. He looked from the guard to the Administrator and to the various faces all staring at him. He began to sway and the room was losing its focus and spinning faster. He heard the guard shouting again, but it was indistinct. Blackness closed in.

Chapter 5 - Flickering flames

Garamon felt heat from a fire and opened his eyes. Flames flickered only a few feet away and he could just about see movement through them. He sat up. What he saw made him think that he was still asleep and dreaming. He blinked a few times.

'Mee-yow,' it said, punctuating the words distinctly.

Well that confirmed it, he was dreaming. He waved his hand absently through the fire testing his assumption. Searing pain shot through it and he jerked it back. Scrabbling around he found his axe and he leapt to his feet, his mind racing in confusion.

'I said, Mee-yow. You know, like a cat?'

'What *are* you?' he demanded.

'Oh come on. The red scaly skin and horns give it away.'

Garamon continued to stare, trying to understand what was happening. 'Demons are not real.'

It picked up a small stone and gently threw it at him. It bounced off of his head.

'Ouch!'

'My name is Chantel,' it said. 'Well in fact it's something you cannot pronounce without a forked tongue and a lot of hissing, but you can call me that.'

Garamon responded by gripping his axe tighter.

She placed her hands upon her sides and stared at him with an accusing pose.

'Are you staring at my breasts?'

Garamon shook his head in some effort to gain a grip on his reality.

'What!'

She waved her hands towards her upper body. 'It seemed to me that you were looking at my breasts.'

Garamon's jaw dropped. This wasn't going the way he expected at all. He'd read about demons in story books where encounters always led to a fiery and painful death for the hero's hapless sidekick. His eyes fell slowly to her chest, and then continued down seeing her naked body for the first time. Apart from the hoofed feet, finely-scaled red skin and fine fur in all the right places for modesty, it was as fine a female body as he could imagine.

'You're naked,' he said, blushing slightly, pointing roughly into her middle, avoiding the more sensitive regions.

She looked hurt. 'Well I don't understand why you wear the skins of other creatures. I mean, what's wrong with your own?'

Garamon's mind was at the point of flipping out and leaving, whether he went with it or not.

'Look,' she continued, 'while that's a splendid example of a weapon you have there, would you mind putting it away? It's rather giving me the jitters.'

Garamon responded by gripping his axe even tighter.

She tilted her head to one side. He noticed how the straight lines of her long, jet black hair, bunched up on top of her shoulder, its silky sheen reflecting the dancing firelight.

'Now look, if I was going to hurt you, why didn't I do so while you were asleep?'

'Maybe you were just about to, and I woke up in time.'

'So why did I drag you, from your certain death I might point out, into this cave?' She then pointed to the tracks of someone being dragged into the cave to where he had been lying.

'Ermm …'

'And cover you with your blanket …'

He glanced at his blanket.

'… and then made the fire.'

'You made the fire?'

'Yes, I made the fire. In fact I'm quite good at it. Look.' She faced the palms of her hands downwards. The ground ignited into a ring of fire up to her knees.

Garamon jumped back involuntarily and pointed his axe in her direction once more.

'Oh dear me,' she said shaking her head, 'you are such jumpy things.' She closed her hands and the summoned fire disappeared as easily as it came.

As bizarre as the situation was, Garamon started to feel that he was in fact in no immediate danger. He lowered his axe, although remained alert.

'Could you at least put some clothes on?'

'Don't you like my body?' she said.

Garamon closed his eyes for just a moment.

'It's very nice,' he replied, not able to mask a certain amount of blushing.

She gave a terribly infectious giggle that he found most disturbing. In fact, just about everything she did created that effect in him.

'Oh, very well,' she agreed.

He averted his gaze into the fire.

'All done,' she said a few moments later.

He looked up to see that she was wearing his spare cotton tunic. It was barely long enough to cover all the important areas that were causing him so much discomfort. He also wasn't sure that it didn't make her look even more alluring. It certainly never looked that good on him.

'Are we happy now?' she said twirling around expertly, showing just a little cheek beneath the borrowed garment.

'Yes,' he stuttered, swallowing hard. 'Only please don't do *that* again.'

She smiled sweetly.

He made his decision about the strange creature and sat back down by the fire, his axe resting beside him. Reaching into his pack he removed some bread, offering some to the creature.

'Demons don't eat,' she said. 'Well not your food anyway.'

He decided not to pursue that line of questioning any further, and simply replied, 'Oh'.

He ate the bread noisily, not being able to contain his manners in view of his hunger. He then pulled out a large wedge of cheese and offered it as an alternative. She flicked her eyes upwards.

'Sorry, it's a ... human thing,' he said shrugging, and began eating the cheese in the same manner as the bread.

'Yes, you are curious things,' she said idly. 'You have such a tiny lifespan, yet spend most of it learning and doing pointless activities.'

Garamon felt offended on behalf of his entire race. 'Well I don't see demons doing anything worthwhile!' he said, through a mouthful of half-eaten cheese.

She looked directly at his mouth and frowned for a moment. 'Well, I saved you, didn't I?'

Garamon was about to retort when he found that he didn't have an answer to that. Demons didn't do that kind of thing. In fact he thought they did the opposite.

'Actually, why *did* you save me?'

'Ah, at last we come to an intelligent question. Well now that's going to *really* surprise you,' she said with a sudden relish. 'Do you like surprises?'

Garamon was starting to find the creature annoying and just looked on expectantly.

'I think it best if I simply do this,' she continued, then stood up.

His eyes glanced by accident under the tunic. He snapped his eyes upwards to look at her face. She grinned and wagged a finger at him, making clicking noises with her tongue. He reddened once again.

'Now this is likely to come as a bit of a shock,' she warned. 'So be prepared.'

He nodded that he would.

There was a shimmering about her body. She shrunk to a much smaller volume, then was gone, just leaving a lump covered by his tunic.

The lump moved.

His hand strayed to his axe.

A furry head popped out through the neck of the tunic, looked at him and meowed.

It was Fireball.

'!' said his face, expressing surprise, understanding, confusion and amazement all at once.

The shape shimmered again and returned to the form of Chantel. 'I rather thought that would help to explain a few things,' she said.

The impossible faced down the obvious in a contest for believability.

'So ... you're ... Chayne's ... cat then?'

She nodded, eyes wide and mischievous.

'But he never mentioned this to me. I've known him years.'

She laughed her infectious laugh. '*He* doesn't know.'

'*What?*'

'I know, it's delicious, isn't it?'

Garamon didn't know whether to shout at or laugh with this strange apparition. He was totally out of his depth.

'What are you doing with him?'

Her head tilted back at this, she peeled off a beautiful ringing laughter. 'Well that's the best bit,' she said. 'He summoned me!'

Garamon, knowing less about magic than he did about women, just looked at her with his mouth wide open.

'You see, Chaynie isn't too clever with magic. During one of his more daring experiments, I was conjured by mistake. It's not supposed to be possible.'

Despite all the questions that formed in Garamon's mind fighting for first place, one came out a clear winner.

'*Chaynie?*' he asked.

Now it was Chantal's time to redden. Not something easily done by a demon. She stopped smiling and looked down at the floor.

'It's just my pet name for him.'

'You have a *thing* for him.'

'I most certainly do not!'

He started laughing.

'That would be ridiculous,' she continued, with increasing desperation. 'I could never like such an inferior creature.'

The laughter grew.

'It's ridiculous, completely absurd!' she cried.

But it was no good. With some irony, she realised that the cat was out of the bag. The nasty thing rolled onto his back in a fit of laughter. She raised herself up. The fire flared for a moment, surprising him and dampening the horrible noise. But then it came back even stronger.

She stormed out of the cave, still hearing his laughter echoing behind her. As she walked out into the blizzard the snow melted and turned to water for a foot around her.

She didn't understand these smooth demons at all. The one who summoned her she had learned to pacify by taking up the form of a cat. But the shape didn't work on the silver-clawed ones that stole him. In fact, she was badly hurt by them and had ran away to recover. The laughing one in the cave had also tried to leave her behind at the cabin. So she followed it in the hope that it would lead her to the one she wanted as a mate. When she saved its life from the cold she decided to make contact in another form. She observed the effect that their own female kind had on the males, and although she hadn't yet mastered the smooth female body, her own form was not that dissimilar. She saw how the females in the large settlement preyed on the males, their bodies hardly covered

42

with artificial skin. She assumed that having none of the fake skin would be even better. That just seemed to frighten the one in the cave. So she tried the moves and copied the way the females spoke, but this just made things worse. Then the thing embarrassed her. They were so confusing to grasp.

She looked about and spied a small bare bush struggling to exist in these harsh conditions. Raising a hand she pointed an accusing finger at it. It burst into flames and shrivelled to ash, dissolving in the water created from the melted snow.

She gave a 'humph' and tried to convince herself that she now felt better for it.

Crossing her arms, she stamped a hoof, and disappeared into the night.

Chapter 6 - The Master

Lathashal looked down, listening to the pleading of the student kneeling at his feet.

'Master, I am sorry. I try so hard, but it's so difficult. Maybe if I could have more time.'

'Time boy!' snapped the master magii. 'It is not time that you need, but concentration. You need to focus your eyes on the various energies as they interact within the spell. Once again you are not observant!'

'Oh no, please Master, not that. I beg you!'

Lathashal looked on with pleasure at the dread on the face before him.

'Oh, but I must boy. It is for your own good. If you do not use your eyes effectively, then perhaps losing one will help you appreciate them more.' He pulled out his wicked thin-bladed knife. The student started to shuffle backwards on his knees, his head shaking back and forth unable to accept what was about to happen to him, yet again.

'Be *still*, or I shall send you to the dungeons to teach you obedience also.'

The young man stopped moving, he was close to panic and running away. Only the threatened penalty held him, which he knew was far, far worse than that which he was about to receive.

Lathashal advanced the blade and heard a satisfying whimper as he levelled the ornate knife with the student's eyes.

'Which one today, eh boy? You choose.'

'Please Master, no. I cannot. Have mercy.'

But there never was any.

Lathashal unhurriedly pushed the point into the right eye until it touched the rear of the socket. The student screamed. And then again as the blade was twisted from side to side and up and down until the socket had emptied onto his cheek and down his robe.

'Now get out of my presence! Deliberate your failings through the night, the pain will help you to concentrate perhaps.'

'But Master, may I not see the Mage-Surgeon now. My punishment is surely served. The pain will otherwise keep me awake and I will not be able to concentrate for tomorrow's test.'

Without a word, Lathashal stuck the *Latshoutee*, the Blade of Correction, into the student's other eye. The young man screamed again, and fell to the floor, violently sobbing tears into eyes that could not receive them.

'Would you like to question me further, so I may start on more vital organs?' Lathashal watched the writhing student until he saw his head indicate no. 'I thought not. Now leave me and be better prepared for tomorrow, we begin at one hour after dawn.'

The student got to his feet, staggering off blindly. He crashed into a table and fell over.

'Oh for pity sake boy, can't you do anything yourself!' He clicked his fingers. Two servants jumped from one of the many recesses and guided the blind young man out of the room.

Lathashal placed the blade on the bench and snapped his fingers. Another servant crossed to him and cleaned the weapon.

'Lessons going well, Lath?' came a familiar voice from behind him.

He didn't give the owner the satisfaction of showing surprise. Indeed, there was none. He was used by now to the silent approach of this particular brand of hated colleague.

'Your stealth is as incompetent as your magic was, my dear. I heard your approach from the moment you entered the room,' he casually lied.

'My approach was flawless as we both know. And I was an excellent student. One of the finest in your lessons, I seem to remember.'

'Finest, ha!' he blurted, turning to face her. 'You were a terrible student. The most disruptive and incompetent I've ever taught.'

The figure approached him and placed a finger under the collar of his robe, expertly sliding it up around his ear. She exhaled her warm breath on the side of his face. 'I seem to remember scoring *very* highly in the lessons,' she purred. 'At least you would have thought so from the groans you gave.'

His face remained passive and unemotional. 'That was a long time ago. Your seductions are weak and ineffectual now.'

She withdrew her hand sharply, recoiling from the insult. 'Perhaps it is you that is impotent old man? After all, four hundred years is a long time to stay capable!'

'Oh, I can assure you that I am perfectly capable. The screams of ecstasy of the young woman from my bedchamber most nights are a testimony to that,' he said smugly.

'Oh yes, and I am sure that it must be most gratifying for you, knowing that you have to drug them so heavily first.'

He gave no retort this time, the truth biting deeply.

'What do you want?' he said too harshly.

She smiled, delighted to have riled him so. 'You have a new recruit. A young mage from the Tiburn woods in Mlendria?'

His eyes narrowed. 'Yes, I have only managed two lessons with him so far. A very mediocre student, what of him?' This was not at all the truth. He recalled the student's name was Chayne, something that he almost never could. He was not only one of the best magic students in a century, but his thirst for all knowledge was considerable. He didn't know what the

46

Yhordi wanted with him, but he wasn't going to give him up without a fierce challenge.

'I heard reports that he is a gifted student, one for which you have cut out for special lessons.'

Lathashal inwardly cursed. The Yhordi were the spies of the Empire and existed everywhere. Once they found something out it was dangerous to lie to them. But he was an old hand at playing the game.

He changed tack. No Shodatt would have had enough time to concoct a good reason to justify taking him.

'I am the Master of Magile within the city. I say he is mediocre. Do you wish to challenge my judgement?'

This placed the onus on the side of his opponent, for challenging a Master's decision without solid proof was punishable with whatever horror the Master could dream up short of death, which usually was preferable. And the only proof she could muster, he guessed, would be through her informants in his staff, whom she would have to formally expose, and thus be forced to have them executed for spying within another Shodatt's domain.

Her face changed. The initiative was his again.

'Oh, just hearsay in the dungeons. Prisoner talk,' she said indifferently, avoiding his gaze. He watched as she ran a finger over a nearby work desk. 'This place is so dusty. You run such an undisciplined workforce. You should have your servants more regularly tortured to show them their place.'

A pitifully transparent diversion he observed, not worthy of her at all, for they both knew it would be spotless. Whatever had happened to force her into being so unprepared, needed investigating. He made a mental note to have his spies look into it.

'You have overstayed your welcome my dear, please leave now, I have much to do.'

She seemed to be pondering some decision, but then turned and left the room. He watched the sway of her hips as she moved away. It stirred his loins as ever. 'You still have it,

Illestrael,' he reflected quietly to himself. 'Even after so many decades.'

When she left the room, he indicated to one of his servants to bring the novice Chayne to him immediately.

Illestrael left the master magii's room in a terrible mood. She should have been better prepared, and berated herself. Maybe the drugs needed increasing again. She felt the aches returning to her bones, and her skin was starting to show disgusting tiny lines around her neck. She despised aging, even at the slow rate achievable by those who could afford the high price of the treatment. She wanted to head for the dungeons immediately, but the Yhordi Masters were particularly intolerant of failure. No, she would have to wait. She needed to deal with the irritating problem of the Mlendrian mage first.

Chapter 7 - Sinserti Plain

Kinfular waited until ThreeSwords held up his hand to indicate that it was safe to advance. Keeping low he moved up the ranks of his men, placing a reassuring touch onto each warrior's shoulder as they stayed crouching. He reached ThreeSwords and knelt down. Through the heat haze he could just make out Rainen far ahead, keeping still and low, his advanced position from the group providing early warning of trouble ahead. The scout raised his hands and made a series of movements.

'Twenty large animals at the waterhole. Elktari I guess,' said ThreeSwords reading the distant signalling.

Kinfular, while having superb night vision, was struggling to see the tiny actions under such conditions. 'Or an army of giant purple Gelingus, playing Heckle,' he replied, squinting.

'I believe it *is* a dozen Elktari, Hlenshar,' the black swordsman reiterated. Kinfular hadn't chosen him for his sense of humour.

They watched as Rainen retreated from his position and returned. The man's easy stride was smooth, almost hypnotic, raising no dust in his passing.

He stopped before them and knelt down. 'There is a herd of Elktari drinking at the waterhole. I believe they have not long arrived.'

Kinfular nodded his understanding. The large beasts were bad tempered, especially if thirsty. They were wandering animals by nature and once watered would move on.

He considered the alternatives. There were few this deep into the plain where no mountain streams ran to replenish water skins.

It was midday and the men were sapped by the heat. He decided to rest, ordering Grast to set up temporary shelter from the sun.

Shinlay saw the group ahead and felt relief again. This was the fourth time she had lost them. It was difficult to track them with Rainen leading. She stopped and let her eyes adjust, picking out enough details to see that they set up a temporary camp.

She set out her own Pitukka, stretching the water resistant skin between a few rocks that were lying around. Using her bow as a pole she created a little height to the structure, providing both shade and gaining the benefit of any breeze. She attempted three times to make a hole in the ground for her bow to act as a support. The baked soil cracked and crumbled under her knife. In the end she resigned herself to resting one end of the bow on the ground and holding it up with her hands. The ground was covered in broken pieces of white shell making it uncomfortable to lie on. She was told that the plains were long ago a seabed under hundreds of feet of water. She didn't understand how such a thing could be possible.

She settled down and lay still, watching the faraway group. Her thoughts drifted back to the tribe. What would her father be doing right now? She thought of his craggy, smiling face, full of warmth. The people loved him as their chieftain. As a child she would sit in his rough arms as he told her of the glorious battles of his past. They were always filled with great victories and amusing stories. She wondered on occasion if he ever suffered any hardship at all during these times. Of course as she grew older she learned to see the sadness in his eyes, and the toll that war took on all old soldiers' souls. She closed her eyes from the glaring sun and began recalling the stories to detach herself from her current situation.

She awoke with a jump, her instinct warning her of some pressing danger. She froze in place until her wits returned.

How did she fall asleep? Her left leg was stinging below the knee and she wondered if she was bitten by one of the plain's many venomous inhabitants. The air was cooler and she surmised that she was asleep for some hours. Her Pitukka had fallen across her, covering her body and head but not her legs.

She felt movement along her left side, judging it to be a snake. Perhaps it was just seeking cover from the sun. She kept still, not wanting to risk provoking an attack as most of the snakes on the plain were poisonous. She cursed again for her stupidity. It was this kind of slip that would be the greatest threat to her survival whilst travelling alone.

The snake shifted again.

Taking a slow, shallow breath she tensed her muscles. In a sudden scrabble she slid out from under the cover and sprang to her feet. The creature hissed and thrashed, caught in the folds of the Pitukka. She snatched up a rock and threw it. It missed the creature and dragged the cover clear instead. She recognised the distinct red and yellow crisscross markings of a Skellat. Without a Shaman's potion, a bite would be fatal.

She kept still, hoping that it might attack the rock and ignore her. It turned towards her and attacked with surprising speed. She attempted to pull her short sword free. With it only half way out of its scabbard, the snake struck.

Instinctively she kicked out her foot. The snake connected. She closed her eyes, feeling nausea sweep over her as the shock hit her.

There was no pain.

She opened her eyes to see that the creature misjudged its strike against the fast moving kick. Its fangs had gone through the tip of the leather boot, just missing her toes.

She slashed her sword across the reptile's body, severing it in two. Both halves thrashed about. She fanatically unstrapped her boot and threw it away, the creature's head still attached. Kicking at the remaining body, she sent that away too.

She slumped down, panting from the fright.

She looked towards Kinfular's camp. Her panic rose as she realised they were no longer in sight. She jumped to her feet and ran forward for a better look.

They were gone.

She judged from the position of the sun that she had slept for four hours. Without knowing how long the men rested she didn't know how far ahead they were. If it was more than an hour then she felt little hope of recovering the ground in time, entering the Hammerheads alone.

Tears stung her eyes, spilling over to fall down her cheeks. For the first time she looked towards home. In that direction lay ridicule and humiliation. Forward and she could die alone, to be food for buzzards and jackals, or capture by bandits.

She made her decision. She got to her feet, dusted herself down and set about recovering her boot and packing her Pitukka.

Rainen slowed to a halt and waited for the rest of the group to reach him. He was tired and his breathing was ragged. Soon after the delay at the waterhole the group detected a nomadic tribe between them and the mountains. Kinfular was incensed. The plainsmen were highly warlike and would attack a smaller group on sight. The resulting diversion took several hours of hard running.

They were at last at the foot of the mountains, although many miles south of their intended entry point. It was now dusk.

'Opinion?' said Kinfular as he arrived.

The scout looked pensive. 'It is enclosed with many overhangs along the path, although the markings show this route was once heavily used.'

'Old trading route?'

'It is likely,' agreed the scout.

'Now abandoned due to bandit activity, perhaps?'

Rainen shrugged.

'We need to use it,' said Kinfular, testily.

'I'll take a closer look,' replied Rainen.

Kinfular looked for his second in command. 'Grast!'

The swarthy barbarian broke away from checking on the weary men. 'Yes, Hlenshar.'

'We enter at sunset.'

'Aye, Hlenshar,' replied the older man.

Rainen caught a troubled look on the Grast's face, but knew he would not openly defy a direct order.

The scout turned his eyes back to the mountains. They looked cold and uninviting, an unusual feeling for a mountain barbarian. He also couldn't shake the notion that they were being watched.

He moved off for a closer look.

Chapter 8 - Accountability

Kinfular was only just holding onto his patience as Rainen called for him again. It could only mean another U-turn or detour. They were being forced to make little more than guesses as to the best path, and their overall progress through the dark hours was poor. He did not blame the scout for this, it was simply a consequence of the decision to travel through unknown terrain under these conditions. The pace improved with daylight, but also the risk of being discovered.

'What this time?'

The scout heard the edginess in his leader's voice. 'There is perfect killing ground ahead: high rock and overhangs.

'How much time do we lose if we go back?'

'At least one hour backtracking to the last fork, and no way to know that it's better,' replied Rainen.

'So this is the best place for a trap,' mused Kinfular. 'We are too large a force for bandits to risk in straight combat, and it would take a vast amount of rock to close the far end. I cannot see bandits being that organised.'

'I could take a look at the far side?' Rainen offered.

Kinfular took another look at the high surrounding rock, his lips pressed with uncertainty. Then he nodded.

Rainen passed his knives, bow and quiver to the leader. They would be of little use to him alone in an ambush. Speed would be his greatest defence.

Kinfular watched him move silently across the clearing like a ghost. He turned to Grast and passed his orders to be fed back down the chain of men behind.

Rainen crossed the clearing without incident and came to a halt at the exit, scanning the area for a trap. He took his time. Eventually Kinfular saw a wave from the scout. It was safe.

The first group of barbarians assembled. Despite being given the all clear by Rainen, it was standard routine for crossing such danger areas. That way, if an ambush occurred it would only catch a few at a time. They moved off quickly, with eyes darting along the high walls of the pass. They were making more noise than the whisper that was Rainen's passing, but most of it was absorbed by the snow and prevented from echoing from the enclosing rock.

They crossed without incident and scattered to form a tight perimeter protecting their end of the pass.

Kinfular tapped the kneeling leader of the second team on the shoulder. They sprinted off next. Kinfular began to relax as they too arrived without incident. He looked to Grast next as the leader of the third group. He had two relative rookies with him: Olan and Queal. Both looked to the older warrior as a second father, as did many of the younger men. Kinfular made his last check of the pass and patted Grast on the shoulder.

'May Rolk be with you, friend.'

'Aaagh, Rolk never bothers with us anymore. He gave up worrying with you around.'

Kinfular exchanged a brief smile with the man. Grast led his group away.

They were slower than the first two groups due to Grast's inclusion. Even so, they were at the half-way point soon enough. Kinfular turned to assemble the fourth group when he heard something that alerted him.

He raked his sight back across the clearing for the source of the sound. A single rock, about the size of a fist, was tumbling through the air close to one of the vertical walls, followed by a string of smaller ones and some snow. It was far from the traversing group and represented no danger in itself. It hit the ground with a thud, scattering some snow.

Kinfular followed the falling snow trail up. A puff of dust was still dispersing at the top of the ridge.

Nothing else happened. He looked to Grast. His team were frozen in place. Grast was looking back, anxiety showing in his eyes, waiting for orders.

Kinfular knew a random rock could have fallen due to the crossing of his men. It was unlikely though, especially with the snow helping to keep things in place.

He waited a little longer. There was no sign of anything more. He waved to Grast to continue.

The warrior restarted his run. A sound shattered the quiet of the snow laden Hammerheads. It was a horn.

Dozens of hand-sized rocks began to rain down on the exposed men from the high rocky sides of the pass. The training of the men took over and shields were joined overhead to form a protective barrier against the missiles.

Kinfular needed to make a split decision.

He recalled his men.

Grast and his group turned and began to run back. Rainen and the first two teams began their retreat from further out. Rainen, without the protection of a shield, was like a hare, leaping and dodging through the deadly barrage.

Grast was last in his pack and pounded his powerful legs into the ground. He didn't bother trying to dodge any of the missiles. He no longer possessed the agility. He realised that he was slowing the others down as they attempted to protect him, and bellowed out. 'Don't wait for me, *run!*'

The pack responded and broke formation, sprinting away. Almost immediately, Ginurar took a hit to his lower leg and stumbled to the ground. Illient was following and dropped over the man with his shield raised to protect both.

Ginurar tried to stand but cried out and fell back. 'I can't stand on it.'

Grast caught up, joining his shield with Illient's to extend the cover. 'Come on lad, this is no time for lying around,' he encouraged, and placed his free hand under Ginurar's arm.

Illient did the same and Ginurar was lifted to his feet, crying out as they dragged him up.

Soon the first two groups arrived, adding the extra safety of their shields.

Kinfular went to race out to help them, but ThreeSwords grabbed him and held him back. 'They know what to do. We cannot risk losing both you and Grast,' said the swordsman.

Kinfular bit back a retort to the unemotional Heslarian, but held his position.

Agonising seconds passed as Grast's slow rescue was working.

He was almost across when a second horn blast was heard. Large rocks began falling from the high narrow walls behind Kinfular and onto the men there. Cries filled the air and the area soon became filled with choking dust making it impossible to see what was happening.

'Run!' Kinfular yelled at them, as one by one, the nearest warriors emerged from the dust cloud. Three got out of the thirteen when Sholster emerged from the cloud, his huge shield deflecting the rocks to either side as he gave protection to another two men.

'Terrible weather, Hlenshar!' he bellowed, and turned to disappear back into the dust cloud. The rocks continued to fall.

Sholster emerged once more, this time alone and without his usual battle humour. 'These bastards are well prepared. The rest are cut off,' he shouted over the noise of the falling rocks.

'We'll find another way back to them,' shouted back Kinfular. He led the survivors out into the main pass. There, the island of shields that was Grast's group was arriving. Kinfular's group formed up their own combined protective barrier and joined them.

'Grast!' called out Kinfular under the shields. 'No escape here, we must go back across.' Kinfular saw the momentary look of dismay in the old warrior's face at the order, but the veteran turned and began to lead his team, once again, back across the killing ground.

'Out of my way!' bellowed Sholster, ducking under shields and all but barging Grast and Illient aside as he scooped Ginurar from his feet and started running with him under the protection of his shield. The instant this happened every man broke into a run towards the safety of the other side of the pass.

The rocks continued and now the ground was littered with hundreds of the missiles, making the footing treacherous. As the group broke half-way again, a third horn blast was heard and the far side of the pass was engulfed in dust as their only remaining escape route was sealed. The rock barrage stopped and ropes were thrown down the high pass walls. A ring of bandits appeared atop the rock, outnumbering the barbarians three to one. They dropped down the ropes into the pass, surrounding the group.

Kinfular gave the command and his men formed up a fighting circle with the badly injured in the middle.

The bandits rushed in, three deep to surround their captives in a tight ring.

The clash of steel began and Sholster launched his first attack as a downward blow that drove the recipients head halfway into his shoulders. 'No need for that scarf now laddie!'

The fighting was fierce. The bandits were falling at twice the rate of his men. Even so, Kinfular heard the calls to close up the gaps in the circle as his warriors fell. The knowledge of the loss of each man fuelled his strokes as he swept away one attacker after another.

Grast fought with the younger warriors, Olan and Queal, one on either side. Olan had been unlucky and drawn an experienced fighter. Grast knew the bandit would soon open up the young man's defences. He kept his own foe at bay whilst trying to watch for the inevitable strike. It was only a few moments more before Olan overstretched, tempted by an apparent opening in the bandit's right side. It was a ruse by the bandit, and he smiled as he turned aside the incoming sword with his shield and thrust out his own.

Grast reacted instinctively to block the killing strike, managing to clip the attacking blade and deflecting it passed Olan's hip. Olan gasped as he expected the bandit's attack to hit, and quickly recovered his position. But distracted, Grast could not fully defend his own position and his opponent's sword sliced down into his groin. Blood spurted from the wound indicating a major artery was cut.

Grast attempted to continue, but shock flooded through him. His attacker was about to strike again when Olan, heedless of his own safety, yelled out and threw himself at Grast's attacker overbalancing them both backwards. As they hit the ground so Olan's sword thrust into the bandit's chest and was pushed up into his throat, his bodyweight snapping the blade off at the hilt. Olan died as strikes sank into his back.

Kinfular, hearing Olan call out, trapped his current attacker's sword in his shield snare giving him a short opportunity to see what happened. He watched the oldest warrior fall backwards into the centre of the circle as the youngest carried out his suicidal leap forwards.

'Cover here!' he shouted, pulling his attacker with him, tripping him and thrusting his sword through the back of his neck. Sliding his shield free of the dead bandit's sword he crossed the centre of the diminishing fighting circle to where Grast lay. Dropping his sword, he pushed his hand over the wound trying to stop the blood from escaping. Grast reached up to hold his arm. The grip was weak and tears created streaks through the dust and blood on his cheeks.

'One to remember, Kin,' he said through fading breaths. He was already deathly pale and he tried to say something more, but no words came forth. His grip tightened a little as if he was trying to hold himself to life. Then his hand fell away and his head sagged back. The blood stopped pumping from his leg.

Kinfular, his shame and grief absolute at his decision to risk the crossing, stood and looked around as if in a dream. More of his men were falling. He could no longer see Rainen. The scout was never suited to defending against so crude and brutal an assault. Kinfular then watched as Queal's luck finally run out as two bandits overrun his position and charged through to the injured Ginurar who, after all the efforts to save him, fell to a swift strike through the chest.

All hope was now gone, the bandits tore into the exposed flanks of the remaining barbarians and headed for Kinfular, almost stumbling over each other to take the finest prize. Only he, and Sholster and ThreeSwords back to back, remained.

The bandits were too many for the three of them to defeat in such a position. It was time to die. After all these years of honour and award he was to face the Mystics in shame, with the blood of the Riaan's finest warriors and his best friend on his hands.

He grabbed his sword and went to meet the nearest of the bandits.

The sound of a horn fell upon them once more. The bandits, as one, fell back.

There was an eerie silence broken only by the sound of men panting. Steam rose from the blood of the fallen and the breath of the survivors.

At the end of the pass a rope slapped against the rock. Another bandit climbed down. He hopped down the last couple of feet with ease and walked towards them with a laidback swagger.

From the red and white feathers tucked into his wide-brimmed tan hat, to his glossy studded boots, the man looked absurd for both climate and terrain. His protection was nothing more than a white woollen shirt and grey fur leggings.

His two sabres sat comfortably on his hips, however.

He halted at a safe distance behind his men.

'You don't look so big down here,' he said, eyeing Sholster.

'Come closer friend. I'll look real small when you see me from hell,' replied the barbarian.

'Oh I dare say I've carved a fine place for myself there,' replied the bandit smoothly. 'However if you don't submit to me now, you'll find yours long before I.'

'I'll smash your head into more pieces than this mongrel band of bitches could find in a lifetime,' replied Sholster, taking a step forward.

The line of bandits took a firmer stance.

Kinfular stayed Sholster with a hand.

'You will kill us either way.'

'Normally, perhaps,' replied the bandit. 'But I've lost enough men this day. I reckon you're worth more to me alive in ransom than dead.'

Kinfular's eyes bore into the bandit who took a step backwards, the smile fading from his lips.

'Also, I'll allow your men cut off by the rock fall to escape,' he offered.

Kinfular's eyes narrowed. 'How can I be sure you will honour this?'

'Well as my word will no doubt be of little use to you, you cannot,' admitted the bandit.

'You cannot trust these maggots,' snarled Sholster.

'I agree,' said ThreeSwords. 'I do not wish to die at the hand of these jackals without swords in my hands. Let's be done with it.'

Kinfular paused for a few moments longer. He shook his head. 'My frustration at delays has caused me to kill many good warriors this day. I will not be responsible for killing you also.' He threw out his sword, unbuckled his shield and let it drop to his feet.

'Hlenshar!' responded Sholster.

'You may do as you feel you should,' instructed Kinfular. 'I will not order you in this.'

ThreeSwords and Sholster threw aside their weapons.

Chapter 9 - Crossing the line

It was the fifth day since Chayne passed out in front of the Administrator. Initially he'd awoken from his blackout in a long dormitory for student mages or *Magiis* as they called them. This changed after his first meeting with the master magii, Lathashal, and his passing of many tests set by the man. Now it seemed as if he wasn't a prisoner at all. He was in a private room, there was no lock on the door, nor guards posted, and he could walk freely between the places he was told he could access. One of these was an immense library of books and parchments, the scale of which made the libraries of Tiburn look no better than market stalls. He was particularly captivated by its vast supply of tomes and scrolls relating to magic. He never dreamed of such a place existing. He knew it was wrong to bring him here against his will, but admitted that for now he was happy to stay and learn their magic. Especially considering the tremendously skilled Lathashal taught him often and, he discovered, at the expense of the other students' training. The man delighted in his ability to grasp the teachings so quickly.

There was a knock on the door. He expected it to be his newly appointed servant. He was told that servants were forbidden to speak, except between themselves, and even then never within earshot of their 'superiors'. He opened the door. The servant made the sign to follow and the symbol for Lathashal. At no time did his eyes avert from the floor. To get their attention you were supposed to snap your fingers. This appalled Chayne's sense of morality and had resisted signalling in such a way.

'Thank you,' he said automatically. The servant blanched. They were punished if caught being spoken to.

He picked up his tall stack of notes and allowed the servant to lead him up two levels to the master magii's lab. The servant knocked on the unadorned service door that led up the final stairs. The door was unlocked and opened by a servant on the other side.

Chayne stepped through and climbed the twenty-five tightly-winding stone steps up the spiral staircase, trying not to let his pile of notes erupt from his hands. Near the top he became aware of an orange glow from the lab. He stepped up into the lab looking for the source of the illumination. He was caught by a breathtaking sight.

The lab's west wall was always a curiosity. It had been a polished dark grey material. Now it was replaced with lightly smoked glass, embedded with thousands of crystals. It covered from wall to wall and floor to ceiling. It was supported by an intricate criss-cross of metal strands, inlaid into the glass in thin, flowing curves. The delicate structure gave it strength without cumbersome struts that would otherwise detract from the beauty of the view.

The window faced west and the angle of the crystals caught and refracted the setting sunlight, splitting it into a colourful display on the room's white domed ceiling. It was an achievement of creative and architectural genius. Even so, the finest efforts of man could not match the spectacle that nature created beyond the sparkling panes. He stood transfixed by the scene. The bloated, crimson sun loomed amidst the red and orange hues of a spectacular sunset setting over snow-capped mountains on the horizon.

The window stood before a wide gorge, forged by millennia of water flowing from a vast river far below. The sunlight glinted across it in countless ripples under the light breeze. Unfamiliar birds with incredible wingspans gracefully circled on the updraft created by the gorges steep moss and fern-covered sides.

'You have more favoured treatment than you could appreciate. However, if you continue to test my patience another second, you will suffer my displeasure.'

The sound of Lathashal's steely tones tore Chayne away from the window. He turned to the magii who was sitting before a polished silver-golden sphere suspended from the ceiling by two wires making a V-shape. They were as fine as spider silk and seemed impossibly thin for the task. The sphere was roughly twice the size of a man's head and with many small, evenly spaced holes over its surface. Chayne had seen it before, but learned from the first moments with his teacher that deviations of any kind, including questions or even looking at something not the focus of the lesson, brought immediate wrath from the quick-tempered magii.

The other students in the dormitory also said that the Master would hideously torture them to make them obey. At first he didn't believe it as none of the pupils bore any physical marks in keeping with their claims. They insisted that all injuries were repaired by the Mage-Surgeon. Chayne decided it was just the kind of thing new graduates were told to frighten them. Then one day he passed Pristin, his bunk mate, being carried from a lesson with wounds that left him in no doubt of the punishments.

He came back to the present and looked into the eyes of the magii. He was clearly expected to make amends.

'Forgive me, Master. The wonder of the Empire's craftsmanship surpasses anything I have seen in Mlendria.' He bowed. Such subservience would hopefully sate the man's anger.

'So you acknowledge the superiority of *Straslinian* prowess?'

'Oh indeed, Master. I have never seen its match.'

'Very good.'

Chayne felt this finally confirmed his hypothesis. He'd chosen his flattery to see if the old man would again put his city of Straslin before Ashnoria as an Empire. Internal rivalry was rife at all levels in this Empire. It began between individuals and extended to entire cities.

The magii waved a hand at the glass wall, and it was once again replaced with the bleak grey as before.

'Magic?' said Chayne in wonder.

'Of my own design,' replied Lathashal.

This uncovered a side of the Master that Chayne would never have believed. To create such a breathtaking scene took a soul and creativity to match any of the great artists in Mlendria.

'It was an earlier period in my life when I had time and inclination for such things.'

Chayne saw a look of wistfulness in the man's eyes. Was that regret in his voice?

'Come boy!' he said, snapping out of the only moment of humanity that Chayne had detected in the man. 'In today's lesson you will begin to learn the wonders of the manasphere.'

Chayne balanced his stack of notes on the bench and sat on the opposite side of the table as indicated, eager to learn anything this master of magic was to teach.

'Now tell me the highlights of yesterday's lesson.'

Chayne didn't hesitate. 'Yesterday we discussed that mana is to be found in almost everything around us: plants, rocks, water and even the air. However, it is so weakly concentrated that we cannot ordinarily feel its presence. The act of forming a spell creates a concentration of mana that with skill and practice can be channelled in many forms from healing wounds to blasting your enemies.' Chayne remembered thinking how typical were the chosen examples.

'And what would happen after you have blasted away the gates of an enemy's fortification?'

'Such a powerful spell would have depleted the mana for a great distance. Further magic would not be possible in the area for days.'

'And if the magiis were then attacked?'

'They would be defenceless.'

Lathashal smiled. 'Excellent. Today I am going to expose you to a fifth gradia test.'

Chayne was taken aback. One of the first things he was taught was the magical grade structure. First gradia was for complete novices, covering the basic theory with no practical. Second gradia occurred a few weeks later, consisting of an attempt at casting the most minor of spells. At seventh gradia, which normally took five years of concentrated learning by even the most adept of students, you would be able to heal moderate wounds, levitate tables and cast a bolt of energy capable of killing a man at thirty paces. At tenth gradia you became an honoured Shenwhi Shaska or Master First Class. It was the lowest of the Master grades. Few people reached, even survived, to this level, as most died attempting the hazardous elevation in control demanded by casting a ninth gradia spell.

Chayne, according to all who spoke of him, possessed an exceptional talent, but even so was still only at second gradia. Lathashal, by making him face a fifth gradia test so early made him feel highly honoured, but also hugely daunted. He felt he couldn't possibly know how to achieve such a feat.

Lathashal continued. 'Although high intensity mana cannot be brought together more than once in a single place at the same time, for as you have correctly stated it suffers local depletion. It can, using the correct devices, be stored.'

Chayne was stunned. The implications for this were enormous.

'Yes boy, I can see you understand the gravity of the statement. It is not known outside of the Empire, and it is our closest guarded secret. For it makes us undefeatable.'

Chayne knew the stories of the Ashnorian mages were legendary. They were capable of casting spells of great power and frequency beyond those outside of the Empire.

It was then that the full implications of the thought struck him. It meant he would never be allowed to leave the Ashnorian Empire or see his cabin again.

'Place your fingertips on either side of the sphere. I will show you how to store the mana.'

Chayne did so.

'I want you to concentrate on the mana surrounding you, and *pull* it in.'

Chayne closed his eyes and settled into his usual semi-meditative state as taught. He could feel the particles of mana around him. He began to focus his will on drawing them towards him. The air warmed as usual and there was a tingling on his skin. Included this time though was a slight warming of the ends of his fingers where they were in contact with the manasphere. Strangely too, it felt as though the manasphere was pulling at *him*.

'That is good, very good indeed. Continue.'

His concentration deepened, increasing his range of influence over the mana, pulling it from further away. His body was now starting to feel the first effects of the magic flowing through him. It felt like a fire was just a few feet away. This is where he previously would have completed the spell, discharging the energies before they built to a level beyond his skill to control them. His hands were now hot to the point of being uncomfortable. The manasphere seemed to be pulling the mana through his body at an ever-increasing rate, and he began to feel that he wasn't in control.

'Master I -'

'Quiet boy, I did not instruct you to speak.'

He tried to slow the flow of mana. To his dismay he found that he could not. It was then that he first sensed something else about the object in his hands. It was almost as if it projected feint malevolence.

The flow of mana was now considerable. His body was beginning to vibrate from the energy. His fingers were in pain and it was spreading to his hands.

'My hands -'

'*Silence!* Speak again and you will be *corrected!*'

Hearing those words caused panic in him and he opened his eyes, breaking his concentration. He stared in wide-eyed revulsion at the tendrils of smoke rising from his fingers. Veins of blue energy were flowing over the sphere and being consumed by the holes in its surface. He looked at the magii, who to his horror, was grinning with undisguised pleasure.

'Help!' he begged through gritted teeth. His body began to rack and spasm, the energies growing in him as the manasphere continued to increase its pull on mana. He could feel it was being drawn from as far out as thirty paces now, and emptied the large room.

He tried to call out through clenched jaws, but made no sound. His fingers were melting onto the manasphere. His body was in a constant spasm of racking pain. He felt his heart was going burst. He was helpless to stop his own destruction.

Lathashal moved his face close.

'Next time you come into my lesson boy, you pay immediate attention to *me*. And if you ever try to manipulate my favour again, I will strap you to this device and leave you until your body is nothing more than charred remains in the cracks of the stones under your feet.'

And with that the master magii placed a hand upon the orb. The manasphere stopped.

Chayne slumped to the floor finding that none of his muscles would respond. His body, especially his hands, were still in terrible pain and continued to twitch. Breathing was painful and he felt that damage had been done to his lungs. He heard a snap of fingers, followed by approaching footsteps. He was handled by the servants and yelped in pain at their touch where his skin was blistered. They lifted him from the floor, the smell of burnt flesh strong in his nostrils.

He was carried back down the small stone stairway, the servants displaying an expert gentleness with his wounds that could only come from practice. Despite this, anything they did caused him pain, and he often cried out.

After what seemed like an age, they stopped and one of the servants knocked at a door. The door opened and he felt himself carried through and laid down on a hard surface.

He then heard the servants quietly shuffle out and the door close.

'So what have we here?' Chayne couldn't open his eyes to see the speaker. The voice had a deep timbre that was both comforting and soothing.

Chayne began to feel a slight tingling over his body that he knew meant magic was being used upon him.

'Degenerated cellular structure, burns over most of the body, especially the hands. Looks like somebody lost control of a manasphere. You should take more care, those things will kill you, as this one nearly did. Lie still and I will repair the damage. There will be a little discomfort. It will pass.' The voice was sympathetic. The first he'd encountered since waking in this land.

The magic built up once more in his body. The air began to grow warm and was painful to his burns. He tensed at the feeling.

'This is delicate,' said the voice. 'If you move I may miss some of the damaged areas.'

Chayne did his best to comply.

The magic continued to build. It felt similar to when Lathashal punished him, only many times less intense. Even so, with his body in its current state, he was suffering. It took all his effort to maintain his position while the magii performed his art. Slowly he felt his skin changing until at last the pain was receding all over his body and strength returned to his muscles. It continued for a little longer until he was finally pain-free. He then began to enjoy the sensation of the magic coursing through his body.

Then it was over. The feeling subsided and he lay still, waiting for his next instruction.

'Well get up, you're done.'

He opened his eyes and tentatively sat up, testing every movement before fully committing. Facing him was a heavy-set, middle-aged man dressed in a long cream robe. It displayed the green and white symbol of a hand that Chayne recognised as that of the healing Shodatt. The healer was holding a two-foot long staff. A finely crafted wooden clasp at the top held a small version of a manasphere. He shrank away from it.

'Thank you,' he managed.

'Mana isn't free. It takes students a good deal of time to gather enough to treat wounds such as those. You can thank *them* by learning to control manaspheres of such power before attempting to use one again.'

Chayne's expression dropped. 'It was a punishment.'

'I see,' responded the Healer, his face losing some of its sternness. 'What happened?'

Chayne told of the encounter with Lathashal. He thought he saw momentary anger in the man.

'You must not cross him, even in the slightest. He is the most powerful magii in Straslin and commands almost total immunity for his actions. He could have killed you and nobody would have stood forward to accuse him.'

Chayne nodded his understanding.

'You did well though. The manasphere you mentioned is rated gradia nine. For you to lose control of such a device and survive, even for a few moments, shows you have an exceptionally high coherence with mana. It indicates that you have an unusual potential as a magii.'

Chayne nodded again. 'Master Lathashal told me this also.'

'Well, I am Stalizar, the Mage-Surgeon General. I'll be here should you have any more mishaps. I will not be pleased if I see you here too often.'

Chayne jumped to his feet, bowing slightly, as was the custom before a Master. 'I am Chayne, and I am in your debt,' he said.

71

The magii's expression changed.

'So you are the new Mlendrian recruit.' It was a statement, not a question. 'A word of advice; our Empire is based on who has the greatest influence with the Emperor, and magic has long been the favoured power of Emperors. Shodatts fight constantly between themselves to improve their position. An exceptional potential such as you will be exploited to the full.'

Chayne stared at the magii. He couldn't comprehend what that would mean for him.

The man moved closer and dropped his voice conspiratorially. 'You will be a pawn in many a strategy. You will have to quickly learn the politics of the Empire. Become as much a master of it as your magic. And understand this: a rival Shodatt, if they cannot have you, will prefer to see you dead to prevent another Shodatt from gaining such an influential tool.'

Chayne didn't care much for being described as a tool, but appreciated the warning and bowed again.

He said his farewell and headed back to his small quarters. All sign of pain and weariness were gone and he decided to head to the main library to begin his study of the Empire's politics. He returned to his room first to pick up more parchment for his notes. As he entered, he saw an ornate wooden chest on his table. On the lid was the symbol of a staff crossing a hawk: Lathashal's personal mark.

He wondered what torment there may be within, but realised that it wasn't the man's style. If he wanted to hurt you he would want to see the suffering in your eyes. He lifted the finely crafted lid. Inside were many compartments. There was also a fine quill and a full ink well. Looking in the compartments he found spare parchment and a stack of smaller, thinner parchments. These contained the notes he'd left in Lathashal's laboratory. They were transcribed perfectly onto the smaller area making them far easier to carry and study.

He shook his head in disbelief at this strange land. There was unreasonable suffering for the most minor of discretions, followed by great generosity.

He continued to check the contents.

There was a latched compartment which he opened and found a small book. The title of the book was written in Ashnorian but he did his best to translate it. He decided it read: *Magii Handbook*. He opened it.

Each page was made of impossibly thin paper that, despite its flimsiness, was strong and didn't tear. Each page was edged with gold, and the words and pictures within were exquisite. He opened to the first page and found an inscription on the inside of the front cover. It read:

> *May you study this book well and gain the insight you deserve.*
>
> *Lathashal.*

Taking a moment to consider his confused feelings over the contradictory magii, he then scanned through the pages. He noticed that chapter twelve was underlined in the same ink as Lathashal's written comment.

It was entitled: *Controlling Manaspheres*.

He shut the book and placed it within his robes along with his diminutive notes. Closing the lid of the chest he headed off for the library.

Chapter 10 - The Ranger

Garamon awoke the next morning, shivering. The fire was out and his breath was frosty. He got to his feet and looked for a sign of the strange demon creature. It was nowhere to be seen.

He moved out of the cave, stomping his feet and blowing into his hands to get some warmth into his body. There was light snow falling in the still air, as if the weather was exhausted from the previous night's exertion. Everywhere was rock, with no obvious clue of direction or escape. No sign of his or the demon's tracks could be seen under the overnight fall.

He moved back into the cave and checked his main pack. The only thing missing was the tunic. He took out some fruit to eat and sat back against the cave wall with a slump. He considered resting the day in the cave, but dismissed the idea. He needed to take advantage of the good weather and ensure that he found shelter long before nightfall.

He thought about the strange creature. Was it really a demon? It seemed so absurd. There were plenty of tales about them in children's stories, and she did have a passing resemblance to one. The magical fire she produced was impressive, but then it was nothing more than he'd seen produced by circus mages. The transformation into a cat stumped him though. He'd never seen that nor heard of such a thing being possible.

He half-wished that she was still here. She was irritating and definitely disturbing, but on balance he preferred to have somebody around. She also handled herself far better, and if

74

she genuinely cared for Chayne she might be useful in helping in his rescue.

He finished off his cold meal and gathered his belongings. Setting his pack into place, the tender parts of his shoulders feeling sore, he picked up his axe and headed once again out into the snow. The sky was a uniform grey and gave no indication of the sun for direction. He starting walking, hoping he would come across the main trail.

Half the morning went by with no sign of the mountain road or the demon. It was no longer snowing and even the sun made the occasional appearance through gaps in the clouds. It confirmed his direction, but there was little else to celebrate. He came out onto a ledge, high above the floor of a clearing. He considered jumping down onto some steep scree. It would have to be a last resort.

As he continued to look around, his eyes caught a distant glint from the far side of the clearing. His spirits soared. There were two men. The flash of light had come from one of them holding a sword up towards the other. They seemed to be in a heated discussion. Then to his horror the other man drew his own sword and made a lunge for the first. It was batted away with ease. The unarmed man now put up his hands and started to back off.

Garamon had no idea of the circumstances between the two, but he couldn't stand by and do nothing for the unarmed man. He leapt out onto the steep slope, hitting it hard and creating his own avalanche of loose rocks and snow. He picked up speed and his body began to flood with adrenaline, giving him the strength and reactions to ride the falling scree. With a grunt he crashed into the clearing floor, tumbling over several times before coming to a halt. Shaking his head he jumped to his feet to clear the snow to locate the two men. He began running.

The swordsman pinned the other man up against a rock, his free hand around the throat of the other. Garamon, part way across the clearing, shouted out. He was ignored and saw the man draw back the sword while the other starting fighting back with his hands. Garamon, eyes wide in horror, watched as the swordsman thrust the sword into the other man's chest.

Garamon screamed in defiance.

The killer snapped his head around, and then relaxed at seeing him, returning his attention to the dying man. Taking his time he pulled the sword free and wiped it across his victims clothing. He then turned to face the new challenge.

Without missing a step, Garamon shrugged his shoulders, dropping away his backpack. He then placed both hands over his head to grip his axe handle, and pushed sharply downwards. The two-handed weapon sprung free of its special release bindings and he pulled it into view. This changed the killer's expression. He retreated to the nearby high rocks and climbed them. Garamon bellowed out his anger at the man's cowardly act and raced to the point where the killer climbed. The rocks were vertical and he had no idea how the man how ascended so quickly.

He heard laughter coming from above. The killer stood gazing down from the rocks. Garamon, realising that he could not climb with his axe in hand, snapped it back into its bindings and leapt onto the first rock. Getting his first footing he jumped and caught hold of an overhang. He pulled his head up level with it. He was met with the tip of a sword placed on his cheek. He kept his nerve and moved his eyes from the tip of the sword up into the eyes of the man holding it.

'You are either incredibly foolish or stupendously courageous,' said the killer. 'You cannot climb *and* fight.' He flicked his wrist. The blade tip cut across Garamon's cheek. Garamon tried to move his head away but felt a sting followed by the trickle of blood running down his cheek.

'Your first scar it seems. And if you let that temper get the better of you again, it won't be your last.' He turned and disappeared from view, moving over the rocks like he was born to it.

Garamon couldn't speak, seething with the humiliation of the words. He wanted to pull himself up and chase the man down.

There was a groan from below.

He let go and dropped back to the ground, hurrying over to stabbed man. There was a lot of blood pooling in the snow as it pumped from the opening in his chest. Garamon felt helpless and pushed his gloved hands over the gash. Blood forced its way between his fingers.

He looked around frantically for something that might help, not even knowing what that might be. The man gave another groan and rolled his head. His breathing was becoming faster and more ragged. Garamon's young soul had never witnessed another man dying, especially in so sudden and harrowing a way. Tears fell, stinging the cut on his cheek.

'I'm so sorry,' he repeated over and over. The man tensed and slumped, his last breath escaping his blooded lips in a horrible rattle that Garamon knew he would never forget.

Removing his hands he sat back, staring at the corpse. He felt a terrible loneliness, wishing somehow for his father to arrive with the Rangers. They would seek out the killer and bring him to justice. He pictured the attacker's face, with his cocksure smile fading as the noose tightened around his neck.

He looked down at his gloved hands and noticed that they were crimson with congealing blood. Bile rose up into his mouth and he turned and vomited into the snow. He pulled them off and threw them away.

He forced himself to look at the corpse again, wondering who he was and whether a family was waiting at home for him. He decided that he wouldn't leave him here to be devoured by wolves, and began to think how he would bury him.

A crack came from behind. Without looking around he dived away, releasing his axe.

'Lucky you have an axe. That wound was from a sword.'

The speaker stood only a few paces away, holding a short sword. It wasn't the killer, although he was dressed in similar heavy, well-cut furs. A long thin dagger was still sheathed on the opposite side to his sword scabbard. His overall appearance was one of quality and he wore his clothing comfortably. He radiated relaxed confidence, similar to the killer, and his eyes were steady and alert. Garamon was left in no doubt that the man knew how to handle himself. He then noted that one of the stranger's boots was lifted at the front. Under it was a dead branch of a tree protruding from the snow. It was not likely to have been missed. The stranger lifted his foot and placed it down beside the branch, as if emphasising the point.

'Is he dead?' It was a voice accustomed to asking questions and getting answers.

Garamon nodded. 'Another man, dressed like you. Mocking green eyes.'

The stranger showed no surprise.

'I tried to save him,' said Garamon, looking to the dead man. 'I didn't know what to do.'

'Mortal wound. Nothing you could have done,' replied the newcomer as he began inspecting the markings in the snow. He moved to where the killer climbed.

'Wait here,' he ordered. He sheathed his sword and leapt high onto the rock face, pulling himself up in one smooth motion to disappear from view.

Garamon felt numb. His eyes fell upon the dead man and he averted his gaze, wanting to look at anything else.

The stranger returned a few minutes later. Garamon noted how economically he moved over the rocks. His final drop to the ground, he didn't so much hit it, as merge with it.

'Did you see him?' asked Garamon.

'He's gone,' replied the stranger, walking over to the dead man and checking him closely.

'Will he return?'

'He only wanted to remove the members of my hunting party. He won't face me,' said the stranger.

'You seem to know him well.'

'Yes,' replied the stranger, offering no further explanation.

Garamon watched as the stranger removed the valuables from the dead man, wrapping them carefully in a cloth and tucking them inside his own tunic. He worked quickly as if he'd done it many times before.

'What will you do with those?'

'They belong to his family now. I shall return them.'

'Are you a trapper?' he asked.

'No,' the stranger replied. 'We'll bury him in a shallow grave to keep the scavengers at bay until the Rangers can get here.'

'Was he a good man?'

The stranger shrugged his shoulders as he continued to work.

'I mean, did he do good things?'

The man turned the body over onto its front. 'There were stories that he beat his wife when he got drunk, if that makes you feel any better.'

Garamon felt a little ashamed that it did.

The stranger finished up his work and wiped the blood from his hands on the dead man's clothing before standing. He peered at Garamon's cheek.

'That needs to be stitched or it will become infected. Come over here and sit down. If the cut is clean enough you may get away without much of a scar.'

Garamon sat down on a rock next to the man.

The stranger pulled a small cotton bag from within his tunic, untied the drawstring and removed a delicate curved needle and a length fine of gut. Garamon moved his head away at the sight.

'I won't lie to you,' admitted the man. 'This is going to hurt like all the hells in the cold. But unless you want your cheek to turn into a pus-filled mess, I suggest you put up with it. It won't take long. I have done this many times.'

'You have many scars?' asked Garamon, trying to make any conversation that took him from his field surgery.

'Enough. Now keep still.'

Garamon watched as the man threaded the needle with as much skill as his mother. As it was brought to his face he tensed his cheek.

The stranger stopped. 'I'm happy to sew your face up that way, but you need to relax if you don't want a permanent smirk.'

Garamon did his best to let his cheek muscles relax. The stranger waited a moment and then continued, patiently stopping at each of Garamon's involuntary muscle spasms.

As promised, it was over quickly.

'Thank you.' he said, the effort of speaking pulled at the stitching causing him to grimace.

'You'll soon get used to that,' said the stranger. He pulled back and observed the final result. 'Not bad. That should be a fair ladykiller.' He started packing away his medical items.

Garamon's gaze slewed across to the dead man.

'First time seeing a man die?'

Garamon nodded.

'Well I carry a book of O'lim with me. I'm not a religious man, but out of all the gods, his priests seem to be the least insane. Let's bury him, and if it makes you feel any better, I'll say a few words for him.'

'Thank you. I would like that,' replied Garamon.

The digging was hard in the frozen ground. They settled for a shallow grave covered with rocks in a long square pattern. The stranger explained that the rocks prevented the animals from disturbing the body and it assisted the Rangers when attempting to locate it. He then read a few verses from the tiny bible. They spoke of happiness in death and asked O'lim to help the man's soul to find its way home, resisting the Angel of Desires who would attempt to entice him from his path. Garamon thought the prayer was well chosen for the dead man.

When the stranger finished, he paused for a few moments in some private contemplation before returning the little religious book to its pouch and tucking it away inside his tunic. He took a look at the sky.

'It will be snowing again by nightfall. You need to find shelter. Here,' he said, throwing over the leather gloves of the dead man. 'These are better than yours.'

Garamon was reluctant.

'He's dead, you're alive. It's the way of things. You're ill-prepared for the mountains and it's a lot easier stitching up scars than sewing on frostbitten fingers.

Garamon saw the vision and took the gloves.

'Where are you heading?' asked the stranger as he continued his work.

Garamon didn't reply.

'Well it's none of my business,' continued the man, 'but you're a long way from any settlement. With the clothing and provisions you show you are not experienced in mountain travel this time of year.'

Garamon could do no more than stare at the man helplessly.

'I know of a good place to hold up for the night about an hour's run from here. We can be there before the light fades, and maybe have a little time to hunt something to cook.'

Garamon's stomach growled at the thought. He nodded. 'I dropped my pack while running across the clearing.'

'Get it. I'll bury your old gloves. They will attract animals.

Garamon did so and soon after they set off. He settled into an easy stride behind the man, noting again how effortlessly he moved. He realised he didn't know the man's name.

The stranger then slowed his pace and called back. 'Looks like we cannot cut through up ahead as I'd hoped. The drifting snow yesterday has left many of the smaller paths blocked. We'll need to pick up the pace if we are to make it before dark. How well do you run?'

'Well, sir.'

'No need to be so formal out here. This place cares nothing of rank.' The stranger increased his pace.

Garamon responded.

'Could I ask your name?' he called forward, while leaping the trunk of a fallen tree that the stranger just landed from.

'Falakar,' came back the reply.

Garamon stopped so quickly he lost his footing on the snow and his feet shot out from under him, landing him on his back. The stranger stopped and looked back.

'Are you alright?' he called.

Garamon didn't respond. He was staring back, open mouthed.

The stranger walked back and put his hand out for Garamon to pull on.

'Falakar!' Garamon said incredulously. 'The Ghost Ranger. The Mountain Stalker. The Silent Avenger!' He put his hand up and grabbed the one offered.

Falakar pulled him to his feet. 'Such titles are bestowed by tavern story tellers and minstrels looking to improve their meagre takings by embellishing small facts into unreasonably heroic deeds. But yes, I believe I am the one to whom you are referring.'

Garamon went silent again.

'Come, we can swap histories by the fire when safely out of the cold of the night. Perhaps then you can make up your own mind,' said the Ranger, and set off again.

Garamon followed, a thousand thoughts racing through is mind. The man was a living legend, the greatest Ranger that ever lived. He was said to be a master of all weapons.

Not long after, Garamon saw a Perlic, a mountain hare often hunted for its thick fur. It sprang out in front of them, nervously kicked its back legs and jumped away, high and far into the air. Falakar plucked a throwing knife from its sheath and flicked his wrist without pausing to aim. The blade cut through the air to strike the creature, killing it in mid-flight.

He went to work, trussing the animal's legs together for travel. Then he was up and running again with hardly a pause.

They were running until the light was almost gone when Falakar made a few sharp twists and turns and stopped at a dead end. He removed long branches stacked against the rock, exposing a fissure just large enough to allow a man to get through. He climbed in. Garamon followed.

Inside it was narrow, but long enough for the two of them and a fire. There was a pile of dried branches and sticks at the back.

It wasn't long before they were both sitting by the fire eating the cooked Perlic with some of Garamon's bread.

'What's your name?'

Garamon, realising that he hadn't told his travelling companion his own name, felt embarrassed. 'I am sorry, it was rude of me not to mention it.'

The Ranger waved the comment away.

'I must seem young and foolish to you.'

'You are certainly foolish to travel this deep into the mountains at this time of year, and you were reckless in facing Jontal, but in those acts you show you are a man of principle and courage. You also put your own life at risk to help a stranger. Such traits are rare, especially in one so young. But know that you have been lucky so far. If I hadn't been tracking the man you faced and he knew that I was close by, your story may have ended differently.'

'Who is this killer, Jontal?' asked Garamon.

'He is a bandit who lives in these mountains and preys on those using the pass. In the winter when pickings are low he ventures out into the nearby farms, stealing food and robbing individuals he finds on his way.'

'You track him for the Rangers?'

'Not any longer. I work for myself.'

'So you are a mercenary now?'

Falakar grimaced at the title. 'I guess that is one word. People pay me to find things, so long as the task is an honest one. I still follow the codes of a Ranger.'

'So, do I get your name?' requested the Ranger again, finishing off his water and refilling his cup from a water skin.

'I am Garamon. Son of Renous of Tiburn.'

Falakar smiled. 'Renous. I had half-guessed as much. You have the features and trustful eyes of the man.'

Garamon felt fear wash over him. This was a connection back to home that he hadn't expected.

'I see that troubles you. I hope you have not run away from home with your family's fabled axe and a young man's thirst for adventure. If so, then I shall escort you back and delay my hunt.'

Garamon began to show signs of panic.

Falakar lifted his hand. 'Calm yourself, but I now wish to know more. You have placed yourself in mortal danger leaving your home, and I'm guessing it is not with your father's blessing. Please tell me the truth.'

Garamon considered his options and how much to say. In the end he decided that he would tell the truth and be judged.

He explained about Chayne's abduction, his likely destination and what awaited him. He spoke of his father's refusal to help, and of his mother's distress, and that despite it all he was compelled to leave and attempt to find his friend. He even mentioned his brush with death in the blizzard and his dealings with the Demonette. At this point the Ranger showed doubt, but Garamon expressed his own disbelief at the bizarre encounter in response.

'The next day I travelled the morning and stumbled across the clearing where I saw two men arguing and raced across to help. The rest you know.'

'And now you wish to find a way over the mountains and into the Ashnorian Empire, somehow to reach and enter the heavily guarded city of Straslin, find your friend, snatch him back from the clutches of a formidable enemy, and get back home without being captured, killed or tortured?'

'Yes,' confirmed Garamon, placing conviction into the word. 'Or die trying.'

'I'd say that was something of a certainty!'

'I don't care! He's my friend and I cannot leave him in such a place without doing everything I can to rescue him.'

He watched as Falakar studied him. He expected to be chastised for his stupidity and told that he was to be returned home.

'I can guide you across the mountains to the Ashnorian border, but I'll go no further.'

Garamon sat staring at the man. 'You're going to help me?'

'To the border only,' confirmed Falakar.

Garamon sat stunned. 'I don't wish to seem ungrateful, but why?'

Falakar looked up from his last piece of Perlic.

'I was like you once, about your age too. I did something similar to what you're doing now. It made me who I am.'

'So you succeeded in your quest?'

'My undertaking was as impossible as yours. I failed and was never reunited with my people or parents again.'

He rose from his position and moved to the back of the cave. 'Feed the fire for the night and get some sleep. We have a good deal of travelling to do tomorrow and you will need rest from your ordeals today.'

And with that the legendary warrior wrapped the blanket around his shoulders and sat against the back wall facing the slim cave opening.

Garamon did as he was told. As he lay near the fire, his exhaustion washed over him. Despite the uneven floor and his jumbled thoughts trying to make sense of everything that happened during the day, he fell asleep.

Chapter 11 - Sleight of hand

Chayne followed his memorised path of corridors and stairways to the library. Straying into areas not assigned to you was punishable. He did his best to look down the many corridors and into rooms to gain whatever information he could about the place. If Stalizar's warning was correct, he would have to stay alert and know as much about his surroundings as possible. He would also have to make allies fast, although at this time it was impossible to know who to trust.

What a contrast to his cabin back home. Spring would be bringing the animals out of hibernation. He thought about the badger he befriended two years ago. It would be appearing about now. He'd read that they didn't hibernate. It was always his intention to go find out why it wasn't around during the coldest part of the year. Fireball hated it with a vengeance of course, and was chastised for challenging the badger during the first encounter. Oddly enough the cat tolerated the visitor from then on.

Such thoughts brought him to thinking about his other early spring visitor. It must be around now that Garamon would make his first trek out to see him. He wondered what the woodsman would make of his disappearance. It made him feel homesick.

He reached the library's door for students, plain and functional without the trappings of the main palace entrances. The servant opened the door.

As always he paused for a moment when entering, casting his eyes over the magnificent hall. As wide as a town square and four times as long, it easily surpassed the great museum of Quelt which Mlendrians believed to be the largest in the land. He gazed again over the galleries running the full length on either side. Each one contained thousands of bookshelves, and every space was used. The galleries were wide enough to include huge oak study tables, each inlaid with gold relief maps of all known lands. His eyes ran along to the far end of the library where the galleries twisted back on themselves to merge with one another to create a wide stairway to the ground floor.

But he was taking too much risk. He dropped his eyes to the floor as was demanded of his position and walked noiselessly on the soft wall-to-wall carpet. The place was busy, as usual. Servant recesses were every ten paces but few were ever occupied, the residents either carrying out a task for a scholar or putting back books. All instructions were given in written note form to the servants as the sign language wasn't capable of describing individual book titles. He shut his eyes for a moment and listened. There was a sound similar to light rain. It was the turning of hundreds of pages as the students and scholars thumbed through their tomes.

On reaching the middle of the hall he stopped at the librarian's desk to sign in. A grand affair, the desk was in the shape of a crescent moon supported on carved wooden legs modelled on some vast hoofed creature. It was positioned in the centre of the hall and appeared the most dominant feature on entering the library from either the main entrance or the student doors.

After signing in, he walked to the low-gradia magic tome shelves on the ground floor. Keeping his eyes down, he found a seat at one of the round study tables where sat ten students already. A servant arrived. Chayne took a quill and wrote his request for two books on a pre-cut parchment square from the desk. The first was his current book to support his lessons in magic training. The second was a two-way dictionary between the Ashnorian language and his own. On his first trip to the library it took him three attempts to get the servant to understand his novice writing for a dictionary. He'd first ended up with a huge tome filled with pictures of animals and plant life, while the second was exquisitely drawn erotica. Upon opening it he almost laughed aloud.

He completed his request and gave it to the servant, then set about laying out his quills and notes in a methodical fashion.

The servant returned and laid the books on the table next to him. He was glad to see they were correct. Without raising his head he gave a light nod and the servant bowed in acknowledgement and withdrew.

He had gathered together many books and scrolls over the years in Mlendria, but none compared to those here. He opened the book on magic at the page he'd last finished. For this session he turned to pages twenty-one to thirty-six and would be tested by Lathashal in the afternoon. He shuddered at the thought of the uncompromising Magii, but felt confident that he would achieve his given tasks and avoid correction.

A student walked passed and caught the corner of Chayne's notes, scattering them to the floor. Immediately servants left their positions and began collecting up the fallen pieces. The student picked up a piece of parchment and scribbled out a note and passed it to him with a bow of apology, and left. The servants completed their tidying and Chayne glanced at the note. He stared at the words in disbelief. He removed the note as nonchalantly as he could and placed it onto the table, close to his body. He kept up the pretence of studying as normal for a while longer and then purposefully removed from his robe the note-book Lathashal had given him, pretending to read a section. As he closed it again he slipped the note inside and returned the book within his robe. He read and absorbed the remaining pages for his lesson.

Completed, he packed up. As he rose from his position he caught movement in his direction in his periphery vision. He pretended he hadn't noticed it and went to leave the seated area.

Two figures approached. He stopped, waiting to be seized.

The first one moved passed in front of him; close enough to be made out as a servant on some errand. The other went behind him. He heard his books being picked up. It was only a servant returning his books as usual.

He tried to be calm. The chance of anyone seeing him store the note in such a vast place was unlikely.

He left the table area and headed back towards the student entrance. As he walked he tried to be coolheaded, reasoning that if somebody had seen him then he would have been intercepted by now. Even so he started to walk a little quicker, unable to completely quell his fear.

Halfway to the exit his heart was starting to race. He chanced a glance up at the end door.

It looked so far away.

He realised that his pace quickened and tried to check it without being too conspicuous.

He wanted to run.

Five paces remaining. His heart was pounding and his throat was tight. The servant extended a hand to open the door.

'Halt!'

The shout came from behind him, some way back. Within the soundless library Chayne responded to it like the crack of a whip. He jumped to a stop.

He didn't look around, hoping that it wasn't directed at him.

He heard the approach of guards, their padded chainmail armour chinking faintly and giving away their progress.

They reached his position and stood either side of him.

A third man walked around in front, blocking his way to the door.

With his downcast eyes, Chayne could only make out black leather boots and dark leggings.

The man forced his hand into Chayne's robe like the strike of a snake and fumbled for a moment before pulling free the note-book.

It was opened and the pages shook. A piece of parchment fell out onto the floor. He could feel the man's eyes burning into him with triumph.

The note-book was cast away and a snap of the man's fingers brought a servant to pick up the parchment for him.

He was close enough for Chayne to see it unfolded to reveal a blank side. It was turned over. The other side was also blank.

The paper was again turned over to its first side. The man then rubbed at it with his fingers, breathed on it, and even smelled it. He then screwed it up and threw it to the floor. He gave a sharp hiss in Chayne's direction and walked away, taking the guards.

Chayne took the discarded notebook from a servant and walked the remaining paces to the door. The servant opened it for him, and he stepped though.

As the door closed behind him he fell sideways to the wall for support, feeling the cold stone through his robe cooling his skin. He took a moment before continuing back to his room.

Upon entering he headed straight for his bed, foregoing the usual ritual of logging his notes for the session, and dropped onto the mattress. He flicked his hand and a piece of parchment appeared as if from nowhere. Even at a young age his fascination with magic led him to learn magician's parlour tricks. He was glad he hadn't lost his touch.

He read the words again, but there was no doubt as to the translation:

You are to be terminated at 3am, do not be in your room. Trust no one. Search your room for that which isn't right.
Lan-Chi

He closed his eyes, at a loss for how to come to terms with this alien land. He'd managed to handle himself in the library using sleight of hand, but he wasn't fooling himself. He was steering blind, adrift in an unforgiving ocean, not knowing which of his actions would lead him unto the rocks.

For a while it all seemed unreal, and a part of him was waiting for somebody to say it was a mistake and he could go home. But his punishment at the hands of Lathashal had dispelled that. His life was forfeit for reasons he didn't understand and he had no idea how to counter. And who was the benevolent stranger who provided him the warning? Whoever it was took a considerable risk, which meant they gained a lot to keep him alive, or at least believed that gaining his favour would be worth the risk of terrible torture.

He began his search of the room for something "that wasn't right". He found nothing obviously out of place. He sat on his bed and picked up his pillow to puff some air into the feathers. It didn't feel normal. The stitching wasn't the usual perfect handiwork expected of everything created in the Empire. He took a paper knife and cut the thread. Inside he could see the edge of some pale cloth. He pulled the material free.

It was a servants uniform.

As he was holding the garment and pondering its purpose, there was a knock on the door. He flinched. He saw a vision of armed assassins waiting on the other side preparing to thrust cold steel into his chest.

Wouldn't they just burst in?

Hiding the uniform, he opening the door and was met by a servant who made the signal for Lathashal.

Chayne opened his hand with his fingers together and made a single chopping motion downwards. The servant backed away from the door and stood waiting outside.

Chayne gathered up his things for the lesson and left, heading once more to the scene of his first experience of torture. His stomach twisted in anticipation of what would occur this time.

Chapter 12 - Vindication

Splitter laughed explosively at the antics before him, spraying the beer from his mouth and adding to the pieces of food already contained within his matted beard. He was in good spirits. Tonight he wouldn't have to enforce his will to break up the fights that would occur within his bored feral bandit following, nor quell dissent about his aging leadership.

He looked towards the camp's blazing fire and his eyes fell upon the stricken forms that were the reason for their celebration. Three barbarian fighters: a huge one that killed ten of his men with his ungodly sized club; the black dual-sword wielder, swift and controlled; and the third, the dancer. He was the leader and an amazing killing machine. It was reported that he moved with grace and economy that none had ever seen equalled. Like the other two, he now looked powerless in Splitter's realm.

All were strapped to the underside of wooden beams angled towards the fire. Hollowed out trunks were placed under each of their heads so that when removed from their bodies they would roll into the fire. Splitter heard that the brain did not die immediately when severed from the body. He made sure his victims were aware of this before execution.

Their group were skilled but they were foolish to enter *Credes Folly*. He wouldn't have done so. It had reconfirmed once again his choice for the camp's location, contained within a large clearing and protected from the elements by fifty foot rocks. With few ways into the bowl it made for easy defending and was difficult to find. Little sound escaped and their fires were not detected at night.

Tonight the sound of laughter and music echoed within it and the air was filled with energy, making him feel alive.

He judged the party was at its peak and so the time was right for the main event. He banged his mug on his chair three times, heedless of the beer that flew from it. He waited until the camp quietened. He raised his mug high into the air.

All eyes were upon him eager for his next action.

He scanned them all with his bloodshot eyes, pleased that he could still command such attention. He turned his mug, allowing the remaining beer to slowly spill. The camp started chanting the executioner's name: *'Rolac, Rolac, Rolac'*.

The chanting grew louder and more frantic as the flow reduced to just drips. He timed the slowing rate of drops to perfection, creating a fever pitch. As the final drip fell he righted the mug again and the chant abruptly stopped. Waiting a few moments longer for full effect, he slammed it down onto the arm of his chair.

All eyes snapped to the huge mute who positioned the shining axe blade under the first neck. Splitter could see the dark barbarian close his eyes.

The axe was pulled up in a high arc. The camp was silent of all human activity, only the crackling and spitting of the fire could be heard.

The mute's muscles tensed for the return stroke.

On the edge of hearing came a sound. Only just perceptible at first but it grew rapidly. It stopped abruptly as the mute gave a grunt and dropped the axe to the floor. He turned to Splitter for explanation, an arrow through his neck buried up to its flight. Then he tipped forward to land with a thump to the ground.

The camp scattered for cover and began scanning the rocks for the source of the attack.

Splitter remained standing, crimson with rage.

'Up there!' came a cry.

Splitter looked. High up on the rock, feet spread, was a barbarian woman. Dressed in light tan leather and white head feathers, she lit up blood red from the camp's fire like an avenging demon. He could just make out broad black streaks running across her face. In one hand, she held her bow. In the other were the severed heads of two guards sagging lifeless by the hair. Glistening droplets of blood fell to the rock.

The camp was transfixed.

Slowly she brought the heads forward. Then, with a flick of her wrist, dropped them out towards the camp. They fell onto the rocks far below with a wet thud.

Splitter's bellow broke the spell.

'Bring her to *me!*'

The camp exploded into action.

He watched as the apparition backed off slowly into the shadows as if unconcerned. Irritated, he waited as his men, drunk to a man, struggled to make progress up the steep rocks. He was already thinking up ways to bring about her agonising death.

The first of his men reached the top and disappeared for a few moments. He reappeared, and shrugged.

Splitter snarled, enough of ceremony.

He turned to the barbarians to dispatch them himself. He looked on in disbelief as he witnessed the release of the last of them by the female. He gave out a primal cry that made all but the barbarians cower. As the group raced away he took up the chase ahead of his men who were still up in the rocks. He passed the dead axeman, snatching up his weapon.

Many years of sending others out to do his bidding made him slow, but he knew these mountains like no other and wasn't to be denied his revenge.

He saw them take a turn and he diverted down a narrow path that would shorten the time to the next clearing. Five more corners and he broke out into the clearing. He saw them fleeing, the leader only ten paces ahead.

He roared in triumph, the clearing was a dead end.

The barbarian slowed and Splitter took aim at his back for his first strike.

The barbarians were forced to stop at the rock face.

Splitter raised his axe. This was going to be sweet.

The woman threw something to the barbarian leader from a covered bundle at the base of the rock, his back still turned.

Splitter steadied his axe, his muscles bunched for a strike that would cleave the barbarian in two, and pulled the axe down.

The barbarian leapt out to meet him and spun around low, flashing a sword across in front of him releasing a sharp pain from Splitter's stomach. He grimaced and could only watch as his now attacker used the momentum to pull himself out to one side. In a continuous movement the barbarian pulled his blade up and over to fall back down upon Splitter's wrists, now held out in front of him were the axe had missed its target. Searing pain shot through his arms and he watched his axe fall away with his hands still attached.

Transfixed by the sight, he was barely aware of the barbarian still moving around behind him. A second later and he felt fire rip down his spine. His head sank to his chest and he saw his bowels pouring out from a stomach wound stretching from hip to hip. He slumped down onto his heels. He was aware of agony from almost every part of his body. He felt the pain fading, knowing what it meant.

Splitter's nearest rival for leadership, Crase, broke out into the clearing first. He slid to a halt on the loose surface. The sight before him filled him with confusion and fear. As many more attackers filed out into the area behind him they all stopped just as suddenly, not knowing what to do next.

Ahead of them stood the barbarian leader holding a torch in one hand and the executioner's axe in the other. Splitter was sitting back on his heels with his head bowed and his back to them, blood was pumping from a long wound down his spine. All of the barbarians now held weapons and flanked the leader, including the devil woman, whose bow was aimed at Crase's throat. He remembered her precision shot back at the camp and swallowed hard.

The barbarian leader looked at them with a malevolence and hatred that drained Crase's courage to the core. At that moment he believed the man could kill them all. The barbarian then moved slowly around to the side of Splitter and raised the axe high above his head. His eyes then raked from one side of the bandit group to the other, imparting the message to each of them. He brought the axe down hard. The nauseating sound of flesh and bone being parted was followed with Splitter's head falling to the floor. His body remained upright. The barbarian pushed the body over with his foot.

Crase looked around to the men, *his* men now. They outnumbered the barbarians five to one. He looked back again at the warriors facing him and the hateful look burning in their eyes.

The standoff was broken as the barbarian giant roared and started to charge. Crase's survival instincts took over. He dropped his weapon and ran into the men behind him, noticing that each of them had the same idea.

Kinfular watched as Sholster thundered across the clearing, scattering the bandits. They fled over the rocks or back down the trail.

He turned to Shinlay, controlled anger flowing within him.

'You disobeyed me, woman.'

Shinlay held his gaze for a few seconds, incensed that her mate should show such ingratitude.

'I saved your life!'

'You have shamed me!'

Shinlay's glare intensified. 'Is it shame, or are you simply too proud to admit that the great *Hlenshar* owes his life to a woman!'

Fury boiled in Kinfular's eyes. Shinlay was suddenly afraid that she had gone too far and that he would strike out. She could see the inner battle raging within him.

'Rainen is dead,' he pushed out through gritted teeth. 'You will be our scout. Lead on.'

She held her position a moment longer, not wishing to show subservience.

'Go, *now*!' he barked.

Flinching at his final words, she snatched up her pack and climbed over the rocks.

Kinfular waited until ThreeSwords and Sholster followed her. He then took a moment to look back at the mutilated bandit chief. His brutal death seemed to do little to suppress the guilt and loss of so many good warriors and his long-time friend. He wanted to wake up the vile pig so he could drive his sword into his heart again until he exorcised the demons and his crushing grief. But he knew the memory of this day would bury itself in a tainted corner of his soul to fester for the rest of his life.

'A pox on you all,' he spat. Then turned and followed after the others.

Chapter 13 - Left to die

Garamon was walking along the banks of a picturesque lake, holding hands with a woman covered in orange fur and long, jet black hair. He heard his name being called in the distance. She turned and shook him.

He awoke suddenly with Falakar kneeling over him, shaking his shoulder.

'That must have been a fine dream. You've been grinning for twenty minutes. Anything you'd care to share to brighten up my morning?'

Garamon shook his head, trying to dislodge whatever madness lay within. 'Not really,' he replied.

Falakar cracked a smile and took a bundle of fresh wood he carried to the back of the cave.

'Get your things together. An early start with this weather will see us half-way across the rest of the mountains by dusk.'

Garamon did so and soon they were jogging again. The sun was far below the mountain line and the sky was a glorious blue, making Garamon feel refreshed and optimistic once more. With every footstep there was a crunch as the surface crust broke underfoot, a sound he always enjoyed. Even so when he looked up at the call of a bird of prey floating on the updrafts, he found himself envious of their ability to float over the difficult terrain.

He noted that Falakar's footsteps were considerably quieter than his own. It seemed to him that as each foot touched the snow it would slow imperceptibly and tilt downwards at the toe allowing the foot to enter the crust more slowly and at an angle. This prevented the crack that he himself made. He

99

attempted for several minutes trying to repeat the action without success.

'How do you land so softly?'

Falakar didn't slow, his eyes always scanning the surrounding rocks

'I spent many years of my life in the Eastern lands. There I met Grand Master Kfansh. He was part of an order with great powers of discipline over their mind and body. I needed work so I carried out tasks for him. In exchange he taught me their way.'

'Was it hard?' said Garamon, and began playing a little game with himself trying to land exactly in each of Falakar's footsteps and getting as close as possible to the man without catching his heels.

'At the time I remember having moments of doubt.'

'But you continued.'

'Kfansh taught me ways of controlling pain and exhaustion with mental discipline. Eventually I took their test to become a Shourai Warrior.'

'And did you pass?'

'Failing would have permanently crippled or killed me.'

'That doesn't sound fair.'

'Perhaps. Most fail the initial tests which are not harmful. But you have to understand that their people live in poverty. To be accepted as a Shourai means a life wanting for nothing and living in comparable luxury. Letting the people know the danger they face in the tests keeps the masses away.'

'Makes sense I guess,' said Garamon, swiftly leaping a knee high jagged rock that protruded from the path that had been obscured by Falakar ahead of him. He glanced back and noticed that there was plenty of space on either side of the rock to pass by. He suspected that Falakar had caught onto his game.

Still looking behind he was brought to an abrupt halt by the Ranger.

Ahead of them on the trail stood Jontal and three other men of equally dubious character, swords in hand.

'At last,' said the bandit, sociably. 'I've lost all feeling in my toes. I remember a time when you would have been out at first light.'

Falakar pushed Garamon back the way they came. Three more men dropped down from hiding places to block the return path. Falakar scanned the rocks around. The location of the ambush was well chosen.

'No way out, Fal. Well not for the boy anyway, and I know you wouldn't leave him behind, you being the perfect example of an honourable man.' Garamon detected a hint of bitterness in the comment.

'What do you want?' said Falakar sharply.

'Well you of course. You'll provide my retirement ransom I reckon.'

'The lad's valuable too,' said Falakar.

'Really?' replied Jontal, sounding dubious.

'He's the son of Renous of Tiburn.'

Garamon snapped up to look at Falakar.

'Don't worry lad, old Fal hasn't betrayed you. He just knows that if you're worth money to me I'll keep you alive.'

The bandit looked to be considering the proposal.

'Okay, I'm game.' His voice changed to one of command as he spoke to his men. 'Tie their hands and bring me the lad's axe.'

Falakar drew his short sword and long dagger and moved in front of Garamon. The men stopped.

'Come on Fal, if we get into a fight here the boy's misguided courage is only going to get him killed.'

Falakar stared at the bandit for a long moment, then pushed both weapons back into their scabbards.

'I have your word you won't do anything unfriendly?' said Jontal.

Falakar nodded.

Jontal's men remained still, looking for instructions.

'Go on lads, don't worry about old Fal, he's far too principled to go against his word. Take care with the lad though. I don't think he has too many morals about killing the likes of us.' Garamon shot the man a cold stare.

The men, still tentative, moved forward. One of them disarmed Falakar while the other rested his sword on the Ranger's chest. Falakar's hands were pulled behind his back and bound.

The men approached Garamon. He batted away an arm. The mercenary kicked out his boot connecting with Garamon's knee, taking him unawares and causing him to buckle to the floor. As he fell, the mercenary followed up with a heavy punch to his head, dropping him to fall face first into the snow. The other one placed his boot on Garamon's head and applied enough pressure to keep him down. The first man studied the straps holding the axe but couldn't work out how to release it.

'Try pushing it sharply downwards,' suggested Jontal.

With a few tries, the axe came free.

'Leave the lad,' said Jontal. 'We'll barter with his father using the axe as proof that we have his son.'

'No!' shouted Falakar, kicking up with a foot into the ribs of the nearest bandit, creating a loud crack and throwing him backwards to the ground.

The other man drew his sword and calmly placed it against Garamon's neck.

Falakar stopped. 'You bastard, he'll die out here!'

'Probably true,' replied Jontal. 'But the lad's got too much spirit and he'd be sure to try some ridiculous escape and get himself killed anyway, so this way it's the same result without the trouble of further interference to me. Now let's go, we're a couple of hours from my nearest hideout.'

The man who was kicked got to his feet, holding his chest in obvious discomfort. He spat on Falakar from a safe distance. The other then pushed him hard in the back forcing him forward.

Garamon looked up at the retreating figures. He could see Falakar looking back at him until the final moment.

When the last man moved out of sight he tried to stand. He caught himself as the pain in his knee stabbed. He held onto the rock to steady himself until the pain eased enough for him to apply weight onto his foot. He considered his position. He was in dangerous territory without weapon, food, water, survival skills or clue about which direction to travel. Having no better idea, he limped in the direction that Falakar was taken.

Chapter 14 - The Lan-Chi

Chayne heard the chimes indicate three am, the reported time for his assassination. The palace enforced a curfew from dusk until dawn. Other than guards, palace elite and Masters, only the 'invisible' servants moved during this time. And so he came to understand the purpose of the garment left in his room.

He was now wandering the lower levels of the palace dressed as a servant and pretending to be on some errand. He was running the risk of being checked by a guard for his papers which were not included with his disguise.

He reached another T-junction and didn't pause, as servants would never do so. He walked straight into two guards in front of a doorway just after the turn.

Orders, said one of the guards in the sign language.

He didn't have any.

Orders, repeated the guard with stronger gesticulation.

Chayne bowed and turned away.

'Halt!' said the guard aloud. Swords were drawn.

'Identification!'

Chayne stopped, keeping his head down indicating subservience.

'Come with me,' said the guard.

Having no choice, Chayne followed.

He was led along identical looking passageways, enough for him to be lost, before they emerged into a wide corridor. Unlike the grand affair he'd seen on leaving his prison when he arrived, here there were no windows, drapes or servant recesses. It was functional in its pale grey decoration and bare wooden floor. Pairs of guards were walking in step, to and from a set of doors at one end. It looked like a major guard post. The guard led them towards the doors.

Inside was an antechamber, decorated in much the same fashion as the corridor. Soldiers milled around in pairs here too, coming and going from an internal smaller passageway. A single desk sat off to the left with a soldier processing parchments. Chayne guessed these were orders as each pair that came to him received a parchment and then disappeared from the room into the main corridor. The whole scene was one of unquestioning obedience and mechanical efficiency.

Chayne's guard approached the desk.

'Soldier?' said the desk soldier.

'Sergeant, this servant turned to enter Ha'Jakurian's quarters, but has offered no orders upon request.'

The Sergeant looked to Chayne. *Orders*, he mimed, with hands younger than should belong to the voice.

Chayne again did not move.

'Take him to the inquisitor on level two for interrogation and correction.' He wrote into a large log book and then wrote on a small brown parchment which he passed to the guard.

The guard saluted the sergeant and snapped his fingers at Chayne to get his attention. The guard displayed the instruction for *follow me*. Chayne nodded once.

He was led from the room to continue on another journey. At the point where they dropped down a level, he was handed over to another guard.

This part to the journey was even longer. The corridors became less populated until they were the only two travelling. They turned down a poorly-lit passage, the first he'd come across in the palace, which was unusual. At the end of the passage were stairs leading down. These were not lit at all.

The guard picked up a lantern from the floor. It gave out a weak light, barely enough for a good footing. As they descended, Chayne noted the stairs were poorly maintained, which was never the case in any part of the palace. At the bottom of the stairs the usual guard presence was absent.

The low light outlined a barricaded wooden door. Chayne's unease was turning to fear. Was this the fate for unwanted servants, humans who were valued less than household pets, a short sword in the back and disappear without trace? Or perhaps his assassins had infiltrated the palace guards. After discovering his absence in his room, they tracked him down to make alternative arrangements.

The guard carried out a series of gentle taps on the wood that were obviously a code. A small panel at head height was removed from the inside which revealed darkness beyond. A pair of eyes appeared and inspected the visitors. The panel was replaced and several securing bolts could be heard being pulled back. The door swung away into the blackness beyond.

'Enter,' said the guard. No sign language.

Chayne went to back away. The guard grabbed his arm and drew a sword, dropping the lantern in the process and plunging the area into complete darkness. He felt the tip of a blade against his stomach.

'Enter,' repeated the guard.

Chayne edged forward over the threshold and was tripped to the floor. He was held down as a hood was forced over his head and tied while another pair of hands searched his body.

He heard the door close behind him and the bolts thrown.

'Do as I say or you will meet a quick death. Understand?' The words were whispered close to his ear, but forceful.

Chayne nodded.

He was helped to his feet and could see specs of light breaking through the thick fabric of his hood, but nothing else. Two pairs of hands held his arms. He heard a door open in front of him and the smell of damp wafted through.

'We must move quickly from here, the footing will become slippery at times.'

'Who are you people?' he whispered.

'Do not talk or even whisper until we reach our destination. Another word and we will gag you also.'

Chayne nodded again before being guided forward.

The resonances changed to indicate that they had entered another corridor. The door was closed and locked behind them. The men around him moved quickly and silently. Nobody spoke. Chayne occasionally heard sounds that he recognised as the gentle slap of fingers against palms from hand signalling.

He was led along more passages and down more flights of stairs. All the time the footing became more slippery and the smell of damp and decay increased. The sound of flowing water could now be heard and was getting louder. He turned another corner and the sound of the water increased alarmingly and he faltered. Were they going to drown him?

A mouth was pressed close to his ear.

'We must climb down here. The footing will be difficult. We will guide both your feet and hands. A fall wouldn't kill you, but you could break something.'

Chayne nodded again, relieved to hear such an affable tone being used.

His first footing was onto a small surface barely larger than his foot. It was at a slight angle down and away from him. His foot slipped away and he was grabbed by several pairs of hands that stopped him from falling. A hand grabbed his foot and pushed it down onto the surface again. He was helped to regain his balanced and gathered his weight back onto his foot. This time it held firm.

The descent was slow. After his first slip both his hands and feet were guided meticulously to each foot and hand hold. Some were cracks in rock and others rough pointed stone. The time was thankfully short before he was standing on a wider, flat surface able to take both feet.

'You must jump here,' said a voice. 'It is only a few feet and we will catch you at the bottom.'

'I don't think I can,' replied Chayne, and took a step backwards.

'I'm sorry but there is no other way,' said the voice. 'Please hurry.'

Chayne took a tentative step forward, and then stepped back quickly.

'I-I-I'm sorry. I cannot do this bli -'

But before he could finish, hands gripped his arms and threw him forward. He attempted to remain upright but his third step met nothing and he fell forwards with a shout.

No more than a second later he was caught by several pairs of hands and safely righted to his feet. His legs gave way, landing him with a thump onto his backside.

'Get to your feet,' came another command, urgently whispered into his ear and only just heard over the sound of running water which was far louder here, as if a river were nearby.

He attempted to stand. His legs had yet to recover from the shock of his fall. Then there was a sound that froze Chayne's blood. It was primal and animalistic. It sounded a long way off. That only suggested to him how loud the noise must have been and the size of the thing that made it. He was promptly hauled to his feet and half dragged along.

'What was that?'

A head was pushed hard up against his ear. 'Shut up you idiot, do you want to kill us!'

He was pulled and pushed along in a half run. The sound of the creature grew louder.

There was a thunderous rush of water from not far behind them and the air was split with the sound of the creature's squealing cry. Chayne placed his hands over his ears to block the noise. At the same time the men let go of his arms.

'*Run!*' one of them shouted.

Chayne heard the men running off ahead of him. He tried to remove his hood but it was secured by a knot. The creature bellowed again, much closer. He left the knot and just started running blindly in the direction of the retreating footsteps. Slipping he stumbled onwards as fast as he could, heedless of whatever might be in front of him, for whatever it was it couldn't be worse than the thing chasing him. The sound of the running footsteps ahead ceased and he panicked, sprinting on.

'*Help me!*' he yelled, but there was no response.

He continued to run, the thing cried out again making him duck away from the pain in his ears. The movement made him lose his balance and he fell headlong to the floor, sliding on the slippery surface for several feet on his chest. As he came to rest he could hear the creature approaching, making a slapping and sliding sound.

He got to his feet again and ran. He took only a few steps before impacting on something hard like stone. His head cracked against it and he recoiled from the collision.

He was grabbed by hands that wrenched him from his feet forwards. He heard a door slam shut behind him and bolts hastily slid into place. There was the sound of a huge impact on the door. The bolts rattled violently but it sounded like they held. The door creaked again as if some huge pressure was being applied. There was the sound of snuffled breathing, as if the thing was sniffing them out. It was followed by a smell of rotten fish strong enough to almost make him gag. He placed his hand over his mouth to stop any sound he might make and could hear faint shuffling indicating that the other men were having similar difficulties.

Stealing himself against the stench, he tried again to remove his hood. A hand was placed over his, stopping him.

The door creaked again and the bolts rattled loose in their fixings, indicating that the pressure had been released.

Minutes passed before one of the men spoke. 'I think it's safe.'

Chayne was pulled to his feet. 'Are you fit to travel? You hit that wall pretty hard?'

'I'm okay. My head broke the impact.'

There was the merest murmur of approval of his humour from the collective around him.

'It is safer from here on and there is no danger from the creature.'

'What *was* that thing?'

'No questions will be answered until we reach our destination. It isn't far now.'

They continued their journey without further incident. The smell of damp persisted, but lessened the further they went. They finally halted and Chayne heard the familiar dull tapping of a code on wood. A door opened and he was pulled through. The door was closed behind him and he was directed to a position.

'There is a chair behind you, sit down.' The words were spoken by a new voice from in front of him. A voice that was used to conveying authority.

He did so.

'We are going to remove your hood. It will be bright. Do not attempt to cover the lamps with your hands.' Chayne felt the twine around his neck loosen and the hood was pulled free. Intense light poured into his eyes and his hands came up instinctively to cover them.

'Lower your hands!' spoke the voice urgently. 'Do not attempt to cover the lamps or you will not leave this room alive.'

Chayne complied and was left squinting heavily into two lanterns. The lantern light was being concentrated through lenses, focused onto his face. With no other light in the room this created complete blackness from where the voice came. He scanned around the rest of the room that he could see behind him. It was another room in poor condition and had the look of being abandoned. Other than his chair he could only make out the small table ahead of him upon which the lamps were placed. Behind him were three men standing across the door. All were wearing black hoods with holes for eyes, ears and mouth. He turned back to the source of the voice, the lamps blurring as his eyes watered in the light.

'I have no doubt you are confused by this abduction. Unfortunately, our attempt to rescue you from the assassination attempt tonight was hastily constructed and as such didn't go to plan. We didn't expect you to travel so far from your room and we couldn't find you. Eventually you were handed into one of the guard stations where we have a presence and we managed to divert you from your appointment with the interrogator. All of this has been done with considerable risk to us and not without dissent in my ranks for attempting your rescue. However, you are here and it appears we have managed this without exposure.'

'May I ask who you are and why you have any interest in rescuing me?'

'We are the Lan-Chi, and you are here because you may be of some use to us.'

'The re-sis-tance?' said Chayne, trying to translate.

'Your interpretation is a little peculiar, but yes, you have the idea.'

'What use could I be to you that would justify the risk you have taken?'

'I cannot fully reveal that at this time. If you are who we hope, then we can use you, or at least what you are to become.'

'Use me? Become?' queried Chayne.

'You are a pawn in a complex political struggle for dominance between different factions within the Empire and certain powerful individuals.'

'You're talking about the Shodatts and Masters?' said Chayne, once again noticing himself being referred to as a pawn.

'They are two of the groups, yes. There are others.'

'And how could I possibly be important to them?'

'You have been identified as the Zil'Sat'Shra.'

Chayne paused for a moment attempting to match the word with any of the Ashnorian words that he knew, but there were none.

'Should that mean something to me?'

There was a pause as the leader spoke softly with another unseen person.

'The term is largely obsolete in common language and is something of a myth. It claims that a man, not of Ashnorian blood, will one day arrive and be the salvation of the common people from the tyranny of their evil masters.'

Chayne only just withheld a laugh. 'And that's me?'

'I am an educated man, Mlendrian, and in my normal life not unreasonably positioned. The Zil'Sat'Shra is no more than another false hope amongst the servants and low-born, as they believe in one saviour after another to bring them out of their oppression. But that is irrelevant to us. If you have the potential for magic as we've heard, and you are being believed as this saviour, then the Shodatts will fight for you, or prevent you from being beneficial to rival parties if they cannot have you for themselves.'

'Like tonight you mean?'

'Precisely. However, if we handle things carefully we can play one off against the other to our advantage.

'Using me in the middle?'

'Yes.'

'And I'll do this because?'

'You owe us your life.'

'I only have your word that the assassination was genuine. How do I know that you didn't plan all this and that it wasn't you that planted the warning note?'

'I have no proof to give you. There is an element of blind faith here.'

Chayne paused. Stalizar said that the Empire was based upon who held the greatest influence with the Emperor and that magic was the favoured power. He could believe that he was saved as these so-called Lan-Chi were claiming. It was also just as reasonable that they could be manipulating him. It was impossible to know which was true, or come to that, which was the lesser evil.

'I can see you are not easily swayed,' continued the voice. 'I consider that a strength. So perhaps there is another reason that you will do it.'

'The Emperor is preparing his armies to invade Mlendria across the Hammerhead Mountains.'

Chayne's eyes went wide. His thoughts went immediately to his cabin in the woods and he looked on as soldiers marched across his clearing, ransacking and burning everything to the ground. Then his thoughts turned to the small town of Tiburn.

'They are just farmers, woodcutters and their families. The Rangers are only there in small numbers to maintain law enforcement and protection from bandit trouble. They wouldn't create any resistance to an organised army. You must stop it!'

'We would like to.'

Chayne continued to stare in the direction of the voice, waiting for more. Realization then struck him. 'You want *me* to help?'

'If we tell you how.'

'What possible difference could I make against the most powerful Empire in the world, bent on war?'

'Because Lathashal is the most senior magii in Straslin and the new Emperor has assigned him the position of Attack Magii to General Zanthak.'

'But I have no influence over Lathashal. He is my teacher, that is all. I cannot speak out of turn or even discuss anything that isn't related to a lesson.'

'He is going to discover that an attempt has been made on your life.'

'How will that make a difference?'

'He wants you alive and under his control. We believe we can exploit that fact to achieve our mutual aim.'

'What will I need to do?'

'You will tell him of the assassination attempt, at your training session later today.'

'He will believe me?'

'In all likelihood he will already know. His is an old hand, his spy network extensive. But if not then such a serious accusation will not go unchecked. He will discover the truth and will be enraged, although unable to release his anger as he has yet to officially announce your true potential.'

'Why so?' said Chayne confused as to why someone in such a high position would be troubled with the simple announcement.

'He is afraid he will lose you to one of the more powerful cities.'

'I don't understand. If the Shodatts are fighting over me then they all must know of Lathashal's judgement of me in this matter.'

'That is correct, but you must understand, everything is not as it seems and nothing you hear is the full truth. The Empire is riddled with spies, and spies spying on those spies. Everybody is doing it, *but it is strictly forbidden*. So although a Shodatt may know of another Shodatt's secrets, and the second Shodatt knows that the first Shodatt knows of the secrets, if you follow me, neither can expose the other without implicating their own guilt in spying. The penalties for such are extreme. The Emperor knows all of this and in fact uses it to his advantage as it keeps the Shodatts busy fighting amongst themselves instead of uniting against him. It has worked perfectly as the source of the Empire's paranoiac control for six hundred years.'

'But again, what could I possibly do to stop the invasion plans of an Empire, or even Lathashal for that matter?'

'We believe that the only way Lathashal could protect you is to make you his Zintar: his apprentice. It would be a daring move because it will provide you with unprecedented access to him, his politics and his power. It has not been done in many generations by any Master because of that.'

'What if he doesn't think to do that?'

'Then you must find a way to make sure that he does.'

'Won't he be suspicious?'

'Of course. However, it is our hope that you being an outsider and not knowledgeable of such an antiquated custom that he will allow himself to believe that you simply stumbled across it in your reading, which we have come to be informed is most studious.'

'And if he doesn't believe *that*?'

'Then you will be tortured for the truth.'

Chayne's mouth dropped open.

'Are you aware of the Rite of Rakasti?' said the voice.

Chayne took a few moments to register the new words and shook his head from the vision of his agonising potential future.

The voice took the movement as indicating no.

'That is to be expected. It is one of the many secrets amongst the Shodatts. Before a major attack on another army, a powerful and dangerous series of spells are cast by the Battle Magii, in this case Lathashal. I'm afraid I am not a magii and therefore cannot explain the technicalities as you might, but the spell somehow provides the Attack Magii with a complete picture of all enemy locations within the intended invasion point. This has always provided us with accurate strategic and tactical information on enemy scouts and locations of points of resistance. It is why we are able to penetrate in such large numbers with total surprise.

'But that would take energy in unthinkable quantities,' replied Chayne.

'As I said, the spell is extremely powerful. It is also dangerous to the casting magii. Those who fail at such spells shrivel within a fiery blaze or die screaming. This is why only the master magiis dare attempt the spell, and even then they take extreme precautions in their preparations and isolate themselves during casting to avoid any distractions.'

Chayne thought he understood. 'So by placing me as his Zintar you hope I can get close enough and disrupt this spell, thereby both destroying the most powerful magii in Straslin, and stopping the attack.'

There was a brief pause from beyond the lamps. 'I see your reputation as a quick learner is no exaggeration.'

'But another magii would take his place?' continued Chayne, ignoring the remark. 'I would only delay the attack.'

'As I said, the spell itself, and those that must be cast to protect the caster from potential side-effects, take many weeks to complete. However, that will be as nothing compared to the ramifications of such a potent position becoming available. There will be months of political manoeuvring. In that time your people could be warned and prepare themselves for an attack. It may even make the Emperor rethink attacking your land.'

'How so?' said Chayne.

'We have certain operatives in key positions in the politica that are poised and ready to sow dissent regarding the wisdom of the attack. It is possible, given a delay, that my people will be able to create a split between the Emperor's advisors and have them change their plans.'

'What if I fail?'

'I will not lie to you, Mlendrian. It is a dangerous gamble. There are many things that could go wrong.'

'What if I think it is too risky and declined your offer?'

'*Do* you decline?' came the quick response.

Chayne paused for only a moment.

'I know little of these matters at this time. If what you say is true then I will attempt to do what you ask.'

'Then you will leave this room alive.' And with that the lamps were extinguished and the hood was forced over his head once more and tied.

'Wait! I have many more questions. How do I achieve my task? When should I act? *How will I contact you?*'

'Use the word *Whitehawk* in conversation around the palace guards. We will be listening.'

And that was that. The discussion was over. The door was unlocked and he was led back via many twists, turns and stairways until a voice was heard some way ahead. His escort pulled sharply on his arm, bringing him to a halt.

'I cannot take you further!' The words were spoken in panic and Chayne could hear the sound of receding footsteps as the man left him.

Chayne now recognised the angry voice as Lathashal's. He scrabbled at his hood to untie it. He had to get out of his servant robe.

The voice was getting closer. The muffled echoes indicated that Lathashal had yet to navigate one or more corners. Chayne managed to release the knot securing his hood and pulled it clear. He found himself back in the familiar lit passages of the palace. He looked around for his escape and noted a bundle of clothes at his feet. It was his training robe.

He threw off his servant disguise and began putting on the robe. It was still only half way over his head and blocking his view when he heard Lathashal enter the corridor directly ahead giving frenzied orders. As the garment fell into place he expected to see the magii bearing down on him ready to inflict terrible retribution. But the man entered from a side corridor and must have looked the other way first. That precious second was all that was needed.

The magii advanced almost in a run, leading four guards.

'Are you harmed?' He was red in the face. His voice was filled with anguish, not anger. Chayne then knew what to do.

'No Master, but I was so frightened, he replied and ran forward, trying to disguise the bulge of the servants uniform under his robe.

The look on Lathashal's face was one of great relief. Chayne would not have believed that the man was capable of such an emotion.

'That is good news, boy,' said the magii, reaching his hand out to clasp Chayne's shoulder. The act of affection almost made Chayne recoil.

'What in all the mysteries of known existence compelled you to leave your room?'

Chayne's mind raced. He could not show a moment's delay in answering.

'I am sorry Master. My room, whilst generously sized, is smaller than my old cottage, and I am ashamed to say that I felt claustrophobic. I slipped out for a brief walk. Upon my return I saw men with swords drawn entering my room and I panicked and ran, getting lost.'

'You have the luck of the gods, boy,' replied the magii shaking his head. 'Those men were ordered to kill you.'

Chayne faked a gasp.

Lathashal addressed one of the guards, 'Take him back to my lab and guard all entrances. Your life depends on his safety.'

The soldiers acknowledged the instruction with a stiff-backed salute and bundled Chayne away. Chayne risked a glance over his shoulder to see Lathashal inspecting the area for a few moments before following.

Later that morning, Chayne received his thirtieth lesson from Lathashal. The drama of earlier seemingly forgotten by the man. The sessions were going unusually well according to the magii. Chayne had increased his understanding of magic a hundred-fold and was now capable of safely discharging the energy from the smallest of manaspheres. For this reason Lathashal took a gradia two sphere from the training cabinet. Chayne looked at it with both eagerness and anxiety.

'You fear the step up?' said Lathashal.

'A little Master. My punishment with the gradia five sphere during my early days with you is hard to forget.' This predictably pleased his tutor.

'There is nothing to fear now,' replied Lathashal. 'I will not allow harm to come to you unless correction is required. Since then you have behaved impeccably and listened flawlessly.' He placed the box with the manasphere onto the table. 'Open it and raise the manasphere.'

Chayne flicked the latch on the box and lifted the lid. He was surprised to see that this manasphere was the same size as the gradia one sphere he had already been using.

'Master, may I ask a question?' he said as he levelled the sphere to its upper position.

'Continue.'

'Is not the size of a sphere related to its power?'

'In part, yes. There is another factor at work that you are unaware. Place your fingers upon it as you have been taught.'

Chayne placed the fingertips of both hands gently upon the surface of the orb. As he did so he felt a little light-headed and his hands tingled faintly. This reminded him of his experience with the sphere that Lathashal burned him, but this was far less threatening and he resisted the urge to pull away.

'How does it feel?' asked Lathashal.

'A little uncomfortable, Master. My mind is having trouble focussing as well as usual.'

'Levitate the glass on the table before you.'

Chayne began to concentrate on the glass goblet, allowing the energy to flow from the sphere to push up under the glass.

The glass rocketed upwards. Before Chayne had a chance to react, it smashed into the ceiling, shattering into hundreds of pieces that rained down within the room. Lathashal snapped his fingers and several servants left recesses and began clearing up the debris.

'Master, I am sorry. I do not know that happened. There was too little time to react.'

But Lathashal was amused. 'How does it feel now?'

'A little warm, Master. And I am having trouble gaining focus.'

'You remain a wonder to me boy. Each lesson I try to push you beyond your limits and between lessons you learn evermore to keep pace.

The manasphere in your hands is not a gradia two but a gradia three. By rights the glass should have simply exploded on the desk and you should be experiencing significant disorientation, and pain in your hands. But instinctively you reacted to gain some control. Do you think if you tried again you could do better?'

'I'm not sure, Master. My mind is being pulled from its train of thought.'

'Let us see,' insisted the magii. He pointed to the table. A servant replaced the destroyed glass with a new one.

Chayne closed his eyes and attempted to gain full concentration. Again something seemed to be interfering. He battled before getting control of the interruptive force. He opened his eyes to focus on the glass.

Once again it reacted violently, speeding to the ceiling. This time he was ready and fought to hold it. It stopped inches from destruction, pulling this way and that, tumbling and twisting. He appeared to get the upper hand and he felt his control winning and brought the glass back down to hover in front of him, turning slowly. Now that he had control, he relaxed a little.

'You are in control?' asked Lathashal.

'Yes, Master. I had trouble at the start, but now I am -' His mind was struck as if by a whip, his hands seared with heat. The glass shot directly towards him and he ducked as it flashed passed his head and smashed once again into pieces, this time on a far wall.

He released his contact with the Sphere and shook his head in disbelief.

Lathashal chuckled, 'What did you observe that time?'

'I thought I was in control of the glass. Then just as my confidence grew and my guard was let down the sphere became hot. It felt like *something* was fighting for control of the glass.'

'And it looks like it won,' said the magii with a smirk.

'Yes, Master. I have failed a test,' said Chayne dropping his head in the knowledge that this meant correction.

'Worry not boy, this was not a normal test and you shall not be punished. But it has finally confirmed my assessment of you. You shall be leaving my training programme forthwith.'

'Master, I do not understand.' replied Chayne, distraught. He had to stay within arms reach of the man to accomplish his mission for the Lan-Chi.

'You may well look distressed boy, and not for leaving my training. You are to become my Zintar, the first for three hundred years.'

Chayne couldn't believe it. Had Lathashal gained knowledge of his covert liaison with the resistance and was playing him to gain information from within the Lan-Chi?

'The position will carry considerable authority,' continued the magii, 'and even give you some standing within the Straslin royal court. I shall be devoting my teachings solely to you. The training will be gruelling.'

'Master, may I ask another question?'

'You no longer require permission to speak,' said Lathashal. 'As my Zintar you have the privileges and freedoms similar to my own.'

Chayne pondered for a moment exactly what that meant in such a place. He parked the thought for later.

'I have not come across any mention of such a position in any of the texts I have read?'

'It is not mentioned. Zintars are almost unheard of due to their purpose. To be trained to replace their Master so that the Master can be elevated into a higher position, knowing that he leaves behind somebody he can trust to fulfil his old post as he would have done. The post is rare because there are many powerful Magiis who have waited for decades to be take such a position. A Zintar has first rights on the position of his Master. If I die, or am favoured with the Emperor for elevation in rank, then you will replace me. For that reason few Zintars live long enough to claim the position. You have already attracted dangerous attention. Now I will take personal care of you. From now on, when you are not here in this protected laboratory, you shall be with me learning the roles of the new posting. All texts that you require from the library shall be magically delivered. I will announce my intentions to have you made my Zintar within the hour. Remain within this laboratory.'

'I am honoured by your kindness and generosity,' said Chayne.

'I care nothing for either, and you will not be honouring me in a few days. I will push you far beyond even your limits. You will learn at a vastly accelerated rate that will create huge stresses on your mind and body. You will be lucky if you survive.'

'I look forward to the challenge, Master. When do I begin?'

'I have already prepared your workplace,' replied Lathashal indicating a small workbench in the corner of the laboratory. There was also a small bunk and a cupboard. One of the lab basins was adjacent and was converted for personal use. 'All of your belongings are here so there is no need for you to leave this room.'

'Thank you, Master,' replied Chayne, surprised at the speed with which his circumstances changed.

'I need to make my announcement. Your next lesson is laid out for you. Be ready for the tests on my return,' said Lathashal. He left the room.

Chayne walked over to the bench and inspected the items laid out upon it. Some were to do with the lesson, but a small wooden box stood out that didn't belong. There was a note lying on it with Lathashal's mark. He unfolded it.

It welcomed him as his Zintar. It was short and without warmth. It explained that the bench was now his personal area and that the wooden box was a gift. A footnote read: *'The tertiary radial to the fifth juncture'.*

Chayne inspected the box. He had seen many like it. It was a manasphere container, as usual made with exquisite workmanship. Polished wood with brass hinges and latch. He tried to lift the latch but it would not budge. As it was inconceivable that the mechanism would be anything other than perfectly manufactured, Chayne knew that there must be another method of opening the container. He recalled that Lathashal would whisper something while opening the latch of manasphere boxes. He looked at the note again: *The tertiary radial to the fifth juncture.* This referred to the teachings at the end of the fourth gradia and something that he would not normally learn for some time. He was guessing that Lathashal had assumed that he might already know the answer. Chayne touched the latch and whispered the words, *'Ithalical Malitrolii.'*

The latch popped open.

He lifted the lid to reveal his first manasphere.

Reverently, he raised the sphere from its box using the lifting mechanism and locked it into place. He placed the fingertips of his right hand on the sphere and concentrated for a few seconds. Mana began to flow into the holes.

He stopped and wondered about how to test out his new acquisition. He looked to the note from Lathashal and knew that the clue to his pass phrase should be destroyed. He decided that that would be his first spell with the sphere.

Returning his hand to its previous position, he placed the other over the paper.

'Burn.'

The note erupted into an intense blue flame and was consumed. Not even smoke survived.

He had only meant to release enough energy to erase the ink. Startled at his lack of control he attempted to let go of the sphere. Something pulled at his mind and attempted to hold his fingers to the sphere. He pulled away sharply, both with his mind and fingers. As he broke contact, so his fingertips stung and there were tiny cracks of sound as they released from the surface.

He shuddered and decided to lower the sphere back into its box for now.

He closed the lid, the latch reset with a gentle click. He pushed the box to the back of his bench and began unpacking the items for his lesson.

Chapter 15 - Mountain allies

The tantalising aroma of cooking once again drifted across Garamon's nose. He'd been trying to track down the source for over an hour and was beginning to think that he was imagining it. He'd doubled back, crossed paths and sought higher ground. It eluded his poor tracking skills until at last he caught a glimpse of a column of fine white smoke rising from a crack in the rocks. It carried the smell of cooked meat, herbs and spices. His stomach growled and he moved back from the small opening. Would the occupants be friendly? He felt he had nothing to lose and made his way down through the rocks.

The entrance was well hidden. Without the smoke giving away the position he would never have found it. He worked his way down to hide behind a snow-laden bush just outside the cave entrance. He peered through the gaps of the snowy branches.

The cave opened out from its entrance into a good-sized shelter comfortable for the small group. Suspended above a fire were five small pots and some skewered meat cooking. It looked the most appetising meal he'd ever seen. He pulled his eyes away and scanned the rest of the cave. There were four people. From their leathery clothing they looked like barbarians. He'd seen envoys from the mountains west of Mlendria dressed the same. One sat, crossed-legged and straight-backed in the far right corner of the cave. His skin was black and he was almost lovingly cleaning and oiling two swords that lay out in front of him. Near him was the second barbarian. He was asleep, laying length-ways from the back wall with his head nearest the cave entrance. It was difficult

125

to make out his proportions well from this angle, but from the size of his head he had to be huge.

The third was a striking young woman. Slim, but strong for her size. She wore a dagger and small sword around her waist and there was an unstrung bow leaning against the wall next to her. She sat alone with her knees pulled up under her chin and her eyes closed. Her face looked sad.

The last occupant was close to the fire. He was lean and powerful with an unusual metal shield resting over his sword nearby. He opened a small pouch and added a pinch of something into each pot. A puff of steam lifted from each one and the air current wafted it passed Garamon. He recognised the herb as one his mother used. His stomach growled again and turned over like it was trying to get out.

The minutes went by. These people were dangerous. Would they consider him an enemy? The mood in the cave seemed heavy. The cook stood and tested the meat with a slender knife, smelling and inspecting the juices on the end of the blade. He then cut off a long piece of meat and scooped up a pot with his knife under the handle and walked to the back of the cave with the other two men.

As he arrived so the dark-skinned one pushed up from his cross-legged position and walked across to the fire. He too sliced off a piece of meat and took one of the four remaining pots and returned to his position. He gave the big-headed one a kick as he sat.

The giant responded with a gruff snort. He raised his head and his nose sniffed the air. 'Ah, at last!' he said in rough tones. He got to his feet and Garamon looked on in awe. Apart from those that travelled with wandering circuses, he was the largest man Garamon could ever remember seeing. He looked almost comical in an assortment of ill-fitting furs. As he walked so he had to weave his way through the uneven roof of the cave. One of his legs looked to contain more muscle than Garamon's whole body.

He reached the fire and sliced off a huge piece of meat and stuffed it straight into his mouth. The majority of the meat was still protruding from his lips as he chewed, but not for long. A second piece suffered the same fate. He gave a loud grunt of satisfaction and sliced off another piece, waving it back at the cook indicating his approval. The cook nodded in reply.

The giant finished consuming the second piece of meat and folded the third up. He picked up his pot and was about to head to the back of the cave when to Garamon's shock he looked towards the bush where he was hiding.

'*Eat!*' ordered the giant, pointing to the food.

Garamon remained still.

The giant tapped his knife against the last pot and pointed back to him. '*Yours!*' Then he returned to the back of the cave with the others.

The fifth pot was for him? But it was already cooking when he arrived.

The woman then got to her feet. With subdued movement, she walked to the fire. She lifted one of the two remaining pots and walked to the front of the cave, kneeling down on the other side of the bush. She looked directly into his eyes through the foliage and gave a smile.

Garamon shrank back out of sight.

'You are welcome to join us.' The voice was as delicate and pretty as the face.

Garamon still didn't move.

'We lost our guide to bandits and I'm not experienced in these mountains. We wanted to exchange information for food and shelter.'

She held out the food pot.

He gingerly moved out from hiding, staring at the pot and licking his lips much like a starving kitten torn between the danger of a stranger and the offer of fresh milk.

He took the pot.

'It is warm by the fire,' she said, and walked back into the cave, collecting her meal along the way and returning to her position away from the others.

He crossed the threshold into the cave and was enveloped by the warmth. The cook rose from his position at the back of the cave and approached. As he came closer, Garamon could see that he walked like Falakar, with grace and fluidity. His face was broad and strong-jawed.

'Welcome, I am Kinfular of the Riaan.' The voice and eyes conveyed a man that didn't need to prove himself, and invoked immediate trust.

Garamon found himself bowing a little. 'I am Garamon of Tiburn,' he replied. 'I thank you for letting me share your food, fire and shelter.'

The barbarian lowered into a cross-legged position by the fire. 'You should take off those damp clothes and hang them near the fire.'

Garamon looked down at his clothes and noticed steam rising from them.

'I have nothing else to wear.'

The barbarian shrugged. 'It is warm in the cave.'

Barbarians obviously didn't share the modesty of Mlendrians. He took off his coat and gloves only and laid them across the nearest rock.

'Your boots too. Bluetoe will remove toes up here.'

Garamon resisted the urge to say, 'Yes sir.' He removed his boots and sat down by the fire, steam now rising from his thick woollen socks also.

With nothing else happening he picked up his pot. The first sip was cool but after breaking through the surface skin the second was hot and he burned his lip, spilling some. He looked up to see his host looking at him.

'The meat is not so hot.'

Garamon looked to the glistening roast. The succulent meat was moist and occasionally dropped a globule of fat onto the fire causing it to spit and hiss. He wanted it more than anything at that moment, but felt too self-conscious and just shook his head. He blew on the pot instead and slowly sipped at the thick liquid. It tasted strongly of herbs and was a little bitter for his taste, but he didn't show this.

'You do not like meat?'

Garamon nodded.

The barbarian reached over and cut off a length of the best remaining meat and passed it to him. 'You seem to have had bad luck,' he said, gesturing to Garamon's appearance.

'More than you would possibly believe,' replied Garamon.

The barbarian nodded his understanding, 'I too have not had the best of days.' For the first time his voice held some warmth and less command.

Garamon smiled in return.

'The woman, sorry I do not know her name ...' he ventured. The man gave no indication that he was going to offer it. 'She said that you wanted to exchange information.'

'We are looking for your Rangers. We come each year to help them against the bandits.'

'I thought you came in larger numbers?'

The barbarian looked pained at the comment. 'Bandits west of here ambushed us soon after we entered these accursed mountains. I lost most of my men.'

'It sounds like you came across Splitter's band. They are the most powerful in the mountains and something of a legend.'

'A legend no more then,' said Kinfular quietly and without pride.

'You killed them?' said Garamon astonished.

'Their leader, yes. And many more.'

Garamon looked upon the man before him with a new-found respect. 'There will be a lot of people relieved to hear that news. And there is a huge reward for his capture or death,' informed Garamon, smiling tentatively at the man's good news.

'Rewards will not bring back my men,' replied the barbarian, snapping a piece of meat away from the bone he was holding.

Garamon's smile faded.

'You will return now?' he said, wishing to move the conversation on.

'Our pledge still stands, and we will honour those fallen.'

'A shame you didn't arrive earlier,' said Garamon. I was travelling with a Ranger.'

The barbarian seemed only half-interested in the comment. 'Perhaps we make contact with him tomorrow.'

'I doubt it,' said Garamon regrettably. 'Falakar was taken during the ambush that left me out here alone.'

The reaction in the cave couldn't have been more immediate.

'How long ago was he taken?' demanded the barbarian.

'About five hours, sir,' replied Garamon.

'We have an hour of light remaining,' he called back to the others.

'You're going after him?' said Garamon surprised.

The question was answered as he watched the barbarian woman throw on her furs and disappear out of the cave, leaving her other belongings behind. The two men at the back were already packing their things while Kinfular doused the fire and packed the cooking implements.

'I might be able to backtrack to the place where he was taken with help,' offered Garamon.

'You fight?' asked that barbarian, ignoring his offer.

'Err, not really. I chop trees,' said Garamon apologetically. 'You run?'

'Yes sir, back home I annually win the -'

'We shall run through the night. You follow him,' interrupted the barbarian, indicating Sholster.

'In the dark?' queried Garamon.

The barbarian stopped what he was doing and untied a small pouch from around his waist and held it out.

Garamon took it and pulled apart the drawstring. Light came out. Inside was a smooth crystal, glowing with a blue hue.

Chapter 16 - Fate of men

With the fresh snow falling and the fading light, Falakar's trail was difficult to follow. When it became dark the barbarian woman's progress slowed, and Garamon noted frustration in the barbarian leader. The trek took them through the night and brought them out of the high mountain parts into a less rocky and more wooded area on the southern side. Eventually she had tracked down their quarry and returned from her survey of the area.

'Fifteen in the camp and six are on guard.'

'Could you see Falakar?' asked Garamon before Kinfular had any chance to respond to his scout.

'There was a man, tied up and guarded,' confirmed Shinlay.

'I need to see him, to be sure it's him,' he injected.

Kinfular seemed aggravated at the interruptions.

He looked to the sky. 'Dawn will be here soon. Silence a guard and return,' he ordered. 'Take him,' he added, indicating Garamon.

'Come with me and do as I say,' instructed Shinlay.

Garamon fell into line. As they reached the cover of some nearby trees, Shinlay stopped and looked back. The men were planning the rescue and Garamon could see that this didn't sit well with the woman.

'He seems harsh with you. Is that the custom of your people?'

'Custom?' she replied.

'You know, towards woman. I have heard that it is common amongst the primitive peoples.'

'You think us primitive!' she accused.

Garamon realised that he in fact meant exactly that. 'I guess I have grown up to believe that my people are better.'

'Then do not worry. I believed as a child that Mlendria was full of gutless sages.'

Garamon smiled at the thought.

'No more talk,' she ordered, and set off. Garamon followed her lead.

She moved through the terrain avoiding obvious paths. They stopped behind a rock large enough to give them cover. She unstrapped a sturdy-looking hollow cane. From a wrapped leather bundle she peeled away the layers to reveal six tiny darts. Taking one, she inspected the tip and the flight before pushing it gently into one end of the cane. Once in place she scooped up a stone and threw it over the rock. As soon as it hit the ground she stepped out and blew into the tube. Garamon heard a grunt and Shinlay sat back down and tied the reed back into place. Once completed, she stood and walked out.

Garamon followed to see a man lying on the floor. Shinlay removed the dart that was protruding from the back of his neck and replaced it back into its pouch. She pushed her finger up against his throat and seemed satisfied.

She then led with a series of sprints from trees to rocks until they could hear voices ahead. She held up her hand indicating that he was to stay where he was. She moved forward, crouching down and heading for a pair of young trees that would provide cover. For the last few paces she got onto her stomach and crawled. When in place, she looked through the foliage and then beckoned him over. He did his best to mimic her approach.

She gently pushed aside some of the foliage, allowing him to see through. The camp was no more than a rocky clearing in the trees. There was a fire in the middle and men were scattered around on blankets. Some were eating while others were cleaning weapons, playing dice or sleeping. As he scanned across the area, he saw Falakar. His was resting with

133

his back against a tree, his hands and feet bound. Talking to him was the bandit, Jontal, feeding him slices of fruit from a knife. The conversation looked surprisingly informal.

Garamon looked to Shinlay and nodded. It was the Ranger.

They returned to the others.

Kinfular listened to the report. 'You will stay here and guard the Mlendrian while we rescue the Ranger,' he said to Shinlay.

'You will do better with me covering with my bow,' she countered.

'We will manage fine without your help, woman!' snapped Kinfular.

'You are heavily outnumbered, Kin! We should wait for nightfall and rescue the Ranger under cover of night.'

'You will address me as Kinfular or Hlenshar, and I have had enough of being questioned!' his anger allowing his voice to rise dangerously loud so close to the camp.

Garamon knew little of fighting tactics but it did seem that the barbarian leader wasn't being reasonable.

The woman pursed her lips as if preventing more from coming out. She moved away.

Kinfular turned to him. 'If we should not succeed, she will lead you safely out of the mountains.'

Garamon nodded. 'Thank you for everything. Good luck to you.'

'May Rolk be with you too,' said the warrior, absently.

And with that they readied their weapons and set off.

They stopped one hundred paces from the camp, concealed from direct view. 'This is for the fallen, their families and for the honour of the tribe.'

'For the honour of the tribe,' said the other two in unison.

Without further ceremony, Kinfular lead the sprint towards the camp, threading between the outer guards either side of the one that Shinlay slept. They raced through to the edge of the camp unchallenged. A shout went up as the three burst into the open area and raced to the centre.

The defenders were caught by surprise and took a few seconds to understand what was happening. Scrabbling for their weapons they looked around for the rest of the attackers, but it became clear that there were no more. The bandits turned in to look at the three men standing impudently within them. Without a word they began to create a circle around them.

'Who in the five hells of Abborack are you?' questioned one of the more seasoned-looking bandits.

Kinfular's voice rang out across the camp, sounding crisp in the cold morning air. He didn't acknowledge the man who spoke, nor turn to face him. His words were for all.

'Fate mocks us all. I believed that I was to lead my warriors to aid the Rangers. But today the sun rises, laughing upon my arrogance that I may know my own destiny. I saw my warriors and best friend slain. Now the ripples of that act flow into your lives. For today you woke in the belief that you would see another sunset. This shall not be. Your lives end this day, but at least you can die in the knowledge that your deaths honour ones such as you are not even fit to know.' The Riaan warriors took up a battle stance, positioning their backs inwards to form a triangle of weapons facing out towards the rogues.

The bandit that spoke began to laugh. The rest of the camp joined in. He swung his sword around experimentally, loosening up his arm and shoulder.

'Then I hope your dead friends enjoy the show. For soon you can debate it with them.'

The man attacked.

ThreeSwords watched with detachment at the approach of the man. Without needing to think, he took in every detail about how the man held himself. The length and type of his sword, the weight distribution across his feet that gave away the intended two-handed attack profile. The direction of the

135

incoming first stroke was as obvious as if the scene were rehearsed. The blade approached and ThreeSwords had already committed to his counter. He raised his longer left sword to guide the overstretched two-handed chop harmlessly down to pass his side-stepped position to strike the ground. Simultaneously he thrust his shorter right blade out to take the attacker in the throat, piercing the vein. Without bothering to consider whether the man was finished he was already manoeuvring his body weight and weapons to block the next attacker.

Stensen was still at the back of the circle surrounding the barbarian attackers. He was nineteen and had only joined Jontal's band after his temper left an unarmed man dead in a bar brawl. He ran. Jontal had been there that night and followed him, offering him work. He reluctantly joined the band. Now he watched in confusion as his comrades fell, one after the other, as they came in contact with the ring of death. The mighty club of the giant smashed away with horrific consequences, sometimes lifting men from their feet to be thrown against those behind. None were yet to get close to him. All the time he smiled. The self-proclaimed leader's sword and shield worked with a harmony of defence and attack that struck down each attacker almost without any sign of contact, and with no threat to him. Lastly was the dark-skinned one, wielding twin swords that worked to trap and turn oncoming blades and return a deadly strike. He took slightly longer to kill than the other two, but seemed just as untouchable.

Although outnumbered, the positioning of the tribesman made it impossible for more than a few men to attack at a time, and as they did, they died. The weapons of the three warriors covered each other with a precision that was threatening in its own right. As he was considering this, the line of men separating him from the barbarian leader thinned and he faced him. He moved forward and raised his shortsword involuntarily. There was a flash and all noise faded and time seemed to slow. He took in the surreal scene of the barbarian turning in slow motion and keeping his balance as he slid over the blood and entrails of those already fallen before him. The world started to turn and he couldn't understand why it did so. The sky slipped into view and juddered and he noticed with clarity the contrast of the deep blue morning sky against the puffy spring clouds as they gently moved across the scene. It was so peaceful, he smiled to himself. He wondered briefly why it was getting dark.

Less than a minute passed since the fight begun and already the number of bandits thinned to less than half. Kinfular and his men continued to fight like avenging angels sent from the gods themselves and showed no mercy. When the bandits were down to ten men, one of them turned and fled from the barbarian leader. Kinfular, enraged at the cowardly act, roared his defiance and thrust out with manic power, smashing his shield out into the left attacker and stabbing his sword through the defence of the other, leaving it embedded. Crashing through them, he pulled a throwing axe from its sheath. With berserk strength and guttural cry that echoed out into the mountains stopping all who were fighting, he hurled the axe end over end.

The fleeing man reached the edge of the clearing, only a heartbeat away from the cover of the bushes. The axe struck the back of his head with a sickening thud and a power that split his head open, scattering his brains in a spray.

Kinfular stopped, still facing away from the main fight and panting heavily.

One of the men in the camp dropped his weapon and made a run for it. No action was taken to stop him.

The rest took the lead, throwing down their weapons and running from the clearing.

Kinfular remained still, feeling his heart thumping. Slowly the world came back to him, almost as a surprise. He blinked and looked at the scene around him. It was a scene from a nightmare. Sixteen men lay dead surrounding his two tribesmen. The snow turned to a crimson slush around them.

At the edge of his vision something moved and Kinfular saw that it was the Ranger, still bound, but now standing. He looked at him with puzzlement for a moment. His head cleared to remind him of the true purpose for the attack and the rescue of the man. A memory came unbidden to his thoughts. He walked back to the body of the young man who hardly raised a sword in defence and died from a single thrust into the heart from the *Hlenshar*. The lad looked so young, perhaps not even twenty. His eyes were still open and he seemed to be smiling. Kinfular moved his hand across the serene face and closed his eyes. ThreeSwords approached the kneeling leader.

'I do not feel right,' he said in his usual emotionless monotone.

Kinfular shut his eyes. His anger and loss had driven this honourable warrior into the slaughter of men who, while probably deserving of this fate, were not those that slew his men and should not have been held accountable. He had enacted a death sentence upon them, including a young man who didn't even know how to fight.

He then thought of Shinlay and the way he'd treated her, taking out the loss of his men upon her. She followed him out of love. He spurned her out of misdirected guilt and pride.

There was a nervous cough from behind and both men turned to see Sholster standing behind them with Falakar. He had been untied and was rubbing his wrists where the bindings had been.

Kinfular looked up into his eyes. They held no judgement, fear nor recrimination. The barbarian flicked his head toward the young man's corpse. 'You knew this boy?'

Falakar looked at the dead young man. 'No. He behaved like one of Jontal's new recruits.'

'He barely raised his sword. I didn't even see his face. I just lashed out at yet another soul to steal in an attempt to ease the pain in my own.'

Falakar didn't know the source of this warrior's trouble, but he knew that look after battle. Some things had to be worked out alone.

He turned back to the huge barbarian who released him.

'Thank you for setting me free. I don't wish to seem ungrateful, but I must leave you to search for another young man. He was left to die when I was captured.'

'Thick set, dark hair, about this high and underdressed?' ventured Sholster, holding his hand up around Garamon's height.

'Yes!' said Falakar.

'He is why we are here. Come, I'll take you to him.'

Falakar collected his weapons and Garamon's axe and re-joined the barbarian.

'I am Falakar.'

'The lad told us. You are a name known to us. I am Sholster. The dark-skin is ThreeSwords, the troubled one is Kinfular. We are Riaan.'

'I guessed as much,' replied Falakar. 'I fought alongside your people many years ago and recognised your fighting methods, although never with such ferocity and skill.'

'I do not remember you,' said Sholster.

'It was a long time ago,' replied Falakar. 'I doubt you would have been a warrior then. Also, I would have remembered one of your size.'

They began their walk to Garamon and Shinlay.

'Axe man then?' said Sholster, seeing the axe.

'No, it's the boy's,' replied Falakar. 'In truth he hasn't got a clue how to fight with it yet, but he's learning. The axe is something special.'

'May I see,' said the giant.

Falakar held out the axe.

Sholster took it and swung it around experimentally like another man would wield a single handed axe.

'Unusually light, it almost guides itself. What do the runes mean?'

'You can see them?' said Falakar surprised.

'Of course. How can they be missed? They are all over it.'

'It may surprise you to know that few people can. I most certainly cannot.'

'Magical!' said the big man, holding out the axe as if it suddenly turned into a dozen deadly snakes.

'So folklore has it,' said Falakar.

'Take it off me, quickly!' The man's urgency was genuine and fear could be seen in his actions.

'My apologies, I should have remembered your peoples' aversion to magic.'

'Just keep that thing away from me,' said Sholster, visibly relieved at letting go of it.

Shinlay watched the others go to rescue the Ranger. She turned back to Garamon and smiled weakly.

'Do you not wish to go with them?'

'I am not a fighter. Kinfular said that his plan relied upon each warrior protecting one another whilst fighting. I cannot do that. He was kind about it really.'

'Yes, he has a way with men,' she said, emphasising the last word a little sourly.

'You do not like him?'

'Before we left, he and I were mates. I followed him on this journey against his command and my father's will. Since then he has hardly spoken to me.' Shinlay then realised what she had said and wondered why she was so open with the young stranger.

'I too left my father,' replied Garamon.

'You are not old enough to do so? Our young men are sent alone into the mountains at your age to discover their courage.'

Garamon shook his head. 'My brother was lost to an accident while he was out hunting alone. My sister and I have been overly protected ever since.'

'Then why did you leave?'

'My friend was taken by the Ashnorians.'

'Did your clan not help you?'

'My father believes it pointless. Ashnorian borders are impenetrable, and they torture anyone found from the outside.'

'Then how can you achieve such a task?'

'In truth I have no idea. In fact without a lot of luck over the past few days I would have died three times already,' he replied solemnly.

The dulled sounds of fighting began from the direction of the bandit camp. Both flinched a little.

'You are a man of loyalty and courage then,' said Shinlay matter-of-factly, forcing her thoughts from the nearby conflict.

'Or just stubbornly stupid,' replied Garamon.

'Perhaps they are the same,' she said, partly distracted.

'You think I am foolish?'

'I do not demean your quest,' she said. 'In my tribe you would be granted great honour for attempting it.'

Garamon flushed at the compliment from the pretty tribeswoman.

'Well, well. What have we here?' The voice came from the side of them.

Both turned sharply to see Jontal walking towards them, sword drawn.

'*You*!' said Garamon.

Shinlay, hearing the venom in Garamon's voice raised her sword towards the newcomer.

'Ah, the boy-avenger. You've done well to survive. And who is this exquisite specimen from the tribal lands? You have good taste,' said the bandit, radiating confidence and not faltering in his approach at the sword drawn against him.'

'You leave her alone!' shouted Garamon.

'Come no closer,' commanded Shinlay, now setting herself into a combat stance.

Jontal continued until he was just inches from her sword tip pointed at his chest. He was still smiling. He sheathed his sword and brought his hands up quickly, attempting to unnerve her, making her jump.

'I have no sword drawn. It would be criminal to endanger one so beautiful.'

'What do you wa-' But that was all Shinlay said. Liquid squirted from the bandit's left hand into her eyes. She closed them in pain and swung her sword blindly, keeping the man at bay. Garamon then watched in horror as Jontal brought his right arm forward sharply to release a rock that struck the barbarian woman on the temple. She cried out and slumped to the floor, unmoving. Garamon stood dismayed for a moment. He'd seen neither where the rock, nor liquid came from.

'*What have you done!*' he shouted, turning to attack the bandit.

Jontal's sword was already resting on Garamon's chest. He was wearing that smirk, as ever.

'Distraction and expectation. I distract her. She expects me to draw a sword and so seeks blindly while I have a clear attack to her head. You were distracted by her body falling, caring for her. This I expected and gave me time to draw my sword. I have been doing this for a long time. Everything that transpired here was planned from the moment I walked into the clearing.'

At that moment they heard the sound of primal rage from the direction of the bandit camp, even Jontal seemed momentarily unsettled. He refocused.

'You are a persistent pest,' said the bandit, the smile fading from his lips.

'Give me a sword and I'll show you exactly what I am,' replied Garamon with pure hatred in his voice.

'I could, but your raw emotion is no substitute for proficiency. We both know that you wouldn't get the slightest chance of harming me.'

'Then you have nothing to lose,' contended Garamon.

'You're an irksome brat, but there is something about you that makes me not want to waste your life. Get on the floor and put your hands behind your back.'

'Go to hell,' replied Garamon hotly, and pushed his chest against the tip of the sword.

Jontal kicked out without warning into Garamon's stomach, forcing him back. He followed in one move by placing his sword against Shinlay's throat.

Garamon halted. 'You must feel very brave, threatening the life of an unconscious woman.'

Jontal sighed. 'You really are starting to aggravate me lad. Now do as I say or I'll kill you both and be done with it.'

Garamon stood his ground until Jontal made to deliver the strike. He held up his hand and slowly laid face down on the ground.

Jontal approached. 'Now we both know you're preparing some foolhardy attempt to attack while I don't have my sword in hand. If you try, I *will* kill you both.'

Garamon relaxed his posture. The bandit landed heavily with one knee on his back, causing him to grunt the air from his lungs. His hands were pulled behind him, bound tight.

Jontal was walking across to Shinlay when the sound of voices drifted into the clearing. One of them sounded like Falakar to Garamon. The bandit looked around. His eyes locked onto Shinlay and he scooped up her bow and a single arrow and ran back to Garamon.

'Get up, now!' he said, trying to drag Garamon to his feet. Garamon responded sluggishly.

Sholster and Falakar broke through into the clearing.

Jontal stepped away until his back was against a tall sheer rock face at the edge of the clearing.

Falakar dropped Garamon's axe and drew his sword. Sholster pulled out his club.

'Do not raise the alarm or I'll kill him,' said Jontal, bow in hand and levelled at Garamon's chest.

'Most of your men are dead, the rest running,' said Falakar. 'It is time to give yourself up.'

'They were worthless to a man,' snorted Jontal. 'This is what's going to happen. You will throw *your* weapons far away into the shrub.'

'You cannot escape this time, Jontal. It's over. Give yourself up,' urged Falakar.

'That's never going to happen. I'll count to five and then your new recruit gains another hole to breathe through,' answered Jontal.

Nobody moved.

'One.'

'If you let that arrow fly, you will die bandit,' said Sholster.

'Two,' said Jontal, ignoring the threat.

Falakar started scanning the area for some way out of the situation. There was clear ground either side of the bandit and no way to get behind him. The only option would be to rush him. He would never reach him before he loosed his arrow.

'Three!'

'You said you only killed people who threatened you,' said Garamon, desperation edging into his voice.

'I seem to remember that you wanted to bury your axe in my head yesterday. I just didn't get a chance to thank you properly back then,' replied the bandit.

'*Four!*'

Garamon prepared to dive. His heart was beating fast and although he doubted that the bandit would miss, he didn't see another choice. He saw the bandit pull the string back another inch and press his upper teeth to his lower lip in preparation to speak the final word.

'*Mee-yow.*'

Jontal lost his breath in an explosive exhale and, for the first time that Garamon had seen, his composure.

The words were spoken clearly, high up on the rock behind the rogue where there was no possible purchase for a human.

Garamon looked up and saw two large paws hanging over the edge of a tiny ledge, twenty paces further across and forty feet high up on the rock face. A furry head peered over.

It winked at him.

'What was that?' said Jontal, his eyes wide, but not moving from his target.

Fireball got to its feet and stretched lazily. It wiggled its backside a few times first, then, to Garamon's wonder, leapt gracefully from its distant perch and began an elegant arc across the impossible distance towards the bandit's head.

The woodsman looked down at the doomed man, smiled, and said:

'Five?'

Faced with the expression of utter confidence before him, Jontal was forced to spin around. At that moment, Fireball was completing the last seconds of free-fall and pushed all four legs out in front. From the paws extruded sixteen of the longest and most vicious-looking claws no cat had a right to own, and plunged into its target's head.

Jontal threw his bow to the floor, his hands moving frantically to dislodge the animal. Each time his hands attempted to catch the thing it had already moved. It was impossibly quick.

Garamon watched, unable to tear his gaze from the attack. Small tufts of hair were torn from the bandit's head and thrown in various directions. Jontal yelled and continued frantically to scrabble for the cat to relieve the agony he was suffering. In desperation he attempted to squash it by head-butting the nearby rock, only managing to hit his own head instead and staggering back from the impact.

He sank to his knees pleading for help as the onslaught continued.

Falakar approached, sword pointed more to the cat than the bandit. 'Your demonette?' he said over the commotion.

Garamon nodded.

'Can you call it off? I think we can say he is no longer a threat.'

As if responding to the request, Fireball leapt from the beleaguered bandit and landed front paws first into a drift of caked snow lying in the shadow at the bottom of the rock face. The thin crust cracked open, swallowing its new tenant and leaving only a backside and tail sticking out. Both wiggled a few times unsuccessfully to be free, then stopped. Smoky wisps appeared around the animal and it shaped-changed into Chantel. She looked down at the snow with contempt and it disappeared into a pool of steaming water.

'I truly *hate* that stuff,' she said.

She turned around to face the rest, all of whom were staring, ready to attack. Except Garamon who was only staring.

She looked down.

'Oh, sorry,' she said with a shrug. 'Lost the shirt.'

Nobody spoke. All maintained a battle ready stance.

'I think the words you're looking for again are: thank you Chantel, most kind Chantel, what would I do without out you Chantel?'

'Is it dangerous?' said Falakar to Garamon.

Garamon gave a silent shrug.

'*It!*' exclaimed Chantel. 'I'm not an *It*. I'm at least a *She*. Which under the circumstances I find hard to believe you cannot tell!'

At that moment Kinfular and ThreeSwords burst out of the bushes responding to the cries of help they heard, not knowing they had in fact come from the bandit. Everybody turned to see who it was. Turning back, the demonette was nowhere to be seen.

Kinfular saw Shinlay lying on the ground and rushed to her side.

146

'Guard him,' instructed Falakar to Garamon, then crossed to tend to Shinlay. He packed some snow and placed it upon a large blue welt on the barbarian woman's forehead.

Kinfular took over, holding it in place and cradling her in his arms.

ThreeSwords joined Garamon.

'What happened to him?'

'He was attacked by a cat that turned into a demon,' replied Garamon.

ThreeSwords looked at Garamon for a few moments. 'Your jokes escape me, Mlendrian, as much as the Riaan's.' He turned away and joined the others.

Garamon reasserted his vigil over the bandit, who was looking around nervously.

Chapter 17 - *Zystal*

Chayne sat at the lab's main bench deliberating the next series of magical undertakings provided by Lathashal. The bench was covered with containers of various interacting liquids, materials and magical trinkets capable of all manner of subtle and not-so-subtle reactions. His manasphere was close by. His desire for the object to stay within arm's reach was beginning to concern him, for each time he used it he wanted to do so more than the last. It was intoxicating to have so much power at his command and he had spent the last three months absorbed in his urgency to increase his magical skills. Lathashal was spending less and less time with him, showing increasing tiredness and even greater irritability than normal as the days went by. Chayne put this down to the magii's heavy involvement with the impending strike on Mlendria and the preparation of the *Rite of Rakasti*.

Chayne attempted to learn as much as he could about the Rite. All the most sensitive books were kept within Lathashal's personal bookcase, protected by a powerful spell for which Lathashal had a magical key to bypass. The key was kept within one of the many pockets within his robe.

So far he had discovered nothing to disrupt the Rite, but was sure that the answer lay within the bookcase. He once asked if he could study the books contained within it. Lathashal's response was sharp and final.

As he thought about overcoming the magic of the bookcase, so his hand involuntarily moved over to his manasphere. His fingers began to tingle and alerted him to its presence. He quickly closed his mind and pulled away. He pondered the orb once again, wondering why it had such an addictive nature.

His knowledge and control of magic was growing at an exceptional rate, according to Lathashal. He already had his own gradia five orb that he was safe to use without supervision. Lathashal explained that even a gifted student would take two years to get to such a gradia.

Chayne looked at the orb and believed he could feel it calling to him. He shook his head at such notions. At no time did Lathashal hint that the spheres contained any degree of sentience. And anyway, to create such a feat through magic would be too complex to imagine, even by Ashnorian standards.

He pulled his eyes from the object and continued reading his book: *Counter Magic, the Art of Negating Other Spells.* It was in addition to those ordered by Lathashal from the library. He glanced briefly at the bookcase, as if it would provide the inspiration necessary for him to understand how to overcome the protective barrier.

So far he believed he established the form of magic that was used. It was an adaptation of Energy Armour coupled with a Sustaining Field that maintained the armour magic even in the absence of the caster. There would be a manasphere within the cabinet somewhere providing the energy to maintain the Sustaining Field, and this would require recharging on a regular basis. The book explained that the normal way to defeat such a defence would require either an Energy Attack spell, powerful enough to exhaust the defence spell, or a more subtle approach that disrupted the Sustaining Field, thus causing the armour field itself to collapse.

Chayne was certain that his meagre skills were no match against spells that Lathashal produced, but the book explained that there was a riskier third option. Smaller spells could have a chance of temporarily interfering with the phase interaction between the Sustaining Field and Energy Armour that would allow a short period of access using Telekinesis - the act of moving something without touching. Chayne thought back to the glass smashing incident and knew that, while he was now capable of moving an object the size of a book, he would be controlling the counter magic at the same time, and that this may be too much for him. However he felt that he'd waited long enough, and that he'd have to risk it if he was to stand any chance of helping to thwart the invasion. He looked across to his manasphere. He somehow felt it was eager to help.

He took several minutes to place himself into a careful meditative state, providing him with the best mental discipline he could attain. The cabinet, apart from the magically strengthened glass in the doors, was made from solid thrinium; a strange silver-golden coloured substance that was not only light and incredibly strong, but as Chayne came to learn, was almost symbiotic in its reaction with magical energy, being used extensively by Ashnorian magiis. All manaspheres were made from it for instance. Chayne had never heard of the metal before entering Ashnoria. It was rare and incredibly expensive, even by the standards of the affluent Empire.

He began the task, placing the manasphere onto the bench and lowered the fingertips of both hands lightly onto its surface. As usual there was the immediate mental grab from the orb which he countered. He let part of his consciousness fall into the manasphere to gain access to the stored energy. The further he opened himself to the orb, so the more energy he could release, but the greater risk there was that he would lose control of the magic and it would behave unpredictably.

He placed his control at a comfortable depth within the manasphere where he was confident it would be stable, and began to probe his consciousness out towards the cabinet. He closed his eyes so that he could better *see* the cabinet's magical fields and his own probing magic extending out before him. The energy armour was a mixture of dark, almost

150

solid greys, as if even light itself was hindered by the spell. Interwoven with this were the green and blue hues of the Sustaining Field, constantly moving through the armour spell to maintain its structure.

He held his magical distance for a moment, once again being struck by the level of complexity that Ashnorian magic could attain, and also the sheer beauty of the scene. His manasphere tugged a little at his mind reminding him that the longer he stayed connected to the sphere the more it drained his mental reserves. He concentrated on his probing magic and pushed it gently forward. Predictably, as he reached the edge of the barrier, it resisted. It felt like the sliding-away effect of two magnets when brought together. He could see his probe bending around, trying to avoid interacting with the surface of the protection spell.

He dropped a little lower into the manasphere, allowing him to pull faster upon its reserves. The probe straightened up. He began to push forward again, attempting to make fuller contact with Lathashal's spell. As he pushed, so the resistance increased, forcing him to drop even deeper into his sphere. Although still confident in his control, he was aware that the orb was starting to interfere with his concentration. He continued.

He watched with satisfaction as his probe finally mixed with the outermost edge of the opposing magic. He felt a mental snap as the energies interacted, noticing a slight warming at his fingertips, although not enough to concern him yet. He waited for the energies to settle down before beginning the task of monitoring how the sustaining magic interacted with the armour magic. The minutes passed until he gained an insight into how the defensive spell was formed. Finally he decided that he knew enough to create the magic that could make his first attempt to destabilise the combined spells.

He pulled his probe clear to give himself a little time to recover his mental strength. His fingertips were warm now and the manasphere was beginning to gain confidence. There it was again: his notion that the thing had a thinking mind of its own. He shook such thoughts from his head and began to concentrate on changing his probe magic to one that would enter the armour field. His idea was to disguise his own magic to look like that of the Sustaining Field, and allow it to mix. Once there, he would invert his magic's polarisation, causing a phase divergence in the bond between the two entwined resident spells. This could disrupt the Energy Armour long enough for him to telepathically open the cabinet and levitate the required book from the shelf. It all looked reasonable on parchment.

He watched as his magical probe changed colour until it looked like the sustaining magic. He pushed it back into the armour field.

This time the spells did not repel, instead his probe was accepted as part of the Sustaining Field as hoped. But something was wrong. The probe was being pulled into the mix of spells.

He pulled back.

The probe continued to be drawn in. It was like watching twine being spun back onto a ball. The manasphere responded and fed the increased length of the probe. He struggled against the pull, having little effect. He could no longer make out his own magic from Lathashal's, so complex was the interaction.

The strain was becoming considerable. He could feel the increased heat of his body as he began to lose control of the magic coursing through him. His fingers were starting to burn and he attempted to release them from the sphere. He began to panic and realised he only had one choice remaining. He had to risk taking more control in a short burst that would break the connection of the probe. To do this meant lowering his hands into full contact with the orb. It was a desperate manoeuvre as it provided the orb with greater ability to take control. It would also break the first law of handling manaspheres.

He had no more time to think as the burning was going to break his concentration. He dropped his hands.

A surge in pull of the orb took control and he was wrenched deeper into its essence. He struggled to lift his hands away. They felt as if glued to the surface.

Now there was a new problem. He was losing awareness of his body. He was going to die.

Suddenly, all the months of fighting with the orbs and vying for control incensed him. He lost his fear and became enraged, wanting to punish the thing. On instinct and against all reason he released his fight and *dived* into the orb. The Orb sucked him down.

It was only moments later he was aware that the sensation had stopped. There was no deceleration. He was speeding in a fall and then he was still. Everywhere was blackness. He could no longer feel his body, so at least the pain was gone.

He tried to make sense of the strange situation. There was no air movement, not even from his actions. He also had the strangest feeling that there was something out there, something malevolent. It was like the feeling he'd felt before with the spheres, but far more tangible.

'Hello, is there someone there?' His words created a distance echo that rebounded from all directions at once.

He heard a skittering sound. It was like nothing he'd ever heard before. Like if a bat could laugh.

'I can hear you but not see you. Can you help?'

More skittering.

It appeared to be moving around him, without getting closer or further away.

'Can you at least show yourself? I won't harm you, I promise.'

This time the skittering became more a mixture of insane high-pitched laughter and chattering.

'*Treacherous human.*'

'I can assure you I mean you no harm. I came to be here by accident and would like nothing more than to leave you alone if that's what you want. I'm currently floating and cannot move.'

The response was more cackling laughter, but that was followed by frightened skittering, as if the thing was not sure of itself. '*I cannot move,*' it mimicked his words in mockery. '*Stupid human.*'

Chayne tried to gather his wits and understand what was happening. Had he lost control of the magical energies and been driven mad? Although that would surely have meant that the manasphere would have gained control of him and consumed him in fire. He recalled that Stalizar the Mage-Surgeon had said that Lathashal burned him with a gradia nine sphere. Maybe his gradia five didn't have the reserve energy to do that and instead he'd been sent insane.

'*Now I go.*'

Chayne jumped at the nearness of the creature's voice. Its tone had lost most of its frightened edge, and the sense of malevolence was far stronger with the closeness of the thing. He reasoned that it was a just manifestation in his mind of the feeling of sentience he felt when using manaspheres. This was therefore a bizarre battle of wills between his mind and the strange creation formed by his subconscious within the magic.

'No, you will let me free,' he said.

His comment was met with a manic laughter, closer now.

'*No-no-no-no-no-no, Tiny Mage. I will go and you will suffer terrible agonies.*'

Chayne felt its will begin to press on his own. It was like having his head pressed simultaneously from all sides. He responded by snapping his own mental control towards the creature. Instantly it released its attack and began jabbering as if in pain. Again it sounded afraid.

Chayne was nearing the point of exhaustion. The thought of his body in the real world fighting for life gave him some strength. It seemed a strange notion to be fighting with your own illusion of sentience. But he knew that however his mind and the magic were creating the fight, he had to win.

He bent his will again against the creature. He heard it squirm and the grovelling increased. His priority was to have the sphere's magic release him, but something about all this forced his curiosity. He focused his thoughts.

'Light!' Immediately a small globe of light appeared. A pitiful cry came from behind him.

'Nooooo, Tiny Mage, pleeeeease, no light, it hurts me.'

Chayne turned to look at his creation. It was floating a little way off. Twisting on the spot, it was a small, demon-like creature, no taller than his knees. It looked like the minor demons he'd seen pictures of in books on demonology back home. That was hardly surprising in that the vision was from his subconscious. It looked real and the detail was incredible. Chayne was amazed that his mind would go to so much trouble. He tried to dismiss the vision, seeing it as a pointless distraction. The vision responded with a terrible scream and squirmed in pain, its flesh began to shrivel and its bones twisted out of shape.

'Arghhhhh, no more pain Tiny Mage, Zystal will not challenge you again. I will let you go.' It now looked a sad and pathetic thing.

Chayne decided it was time to attempt to return to his body. He did the only thing he could think of and concentrated on rising. Nothing happened. It was as if something was holding him here. He looked back to the creature. It was staring at him. He tried to rise again and saw the creature's brow furrow in response. The battle for dominance wasn't over yet.

He decided on a different approach. What if, as crazy as it sounded, his subconscious could provide answers that his conscious mind had still to work out. At his current level of

155

control there seemed no immediate danger. It was worth a try. Odd though, that he'd given it such a strange name. He certainly could not recall ever hearing anything like the odd-sounding word before, and it was spoken in such an alien way, as if it was not meant for human mouths to form.

'What did you mean when you said you would go?'

'*This is not my home. It is cold here. Many Grillels to torment and chase at home.*'

'Grillels?'

'*Grillels are my tiny brothers. They are small and weak and make such a lovely scream when you crunch their bones.*' It said this with curiosity; as if this was something that ought to have been known.

Chayne was becoming more confused with each question. He had no idea how such a vicious act could be imagined by his mind, or what it could possibly represent. It was starting to confirm his theory that he was being driven mad.

He decided to try making sense of it all one more time and chose a more direct route, although it probably broke the rules of the game with his subconscious.

'Why have I created a demon, and how would I go about releasing you?'

The creature looked puzzled for a moment. A vile look then came over its face and it stopped cowering.

'*Tiny Mage does not know where he is.*' It was less of a question and more of the thing thinking aloud.

Chayne responded quickly and with confidence. 'I'm in my own mind, and you are a manifestation of my subconscious doing battle for control of the manasphere.'

The creature laughed a high-pitched cackle and span around on the spot, jumping up and down on the imaginary surface as he floated.

'*You are not inside your mind, Tiny Mage. Your mind is trapped here with me, in my prison*!' More manic laughter followed and then abruptly stopped. '*And now you are mine,*' it said. It began to drift closer, raising its wicked-looking claws. Although the creature was no more than two feet high, its innate weaponry could tear deep wounds upon the body of a human.

The light above Chayne began to dim and flicker. He responded with a mental snap towards the creature, halting its advance. It drained his almost exhausted reserves and he doubted he could conjure another one.

'*You have waited too long, Tiny Mage,*' said the demon, already recovered and advancing once again. '*Your strength is almost gone, and now Zystal will pull mana through your dying body to return him, and take your soul and devour it. Zystal will become strong. Grow into Lazamadd. Then Zystal will be able to crush many demons before him.*' The look on the creature's face was one of utter evil and triumph.

Chayne didn't know what to do. As the demon came within arm's reach the globe of light died. To his horror he felt one of the creatures scaly hands wrap around his upper arm and begin to squeeze, its claws digging into his flesh. He cried out. The demon cackled and probed the claws of his other hand across Chayne's chest.

'*Where's your heart, Tiny Mage,*' it said playfully. '*Zystal must have your heart to take you back.*'

Chayne involuntarily shook his shoulder to remove the creature. It connected with it and pushed it back a little. The creature cackled again and began to push against his chest with his claws.

'*Not enough, Tiny Mage. Not nearly enough. Food now for Zystal.*' As he spoke so a glowing redness began forming in the air before them. It swirled as if made of smoke. Chayne felt himself beginning to drift from consciousness. '*Sleep, Tiny Mage. Sleep for Zystal. He will take you to his plane where things will be very different. Oh yes, veeeeery different for Tiny Mage.*'

Chayne felt the creature's claws push against the skin of his chest and pierce the surface. The pain shook him awake. He realised that if he was to do something then this was his last chance. He thought furiously, with no idea how he could fight his own mind as it made manifest the manasphere's grip on his failing control of the probe magic.

His mind raced as he tried to recall something the demon said, something unexpected. The demon was to take his heart, as it contained his soul and gave him power. He would take it back to his home.

No, not his home. It said 'plane'. But why use such a term. Chayne didn't even know of the word, or what it meant.

The swirling smoke in front of him was growing, and now a small opening could be seen at its centre. He felt the demon continue to push his claws into his flesh around his ethereal heart. The pain was excruciating and made him swoon. Fighting it he continued to think hard about what was said, and what was the significance of the smoke. The creature stated that it would draw mana through his human form until he could return him home, to his plane.

The opening was now almost six inches across. Through it Chayne could see details. A red surface littered with rocks and boulders. Other creatures wandered there. All demonic.

Then it struck him.

This was no manifestation of his mind. Demons were real! The thing before him was real. The swirling mass growing before him was a gateway to another place. A *plane* where demons came from. Some demonic place of existence. The mana pulled in through his human form was being channelled by the demon into creating a doorway back to his place of existence. *That* was the secret the Ashnorians had kept for centuries, the secret to their magical power. Manaspheres held the souls of demons captured from their plane! The demons would always draw in mana and hold it, for if they could harbour enough they could open a doorway and return home. That was the malevolence Chayne felt. The battle that went on when trying to release a sphere's magic. It wasn't control of the magic. It was mental domination of the demon within, attempting to pull mana in through the magii for its own purposes.

The ramifications of the discovery rocked Chayne. The shock gave him a flare of strength to fight. Light burst all around and the demon screamed in frustration.

'*Nooooooo, home, home, my home.*' He released his attack and attempted to jump through the too-small opening in the smoke.

Chayne concentrated. The portal slammed shut with a pop. The demon fell to its knees, sobbing.

'Release me or face the consequences,' Chayne demanded.

He felt his consciousness drift upward, gaining in speed, leaving the wailing demon behind him.

Chapter 18 - From the dark

Illestrael stood in one of the servant recesses, covered in shadow. As one of the Yhordi she knew all the secret ways to conduct covert observations within the palace. Even somewhere as well protected as Lathashal's lab.

She watched as the young magii eyed up Lathashal's protected bookcase, wondering about his intent. The reports said he was suspected of being unusually gifted. She knew something of magic from her early teachings with Lathashal. The cabinet was protected by a spell far beyond anything that the young magii would have a chance of overcoming.

She looked him over. He held an intriguing countenance. Most people walked through life being part of its complicated web and trying to avoid the worst. A few managed to manipulate circumstances enough to provide them a brief existence of wealth and perceived power. With this Mlendrian she got the feeling destiny was looking on to see what happens next.

She watched him get positioned in front of the bookcase and begin using his manasphere. After a few minutes he was showing signs of losing control. His body went through the normal steps. His face distorted with the effort of concentration, followed by a reddening of the skin and sweat on his brow. To her surprise she saw him lower his hands onto the orb, breaking the first rule of manasphere control.

The result was as expected. His features twisted and he was showing signs of panic. There was a faint smell of burning flesh at that point, which without the aid of a master magii marked the irrecoverable demise of the student.

She was disappointed at the impending loss. At least she no longer needed to undo the advantage Lathashal and the Magile Shodatt gained.

She continued to watch the final moments. Soon the magii would lose his contest with the sphere and collapse into a burning heap, his mind lost. She heard that on rare occasions some magiis would be found with their hearts missing. Such stories kept students in line.

Then, curiously, the Mlendrian's face began to relax. A few minutes more passed and he released the orb.

She watched him as he opened his eyes. He looked terrible. Smoke drifted from his hands into his face, making him choke. He staggered from the bench, knocking over a stool. He collapsed onto his bed, unmoving.

Waiting until she felt sure he was sleeping she left her hiding place. Her orders were clear: convince the novice magii to spy on Lathashal, or prevent his further advancement in his care, which was one of many Yhordi euphemisms for assassination.

She looked down on his unconscious form. His hands were burned and there was blood on his robe around his chest. She lifted the loose folds of his robes and recoiled. There were five spots of blood surrounding his heart, an organ for which she knew the position exactly. She shuddered.

She felt his pulse. It was weak and fluttering. It would be all too easy to stop the beat. The reason would be attributed to loss of manasphere control.

She pricked his skin with a sedative and pulled his hood over his face. She snapped her fingers and pointed to his body. Three servants left the nearby recesses and lifted him. She made the sign for follow and left the room via the spiral staircase down into the lower quarters.

She headed for the Mage-Surgeon Stalizar's Medicinii. Decades before, he was the personal Mage-Surgeon to the Emperor. He eventually turned his back on the politics and offered his services to the Vigoratii, the non-political Shodatt for magical healing. She tried to remember if she'd ever given herself to him, but such a thing was impossible to recall within her hundreds of lovers over the decades of her extended youth. Such was the price a woman paid to attain a little power in a society created and crushingly dominated by men.

She was now in her sixtieth year. Her body suggested a woman in her late twenties. For many years she maintained her age at only twenty, but as the years progressed, so it took more Yan to reverse the effects of aging and the price became too high. So she cut down on the treatments, leaving her to age, albeit at a slow rate.

She was getting close to Medicinii. She diverted from the normal route to the front entrance and turned down a side corridor leading to a minor store room. She stopped halfway along and spread her fingers out upon the wall and pushed. There was a click and the door moved inward. She snapped her fingers, pointing inside. The servants carried Chayne into the dark room. She followed and resealed the secret door.

Once the door was secure she lit a small oil lamp on the wall in the room. It was bare of all decoration and furniture, its dark wooden walls and floor covered in dust. Moving to the other side of the room, she removed a piece of plaster from the wall and peered into a hole. Confirming that the next room was empty she spread her hands out on the bordering section of wall. There was another soft click and a section of the wall became surrounded by a crack, filled with a soft light. This time she pulled at the section of wall and it opened inwards.

Stepping through she ordered the servants to follow and place Chayne on the large four poster bed. The room had the style and trappings of the tastefully wealthy, two words that didn't go together elsewhere in the Empire. She pulled the bookcase back into position to cover the secret entrance.

She was about to leave the room to find Stalizar, when it opened. A servant entered wearing the livery of the Mage-

Surgeon. He jumped back in surprise and for a brief moment looked into Illestrael's eyes. Fear took him and he cast his eyes down to the ground.

Illestrael snapped her finger. The servant raised his left hand with the back facing upward. She took something out of her belt and with it drew a single circle with a dot in the middle on his hand. Next to this she placed the letters 'IL'. This informed the duty adjutant of the crime that the servant committed and against whom. She replaced the item and snapped again for the servant's attention. She clenched her fist and placed it to her chest indicating the symbol for *Master* and then pointed to the floor. The servant turned and left the room.

Illestrael looked around. Much could be told of a person by their private chamber. Clearly the owner took time to bring some luxury to their private life. She had been surprised at his choice of placement after leaving the service of the Emperor. A man of his standing could have had many fine commissions in the Empire. Why he volunteered for Mage-Surgeon General of a moderate healing post within the lower levels of one of the Empire's outermost cities was beyond her understanding. It was well known the man possessed no political ambition. Even so, this seemed to be taking it a bit too far.

She continued to wait, and was about to send one of Lathashal's servants to find out what happened when the door swung open. Stalizar walked in. He towered over most Ashnorians and ducked under the door frame. He had a large head, even by his own bodily dimensions, and this served to create an even more imposing figure. The grey eyes held intelligence and sharpness of perception. He scanned the scene, taking in Chayne, the servants, and lastly Illestrael. The opposite of the order she would have. He looked to the injured first. She would have looked to the greatest threat.

'May I ask how you got in here?' he asked. It was a deep, unthreatening voice. Even so it carried a natural power and authority. It seemed capable of considerably more volume.

'You may ask,' Illestrael replied.

'I have people waiting in my care that are suffering and dying, Illestrael. If you wish to verbally fence with me, I will return to them.' The man's manner and stature made her approach seem trite. She felt like a little girl being confronted by her father after some bad behaviour. She also couldn't hide her surprise at hearing her name.

He continued to stare, waiting for a reply.

'I ... I am sorry,' she said, dipping her head briefly in embarrassment. 'Bad start. Too many years dealing in guile and manipulation, I guess.'

He still didn't reply. She resisted the urge to squirm.

'This young magii is injured. He was using a manasphere and I think lost control.'

Stalizar's brows furrowed and he walked across to Chayne. 'If he'd lost control then he would be dead.' He lifted Chayne's hands and noticed the blackened burns. He checked for a pulse. 'Well he's not dead, but by the look of those burns, I don't know how.'

He lifted Chayne's hood to uncover his face. Illestrael noted the recognition in the Mage-Surgeon. He sat down on the bed and lifted both of Chayne's eyelids, and then checked the soles of his feet. Lastly he examined his chest under the region of blood on his robe. He took a sharp intake of breath and drew back slightly.

'What is it?' said Illestrael.

'I have never seen those markings on anyone alive.'

'What are they?'

Stalizar didn't answer.

He slid his hands under Chayne's body and lifted him from the bed. 'I must take him into my surgery. Thank you for doing this. Did anyone see you?'

'I am Yhordi.'

Stalizar showed a brief flicker of surprise. 'Can you leave as covertly as you arrived?'

'Yes,' replied Illestrael. 'Lathashal will be back within the hour,' she added.

Stalizar nodded his thanks for the information and left the room.

Illestrael didn't like the idea of leaving Chayne. She felt she was somehow tied to him. She couldn't remember having a feeling like it before. She wondered what it meant.

She ordered Lathashal's servants to return through the front of the Medicinii before returning back through the secret entrance.

She knew her choice of actions placed her in danger. She would only have so long before she would be forced to report to her Yhordi field operative. Before then there was an unpleasant duty to perform. She grimaced at the prospect. It would take all of her expertise to achieve, but she suspected that Lathashal still hungered for her *skills*, and it was necessary to exploit that.

There was one other undertaking to perform first though. One that would require more routine skills to execute.

Chapter 19 - Fluffy Pillows

Chayne woke to the sound of pleasant music. It was a mixture of strings, percussion and wind instruments. He knew it to be the invention of the Injesurians, a race of scholars predisposed to natural discovery and art in all its forms. It was rumoured that their music had spread across the entire globe. It was complex with numerous movements that could stir the soul through many emotional states. He enjoyed watching travelling musicians when they came to Tiburn from time to time.

He opened his eyes. He was in a bed, his head propped up with many white fluffy pillows. The room was plain, mostly cream in colour. The air smelled of bleach. To his left a window displayed a pleasant scene of grassy meadows. As he looked he was startled as the scene changed to a snowy mountain range. He watched for a while longer as the scene altered between different calming settings.

The right-hand wall held the door. Both the wall and the door were inset with glass in the upper half. Through the glass was a young woman at a desk, dressed in white. She looked up at him and arose from her seat, moving swiftly, without running, down the corridor.

He tried to get her attention, but whatever mission she was on it didn't include stopping for him.

He tried to recall why he was here and what happened. He guessed from his surroundings that he was in the palace hospital. Had there been another assassination attempt? No, Lathashal would have guards outside his room. There was a whirlwind of movement as the door opened and Stalizar burst in. He looked at Chayne with a broad grin, displaying an array of teeth that must be at least double the size of Chayne's. They didn't look out of place in such a large head. He turned to the young girl who Chayne recognised as the one in the corridor.

'Thank you, Tereen. Please check on the other patients.'

The girl hesitated for a moment before dipping her head briefly, and left the room.

Stalizar closed the door and checked through the window that she was gone. He turned back to Chayne and approached the bed. 'You are looking better. I wasn't sure for a time that I was going to be able to save you.'

'What happened?' said Chayne.

'You don't remember?'

'No. Was it an assassination attempt?'

'Not unless assassins now force their quarry to use manaspheres,' replied Stalizar.

'I lost control of a manasphere again!'

'All the signs were there. Your hands were burnt, even the palms were blackened. I cannot imagine what would have possessed you to increase the contact on the Sphere.'

Chayne started to shake his head in agreement. Then something clicked in his memory relating to the word Stalizar used: possessed.

'I was interacting with another spell. It was too strong for me, I think.' Vague flashes came fleetingly to his mind and drifted away on the edge of memory. 'I was, falling.'

'Falling?' responded Stalizar.

Chayne nodded, 'I think so. Sorry, it's all just a jumbled mess at the moment.'

'Falling is usually associated with one of the final stages of losing control of a sphere. Few people once reaching that point have managed to return.'

'I seemed to fall for a long time,' continued Chayne. 'There were … voices', Chayne strained hard to recall the details.

Chayne saw Stalizar's large brow furrow.

'What kind of voices?'

'I'm not sure. Odd voices, whining, high like a child. No … not a child.'

Stalizar perched on the bed. 'I know you must still be in some pain, but it may be important that you recall. We don't have much time together. Would you mind if I help you remember with magic?'

'You have saved my life twice. I owe it to you to help in any way I can.'

Stalizar produced from a belt pouch one of the smallest orbs Chayne had seen. No more than two inches across it was contained within a leather case.

'It stores only a little mana. I normally use it to start hearts or urgently seal wounds. It may be enough.'

'What do I do?'

'You only have to try to remember. I will attempt to strengthen the connections in your brain that you activate.'

Chayne focused on his memories. He felt nothing of the magic being used.

Then he snapped his eyes open. He looked at the orb in Stalizar's hand.

'Demons . . .' he whispered.

Stalizar dropped the orb to the bed to take hold of Chayne's shoulders and turn his body to face him. He shook once to get Chayne's full attention.

'The manaspheres,' said Chayne, blinking. 'They hold demons. I saw mine within my orb. It tried to trick me and drain my will. It tried to open a portal to its home and take me back with it. Demons, Stalizar. They use demons. All those magiis that have failed to control manaspheres have been taken back to the demonic plane. What happens to them?' he said, distressed.

Stalizar released Chayne's shoulders. He looked ashen.

'You didn't know?' said Chayne.

Stalizar shook his head.

168

'But you are a senior magii, how could you not!' accused Chayne.

'*Nobody* has ever returned from such a deep submersion into an orb before. Stories of demons possessing orbs go back centuries. The whole thing has fallen into myth. People who believe such tales are damned as heretics, fools at least. They are turned into outcasts by the religious and magical communities. It has been made all the more difficult to pursue as there is so little information on demonology. That is the realm of the Ashardii Shodatt. They are a closed order existing on the edge of Ashnoria. It is rumoured that all manaspheres are made by them. Perhaps now it is clear why.'

'So *nobody* knows outside of that place?'

Stalizar shrugged. 'A few of the highest gradia magiis perhaps. I suspect that only the most corrupt would be trusted with such information, probably to help them maintain power.'

'People like Lathashal?' queried Chayne.

'As good a candidate as any.'

The two men brooded in their private contemplations of the revelation until Chayne spoke in a subdued voice. It was without allegation or malice.

'You are going to invade my land.'

Stalizar blinked at the change in conversation, pausing before responding. 'Yes,' he said, almost as an apology. 'I am to supervise the setting up of a Medicinii field unit at the front line.'

'I'm going to stop it,' said Chayne flatly.

'The field unit?'

'The attack.'

'That is not possible,' replied Stalizar.

'I mean it. I will stop the attack, or die trying,' said Chayne earnestly.

'I understand your desire and determination in such an act, but what you intend to oppose is beyond you.

'I could with your help.'

'You are mistaken,' responded Stalizar stiffly. 'I have no desire to be connected with any act that openly opposes the Emperor. I may maintain a degree of latitude with the ruling elite due to my neutrality and previous services to the old Emperor, but I have no power to influence anything as substantial as war. Such a thing will be the new Emperor's will. To oppose it would be suicide.'

'Thousands of my people will be killed and hundreds of thousands will be enslaved,' replied Chayne. 'You cannot desire such a thing.'

'Of course I do not desire it,' snapped Stalizar. 'It is against my deepest ethics. There is simply nothing I could influence that would make a difference.'

'You could help me stop Lathashal complete the Rite of Rakasti.'

'Do not speak of such things so openly,' he said in a harsh whisper. 'And how do you know of such a thing? I cannot believe he would tell you, even as his Zintar.'

'The Lan-Chi informed me.'

The Mage-Surgeon glanced around to check for anybody who might be within earshot.

'How could you know of the Lan-Chi or have made contact with them. They are notoriously paranoid about discovery.'

'They contacted me. But none of that matters. The fact is that all I have said is true, and somehow I am going to prevent Lathashal complete the Rite of Rakasti. He will be consumed by his manasphere, and in one stroke I will deal a double blow to the threat to my land,' announced Chayne.

'I am truly sorry for your people, but I cannot help you,' said Stalizar, rising from the bed, his tones returning to their formal bedside manner. 'Do not enter into such conversation with me or any of my staff again.' And with that the Mage-Surgeon left the room.

Chayne felt drained. He thought he judged the man well to coerce his support.

He heard a commotion somewhere down the corridor. The noise came closer and resolved into a heated argument. The door to his room burst open and Lathashal entered followed by Stalizar.

'He is my Zintar. You have no right to detain him!' said Lathashal shouting, his voice thin and hoarse.

Chayne looked at the man in horror. He seemed to have aged twenty years. His face was haggard and dark rings surrounded his eyes. He walked with a stoop.

'He is not *detained,* as well you know,' replied the Mage-Surgeon in a loud, resonant voice, totally in contrast to Lathashal's.

'Do not argue with me!' screamed Lathashal, almost to the point of hysteria. Chayne never believed the man possible of such loss of control. 'Get dressed at once boy. You are returning with me.'

'He is not fully healed,' argued Stalizar. 'He must rest for at least another day.'

Lathashal spun around on the man who towered head and shoulders above him. Even in the Master Magii's deteriorated state, it was Stalizar that backed away and seemed the smaller presence.

'You work here under my sufferance, Surgeon. I know your views on my work. If it were not for the fact that you keep those views to yourself I would have you clapped in irons without a moment's thought. You may have had protection from the old Emperor, but Estatoulie would back me against you in an instant. Now prepare this boy for immediate departure and escort him *yourself* back to my Laboratory.'

Stalizar stood defeated. 'Very well.'

Lathashal turned back to Chayne, 'Hurry up, boy!'

'Yes Master,' replied Chayne, pulling his covers away.

Lathashal stormed past Stalizar and left the room.

'I fear you will not be receiving the kindest of treatment when you return to your work.'

'*Help me,*' said Chayne.

Stalizar snapped away. 'I cannot! You see the animosity between us. With the old Emperor gone I am in a fragile position at best and watched constantly,' he flicked his eyes to where the girl was sitting earlier. 'The slightest hint of open dissent and I'd be deemed a traitor.'

'But my entire people will be enslaved! You have done many great things in your long life. Please take a risk and help us.'

The Mage-Surgeon stirred from his inner deliberation and shook his head. 'Madness.' He began plumping up the pillows and adjusting the bedclothes. 'A few days good rest should be enough. You are young and strong.'

Chayne remained staring at the man as he went about his trivial jobs. 'I understand the desire to protect your long lives, Stalizar. But Mlendrians are a free people. They would rather die than trade extended life to cower under such subjugation.'

Stalizar turned, his expression angry. He went to speak, but Chayne cut him off. 'I am ready to leave,' he stated coldly, picking up his clothing.

'Wait,' said Stalizar.

Chayne stopped.

'I will try to delay the deployment of the field healing unit. It will buy you a couple of weeks at most.'

'And the Rite?'

'I will not be any part of Lathashal's destruction.'

Chayne gripped the man's arm warmly. It was a start.

--- 0 ---

Tereen completed her shift and requested her leave from the Mage-Surgeon General. She headed in the direction of Lathashal's room with much to report. The conversation between the Surgeon-General and the Mlendrian implicated them both in treason. She didn't hear everything that was said, nor understand many of the words used, but she had a good memory and could repeat much of it, especially when the Surgeon-General had gotten angry. This would please the Master Lathashal greatly. Uncovering a plot to stop him casting a great spell would earn her many credits towards the release of her husband held under false accusations. She hated working for the evil master magii, but the release of her husband was the only thing she cared about. Let the Masters fight amongst themselves and kill each other for all she cared.

She turned a corner to a stairway to the next level. It was dark, which meant some maintenance worker would be in trouble. She approached the first step moving swiftly, light in spirit thanks to the reward she would receive after she imparted the news to Lathashal.

'Hello, Tereen.' The voice was female and as smooth as silk. It carried undertones.

'M ... mistress,' said Tereen. 'I cannot see you.'

'As it should be,' came the voice, now from behind her and so close that it made her jump.

'Who are you? W...what do you want?'

'I am sweet dreams and nightmares. Which do you prefer?' replied the voice, coming once again from another direction.

Tereen span around again, scared and started to sob. 'Why are you frightening me? I have done nothing wrong and I have nothing of value. You must be mistaking me for somebody else. Please, leave me alone.'

'What a sad little thing you are. And once I expose your disloyalty to the Mage-Surgeon General, the pathetic excuse of a man you call your husband will be tortured to death.'

'*No!*' screamed Tereen. 'Please, I beg you. I don't know who you are, but I'll do anything. Please let my husband live.' She began to sob.

'Deceitful girl. I'll give you one chance. Tell me what you were going to report. All of it or your husband will not see this night through.'

Tereen held no clue as to her tormentor, or how she knew so much about her situation. She believed the threat was real.

It did not matter to her if somebody else found out what was said, so long as her husband was left unharmed.

'I'll tell you everything.'

Illestrael listened in the shadows as the girl spoke of demons, manaspheres, the coming war and the intended plot against Lathashal. Normally such information would have been worth a great deal to the Yhordi and improve Illestrael's position. She didn't care about the war or the enslavement of the Mlendrian people, but something inside her wanted to protect Chayne. If this information reached Lathashal then Chayne would be tortured and killed.

'You have been most helpful Tereen. Now I shall send you to your husband.'

'Really!' she exclaimed. 'Oh thank you mistress, I have been a fool. I thought I'd never see him again. I'll never make such a mistake again, I swear.'

'No, you won't.'

Tereen felt a quick sharp nick on her neck and gave a yelp.

'What was that? What are you doing?' Blackness started to change before her into a swirl of dark greys and flashes.

'No!' she tried to shout, but little escaped her lips. 'I just wanted to see my ...'

Illestrael caught the girl as she fell. She snapped her fingers. A servant emerged from the shadows and took the body from her, orders already given.

The Yhordi removed her black hood and gloves and relit the torches, checking that no evidence remained of her interception. There was much to consider. She dismissed the servant girl's nonsense regarding demons in manaspheres. The conversation she had overheard would have been far beyond her comprehension and she fell back on the superstitious clichés of the poorly educated. Chayne's plan to attack Lathashal, however, was of great concern. She couldn't believe that he had any chance of defeating the master magii. But if there was any chance that he could, then she would do her best to help him, as long as she didn't become implicated.

Her first task therefore was to get him access to Lathashal's cabinet, and there was only one way to do that.

Chapter 20 - Traitor

Garamon sat against a pine tree within a sprawling forest that smothered the lower half of the mountain on the southern side of the Hammerheads. They had used every moment of daylight to get as far as possible from Jontal's camp. Nobody expected his men to attempt a rescue after the massacre of the morning, but Falakar wouldn't take the chance.

All was peaceful. For the first time since leaving home, he felt safe. His gloves were off and he was enjoying the warmth of the fire, eating the fine meal Sholster prepared. The winter supplies of the decimated bandit camp, added to the game trapped in the forest by Falakar, was enough to satisfy even the big man's appetite. Shinlay was still unconscious and lay by the fire, her bruise now an egg-sized purple swelling on her temple. Falakar reported no fever though. Kinfular sat with her, watching her intently and troubled by her condition. ThreeSwords, as usual, was sitting just far enough away to feel separated, cleaning and sharpening his swords. Sholster was snoring like distant thunder after eating enough to supply a small banquet. Falakar was sitting near to Jontal who was bound to a tree. The bandit had maintained a foul mood after his painful and humiliating encounter with Chantel. He had flinched at every sound on their journey. Garamon was waiting for a chance to talk again to the Ranger. Now all was quiet he wandered over to him.

The man was carving slices from an apple with one of his curved hunting knives, eating them off the blade. The weapon seemed ludicrously oversized for the task.

'May I sit with you?' Garamon asked.

Falakar looked up and nodded.

Garamon sat, cross-legged in front of the man.

'What will you do now?'

Falakar flicked the knife towards his captive. 'He'll stand trial for his crimes.'

Garamon looked towards the bandit. Despite all that happened he couldn't help feel a little sorry for the man. He looked beaten and his head was a mess of matted blood and missing hair.

'What is likely to happen to him?'

'That's for the judge,' replied that Ranger. 'My guess is that he'll be imprisoned for some time.'

'I don't like the thought of anyone suffering such a fate.'

'That's because you have a good soul. Life in the mountains will change that.'

'You say that almost as if being good is a weakness.'

'Men such as these live only by one rule: do anything, don't get caught.'

'So what will you do next?' asked the Ranger.

Garamon returned a shrug. 'I don't have any idea other than to keep heading south and try to find a way to Straslin.' The plan sounded ludicrously inadequate.

'Nobody gets into Ashnoria,' said Jontal.

Falakar looked briefly towards the bandit and returned to his apple, cutting another segment from the fruit and eating it.

'You don't know that,' said Garamon. 'I've heard stories of people escaping.'

Jontal snorted derisively. 'Maybe during an invasion before the borders are sealed. Once they are established, nobody gets in or out other than their spies.'

Garamon was angry. Was he just being stubbornly stupid continuing with his attempt to pursue the rescue of his friend?

'I'm just a single person, not an army. Maybe if I'm careful I could get in unnoticed?'

'Not a chance. All roads and towns are patrolled and magic is used to detect wanderers at night.'

'I'll avoid roads then,' said Garamon.

'You have a map?' said Jontal.

'No' replied Garamon. He was being trapped but could do little about it.

'Straslin is a day's hard march on foot from the border. There are no roads on this side. You would get lost without a skilled tracker.'

Garamon was irritated with the bandit's cutting observations, for he had no answer.

Jontal chuckled at the woodsman's discomfort. 'Just out of curiosity, what drives you to such an insane and suicidal undertaking?'

'To rescue a friend. Something that you would never understand,' said Garamon tartly.

'You are correct. Then again, I'm still alive.'

'But soon to spend the rest of your days behind bars,' interrupted Falakar.

'It's a long way back home Fal, with plenty of chances for my men to regroup and free me again. After all, this isn't the first time I've been in this situation and escaped.

'This time, I'll have help,' replied Falakar casting a brief glance over the rest of the camp.

Jontal flinched. 'They are coming with you?'

'All the way,' said Falakar with a smile.

Jontal returned to Garamon. 'You know you won't get a mile across the Ashnorian border before being caught. And even if you survive the extreme torture, they will set you to work as a slave in the mines for the rest of your life, which would be short.'

'Nevertheless, I will try,' Garamon replied without any hesitation.

'I can tell you how to get through you know,' said the bandit.

It was Falakar's turn to chuckle at the obvious ruse. He started on another apple.

'You told me only moments ago that nobody gets in or out,' said Garamon.

'That was before I discovered the quality of my returning escort,' replied Jontal sourly.

'You're wasting your time,' said Falakar. 'You're not escaping the courts this time.'

'Grant, Quail, Stants, Blue-Mockingbird,' listed Jontal.

Garamon didn't know what the bandit was talking about, but the effect on Falakar was sudden and explosive. He threw his knife aside and flew at Jontal, grabbing him tightly by the tunic and pulling the smaller man up as far as his bonds would allow to meet Falakar's glaring face.

'Where did you hear those words!' said the Ranger, dangerously.

'I have your attention at last then,' said Jontal, attempting to sneer.

'Tell me!' shouted Falakar, shaking the bandit fiercely. All the men of the camp were drawn to the sudden rage of the normally controlled Ranger, and drifted over to observe the scene.

Jontal squirmed under the iron grip of the man that held him. 'They were the names of three undercover Rangers that were working inside the borders of Ashnoria. Blue-Mockingbird was their mission code word.' The words came out strangled, being forced past the pressure applied to his throat.

Falakar cried out and struck the bandit hard across the face with his fist and staggered back as if struck himself. Jontal took it hard, spitting blood from his mouth.

All eyes were transfixed on the two men.

'They were some of our finest. Friends of mine, with families,' said the Ranger.

'It was a stupid mission,' replied Jontal. 'You must have known the risks when you sent them.'

Falakar rose up to strike his tormentor again.

'*I* didn't expose them,' shouted back the bandit, stopping the blow from falling.

'And why should I believe you?' answered Falakar bitterly.

'Because I didn't get the chance, *okay!* They were good, but it was only a matter of time. A random patrol discovered them.'

'And how do you know all this!'

Jontal's eyes flitted around the assembled group.

'Because I've been collaborating with the Empire for some months now.'

Falakar grabbed Jontal by the collar again and raised his hand to deliver another blow.

'Look, there is a war coming,' said the bandit bluntly. 'All of this area: the mountains, this forest, will be under Ashnorian military control. There will be no place for people like me. I was just positioning myself in favour of the new regime.'

'Traitor!' shouted Sholster.

'Wait!' shouted Garamon, halting Sholster from his own retribution. 'Did you supply the whereabouts of mages?'

Jontal tore his glare away from Sholster and looked to the woodsman. 'The younger ones, yes. I never found out why they were not interested in the more experienced mages.'

Garamon's face turned red. 'You bastard!' he yelled and snatched up the skinning knife Falakar dropped and made a lunge for the bandit.

Sholster grabbed him around the waist and lifted him easily from the ground. 'Whoa, lad. Knocking a few teeth out is one thing, but let's all agree before you go slitting the man's throat.'

Garamon struggled for a moment until getting control. Sholster let him down and stayed within arm's reach.

'Do you know where these mages were taken?' said Falakar.

'There is a prominent magic presence in all of the cities. I would guess that he was taken to Straslin.'

'Do you know how to get there?' Garamon asked sharply.

'Possibly,' replied Jontal.

Falakar tightened his grip once again on the bandit's tunic, cutting off his airflow.

'Look,' choked Jontal. 'It's a big place. I don't exactly get a guided tour.'

'Can you take me there?' said Garamon.

'Are you insane? If I set foot inside their borders other than my allocated rendezvous time I'd be deemed a traitor and subject to interrogation as would any other outsider.'

'He has to go back for trial anyway,' said Falakar.

'I'll do you a deal,' said Garamon to the bandit. 'Take me to my friend. If you survive, Falakar will let you go.'

Falakar's eyes widened. 'That's not a deal I would be willing to uphold, and it is not your place to make such offers.'

'Think about it,' countered Garamon. 'I need my friend, and you need information to replace that lost by your three spies more than bringing one man to justice, whoever it is. It seems we have a rare chance here.'

'The lad has a sharp mind,' chipped in Sholster.

Falakar looked between Garamon, Sholster, and the bandit. 'I shall consider it.'

'Consider it!' blurted Jontal. 'Never mind what *you* may or may not want to do. *I'm* having nothing to do with it.'

The sound of Shinlay groaning interrupted them. Kinfular spun around to see her sitting up and holding her head between her hands. He raced over to her just as she slumped back to the ground.

Kinfular dropped to her side, his movements gentle.

'Shinlay?'

She stirred and murmured.

Her eyes snapped open. 'The Rogue!' she tried to shout but stopped, pulling her face into a tight grimace.

'He is captured. You are safe,' said Kinfular.

'I am sorry, he tricked me.'

'He is no danger. The Ranger has him.'

'I heard shouting.'

'All is quiet now, you need to rest.'

'My head hurts,' she said, and then fell into unconsciousness once again.

Falakar lifted her eyelids and felt her pulse. 'She is strong, but I do not know if she will survive. If the skull is cracked then she may have bleeding in her brain and that usually means death. We can only keep her warm and continue applying cold linen to her injury.'

An argument broke out between Jontal, Garamon and Sholster. Falakar returned to them and interceded himself into the quarrel. 'It is my desire and duty to return you to the Mlendrian courts for trial. Although trial would hardly be required in your case. You will be found guilty of multiple crimes including many confirmed killings. You will serve much of your remaining life in prison.'

'I have never killed a man who didn't draw a sword against me first.' proclaimed Jontal.

'That will likely only save you from the noose.'

'Money and belongings. Who's to say where it all came from? I was only taking what somebody stole at some time anyway.'

Falakar gave up. It was always pointless trying to reason with the man. Both knew right from wrong, they just chose opposite sides.

'Can you get us into Ashnorian lands?' he asked the bandit.

'I'd be better off rotting in a prison cell. At least I wouldn't get tortured first.'

'If you help us, I will speak on your behalf to reduce your sentence. You may see daylight again before you die.'

'How generous,' responded Jontal.

'If there is an invasion planned then I need information. With good intelligence we could organise a mountain guerrilla force to hinder progression across the Hammerheads, giving us time to assemble a sizeable army to challenge them when they reach the other side. The lad also needs to reach the palace and rescue his friend.'

Jontal's expression took on the look of a man who was speaking with a madman. 'You want me to take you both into Ashnoria, and undetected to the palace!'

'And the others, if they'll come,' replied the Ranger.

'And for the zero chance of surviving this suicidal insanity, you will attempt to reduce my sentence?'

'That's right,' said Falakar.

'See that large blue vein,' said Jontal lifting his head and pushing his throat out. 'Just stick your knife into it would you, it's going to save me a lot of trouble.'

'We are in the grip of extraordinary circumstances,' replied Falakar. 'I am sorry, but you are coming with us.'

'I will escape at the earliest opportunity, Fal. I swear I will leave you stranded to suffer at the hands of their torturers.'

'I expect nothing less,' said the Ranger.

He walked back to Kinfular leaving Jontal's protestations behind.

'I have a difficult request that I have no right to ask of you.'

'I heard enough of your conversation,' replied Kinfular. 'This enemy does not threaten only your people. For the sake of my own we will accompany you.'

'What about her?' enquired the Ranger.

'We will find a shaman over the border,' said Kinfular.

'You think they will help?'

'They will or they will die,' said the barbarian.

Falakar took over watching Shinlay as the barbarian went to his men.

Garamon joined the Ranger and sat with him as he administered a fresh compress to Shinlay's head.

'We are all coming with you,' he said, without looking up.

Garamon was lost for words.

'We will be entering Ashnoria to assess the coming threat. I cannot guarantee that we will travel as far as the palace, but you are welcome to join us for whatever part of the journey coincides with yours.'

'I am in your debt,' replied Garamon.

'A debt paid then. You rescued me today.'

Falakar reached across and picked up Garamon's axe lying nearby. He threw it to him and Garamon caught it in both hands.

'Now, let's teach you to become a fighter. I think that before this journey is over you will have need of it.'

--- 0 ---

Chantel sat some distance from the perimeter of the camp. It was quiet now, and the night had drawn in. This was a strange world. She didn't know how such an inept creature as Chayne could have created the bridge across the void between their planes, but it was certainly an interesting experience. She never found her own plane to her liking and was out of place. She hated the endless killing that her brethren relished. It was a lifetime of hunting lesser demons and brutally tormenting them to death whilst avoiding being captured by demons greater than you for the same fate.

Since she arrived her life was calmer.

These smooth demons seemed devoid of the natural abilities that she possessed. In fact, spending most of her time out of cat form since travelling with the young one, a necessity due to the limited speed and endurance of the small animal, she was discovering more. She arrived here in the odd feline shape. In fact she had no initial memory of her previous life, it had come back to her slowly. Her recent need for faster travel gave her a strange feeling. As she thought about it, she changed into her natural shape. Since then more abilities had come to her. It seemed that this world worked differently to her own. She still had the ability to excite the air to the point of combustion as normal, but there were things that she couldn't do back home. Her shape-changing was the most surprising, although the act drained her. She could also see faint auras around the humans that reflected their moods: green for calm, red for anger, purple for lust, yellow for fear, and blue for control. It was this final colour that was predominantly on display around the older ones when fighting. When asleep they all had a faint white glow to them.

She also found she could influence them to ignore her presence if she didn't bring attention to herself. This was best done in her cat form.

The one named Falakar moved into view again as he circled the camp. She felt safe enough in cat form hidden under a bush, but each time he crossed her location he would stop and look out into the forest towards her position. She watched as his aura changed from a translucent blue to a more solid colour indicating his concentration was deepening. Each time she would concentrate on being ignored, and each time he would shake his head and move on.

She decided to move further away and sleep.

Sleeping was a curious condition. She never experienced it on her own plane. It was quite like dying. She watched Chaynie do it several times and wake again normal. When it was her turn, she resisted it, afraid. After some days she lay down on the soft rug in front of the fire in Chaynie's cabin, exhausted. The next thing she knew she opened her eyes. It was now dark and the fire was just embers. She was confused and her head didn't seem to work as it should. She searched the cabin in panic for Chaynie and found him in the same position on his bed. Since then she learned to accept the condition and even look forward to it occasionally.

She found a suitable hiding place, and once again, resisting the strangest desire to repeatedly flex her front claws into the soft earth, fell asleep.

Chapter 21 - Chameleor

Garamon woke the next morning to the smell of bacon cooking. The previous night's training left him with a strong hunger and he leapt from his bed. He also felt the training deep within his muscles as he limped the first few steps until the stiffness was out of his limbs.

'I had no idea the camp had woken,' he said guiltily to the group who were already eating.

'Your training yesterday was intense,' replied Falakar. 'We decided to let you sleep. Have no shame and sit with us.'

He sat down with them and Kinfular rose to get a small wooden plate onto which he poured a thick broth and placed a chunk of hot bacon. He passed it to him. Falakar reached for the basket of bread, which contained only a few pieces. 'Save some for ThreeSwords,' he instructed.

Garamon took a single piece.

The food tasted wonderful. It was all he could do to avoid asking for more.

As if reading his mind, Kinfular waved a hand at the cooking pot. 'There is plenty of meat remaining for ThreeSwords and another plateful for you should you want it.'

'Hlenshar!' protested Sholster.

'You've eaten seven portions already. The lad is under training, let him have it,' rebuked Kinfular.

Sholster gave a final look to the remaining food as though it was a long lost friend. Kinfular gestured Garamon to the food again. Garamon's stomach won the battle with his conscience and he collected his second portion. As he went past Sholster he pushed half onto his plate. Sholster's head

186

snapped up looking to Kinfular for approval. Kinfular simply shrugged. Sholster's grin was enormous and fought for position with his first hurried mouthful. 'I'll help you with the cleaning of the dishes lad,' he offered beaming and finishing off the half-meal before Garamon even sat down. He then lay back with arms folded behind his head looking up at sky with a content smile.

The group set off within the hour. Shafts of light from the early morning sun did little to warm the chill forest air. Puffs of exhaled air could be seen drifting away from each person in the line. Falakar led as usual, followed by ThreeSwords. Garamon was next, secured to Jontal by a length of rope, then Sholster carrying Shinlay. Kinfular was rear guard.

The morning journey was easy, although the pace was slow through the thickening forest as they fell in altitude. The terrain was still steep but a carpet of springy pine needles reduced the possibility of serious injury in the event of a fall. Sholster ploughed through it all without trouble, even carrying Shinlay. Garamon was continually tested and having to keep his footing in light of Jontal's repeated slips. This stopped only after Falakar suggested that they removed Jontal's boots so that he could better feel his way over the spiky needles.

By late morning they reached the end of the forest. They stopped short while Falakar scouted ahead.

He returned some minutes later, his face grim. 'The land beyond the forest has been levelled for as far as I can see. It's all sand.'

'We'll stand out like beetles on a blanket!' objected Sholster.

'We must wait for nightfall then,' said Kinfular.

'No, that would be worse,' said Jontal. 'They detect you easier at night. Their mages use magic to see a person's body heat from a great distance. It cannot be done in the heat of day.

'Chameleor,' came Shinlay's weak voice. Kinfular dropped to her side. He tried to lift her, but she forced his hands away and pushed herself up into a sitting position. The effort made her almost pass out again.

'How do you feel?' asked Kinfular.

She waved him away. 'You say it is sand?' she asked Falakar, squinting in pain from the light.

'Completely,' acknowledged Falakar.

'Is the colour even?'

'It has been artificially flattened and topped with sand from the Mel-Tasi desert, I would guess.'

'It improves the chances of invaders standing out,' added Jontal.

'Show me,' she said, waving an arm blindly upwards for support.

Sholster lifted her into his arms and everyone followed Falakar to the edge of the forest. She looked out from under a hand shielding her eyes. A few moments of study and she cried out in pain and collapsed into Sholster's arms. He placed her back against a tree, facing away from the desert.

'There is a lookout post on the edge of my sight.'

Falakar turned back to look out across the horizon. 'I can see nothing,' he said.

'They are placed so that each can see to the point the last cannot,' replied the bandit.

Sholster turned on him. 'You filthy snake, you were hoping to get us detected and captured!' He grabbed him, lifting him from the ground and drew back his free hand.

Shinlay gave a whimper and grabbed her head. 'Please stop raising your voices. It is like knives being stuck into my head.'

Sholster flicked the rogue several feet away to land on his back in the needles.

'I apologise,' said Sholster softly to Shinlay.

'The enemy's defence has some merit, but there is a flaw,' said Shinlay. She halted, placing both hands upon her head again as another wave of pain coursed through it. She stopped for a few moments before continuing.

'There is a small lizard-like creature in our mountains called a Chameleor. It has the ability to colour its skin to that of its background, making it almost invisible. If you chop bark from the trees to cover each person's height we could smear the front in the sticky resin from the trees, and cover them with the sand. From a distance we would blend in with the ground. The land is downhill coming from the mountains, and the lookouts are raised. From their angle we should always appear against the sand. We may be able to pass between towers undetected. Where is the sun now?'

'It is past noon,' replied Falakar.

'Then hurry. The sun in this clear sky will generate some heat that will cause the air to shimmer which will help the deception. Beware that later the sun will cast shadows that will give us away.'

She then slumped back, her head dropping.

Falakar checked her condition.

'She has passed out again.'

'This plan is reckless!' said Jontal.

'You don't like it?' said Sholster.

'No I do not. We will be seen and captured for sure!' replied Jontal.

'But you want that,' said Falakar.

'I do not want to get caught out there. We would be interrogated first to provide information for an Administrator to make an informed decision.'

'You have an alternative?' asked Falakar.

'Take a tower,' said Jontal. 'Use the bark to gain surprise and prevent an alert.'

Sholster snorted at the suggestion. 'What distresses you, makes me feel safer, rogue. I say the first plan.''

Jontal waved his arms in the air with a pleading look towards Falakar.

'We remain with our plan,' said Falakar.

The group completed their disguises and each person stood with their sanded bark shield. Jontal was provided one and allowed to walk free on the understanding that there was no escape from an arrow in the back on such level sandy ground. Sholster's shield was extra wide to cater for Shinlay's body as well as his own.

'Well I guess I've been involved in crazier ideas,' said Falakar, assessing the group.

'I bloody well haven't,' said Sholster. 'People normally hide from *me*!'

ThreeSwords spotted the tower that Shinlay reported, and the band set off.

Garamon had only ever seen deserts in drawings. None had ever been so unerringly flat. He now understood why Falakar said this was manmade. It was as though every bucket of sand hand been placed one at a time and smoothed out. It stretched out in front and to the sides for as far as he could see.

As they continued, the heat increased. There was little breeze to dry his sweat and the act of walking on sand was surprisingly tiring. He had liked it at first as it was soft and like walking on carpet. But soon enough the lack of solid surface took its toll and rarely-used sections of his calf muscles burned for relief.

Falakar called a halt at last. The forest trees behind them were a good deal smaller now. Garamon slumped to the floor thinking it was a rest break. He then realised ThreeSwords was pointing to a column of dust to the south-east ahead of them.

'What is that?' said Kinfular.

Falakar needed no time to discern the meaning of the vast cloud. It was like a miniature sand storm. It stretched back over the horizon.

'Marching men,' he replied, grimly.

'How many?' said Kinfular.

'Thousands,' said the Ranger gravely.

Kinfular looked blank.

'A hundred tribes of warriors,' explained Falakar. The barbarian tribes had no use for such a large numbers.

'You joke, Ranger,' said Kinfular. Not even a mighty Emperor could drive so many tribes to fight together.'

'The Ashnorians do not think in terms of tribes, and they have no need for tactical warfare such as you are used too. They swamp you with overwhelming numbers and magic. When they invaded my land they attacked with many times the number before us.

Kinfular looked alarmed.

Falakar studied the cloud some more. 'From their direction of travel I would say they are making for the Hammerheads to the east of here. They are probably massing for a crossing in the next few weeks, now that the winter weather is waning.'

'How can one fight such a force?' said Kinfular.

'I have long speculated that the Hammerheads were a difficulty, even to the Empire,' replied Falakar. 'They are high, wide and connect from shore to shore. Such a barrier will work against their normal approach to war. I'm guessing that is why they halted their advance at Straslin many years ago. From the look of it they plan to cross at the Strakens, not one of the easier points.'

'Why would they choose to cross at such a place? With such army they could cross anywhere.'

Falakar thought for a moment. 'The opposite side is the widest part of a vast forest. They could assemble their entire army in it without detection. From there they would be able to launch a sudden and devastating attack on Tiburn, and secure the town. They would enslave the townsfolk and set them to the task of providing food and other supplies.'

'If I could unite the clans, together we could create a defence that even such a force would struggle to breach before next winter. In these mountains, numbers count for little.'

'Could you do such a thing?' asked Falakar. 'Your people are not known for such cooperation.'

'We have spent generations fighting petty battles between clans. The idea that we must fight as one, and for a threat that seemed to be directed at your people, would be difficult to achieve. But there is much rivalry between us too. I think I know a way that it may be achieved.'

'They will have outriders,' called Jontal, not privy to the conversation and getting agitated at the delay.

Falakar nodded. 'We will have to head across to the tower to avoid detection by the enemy's scouts. For better or worse it seems we have to try his plan.'

Falakar turned to Jontal, 'How many men per guard-post tower?'

Jontal shrugged, 'Ten maybe, but the problem will be the magii.'

'Magic?' said Sholster, fearful.

'He will be a low ranking non-offensive magii,' replied Jontal dismissively. 'He is only there to communicate with the next outpost further south. The signal will be relayed by that mage to the main barracks for the area. From there a sizable detachment will be dispatched to investigate.'

'If a message was sent, how long would we have before this detachment you speak of would arrive,' said Kinfular.

'They would be on camels, so two hours at most,' replied Jontal.

'But ten men could not be expected to hold off an attack that long,' said Kinfular.

'The towers and the men are expendable. They are only there to raise an alert of an attack,' said Jontal.

'These Yellow Skins have no honour,' said ThreeSwords.

'It is how they do things here. Life and death in the service of the Emperor is a glorious thing,' said the bandit not masking his own distain for the Empire's ways.

'Two hours would be enough for us to return to the tree line if we failed to stop the magic message,' said Kinfular.

'How can we be sure that a message will not have been sent?' said Falakar to Jontal.

'The mages use a small golden coloured ball to cast their spells. From my understanding, if you prevent them from touching it, no message will be sent.'

'Where would we find it?' asked Kinfular.

'The few that I've seen were kept in small polished wooden boxes about a foot across. I doubt you would mistake it if you saw it. Also, it won't be far from its owner.'

'Can we expect the guards to be alert, and at what point can we expect them to surrender?'

Jontal genuinely laughed aloud. 'Your sword in their guts would be nothing compared to their fate if they were found not fully attentive at their posts, never mind them doing the unthinkable and submitting to you.'

Kinfular turned to ThreeSwords, 'How are your bow skills?'

The warrior shrugged, 'I could not skewer a man's throat at sixty paces in the dark,' he replied making obvious reference to their rescue by Shinlay, 'but I can silence an unmoving guard at a reasonable range if that is what you are suggesting.'

Kinfular looked to Falakar, ignoring Sholster who's only venture into bow training left the clan's Fletcher hard at work for a week. 'I have heard stories of your skills with all weapons, Ranger.'

'He is renowned with the bow and sword,' replied Garamon, sharply. 'He is a legend amongst my people.'

'I meant no disrespect,' replied Kinfular, tilting his head to Falakar.

'You have a plan?' replied Falakar, smiling at the claim of his young admirer.'

'We use our disguises to get within bow range, kill the guards that would uncover our approach, then storm the tower and stop the mage before he can send the signal.'

There was a short discussion on tactics before the group agreed. Then they reassembled and, facing their new destination, set off.

Chapter 22 - First blood

Grint sat back in his wicker chair. He dropped his quill to the desk after completing his daily report which, as usual, entailed nothing of significance to report. He hated the job of Tower Captain more than any in his rota. It was the nearest border to the unconquered northern lands and the last place that anybody would attack. The mountains saw to that. That and the ten legions of the army on his doorstep. It all made for the most boring place in the Empire right now. And it was so damned hot during the day and cold at night. Only the occasional breeze from the west carrying cooler air from the waters of Li-Senca provided any comfort.

Today was not such a day.

He took another clean cotton handkerchief from his desk and threw the sweat-soaked one into the linen basket in the corner of his officers' room. It made the usual slap as it hit the reed wall before peeling itself off and falling into the container below.

Reeds! Another triumph in design for the great imperial builders he thought sarcastically. Just place your guards above ground in the safety of hot dried reeds, one of the most flammable substances known to man. It wasn't for some years that he came to discover that this was in fact done for a reason. It was likely that an attacker would chose to burn the tower down. This would make the perfect early warning beacon for the defences of Straslin.

He got to his feet and straightened his tunic. Such thoughts would not do. The Yhordi spies were said to be everywhere and he didn't want to get caught appearing to be tiring in his unbending loyalty to the Emperor.

He heard what sounded like one of the lookout guards collapsing to the floor of the terrace that surrounded the tower. Such was the peril of standing in the oppressive heat in a mixture of mail and plate armour with a heavy close-fitted helmet, the ridiculous maroon plume not helping. He picked up his charge book and wandered out onto the balcony to see who was going to get an uncomfortable night in the dungeons upon his return from duty. He looked around to see that it was the overweight Jelili. He started to write down the transgression, but then stopped. His head slowly turned as if not believing what he had seen. There was an arrow sticking out of the soldier's chest.

His battle instinct took over and he dropped to the ground just as more arrows passed where his chest was only a heartbeat ago. He shuffled to the edge of the terrace and gently parted the thin reeds that made up the almost pointless rail. A broad smile crossed his face. It was a Ranger scouting unit with some barbarians, attacking *his* tower. He couldn't believe his luck. Only a few weeks ago he heard of another group that were caught further inland. The captain in charge was handsomely rewarded.

He pushed himself back inside and stood with his back against the wall. He watched as the tower's answer to Spineless Magii of the Decade entered the room. Briknic's face was a picture of horror and disbelief.

'We're under attack,' he said incredulously, and waving the hand that wasn't clutching his precious box in the direction of the doorway adjacent to Grint.

'You catch on,' replied Grint, dryly.

Then, as if only just remembering his duty in the heat of the attack, Briknic started fumbling to open his container to gain access to his manasphere. 'I must send a message to the Guard-Sergeant!' he said urgently.

'You damned well won't!' replied Grint severely. 'The only opportunity I've got for promotion out of this hell hole will not be ruined by a snivelling neophyte caster who calls for help because of a handful of suicidal heathens.' He snatched up his favourite rapier. After a couple of experimental air-splitting swooshes he headed off with relish down the ramp to meet the enemy.

The first of the guards dropped the last foot from the ramp to the sand and stepped to meet the lead barbarian. He raised his two-handed sword, trusting to his heavy armour to deflect his opponent's light rapier first strike and allow the combination of the weight and strength of his own attack to hack through his opponent's leather armour. All seemed to be going to plan as his sword descended and the barbarian wasn't making any move to avoid it. He then felt a sharp pain in his groin and watched as the barbarian used his embedded sword to pull and twist his body towards and under the slower downward swipe, allowing it to harmlessly pass through the air. The act of having his wound used as a lever caused excruciating pain and he stumbled forward partly from the over swing of his large sword, but also from a coordinated elbow in his back as the barbarian passed by him to engage the next man. He hit the sand as more of the attackers run over him. He looked down to his wound. *Lucky bastard.* He looked up in the hope to see the barbarian being skewered by one of his fellow men-at-arms, but found no solace from the fact that his colleagues were falling at the same contemptuous rate. He wondered if even the Captain could take him. He dropped his head back into the sand, closed his eyes and waited until the magii healed him.

Grint joined at the back of his men, the ramp was too full to get into the attack and he started to get frustrated. He didn't wait long though, the lead barbarians were working their way through Grint's men with alarming ease. He noticed that one of them used a light rapier which he twisted with amazing speed to strike unerringly through the gaps in the Ashnorian armour. Grint was an excellent swordsman and knew that his own heavier version of the weapon would snap through such a flimsy blade.

He held back, remaining halfway up the ramp so that he may propose to his chosen opponent a one-on-one contest.

The last of his guards fell, without a single loss to the attackers. He wasn't going to see that promotion after all, however he had waited a long time to face such a rival to his skills. He uttered a pact with his god Shantartar that if he granted him this one victory, he would serve him for a hundred years.

He raised his sword upright against his nose in the normal respectful salute to a challenge, but the barbarian remained at the bottom of the ramp watching something happening behind Grint. The ramp shuddered and lurched to one side, almost throwing him off. He snapped his head around to see Briknic attempting to pull out the second and remaining stake that attached the ramp to the upper tier.

'You snivelling maggot, the torturers will be too good for you!' and he started to run back up the ramp.

The stakes were designed for quick release, even so the magii was not strong and Grint made the distance and took a lunge at the traitor. His weapon would have struck except for the remaining stake coming free and the ramp dropping away. As he was falling, Grint saw Briknic snatching up his precious box and run inside. Grint then hit the sand, which contrary to his expectations wasn't soft at all, the ramp's reeds doing nothing to ease the impact. He felt and heard something snap upon his landing and knew that his leg was broken. He started to curse his luck, but didn't get far as the largest weapon he'd ever seen, wielded by the largest warrior he'd ever seen, headed for his face. In his last seconds he chose some stiff words for Shantartar.

Kinfular swore as the ramp fell. He saw the mage pick up the box Jontal described and disappear into the structure. He knew nothing of magic but guessed he'd never climb one of the tower legs in time to stop the mage from signalling.

198

Garamon raised his axe above his head and struck down into the nearest supporting leg. A large amount of wood exploded outward. The axe came free easily and he struck again removing a sizable chunk of wood that would have taken half a dozen swings of a normal woodcutter axe. Another swing created a three-quarter deep cut into the leg. Sholster roared for him to move aside. As he did, the giant ran and thudded his shoulder into the weakened point. There was a loud crack and splinters shot out from the leg around Garamon's work. Sholster dug in his heels against the moving sand and yelled out in his efforts as he gave a mighty push. The leg snapped in two.

The tower lurched alarmingly and began to fall, but as they scrambled out of the way the new shortened leg hit the sand so the tower stopped on a heavy tilt. Thinking that their plan had failed they heard a wail from above and the sound of something hard hitting a wooden floor and rolling. As Garamon and Sholster looked up they saw a small golden ball pop out of the structure and drop to the sand with a thud a few feet away from them. Both men looked at each other with broad grins. Sholster walked over to the thing, and with the power driven of hatred of all things magical, rammed the head of his club down onto the half buried object projecting it below the surface. He went to repeat the action but Falakar called out, 'Wait!'

Sholster stopped.

Falakar walked over and looked up to the mage who ducked a little back from view, but not entirely. 'Bring Shinlay over here in view of the mage,' he instructed.

Sholster looked to Kinfular, who nodded his agreement. Falakar looked to the mage and made gestures towards him, then the buried orb and then the lump on Shinlay's head. He then followed up with a throat-cutting gesture that made the mage recoil. Falakar then shook his head hoping to indicate that this would *not* happen. The mage tentatively nodded his agreement.

It took a few minutes for the combined resourcefulness of the group and Sholster's strength to re-attach the ramp into its original position allowing the Ashnorian to leave the sanctuary of the tower and join them.

He looked afraid.

Falakar knelt down to dig out the orb. The young mage became agitated, shouting the same words over and shaking his head and pulling Falakar away.

'I guess we shouldn't touch it,' ventured Falakar bemused. He gestured the mage to the orb.

'How can we be sure he won't raise the alarm?' said ThreeSwords.

'They need line-of-sight,' replied Jontal.

'What does that mean?' snapped ThreeSwords.

'It means they have to be able to see the target of the message,' replied Falakar. 'Or at least have nothing major in the way: no hills, mountains or dense trees for instance. The Rangers communicate across mountains using polished metal and the sun's light. It only works if you can see your target.'

'But the ground is flat here, you can see forever,' stated ThreeSwords.

'Not so, the ground is slightly curved,' explained Falakar. The confused look on the Heslarian's face made the Ranger realise that getting into a conversation about the curvature of the world would have to wait for another day. 'He needs to be high in the tower for the magic to work,' Falakar ventured. ThreeSwords looked up at the tower and seemed satisfied with the simpler explanation.

The mage waited until receiving a gesture to continue before scrabbling across to the dip that indicated where the orb was buried. He closed his eyes for a few moments before pushing his fingers into the sand. He flinched at one point, then began lifting his hands up. The orb emerged between his fingertips. He carefully got to his feet, still maintaining his concentration, and walked to Shinlay. He sat down and placed the orb onto the sand while maintaining contact with the fingertips of one hand. The other hand he placed over the welt on Shinlay's brow with the palm facing downward.

Several minutes passed. Beads of sweat had formed on his forehead and the hand over Shinlay was trembling. He snapped his hand from the orb and fell backwards into the sand. Wisps of smoke rose from where his fingers were in contact. Falakar and Garamon went to his side and pulled the Ashnorian into a sitting position.

'Water' called Falakar. None of the barbarians moved.

'*Water,*' he called directly at Kinfular, his manner accusing and angry.

Kinfular stared for a moment before removing his water skin and passing it to the Ranger. Falakar took the skin and poured some of the contents over the mage's head. The young man opened his eyes, blinking out the water. He looked down on the still sleeping form of Shinlay and pushed himself back to her side, inspecting her injury. The swelling had receded a little and some of the purple bruising was gone. He looked at Falakar with an expression of apology and shook his head.

Falakar smiled at the young man. The Ashnorian was relieved to see the response and smiled back.

'The word for thank you is Il-kai' offered Jontal. This made the Ashnorian look around at the rogue.

'You speak their language?' asked Falakar.

'Our truculent neighbours are as guarded about their language as everything else they have,' replied Jontal. 'But being amongst them for a while you cannot help but pick up on the usual basic words.'

Falakar turned to the young mage again. 'Il-kai.'

The Ashnorian replied with a wider smile.

Falakar then rose to his feet and walked over to the Kinfular. 'We need to talk.' It was given an as order and he walked away from the main group. Kinfular delayed a few moments before following.

'You have a problem with our friend?' asked Falakar, when the barbarian leader reached him.

'He is the enemy,' replied Kinfular, as if that was enough.

'Lucky for Shinlay he didn't feel the same way,' replied Falakar.

'We would have made him. He is young and weak, he knew that.'

'He didn't have to try so hard to heal her, we wouldn't have known. He suffered considerable discomfort in his efforts. He also seemed genuinely concerned with her wellbeing. He is not a warrior. Jontal said it was just a tour of duty they must perform. He probably wants to be our enemy as much as we do his.'

Kinfular simply shrugged. 'Our ways are different, Mlendrian.'

'Well while we are on this mission you honour the codes of the Rangers,' said Falakar.

'As long as it keeps us safe, I will abide by your rules,' agreed the barbarian leader.

Raised voices were heard from the others. The men returned together to the main group. There was an argument breaking out between Sholster and the mage.

'The walking wall wants to bury our friend's toy,' explained Jontal.

Kinfular raised his hand to Sholster.

'That *thing* must be buried, Hlenshar. It emanates evil, I can feel it!'

'I feel nothing my friend,' said Kinfular reassuringly, and looked to Falakar, as if making up his mind. 'He can keep the thing. It shall be placed in its box and one of us shall carry it. It may be possible that he can use it again to help Shinlay.'

'It must not come with us!' protested Sholster in an uncharacteristic outburst against his leader.

'I shall carry it,' said Garamon, interrupting the growing argument.

'Then it is done,' confirmed Kinfular. 'Understand though Mlendrian, Sholster has a strange sense for such things, and I have never seen him so disturbed.'

'We have a few hours of light remaining,' said Falakar, looking to the sky. 'Let's get as far south from here as possible.'

The group soon reformed and set off. Behind ThreeSwords was their new prisoner, constantly looking back to Garamon and the orb box.

Chapter 23 - Distasteful undertaking

Illestrael had endured many unpleasant duties in her decades of service with the Yhordi. Her next task, borne of her own volition to help the Mlendrian Chayne, ranked as bad as any she could remember. Under normal circumstances she would have little trouble removing something as simple as a key from a person's pocket, but this was no ordinary key and it certainly was no ordinary person. Lathashal hadn't lived for four hundred years, or risen to his senior position in full favour of the new Emperor, without having the greatest skills in diplomacy, cunning and, most of all, survival. He was also ranked as a Cin'Shantra, a Master Magii - fifth gradia. Only four ranks were higher, and less than one in a thousand magiis achieved even his aptitude.

He had only one weakness.

She remembered back to her days of magii training with him. It was a requirement of the Yhordi to have at least basic training from all the other Shodatts. It helped with infiltrations and deceptions. She hadn't been a good student and Lathashal was ready to expel her from his personal teaching, which would have left her in the lower ranks of the Yhordi. She resorted, as always when failing in the face of a male, to her best talent. She flirted with the man. The response was overwhelming. The man enjoyed the most extreme tastes imaginable and at times it took all of her training at deception to maintain the illusion of enjoyment. Each week she would attend his lessons which would be cut short so he could receive his reward for providing glowing reports on her magical prowess.

For a year she endured the sessions until the training period was over. He was distraught. In his position he had many females at his disposal, but clearly what he gained from her was special. He attempted many times to encourage her to his chamber. Her refusals incurred his increasing frustration and eventual wrath. As the Yhordi didn't officially exist, Lathashal's political leverage to manipulate other Shodatt Masters did not apply, but sooner or later she knew he would achieve his goal. She made herself available for undesirable Yhordi missions that took her far from Lathashal's reach. After some five years of hardship, his hunger diminished enough for her to return. Now she had to approach him once more.

She knocked on the door of his private chambers.

It opened and she brought her fist to her chest and pointed within the rooms, following the servant in.

From the little she could see of the first antechamber, the place hadn't changed in the slightest. Heavy red flock wallpaper lined the walls, adorned with gold relief. The patterns were intricate and impeccably well-crafted. The themes reflected the occupant: deep, complicated and powerful. The floor was carpeted in a deep red thick pile.

The servant returned and gestured for her to enter the anti-chamber. She entered and sat down to what she expected would be a long wait. She contemplated again her strategy to coerce the suspicious mage into accepting her company after so long. She considered simply pulling the tied knots on her soft black leather clothes and let them fall to the floor. Such a transparent ploy would never work though; too much painful history would prevent him falling for such an easy gambit.

She was aware that a servant entered the room to her left on some unknown task and she didn't bother to look up to acknowledge its existence. It came towards her. As it encroached more fully into her peripheral vision she noted that it wasn't dressed in the normal off-white servant uniform, but a multicoloured robe.

She looked up into the face of Lathashal.

It was all she could do not to take a sharp intake of breath. He looked haggard beyond belief, his skin sagging from his cheekbones and his eyes were sunken within dark black rings. He stooped alarmingly.

It confirmed how she was to proceed.

'My dear, such a *pleasure* to see you,' said the magii. The words were spoken with the normal sarcasm, but lacked their usual bite, almost as if he didn't care. She knew the man to be uncompromisingly self-disciplined. It created some genuine pity for him.

'Please feel free to waste my time by staring,' he said.

She recovered from her moment of concern. 'You look well,' she said, with some kindness that took her by surprise, but it was hard to know what to say - '*Hey Lath, you look like hell, let's have sex. It will either give you a reason to live again, or kill you.*'

'Liar,' he responded to her spoken comment.

'Okay,' she admitted. 'I have seen you looking better. What has happened to you?'

'Arrgh,' he said waving dismissively. 'It is only the preparations for war.'

'The Rite of Rakasti? But you have cast it before. I don't remember you ever looking so … drawn.'

'The Rite is nothing,' he snapped contemptuously. The problem is that our glorious previous Emperor decreed that peace was the future of the Ashnorian Empire. So against the strenuous objections of the Magile Shodatt he ran down the stockpile of filled manaspheres.'

'Don't you have an army of sycophantic underlings for such a menial task?'

'Charging manaspheres isn't a menial task, Illestrael. If you had been a better student you would have learned that. And of *course* I have many magiis restoring the shortfall. But the major spheres, such as those required for waging war

206

against an advanced civilization as the Mlendrians, are numerous and draining to charge.'

'I am sorry. I was unaware of the problem. Is there anything I can do to help?' she offered with as much conviction as she could.

Lathashal snorted derisively. 'My dear, I doubt you could usefully fill a thimble with mana, let alone the smallest of manaspheres.'

She ignored the insult. 'I was thinking more in terms of providing something by way of relaxation. It looks like you could do with it.'

'A knife in the heart perhaps?' he sneered.

Illestrael laughed and gave her best seductive smile. 'Oh Lath, your dry humour always used to make me laugh back in the old days.'

She watched his eyes. They tried to hide a buried longing.

She gave another of her flirtatious smiles.

His face took on an uncharacteristic sadness, an expression that looked almost comically out of place on the man.

'You hurt me,' he said.

Illestrael found the strangely honest and open declaration disconcerting, but she knew how to handle men and she knew this one well.

'I seem to remember it was you hurting me,' she said sexily, continuing her merciless attack of erotic looks. She watched in wonder as he transformed and laughed, looking more like a boy receiving his first kiss.

'I know I'm a dunce when it comes to magic, and we have politics between us. But I'm also loyal to the Emperor, and right now it seems the best thing I can do to help is getting you to unwind from your stresses for a few hours.'

The effect of mentioning such a long session created the desired reaction, as Lathashal almost lost the use of his legs.

'My dear,' he said, trying not to show difficulty in getting his words out between his punctuated breathing. 'It is kind of you, but there -'

Illestrael rose from her seat to place the merest touch upon the prepared knots of her clothing which fell away. Her right knee skilfully pushed forward just enough to slow the fall of the material. The dim light of the room cast lazy shadows across her naked form.

Lathashal fell to his knees, not thinking or caring of any subterfuge.

Illestrael moved forward and placed a single finger upon the man's forehead, and gently pushed. He fell obediently backwards onto the soft carpet. She dropped to his position and began unravelling his robes.

He looked up into her eyes with such a look of longing.

'Oh Illestrael,' he said in the weakest of voices. 'I have so missed you.'

Chapter 24 - Demonic dealings

Chayne worked fast. It was two weeks since his failed attempt at the cabinet and he was getting desperate. He knew that the Ashnorians were close to beginning their invasion and that Lathashal's preparations for the Rite of Rakasti were almost complete. The main bench was strewn with books, scrolls and tomes, but he still didn't have the solution to controlling the destructive pulling effect of his probing spell into the cabinet's magical defences.

His frustration erupted as he reached yet another dead end to the latest thread of his research. He snatched up a heavy glass beaker and threw it at the cabinet.

'*Open!*' he cried.

The glass hit the invisible barrier and shattered into many pieces leaving the cabinet unharmed. In his anger he snapped his fingers at the glass remnants and several servants left their recesses to clean up the mess. He saw them move at his command and felt shame at his momentary lapse into Ashnorian ways that he so despised. He slumped back into his stool.

'I'm sure it will be something more sophisticated.'

Chayne jumped from his chair. He reached for his manasphere and drew mana to create a shield between him and the assailant. He was already tired from his research and the effort was a strain.

Illestrael picked up a small paperweight from a bench and tossed it gently towards him. It struck the barrier several inches before reaching him and fell to the floor. She then picked up a heavier bar and threw it with more force towards the shield. It struck as before, but this time Chayne flinched a little at the effort to resist the missile.

'Impressive,' she said. 'It normally takes years to achieve such proficiency.'

'You are not allowed in here,' said Chayne with as much bravado as he could gather.

'Your name is Chayne. You are a Mlendrian who was kidnapped from your land to be forced to work for the Ashnorians against your own people. You are the Zintar of Lathashal, a powerful but loathsome master magii within whose major laboratory we now reside.'

She stopped talking and waited.

'Who are you?' replied Chayne. His forehead was beginning to show beads of sweat.

'My name is Illestrael. I am a member of the secret Yhordi Shodatt. You will have found no reference to it in the library.'

'This Lab is a protected area, there are many magical devices to protect me,' warned Chayne.

'As you can tell from my presence, I already have knowledge of such contrivances and am able to avoid them. Please, I am here to help, you need not continue with your protection. If I came to harm you then I would not have announced my presence and your throat would be slit.

'I don't trust you,' he said.

'Two weeks ago you almost lost control of your manasphere, sitting right there at that bench. Somehow you survived and staggered to your bed. When you awoke you were in the safe hands of the Mage-Surgeon Stalizar.'

'How do you know this?'

'Because I delivered you,' she replied.

Chayne couldn't confirm her claim, but it made little difference. His manasphere was almost dry of mana. He let down the shield.

'I do not know you. Why would you want to help me and what could I need from you?'

'My reasons will for now remain my own. As for what I can do? She pulled at a chain around her neck. At the end of the chain was Lathashal's key.

'Is that?'

Illestrael smiled.

'But how?'

Illestrael raised a finger to her lips. 'We women must have our secrets.'

She dangled the key and chain out before her.

As Chayne reached out, she pulled it back out of reach.

'There is a … price,' she said.

Chayne, almost believing that an act of selfless generosity might have occurred with this despicable empire, cursed himself for being so drawn in. No doubt the price would be something that would be almost impossible to achieve and placed him at great risk.

'Yes?' he replied, managing to fill the single word with both disappointment and disgust.

Illestrael flashed a smile and lent forward.

'A kiss,' she whispered.

'I'm sorry!' replied Chayne.

'Just a kiss. That's all.'

'A *kiss*?'

'You do know what a kiss is, don't you? I mean, they do kiss where you come from?' she said suddenly, looking a little horrified.

'What I mean is: is that *all*?'

'Just that,' she confirmed, puckering up her lips.

'I am afraid I cannot,' he said flatly.

Now it was Illestrael's turn to look surprised. In all her years no one had ever turned down a physical advance. Admittedly, some of the men wanted to run terrified at her boldness, but she was never refused something as simple as a kiss.

'Do you not find me attractive?'

'You are very attractive,' replied Chayne, seeing no reason not to admit the truth.

'Oh the gods, you don't like men do you.'

'No!'

'Then why not?'

Chayne paused for a moment before replying sheepishly. 'I have never kissed a girl before.'

Illestrael's world just became perfect. For the first time in sixty years she felt something that she didn't initially recognise to the point of believing she had a medical problem - her heart had skipped a beat. She gazed across to this almost total stranger and wanted to spend the rest of her life with him.

'It can wait,' she said. She pushed the key back towards him.

He took it almost expecting it to strike out at him with the venom of its owner, but nothing happened.

Hurriedly he approached the cabinet with the key out before him. He was trembling at the thought of the knowledge contained within and the ability to attain his believed lost goal.

He touched the key to the barrier.

The force field collapsed.

He saw Lathashal do this several times. He knew from watching the magii's speed of movement when accessing the cabinet that the field was only removed temporarily. He moved quickly and turned the key in the keyhole to the sound of a triumphant click. He pulled the doors open and reached for the book. In gold script, set against the dark blue of the book's spine, was the title: *The Rite of Rakasti*. Chayne's heart beat faster and in his excitement he'd almost forgotten about the time limit. He raced to close the doors, and with the dexterity borne from his days trying to cast his old Mlendrian magic, he deftly locked the cabinet and leapt back as the spell re-engaged. It caught his hand as he withdrew providing a nasty kick.

'Are you hurt?' said Illestrael, jumping to his position.

Chayne shook his smoking hand a few times, but his attention was on the item in the other. He sat down and opened the first page and began reading furiously.

'I shall return in ten hours. After that you must replace the book and I shall replace the key.'

'Chayne!' she said forcibly.

He looked up. 'Yes?'

'The key must go back in ten hours,' she repeated.

'Yes, yes, of course, ten hours, right,' he replied. He turned back to his work.

She considered staying a little longer. She wanted to be with him and keep him safe, but he was after all in one of the most secure places in Straslin. She left via her normal secret route.

Chayne's tiredness vanished as he read the book before him. He hoped that he could simply skip over the pages to gain some key insight into disrupting the Rite. It became clear that the spell was complex. Far beyond anything he encountered to date. His respect for Lathashal begrudgingly grew further as he realised the true gap between his own capability and knowledge and that of the master magii. The skill required to understand and achieve such a spell was almost unbelievable. The quantity of mana to be attained and then maintained was orders of magnitude beyond his current ability.

He started again at the beginning of the book and began to methodically work his way through. It only took a few pages before he was shaking his head. The foundations for understanding the physics and mathematics of the magic were unknown to him.

He struggled for another hour, hoping that some understanding would begin to form. He made no progress and knew he had no chance of finding the answer within the remaining time. The only useful reference was a vague warning near the back of the tome about the crucial moment of casting, which was true for all spells. He slammed the book shut and sat back feeling all his earlier tiredness wash back over him.

As he gazed at the book, his eyes drifted across to his manasphere. He knew only the basics of Stalizar's regeneration spells, but perhaps he could regenerate some of his physical and mental energy.

He placed his fingers once again upon the device and began to draw from its remaining mana. He started to channel and form the magical energy, creating a probe to scan his body. He found the body to be an immensely complex subject to work with as a whole. This task was different from say, isolating a wound which could be seen to be different from the surrounding tissues. In that situation the job was to regenerate the damage to match and blend in with the healthy normal tissue. It was not easy, but the task was clear. What he was trying to do now was bring *all* of his physical being to a less tired state. The problem here was the many interacting chemicals that formed all parts of the body. The proportions were crucial. Even a slight imbalance and he could cause a breakdown in the body's natural processes and create greater fatigue, spasms, and even increase the chance of cancers or possibly his own rapid death.

He gave up on the body and moved to the mind. But the task here was even more bewildering. The brain consisted not only of chemicals, but an intricate weave of electrical pulses. He remembered when Stalizar used a small orb to help him remember his encounter with the demon within his own manasphere. It had looked so easy, but to him it looked like ants in a nest, with electrical charges flitting in all directions. Worst still was the fact that the electrical structures changed as he thought about the problem, creating new dynamic patterns in his brain that interfered each time he tried to interrogate a section. He knew he could not understand the complexity of the interactions between the electrical, chemical and physical cells and tissues any more than he could comprehend the book he tried so long to obtain.

He released his touch upon the manasphere and felt the usual pull upon his mind to maintain the connection. He thought momentarily of the demon inside, desperate to escape and never giving up. Just how desperate was the demon and what lengths would he go to? He knew he could control it. It was a constant clash of wills, but both knew the relative strength of the other. Chayne decided to do what no magii should ever consider. He replaced his fingers upon the smooth shiny surface, and instead of pulling mana from the orb and directing it outwards, he plunged his mind into it.

Immediately he felt the will of the demon pulling him in. As before there was the falling into blackness which induced a moment of panic. He restored his control and allowed the falling to continue. When he thought he had fallen the same distance as before he used his will to stop. He heard cackling begin and it echoed from all around him.

'*Stupid magii, you are mine!*' it said racing toward him.

As he felt it reach to within a few feet he illuminated the area with bright light. The demon sprang into view and shrank away.

'*Yow! Horrible mage hurt Zystal's eyes, evil light.*'

'Hello, Zystal,' said Chayne dimming the light.

'*Oh, it's you,*' replied the demon miserably. '*Zystal thought he would be able to escape. Cruel Tiny Mage, why do you do this to Zystal?*'

'I need you to help me,' said Chayne. He could feel the demon constantly attempting to push at his will. Each time he resisted.

'*Help from Zystal? Why would Tiny Mage ask? Tiny Mage can rip into Zystal's mind and force him.*'

'I do not wish to hurt you, I wish you to help without being forced.'

The demon laughed his wicked cackle hysterically, rolling onto his back and stamping his feet and hands upon the imaginary surface.

'Would you prefer I hurt you?' said Chayne, not seeing an end to the demon's merriment.

The creature stopped, spinning to its feet. '*Oh no, Master, Zystal does not want pain from the Master.*'

It was the first time Chayne heard the demon refer to him as Master.

'I do not want to hurt you Zystal. I have a task that I need you to help me with, and if you help me I will give you something that you want.'

'*Zystal want nothing from Tiny Mage, and will give him nothing! Zystal trapped and hate Masters.*'

Chayne focused his mind. A portal appeared. Within it was the land he saw when Zystal attempted to create one during their last encounter. The demon jumped for just a moment, then slumped at seeing the illusion for what it was.

'*Why do you torment Zystal? Tiny Mage is cruel, so cruel,*' it said, shaking its head.

'If you help me, I'll send you home,' said Chayne.

'*Master lie! Never let Zystal go. Trapped him here forever.*'

'I did not trap you. Evil Masters did this to you. I am not an evil Master.'

The demon seemed to consider this.

'*And Zystal take heart of Master?*'

'No. And if you ever attempt to do so again or try to conquer the Master's mind, he will fill this prison with light forever and bury it so that no other Master will find you. Zystal will spend all of eternity here never to return home.'

The demon recoiled, '*Wicked Master! Master should return with Zystal. Master make powerful Demon with such wickedness.*'

'So you will help me?'

'*You are truly great Master. Zystal will not challenge again, nor take Master's heart. But what Master want of Zystal to earn freedom?*'

'I want you to store as much mana as you can within this prison,' informed Chayne.

'*Then Zystal will use mana to escape and kill Master!*' said the demon, the words seeming to tumble out of its mouth as if by reflex.

'No. Then the Master would return and stop Zystal and fill his prison with light,' reminded Chayne, as if speaking to a slow child.

'*Oh yes! Terrible light. Wicked Master*,' said the demon, nodding his head emphatically.

Chayne wasn't so sure of his strategy now. The demon had spent so long defeating any attempt to use the orb's mana that it simply took precedence over all other thoughts.

'Zystal must remember the Master's plan or the Master will become angry,' repeated Chayne.

'*Zystal will remember now, not forget*,' replied the demon eagerly.

Chayne sighed, he didn't have any choice. Hopefully if the demon did cross him then Lathashal wouldn't let him live long enough to worry being abducted by the demon.'

'Then we will begin soon. I will provide you with as much mana as I can until I need to release it.'

'*Then Master sends Zystal home?*'

'Yes, Master promise,' replied Chayne.

'*What is "promise"?*' said Zystal with his head cocked.

'That is when the Master will not cheat you. He will do as he says if Zystal does as he asks,' explained Chayne.

Zystal again took a moment to consider this.

'*Then Zystal promise the Master.*'

Despite their pact the demon was still subconsciously pushing at Chayne's mind the whole time. It wasn't a good sign.

Feeling weary, he decided to leave.

He recalled the feeling he felt when Zystal returned him the first time and concentrated. He felt his essence rising. Within a few moments he was back in his own body.

And so that was it. The book warned that the moments just before the release of the Rite's energy, a magii was at his most vulnerable. Care had to be taken not to be overcome by the manasphere. Chayne would enter at that point and throw as much magical disruption as possible at Lathashal. It would cause a fatal loss of concentration allowing the powerful manasphere to overcome him.

The chances that he would succeed were minimal; there simply wasn't anything else he had come up with.

He was now as tired in the physical world as within the sphere. He returned to his bed for a short rest and to contemplate his plan.

He was aware of being shaken. He snapped his eyes open to see Illestrael bearing over him. 'The key, I must return the key. We are out of time,' she said urgently.

Chayne took a few moments to recover his wits and realised that he'd fallen asleep. He rose from his bed and headed for the cabinet, picking up the Rite of Rakasti on the way. He pulled the key from his pocket and repeated the procedure as before, returning the book exactly as found. He removed his hand and the shield reset. He gave the key to Yhordi agent.

'Illestrael,' he called after her as she was leaving the room. She stopped for moment to look back.

'Thank you.'

She smiled for a moment and then disappeared into the shadows of one of the servants recesses.

After a few moments he went to see what she was doing. The recess was empty, with no clue of an exit, secret or otherwise.

---0---

Illestrael returned to Lathashal's rooms. She made her way to his bedchamber. He was still on his bed, sleeping off his drug-induced revelry from their exploits. She replaced the key within his robe and removed her own clothing and climbed back into the bed. She had about an hour before he should wake.

She started to replace her hands within the manacles he'd used. With only one hand in place, he began to murmur. She cursed her luck and forcibly inserted her remaining hand too quickly, taking the skin from her knuckles. She couldn't help but give a stifled yelp.

'Still going my dear,' said the magii sleepily, turning over to view her. 'I must apologise for my rudeness, I seem to have fallen asleep.'

'I'm not surprised,' Illestrael replied smoothly. 'You were quite the stallion.'

'Nevertheless, I am a man known for my impeccable manners. I shall make up for my indiscretion immediately.' He left the bed to walk over to his trunk filled with his favourite 'toys'.

'Honestly Lath, you have done more than enough to satisfy any girl. I wouldn't want to impose any further, and I have duties to attend to,' she said.

'They can wait.'

And with that he pulled something from the trunk that filled Illestrael with dread. It was the one contraption that she had prayed thanks he hadn't used the previous night.

'My dear Lath,' she said, not managing to mask the tremble in her voice. 'You wouldn't consider using that without more drugs. I don't think I could enjoy it at all.'

'Oh but I insist, my dear. No session would be complete without it. And I owe you so much in return for the years you *ripped my soul from me!*' He swept over her and forced the device upon her naked form before she could release herself from the manacles.

'I have no notion as to why you are really here, girl. But by my words you will pay a heavy price for it.'

She squirmed under the clamps as he tightened the straps.

He began turning a mechanism, smiling as she cried out.

Chapter 25 - Tiny lightning

The shadows from the shallow dunes dissipated with the sun as it dipped below the mountain line behind them. Without the sun's rays on his back, Garamon felt a sharp temperature drop. He waited while Falakar and Kinfular surveyed the next outpost, several hundred paces ahead. The further south they travelled the more the mounds began to feature in the manmade flat terrain. Falakar explained that they were now on the edge of the Mal-Tasi desert. Garamon had never been in a desert before. The novelty soon wore off after the drudgery of walking on more soft sand. At least now mounds provided them with some cover.

He watched as the two men slid back down on their stomachs like lizards, leaving zigzags in their wake.

'The outpost is a low-lying, stone bunker,' reported Falakar. 'Upon it is a tower. My guess is that this provides the height for the mage to signal. Four guards patrol the roof, making it difficult for a dash from here without being seen. There is no sign of any mage yet and I suggest we move now before the guard's eyes adjust to the gloom.'

The four fighters in the group started assembling their gear for the dash.

The captured Ashnorian mage grabbed Falakar by the arm. Shaking his head, he pointed to the west and lowered his finger repeatedly to the ground.

'I think he wants us to wait until the sun has fully set,' interpreted Garamon.

'So his colleague can detect us in the dark,' retorted Sholster.

221

The Ashnorian detected the hostility in the spoken comments and cowered away from the barbarian.

'I do not believe so,' said Falakar. 'From his actions at the tower I think there is little loyalty in him for the Empire. He has helped us at every opportunity so far.'

'So he can get us to trust him and set us up for capture!' exclaimed the giant.

'Maybe,' replied Falakar. 'But I do not think so.'

He attempted to gesture his objections to the mage.

He did not understand and pointed to his manasphere box with a pleading gesture.

'He wants this,' said Garamon, making reference to the box with the orb.

'Well of course he does!' replied Sholster. 'He wants to communicate our impending attack!'

'No,' said Falakar. 'He is too young to be so skilled at such a deception. I believe his desire to help is genuine. Give him the orb,' ordered Falakar to Garamon.

Garamon went to obey. Sholster's huge club landed in the ground between the two with a powerful thud, showering all nearby with a dose of sand. 'That is not going to happen.'

Falakar turned to Kinfular. 'Order your man to move aside,' he instructed.

'I favour his view,' replied Kinfular.

'Your distrust of magic is overly cautious. I need you to trust me,' insisted Falakar.

Kinfular locked eyes with the Ranger, but Falakar did not flinch. There was an uncomfortable moment. Then Kinfular waved Sholster aside.

Sholster went to protest. A look from Kinfular made him stop.

Garamon held out the wooden container which the Ashnorian took eagerly. He opened the box and once again went through the short ritual of concentration before placing his fingers on the orb. Then he started to talk.

'P...pleese, nooo haarm yooo,' he said with his eyes still closed.

'Deceiving son of a ...' interrupted Sholster, but was cut off as the mage spoke again.

'Please, no harm you,' he said again with better pronunciation. 'B...bal,' he continued with a strained expression as if trying to understand the right words to use. 'Ma-jik chainge woords forr you.'

To the surprise of the others, he then closed the lid and locked the box.

Falakar touched the Ashnorian to get his attention. 'Can you understand me now?' The Ashnorian shrugged and pointed to his box.

'I guess not,' said Jontal.

Falakar pointed to the box, gesturing for the mage to use it again. The Ashnorian shook his head and repeated his gesture towards the setting sun.

'I believe the "ma-jik bals" have limited use,' said Jontal. 'I don't think he wants to use it on idle chit-chat.'

'He means to counter the detection magic of the mage in the bunker,' said Garamon suddenly.

'That's quite a leap of understanding,' replied Falakar.

Garamon shrugged, 'It just seems to fit,' he said.

'If that is true then we may be able to bypass the bunker altogether,' reasoned ThreeSwords.

'Then we settle in until our friend is ready to proceed,' decided Falakar. Sholster again went to object, but Kinfular raised his hand to stifle argument.

They didn't have to wait long. With the sun dropping below the mountains it took little time before near darkness was upon them. The mage reached for the latch on his box. Everybody prepared for departure.

This time the Ashnorian concentrated for several minutes before lifting the orb from the box using a small brass lever. The orb rose and clicked into position above the box. He picked up the box in one hand and placed the fingertips of the other upon the orb.

He turned to Falakar, 'Bea clos. Noo see yoo,' he said.

The group assembled close to the mage and he began to walk slowly forward. As they rose above the protection of the mound, Garamon could just make out the shape of the bunker ahead and four guard silhouettes on it against the dark sky.

He felt exposed, despite the gloom.

They began moving down the other side of the mound. No shouts came up from the direction of the bunker.

'So far so good,' he whispered, mostly to himself.

With their current pace it would take a few minutes to reach the bunker. Walking so slowly in the face of the enemy was not easy and Garamon's nerves were on edge.

The mage tensed and stopped. A fifth silhouette joined the guards. His eyes started to glow red and he was turning as if scanning the area. At one point when it seemed he was facing them the eyes became brighter and their prisoner made a slight gasp. The eyes locked onto their position and flared causing the mage to make a sound as if struggling. Everybody prepared themselves for the final dash.

Seconds passed, but then the bright eyes dimmed and resumed their previous searching motion.

The Ashnorian dropped to his knees breathing heavily.

'I do not think we have another chance,' said ThreeSwords.

'That rules out going around,' replied Falakar. We take the bunker.'

'Then let it be now before the mage returns his demon gaze,' said Kinfular, moving silently out into the gloom, his men following him.

Falakar removed a length of binding from within his tunic and began securing Jontal's legs.

'Oh come on, at least give me a chance to run if you don't succeed!' he protested.

Falakar completed his task and turned to Garamon. 'Keep your axe blade two inches from his neck. If we don't manage to overcome the bunker, I suggest you use the cover of night to return back to the tree line with the barbarian woman if you can, and leave Jontal to be found in the morning.'

'Yes sir,' replied Garamon.

Falakar clasped a hand to the young man's shoulder. 'Good luck to you son,' he said earnestly.

'And to you sir,' replied Garamon as the Ranger disappeared in the direction of the barbarians.

'This is madness,' said Jontal, immediately Falakar was out of earshot. 'That bunker is heavily fortified. They have no idea what they are heading into.'

Garamon expected the bandit to try something as soon as the others were gone, and ignored him.

'Listen to me! When our band of reckless heroes are killed or captured, the captain will order a search of the area using the mage. How many more times do you think our friend here is going to be able to hide us?'

Garamon was annoyed that the words held reason. Even so he knew the bandit's reputation for a silver tongue and continued to ignore his protest.

'We are going to die if we stay here, the barbarian woman too. You could save her?'

Garamon flinched a little at the mention of Shinlay. He knew that Jontal was simply trying to engage his protective feelings for the prone barbarian woman, but even so he didn't want her to die because of him. What if Falakar and the others didn't return? It *was* reasonable that the area would be checked for others. The mage no longer looked capable of resisting another attempt to detect them. But Garamon remembered that Falakar had survived many encounters in his life. He found it hard to believe that with the skills of Kinfular and the other two barbarians by his side that he would fail.

'Falakar will succeed.'

'You are a fool placing such trust in that old warrior. He is past his time and now only seeks what glory he can find. His life means nothing to him anymore. He will die here, as will the others. Then we will be captured, tortured for information and killed. They take special pleasure in hearing the screams of the women.'

'No!' said Garamon pushing his axe blade to touch the throat of the man before him and raising his voice too loud. He snapped his head around to look towards the bunker. The red eyes stopped their search and turned back to look in their direction, scanning from side to side. Garamon heard their mage whimper. The eyes stopped their search, facing in their direction. They flared again. There was a cry and their mage fell to the sand.

'They know we are here. Quickly, untie me,' said Jontal urgently.

'No.'

'Look towards the bunker, the mage is already starting to climb the tower. He is going to signal for others!'

Garamon squinted in the near darkness. He could just make out a dark shape beginning to climb the tower. He cursed.

'Untie my hands and give me my bow, I can stop him,' pleaded Jontal.

'You could not hope to hit him from here in this light,' argued Garamon.

'And how do you know that!' snapped the bandit. 'You have no idea what I can do.'

Garamon knew it would be a risk releasing the bandit, but the others hadn't planned on his blunder and the imminent signal.

'Just your hands,' insisted Garamon.

'And my legs. If you knew anything about such a long bowshot you would know I need to brace myself for balance.'

Garamon felt he had no time left to argue. 'I will be standing right behind you at all times.'

'Yes, yes, hurry!' said Jontal.

Garamon kept his axe close to hand and ordered the bandit onto his stomach so that he could untie all his bonds.

'You can get up now.'

Jontal got to his feet and collected his bow and quiver. He strung the bow and notched up an arrow, taking aim at the tower. He cursed softly.

'It's no good, I cannot hit him from here, the angle is wrong. I'll need to get closer. Stay here with the girl.'

Garamon stepped in closer with his axe levelled.

'Look lad, you've made your decision. Don't sacrifice us now for the sake of me getting a clean shot.'

Garamon didn't trust the bandit a jolt, but he had no experience with a bow. The bunker mage would surely signal any moment.

He lowered his axe.

Jontal disappeared into the desert towards the bunker.

Garamon kept sight of the tower for any sign that Jontal was successful, but nothing happened. Then some extra shapes could just be made out on the roof of the bunker. There was a flash of what looked like a small bolt of lightning from the top of the tower to the bunker roof. Moments later a tiny shape fell from the tower.

Garamon waited anxiously for signs of Jontal's return, or the others. Eventually he heard the soft sound of footsteps in the sand. Swinging around, he raised his axe. ThreeSwords ran into view and pulled out his Glowstone.

'We have taken the bunker, and the mage is dead. You are to come now. Where is the thief?'

Garamon looked out into the dark in the direction that Jontal left.

ThreeSwords placed his Glow-stone back in its pouch and used his night vision to check the area.

'Gone,' he said indifferently. 'Come, we must hurry,' he instructed, lifting Shinlay over his shoulder.

Garamon followed ThreeSwords to the bunker.

He walked down a few steps into a main area. There was evidence of a fierce fight in the room, but no bodies remained.

Falakar was sitting at a large table in the centre of the room poring over various bundles of papers and maps. Sholster was in one corner by a cooking range and was eating sizzling meat straight from its surface. He raised what looked like an oversized chicken leg and waved it at ThreeSwords. 'They prepared a victory feast for us!' he said, stuffing the meat into his mouth as the grease ran down his chin.

ThreeSwords carried Shinlay down a side corridor.

Garamon sat down at the table, the smell of cooking filled his nostrils and he realised how hungry he was.

Sholster, upon seeing the young woodsman, picked up a plate. 'My boy! I have chosen the second largest leg of … whatever this is … for you. Come share my banquet,' he said in a voice satisfied with life.

'Thank you, I will in a moment,' Garamon replied, although without his normal polite smile.

Falakar sensed the problem and shot to his feet, looking around. 'Where is Jontal?'

Garamon dropped his head. 'He tricked me.'

Falakar's face betrayed his anger.

'I am sorry, I was stupid,' said Garamon.

'Forget it lad. Jontal's tongue could talk meat from the jaw of a starving lion. I should never have left you with him.' The Ranger turned to Sholster.

'Head south and get as much distance from here as you can. Do not wait for me. Hopefully if you travel the night you will reach the outskirts of Straslin and find somewhere to hold up. I will look for you there.'

'You're going after him?' said Garamon.

'I must,' replied Falakar, heading for the exit.

'Take care Ranger. The one you hunt is treacherous,' bid Sholster.

'We have danced this dance many times,' replied Falakar.

Garamon rose and pulled at his backpack.

'Not you,' said Falakar, almost coldly. Before Garamon had a chance to object, he was gone.

Garamon looked to Sholster.

'Don't worry lad. That one's as canny as I've met,' he reassured, tucking into another steaming leg.

'Where is Kinfular?' asked Garamon.

'Damnedest thing I ever saw,' said Sholster with a mouthful. 'The Hlenshar drew back a knife to take the magika from the tower. It raised its hand, lightning would you believe, like from the gods themselves, but *tiny*! The Hlenshar dived, but the bolt blasted down one arm. The Ranger said it was lucky we barbarians carry so little metal. It's all beyond me,' shrugged the barbarian. 'He is resting in one of the back rooms.' He flicked the half-eaten leg he was eating in the direction of the corridor that ThreeSwords had gone.

Garamon headed off, the Ashnorian mage tucked in behind him like a faithful dog. They entered a room filled with beds racked in pairs. Kinfular was sitting up on the nearest lower bed. ThreeSwords was dabbing a leaf on a long blackened section of his leader's arm stretching from his shoulder to his elbow. Shinlay was on an opposite bunk, still unconscious. The mage went to her and checked the bruise on her head.

'Glansce,' he said, looking to Garamon.

'Drin glansce,' he said again, pointing to Shinlay's head.

Garamon shrugged his lack of understanding and then watched as the Ashnorian opened his orb box and pointed to the manasphere.

'Kintoo.'

Again Garamon indicated that he did not understand.

The mage pursed his lips as if thinking. He picked up a jug of water next to his bed. He poured some of the water into an adjacent mug until the mug was full to the brim.

'Shala,' he said, and then poured the liquid back into the jug. 'Kintoo,' he repeated pointing to the inside of the mug. He then returned to his orb and pointed at it. 'Kintoo.'

Garamon nodded. The Ashnorian smiled. He then pointed to Kinfular's injured shoulder and made a striking motion with his hand and a *pish* sound. The Ashnorian then pointed to his own orb saying 'Kintoo', and then looked and pointed straight up to the ceiling, 'Shala'.

'Do you understand him?' said ThreeSwords.

'He is offering to heal Shinlay again, but his orb is empty of magic. I think he wants me to take him to get the one from the mage you killed on the roof.'

'I do not think it is wise to let him have the killing ball,' said ThreeSwords.

'Go with them,' said Kinfular. 'Do not let him touch the thing until he is back here.'

'Yes, Hlenshar,' replied ThreeSwords.

Kinfular got to his feet as the three men left the room. He was still unsteady, although improved greatly since the encounter. His shoulder was sore at the point of contact with the spell. The rest of his arm was still tingling, but he could now move his fingers, and feeling was returning to his lower arm. He made his way over to Shinlay and checked on her condition. There was no change since the mage attempted to heal her. He stroked her head, feeling helpless. He decided to seek out the others.

He joined Sholster, who was tucking into a plate piled with a dry white meat.

'Hlenshar!' said the man through a mouthful of food and smiling broadly. 'This pale meat is like nothing I've ever tasted before. We must find out what animal this is and take a breeding pair back home with us.'

Kinfular gave the briefest nod. It made his head swim and he sat down at the table. Sholster pushed out the meat mountain. The effect was not pleasant on Kinfular's stomach and he waved the plate away. 'Save some for the journey. We do not know when next we will find food.'

Sholster gave a frown and stuffed in one last enormous mouthful.

'Where is the Ranger?'

'Hunting the bandit,' replied Sholster, almost unintelligibly.

'He escaped?'

'Apparently the young lad let him go.'

'Why would he do such a thing?' said Kinfular.

'Some trickery,' replied Sholster. 'The lad was pretty down on himself about it.'

Kinfular rubbed his hands over his face. 'I feel like a Skooner out of water,' he stated, referring to a common fish that would flap about violently when landed.

'Why so?'

'These Mlendrians, they are strange. They enter into a dangerous enemy land, unplanned with an inexperienced boy and a thief who wants nothing more than to see us captured. After only our first encounter with the enemy they take in one of them to trust almost as our own, and a *magika* at that. And now we are deep within the enemy's borders, the Ranger disappears into the night to chase the thief who was let loose by the boy.'

'I am sorry, I am of little use in such discussions,' apologised Sholster. 'But we are still alive, and it does seem to me that the Mlendrian's choice in keeping the mage alive was correct. I would never have done so.'

Kinfular considered the words of the straight-thinking warrior. 'Yes, we are alive, and I trust the Ranger. I am just used to leading and knowing I can trust each of my men to do the right thing.'

The giant walked around the table and uncharacteristically placed his huge hand upon his troubled leader's shoulder.

'You are the Hlenshar, perhaps the finest swordsman that lives and the most respected leader I have ever fought under.

I am a mountain. With Nightface also at your side, if it is your will, we will complete this, even if it means defeating this entire rat-infested Empire.'

Kinfular looked up into the man's beaming face. 'I may have to make you my second-in-command with such rousing speeches,' he said.

Sholster recoiled. 'Rolk, protect us!' he said throwing his hands into the air.

Sholster's face then turned serious. 'The Ranger says for us to move south. He will look for us around the edge of the city.'

Kinfular got unsteadily to his feet. 'Pack food and plenty of water. We'll wear the Ashnorian armour. It may disguise us.'

Sholster looked down at his frame and sighed.

'Yes, Hlenshar.'

Garamon followed as the Ashnorian searched under the tower for the fallen mage. It was dark and the single oil lamp the Mage held illuminated only a small area at a time. He found the box, broken and in pieces. The orb was not with it. Garamon saw a glint some way off. As the mage continued his own search so the movement of the lamp reflected a golden light similar to that of the mage's own orb.

Garamon called out and crossed to the object. He bent down and prodded the thing with a fingertip. Pain shot into his hand and up his arm. His mind felt like it had been hit by a hammer. He was vaguely aware of the mage shouting over the ringing in his ears.

It was all over in a few moments. His hand and arm still ached but his vision was clearing. The mage arrived and moved the lamp to inspect his hand. Garamon could see that the end of the finger was blackened. The mage shook his head from side to side at Garamon as he jabbered something unintelligible.

'Magic is the curse of men,' said ThreeSwords, standing over them.

The Ashnorian took the cloth belt from his robe and manoeuvred the orb into a makeshift sling. When he seemed satisfied with the arrangement they returned to the bunker. Sholster was just coming out and was looking for them.

'We are leaving,' he said.

'What about Shinlay?' replied Garamon. 'The mage is going to attempt to heal her again.'

Sholster shrugged.

Garamon entered the bunker and sought out the barbarian leader who was carrying Shinlay in his arms into the main room.

'We have found the other mage's orb, we can attempt to heal Shinlay again,' he said to Kinfular.

'We are leaving,' replied the barbarian, laying Shinlay on the table.

'I don't understand,' replied Garamon, not seeing what could be better than healing the woman.

'We are not safe here.'

'But it doesn't take long,' protested Garamon.

'The longer we stay here, the greater the risk. And we may need the mage's magic to help keep us hidden as before.'

'But Shinlay needs help!' exclaimed Garamon.

'This is my *command!*' said Kinfular.

Garamon, at first shocked by the outburst, then became angry in return at the seemingly callous way in which the barbarian ignored the opportunity to ease Shinlay's suffering. He spun around and stormed from the bunker to join Sholster with the packing.

Sholster heard the argument and waited for Garamon to calm a little. 'The Hlenshar is a great leader and a deservedly proud warrior,' said the big barbarian, breaking open a wooden box and checking the contents for anything useful. 'He is used to having his orders obeyed without question.'

'Even when they are wrong!' retorted Garamon, using his anger to pull apart another box.

'Do you trust your Falakar?' he asked.

'Of course,' replied Garamon. 'He is a legend among my people.'

'And do you think he has always made the right decision?'

Garamon knew what the barbarian was getting at.

'Trust in the Hlenshar,' said Sholster. 'He has the respect of his people as much as this Falakar with yours. They do not know the future any more than you or I, but history does not lightly make legends.'

Garamon begrudgingly received the words of wisdom. 'I think you are more of a scholar than you show,' he replied.

'Two compliments in one hour!' replied Sholster, laughing and turning back to his work. 'Something must be wrong with the world!'

Garamon began to help him with the remaining items. Maybe they would find another mage to help the woman.

Half an hour later and they were heading south again, under the cover of darkness.

Chapter 26 - Lies uncovered

Jontal took off into the night. The oppressive heat of the day was replaced with a damp, bone-numbing cold. His rapid departure left him without food or blankets. It meant he had to make it to the major command post without stopping, for halting would allow his sweat to chill him. It was possible to die in the desert at night from the cold. The post was hours away and he was tired from the day's hard pace on sand. There was another reason to keep going. Falakar would pursue him. The Ranger would not be far behind and would be tracking the footprints easily. Jontal knew his only hope of getting away would be speed. He was ten years younger and would be able to outrun him through the night, especially since only one of them had been involved in the bunker attack. Unlike the Ranger, he was magically tagged and would be spared immediate interrogation. He hoped his pursuer would give up and head back to the others, or even to the safety of the forest. But of course that wouldn't happen. The Ranger's code held its crusaders to ransom against such unethical choices, and Falakar was the standard against which the rest aspired.

He kept up his pace until he made out the light of the city. Another half-hour and the silhouette of the station came into view. He waited until he caught the glow of the nearest tower-mage's eyes. He stopped and waved his arms. The eyes flared.

He didn't have to wait long before he heard the hoof beats of camels, huge temperamental beasts that seemed to hold all other life in contempt. They had the ability to spit disgusting goo into your face with remarkable accuracy.

The six man patrol reached his position and surrounded him.

'Mor sanka dantia!' shouted the one with a captain's insignia on his breastplate.

Jontal was dressed in Mlendrian leather armour. It was a sure thing that he would be considered a spy.

'Palkak,' he responded, identifying him as an agent of Ashnoria.

One of the other riders dropped from his mount and removed Jontal's weapons.

'Shin tuo,' ordered the Ashnorian, flicking an arm in the direction to go.

Jontal nodded and started jogging.

They reached the outpost. The imposing iron gates were opened to the sprawling compound. One of the escorts galloped ahead to enter a nearby building.

'Shin tuo,' said the Captain again.

Jontal walked to the internal guards, who took over. His escort slid to the ground and walked off with no further interest in their captive or their mounts. Servants led the camels away. The gates were closed behind and his fate was now in the hands of the army. A soldier appeared out of the shadows with a mage. The young robed figure carried a small metal device embedded with a tiny clear glass orb. Jontal had seen one before. The mage shut his eyes and held it up in front of him. The orb began to glow purple. The mage opened his eyes and the orb blinked out.

'Di, Palkak,' he confirmed with the guards.

'Come this way,' said the mage in passable Mlendrian.

Jontal followed. His new escort close behind.

They approached the largest building. People were coming and going at a rate that was normal for the busy Empire. Some were soldiers, many were clerks. He was led upstairs and along a corridor to a set of heavy doors. Outside was a ten-man wooden bench. Two guards were stationed there.

The mage held a brief conversation with one of them. Jontal noted the anxiety in the faces of the six men already seated.

The mage turned back to him. 'We must wait here until the Commander grants us an audience,' he said. 'This may be some time, please sit.'

Jontal sat down in the nearest space. The mage sat next to him while the escorting soldier took up position at the top of the stairway, legs spread, arms linked behind him.

One by one the men queuing before him entered the room. He took the opportunity to check inside the room each time the door was opened. Little could be seen. Occasionally there would be muffled shouting from within. At no time did his mage seem surprised when voices were raised.

Each man left the room looking pale.

When the last man ahead of him had been seen, the mage stood. 'The Commander will see us now.'

Jontal followed the mage into the room.

The Commander was sat behind a polished wooden desk, flanked by two heavily armoured soldiers. There were stacks of papers on the desk, almost concealing a clerk sitting next the Commander. He was receiving instructions.

The mage approached and waited to be addressed.

The door closed behind with an ominous clunk.

The Commander took his time to finish whatever it was he was doing with the clerk before looking up at the mage. There was a brief discussion between the two men and the Commander looked towards Jontal and beckoned him to the desk. Jontal complied.

The Commander spoke in Ashnorian in the tone of a question. It was translated by the mage. 'You state that you are one of our agents?'

'Yes,' replied Jontal.

Another short exchange of words took place between the two Ashnorians.

'Then why are you not recognised by any of my men?' translated the mage.

'This is not my normal contact point, nor my time. I am here to warn you of an enemy scouting party in the area.'

Another discussion and the Commander looked interested.

'Tell the Commander all you know of the scouts,' said the mage. Jontal noted warily that the mage opened his manasphere box and placed his fingertips upon the orb's surface.

'They are a group of barbarians and a young Mlendrian. They captured me in the mountains and forced me against my will to enter Ashnorian territory. They attacked and overcame a tower and a bunker. It was during the bunker raid that I managed to escape. He kept out Falakar's involvement.

The mage translated.

'And where are they now?' he relayed back from the Commander.

'As I said, I escaped before the conclusion of the bunker attack, and so I have no idea where they may be now.'

'Was there a Ranger in the group?' questioned the mage. It was no translation, the man asked without prompting.

Jontal paused for a moment, probably for too long. He did not know why they should ask such a question. It was possible that they simply feared the Rangers discovering their plans.

'The boy, possibly?' he ventured.

The mage spoke to the Commander again. This time the Commander became angry. He looked into Jontal's eyes and gave a command to his guards. They drew swords and approached him.

Jontal looked to the mage, 'What has happened?'

'During the interrogation I was monitoring your emotions. I could detect an obvious untruth,' he replied.

Jontal didn't like the word 'interrogation', but was even more distressed at the thought of them uncovering a lie. Ashnorians didn't respond well to them.

'I do not know what you mean, I have told the truth the whole time. If there was a Ranger in the group then it must have been the boy, or disguised as one of the barbarians.'

The mage translated the comment to the Commander.

The Commander gave a sharp instruction and the doors to the room were opened. Two guards entered dragging the slumped form of a man in just his cloth undergarments. They threw him forward to land on the Commander's rug.

It was Falakar.

Jontal inwardly cursed his luck. The Ranger was a skilled infiltrator. To get caught so soon was not to be expected. He too had been interrogated, but not in the fashion of Jontal's monitored conversation. The man was badly beaten. Jontal knew that no information would be forthcoming from such brutal tactics. The man would have endured much since his capture. That was the reason he was made to wait with the mage. They were expecting to check his story out against that of the Ranger's confession.

The Commander stood and walked around his desk. 'Gil thak, mur dia relcoynact?' he said to Jontal harshly. The mage began to translate, but the Commander waved the man away irritated. The Commander kicked his boot hard into Falakar's prone head. Jontal flinched at the sound. At least the Ranger was unconscious and wouldn't feel it yet.

'I swear I have never seen -' The Commander's anger flared and he struck out with the back of his hand across Jontal's cheek. He was a heavy set military man and the sudden strike knocked Jontal sprawling onto the hardwood floor.

'*Liar*!' shouted the Commander.

The word was heavily accented Mlendrian. Jontal thought it typically Ashnorian to have such a word in his limited foreign vocabulary.

'Speak with Dalmar. *Dalmar* is my contact.'

The Commander gave an order and two of the room guards approached and lifted Jontal to his feet. Falakar's guards grabbed him by the arms and dragged him from the room. Jontal was then pushed heavily towards the door to follow.

'Please, this is a mistake,' he protested. 'I came here to *help*!'

One of his guards struck him with an armoured fist, splitting the skin. He stopped protesting.

--- 0 ---

Kinfular led the remainder of the group south. There was no sign of the Ranger or bandit. After a few hours they picked up the glow of the city and headed that way as instructed by Falakar.

Now though they were lying flat on the cold sand. Somewhere out in the darkness ahead of them was a patrol. They heard the muffled hoof beats in the sand moments before. Kinfular was troubled by the appearance of the detachment. The desert was a vast place; random patrols in the darkness seemed unlikely unless searching for something that was known to be out here. There were no glowing eyes of their magic men so at least they wouldn't easily be detected. Even so the dim glow of the city might provide enough light to expose them if the patrol ventured too close.

The patrol started moving again in their direction. Kinfular slid his hand to his sword. The hoof beats grew louder and then increased in pace; it was possibly a charge. They were now on a direct collision course with the group.

As they reached his position, Kinfular jumped to his feet, drawing his sword. He was forced to dive to escape being trampled as one of the huge beasts almost ran him down. He rolled and regained his fighting position. The patrol continued their gallop away from them. He could make out Sholster and ThreeSwords also standing, weapons glinting in the city glow.

'Whores blackened teeth,' whispered Sholster. 'They didn't see us!'

'They are looking for us,' said ThreeSwords. His black skin made him almost invisible in the heavy darkness. Only eyes and teeth were apparent, flanked by two swords.

'And the closer we get to the city the more it steals the cover of this black night of the desert,' added Kinfular.

'We should leave this land, Hlenshar. It is like the gods themselves have deserted it.'

Kinfular sympathised with the warrior. At least when the riders were upon them they knew what to do, all indecision was lost. Now they were mercy to the unknown again.

'They are coming for our people. We will continue to trust in the Ranger,' replied Kinfular.

Mounted Patrol Leader Vace kept his unit running until he was sure they were far beyond enemy ears.

So the Mlendrian traitor had been telling the truth. There was an enemy scouting party between the city and the northern bunker. His close run past them had been a risk, but in the near blackness it was the only way he could verify their numbers. It was a small force of five or six. He had wanted to stop and attack the party and bring back the heads of the infiltrators. General Zanthak had a particular dislike for enemy spies, and was offering a month's salary for the head of each. But the base Commander's orders had been explicit. Identify and report, do not engage.

It would still be a generous reward.

He turned his mount in the direction of the outpost smiling at his good fortune.

Chapter 27 - Outcast

Stalizar knocked on the door to Lathashal's private laboratory. He wanted privacy with the master magii and he knew that Chayne would not be there. In truth he wanted to be anywhere but here, to do anything but what he was about to do. He avoided conflict during his life, even if it meant making significant sacrifices in his career and lifestyle. He didn't consider himself a coward, he just wasn't a politically ambitious man.

Now he was about to risk all.

He thought back to his initial magic training under Insanthian, a master magii in the capital city. Insanthian was a hard taskmaster, as were all the masters, although not as vicious as Lathashal - few were. Stalizar demonstrated great promise, but Insanthian became frustrated with his lack of conviction with attack spells. It took some months, almost to the point of dropping Stalizar from his personal tuition, before he tried him with healing magic. It was considered a secondary magic discipline given over to lower achievers. Stalizar excelled. From that point Insanthian focused all lessons on the curative discipline until Stalizar attained full Master Magii status.

He was assigned to the Vigoratii Shodatt where his name became known even to the Emperor for his breakthroughs in healing research. The Emperor called for him to investigate a cure for his life-long debilitating headaches. Stalizar began to research the problem and requested to accompany the monarch until his next attack. It took only a single attack for Stalizar's skills to notice the almost imperceptible swelling of the minute blood vessels in the Emperor's brain. Weeks of study isolated the cause and from there the initiator. Stalizar carried out a progressive treatment of the Emperor's liver, slowly changing it to include a deficiency of cells that would remove the acid build-up that normal bodies automatically removed.

The Emperor was euphoric. Stalizar was appointed his personal physician, a valued position and one that offered Stalizar considerable privileges. He set up his own research hospital and, when not in the presence of the Emperor, spent all of his time there heading up teams providing breakthroughs in medical treatments. The Vigoratii were elevated to the status of a major Shodatt and Stalizar became inundated with quality magiis. His name became known throughout the Empire.

His train of thought was interrupted as the door before him opened. A servant stood there.

Stalizar indicated his need to see the Master.

The servant informed him that the Master was not to be disturbed. Stalizar indicated for the servant to stand away. The servant stepped back.

Stalizar entered and crossed the antechamber to the door of the inner room. Steeling himself, he opened the door and walked in.

Lathashal was seated on the far side of the unadorned, windowless laboratory. The place was built for its special purpose: to contain explosions as a result of experimental spell failure, and to minimise the external distractions that could cause them.

It was to this latter consideration that Lathashal responded to the unplanned interruption.

'You brainless imbecile!' he screamed without turning. 'I'll have your organs chewed out by rats for this.'

'I am not a servant.'

Lathashal span around.

'What in all the hells possessed *you* to come here?' roared Lathashal. 'You know full well that the result of your interruption could have been disastrous for both of us.'

Stalizar saw a man drawn beyond all belief. If it wasn't for the usual venom in his voice, Stalizar would think him ready for his deathbed. Behind him along the back wall were a dozen large manaspheres.

'You were simply charging manaspheres in readiness for the war. A task that I know you are perfectly safe to perform,' replied Stalizar.

Lathashal glared. 'What is it that you want?'

'We need to talk.'

'Then make an appointment. Now get out of my presence before I send for the torturers. You are not beyond such measures Stalizar, even as a Master.'

Stalizar ignored the order. 'You must not perform the Rite to Rakasti.'

Lathashal's eyes narrowed and he stepped from his high stool.

'I *must* not?' he replied dangerously, crossing to Stalizar.

Stalizar held his ground. 'There are reports of increased demonic disturbances. It is rumoured that these are linked to the increased use of manaspheres. The Rite is one of the most powerful spells we cast. I am afraid of the consequences to our people and army without further investigation.'

'Nightmares, possessions and strange shapes appearing during major spell casting?' Lathashal scoffed. 'Such reports have no founding to a professional. I am stunned that a magii of your standing and experience would submit to such superstitious prattle.'

'What if the reports are true?'

'Then wouldn't *I* be alarmed? I cast some of the most powerful spells in the Empire.'

'So you have never seen anything of the like during spell casting?'

'I did not say that, but as far as I'm concerned they are of no consequence, harmless aesthetic by-products of releasing such large amounts of mana.'

'Is there a link between the manaspheres and demonology?' he asked.

Lathashal's expression could not have been more telling. His face changed, taking on a sudden look of forced softness, his thin grey lips even attempted a smile.

'What an absurd notion my friend, you must dispel such insane worries. The Empire would never delve into such a hazardous practice.'

Stalizar pulled open one side of his robe to expose his fingers upon his tiny manasphere. The meaning was clear: he had used the orb to detect the truth, a heinous action without the approval from a superior. Both men knew that such consent would never have been given.

Lathashal's face changed again. It wasn't an expression of anger, but something far worse: utter pleasure.

'You have been a thorn in my side for decades, surgeon. What possessed you to act so rashly now is beyond me. There will be no protection for you this time. Such information as you have just uncovered is only known to a few in the Empire. You will not be allowed to communicate this fact to anyone else.' All weariness gone, Lathashal snapped out his arm to catch his staff that leapt from the bench behind him. He spun on Stalizar and released a bolt of energy, just in time to see the Mage-Surgeon's body flicker and fade.

Stalizar, sitting a few rooms away, broke contact with his manasphere and took up his staff. He invoked a mana shield around him giving him some protection from Lathashal's attempts to detect his location. The illusionary projection he performed and accompanying telekinesis to open the door, plus the clairvoyance to give him sight and hearing in the lab was at the limit of his ability and drained his most powerful manasphere and himself. He knew he could only avoid magical detection from the Cin-Shantra magii for a short time. He could hear the furious cries from Lathashal's private lab. The man was going mad. He would stop at nothing now to see Stalizar's head on a pike for treason. He needed to disappear from the man's reach.

Rising to his feet, he left his heaviest and most powerful manasphere behind. He walked to the wall behind him and knocked the code he'd been supplied. Faint clicks were heard and the section of wall opened up before him.

'It is hopeless,' he said shaking his head. 'The man is consumed with power beyond all reasoning. I am with you now.'

'Come then,' came the reply.

He stepped through the breach.

Illestrael closed the secret door behind him.

--- 0 ---

Chayne waited anxiously in the main lab. He did his best to engage in activities that would keep his mind from Stalizar's confrontation with Lathashal. So much was at stake.

Illestrael had secretly visited the lab several times over the last two weeks. She seemed interested in him. He guessed that she was just spying on him and gaining information pertinent to her Shodatt's plans.

He had to say though that he looked forward to her visits. Apart from his magical training, she was the only pleasant distraction in his otherwise forced existence.

But that all changed two days ago when she supplied him a note from Stalizar. He didn't know what the relationship was between the two of them, but any contact with the man was welcome. In the note, Stalizar stated that he was concerned over the use of manaspheres relating to the demons contained within them, and that it could represent a danger to the Empire. He concluded that he was going to attempt to talk Lathashal out of casting the Rite of Rakasti on the grounds that it may cause some catastrophic event. Chayne didn't know what the Mage-Surgeon meant, but at least there was some hope that, if successful, he would no longer have to confront Lathashal himself.

At dawn, Illestrael had visited and relayed that Stalizar was going to make his case tonight. As it was late, Chayne wondered how much longer he would have to wait to know the outcome.

The answer came suddenly when the lab's huge double doors exploded inwards. The shock wave from the blast scattered shards of wood far into the room, destroying many delicate experiments on the main bench that Chayne assembled as part of his training. He was struck by several splinters, barely managing to hold his seated position. Following behind the event was Lathashal, his staff extended in front of him. His face purple with unbridled rage as he stormed into the room. He directed his staff at a large chest that Chayne had not seen opened. It flew from its position on the far lab wall, ripping away the deep spike fastenings from the stone. It landed onto the end of the main lab bench nearest to the master magii, smashing away any remaining glass, metal and other materials that survived the initial exploding door fragments. He spoke a word and directed his staff at the lid. It snapped upwards, crashing back on its hinges. He discarded his powerful staff, raised his arms high above the box, and without a moment's pause for concentration, dropped both hands fully onto the largest manasphere Chayne had seen.

The fury of the man was terrifying. It seemed as though he had lost all control. It was then that Chayne realised the extreme task ahead of him if he were to attempt to challenge such a mental colossus.

As he watched the man struggle with the manasphere, Chayne began to wonder if the intensity of Lathashal's rage had made him incautious to the point where he might lose control of the orb. But a few moments later he snapped his hands away from the orb. Thick greasy smoke swirled out

247

from the contact. He let out a soul-churning scream. Chayne knew it was not from the pain of using the orb, but that whatever his purpose was for using it, had failed.

Lathashal stood by the chest, leaning on the bench, panting heavily.

'Master, what has happened?'

Lathashal swung on him. For a moment Chayne thought that he would strike him down.

'That treasonous surgeon has betrayed the Empire.'

'Stalizar?' replied Chayne, with the right amount of surprise.

'Do not mention that name in my presence again!' screamed Lathashal, hysterically.

Chayne then feared the worst.

'Did you just kill him, Master?'

Lathashal spat a curse. 'Somehow I am unable to locate him.' He spun around and thundered out of the room, his staff flying from where it lay on the floor into his outstretched hand.

Chapter 28 - Sand trap

The first moment Garamon knew they were in trouble came when their Ashnorian mage fell to the ground clutching his head and cried out. An instant later, light blazed over their heads, blinding them after hours in the desert darkness. As Garamon looked through squinting eyes he saw the ground ahead of them appear to come alive. Twenty warriors arose like wraiths, revealing the livery of Ashnorian soldiers.

They attacked.

Kinfular, ThreeSwords and Sholster drew weapons and spread out to form a wall. Garamon drew his axe behind them and stood over Shinlay, pulling the mage in close to him.

The first three soldiers hit the defensive line and fell within seconds. The next layer formed five across before attacking. Kinfular skewered one through the throat, locking the sword of another in his shield and sliding his rapier up the length of the man's arm and kicking him back. Sholster blasted one from his feet, taking out two more behind to fall to the sand. ThreeSwords blocked the nearest of his two Ashnorians by crossing his swords and pushing the attack downwards, then powering his right sword up and right taking the soldiers sword and shield wide to strike in the groin with his left. His high right sword then swiped back over to hammer down on the second soldier, causing him to raise his shield. Kinfular slipped his sword under the shield into the flesh through the soldier's side straps to puncture the man's lungs and heart.

The second wave had been defeated almost as quickly as the first, with two of them still struggling with the heavy armour to regain their feet from Sholster's strike.

The remaining soldiers held back and spread out to form a circle.

The barbarians regrouped to form a triangle around Garamon, Shinlay and the mage.

'Crouch low and do not rise,' ordered Kinfular. Garamon responded, pulling the mage down with him.

Garamon's respect for the barbarians fighting prowess turned to awe as he watched the three against the onrush of the remaining soldiers. It was like a dance, with each dancer's moves synchronised with the other two, practiced to perfection. It would take only one error, only once for one of them to strike and the other not to defend, to destroy it all. Each man implicitly trusted the other to either side to protect him from an incoming strike. It seemed impenetrable and lethal. As the attackers were reduced to ten men and Garamon started to feel that they were going to overcome the trap, another area of light blazed nearby and the sand erupted to reveal more soldiers. The three barbarians did not falter as the number of opponents swelled.

The fight continued. Even against the increased numbers it seemed the barbarian fighting strategy would succeed, for no matter how many were pit against them only a few Ashnorians could get close to them at a time. Tiredness would eventually wear the defenders down, but the three of them looked as if they could keep it up for a long time. They were also aided by the increasing pile of bodies that were accumulating around them. Each attacker needed to pull the body of the previous fallen soldier out before they could replace them. Only fifteen soldiers remained. It looked as though the defenders were going to win through.

An Ashnorian voice rang out from somewhere out in the darkness. The soldiers disengaged from the fight and retreated to form a line, their swords facing upward as if in ceremony.

The mage broke out from between Kinfular and ThreeSwords and started running away from the soldiers. As he left the globe of light around the party so he disappeared into darkness. The strange source of light only illuminated out to an exact radius; beyond that it was complete darkness.

Another globe appeared and caught him in the centre. He glanced back in panic but kept running, the sand reducing his pace to little more than fast walking. He almost reached the edge of the new globe when he came to an abrupt stop. He turned, as if against his will. He grabbed for his magical orb and placed his fingers upon it. His face contorted and he cried out, letting go and falling to his knees.

Into his globe of light walked a robed figure holding a short staff. Atop the staff was a smaller version of the strange magical orbs. The new mage held up his staff. The young man's eyes went from fear to dread. He appeared to be struggling with his own hand as it moved back towards his orb.

'Tra!' he screamed, desperate pleading in his voice. But nothing he could do seemed to be able to stop the steady advance of his hand. He cried out again as slowly his fingers opened and his hand turned over to have the palm outstretched over the orb.

'Besenta, besenta!' he screamed. He shook his head violently, looking to the other mage pleadingly.

Despite his objections his hand lowered, touching the surface of the orb. His eyes snapped to the object and he stopped speaking. His face took on a look of absolute terror. Moments later and his hand began to burn, smoke rising into his twisted features. To Garamon's horror, he watched as the mage burst into a fierce red-blue flame. This inferno raged for only a short while before disappearing as quickly as it had come. The little remaining charred flesh hung loose as the blackened skeleton tipped forward into the sand.

The other mage released his concentration and turned to them. He closed his eyes for a moment and then opened them again. 'Drop sword. You come,' he said in Mlendrian. 'If no, I kill all.'

Kinfular, so fast that it was hard to see, flicked a knife in the direction of the mage. It flew to an inch of the Ashnorian's chest before bouncing away harmlessly. The mage responded by flicking his staff in the direction of the barbarian leader. Kinfular was thrown several yards back to land hard at the feet of the small column of soldiers. The nearest men lowered their raised swords to rest on his chest and throat.

Both ThreeSwords and Sholster took another look around and to their leader. Kinfular would be dead in a heartbeat if they attacked.

They dropped their weapons.

The Ashnorian soldiers moved in and bound their hands.

'What wrong?' said the new mage, pointing to Shinlay.

'She suffered a blow to the head a few days ago,' replied Garamon, pointing to the welt.

The mage turned and called out into the darkness. 'Bilash, Vigoratii tushantila.'

The globe of light covering the dead mage blinked out. Another mage appeared from the darkness. This one was dressed in a cream robe with a green hand motif embossed upon the chest. He carried one of the orb boxes similar to that of the dead mage.

He walked to Shinlay and inspected her wound. He opened his orb box and lifted the orb to click into its raised position. Placing fingertips from one hand upon the orb's surface he held his other hand over Shinlay's forehead. Closing his eyes he began to concentrate. A few moments later and Shinlay murmured. The mage opened his eyes and removed his hand. The bump was almost gone. He removed his contact with the orb and lowered it once again within its box, closing the lid and shutting the latch.

'Thank you,' said Garamon, not knowing if the mage would understand him.

The mage got to his feet and nodded to him and walked away.

Garamon knelt down to Shinlay. He watched as she opened her eyes. She blinked at the brightness around.

'How do you feel?' said Garamon.

'A lot better than I did the last time I woke,' she replied. 'Where are we?'

Garamon grimaced and held up his bound hands.

'In trouble.'

Shinlay pushed herself up and went to draw her sword. Finding that she didn't have it and that the others were bound, she dropped back to the sand with a thump. 'I think it would have been better to have remained asleep.'

A soldier with a binding approached Shinlay. He kicked out, catching her in the back and making her yelp. 'Gil thac!' he ordered, indicating a standing motion with his hands.

Garamon leapt to his feet and shouted at the soldier.

The man sneered back. Without taking his eyes off of Garamon, he kicked out again. Shinlay grabbed his leg and used it for leverage to swing up and around to come up behind the soldier, the act tipping him forward onto his face. Without stopping she dropped heavily onto the man's back with her knees. Garamon didn't know at what point in the manoeuvre she gained a knife, but it was now under his throat as she pulled his head back using the front of his helm.

'Besenta!' came a command from a new unseen Ashnorian voice. Into the globe of light came a new soldier, flanked by two guards. He walked across to stand before Garamon and Shinlay. 'Besenta!' he commanded again.

Shinlay responded by pulling the prone soldier's head further back, exposing more neck.

The man looked to his men surrounding the other barbarians and snapped his fingers at the captives. The soldiers responded by drawing back their swords ready to strike. Shinlay withdrew the blade and pushed the head she held into the sand. She got to her feet and threw away the knife. She spat on the soldier who had kicked her.

The senior soldier looked to her. She blazed back, defiant in the face of her coming punishment. Without looking he kicked out hard into the prone soldier, in much the same way that she was kicked. The senior soldier then shouted a command. The other one got to his feet and left the circle of light. The senior warrior then gave Shinlay a curt, formal bow and turned away.

This time Shinlay allowed herself to be bound.

They were marched across the desert to an outpost. High fencing and guard towers positioned at each corner told of the significance of the place, with enough buildings to house hundreds of soldiers.

They were escorted inside and taken to a fortified structure in the centre, surrounded by a tall fence. As they entered the building, they were passed over to guards who then escorted them through a series of barred doors, each of which was locked behind them. They stopped at a wooden door with a small grate at head height. The leading guard thumbed his way through a number of keys on a ring and inserted one of them into the lock of the cell door and pushed it open. Their bindings were cut and they were pushed forward, almost falling down the two stone steps into the cell.

Garamon was the last to enter. He gasped as he saw Jontal and Falakar already present in the cell. Both men were badly beaten, but conscious. Shinlay ran across to the two men and removed the Locan leaves from her pouch. She placed them upon the worst areas on Falakar's face and forehead.

'Please help Jontal too,' said Garamon.

Sholster stepped forward to block Garamon. 'He deserves to die,' said Sholster.

'I think we now share a common enemy,' replied Garamon.

The woodsman is right. 'His skills may be useful if we're going to escape,' added Kinfular. 'Heal him.'

The door to the cell opened and a middle-aged man walked in. He was dressed in a green cloth uniform that was decorated with an array of medals. He had the determined features of a man who didn't suffer fools. He was flanked by four guards with drawn swords. Behind him was a mage holding an opened orb box.

The officer walked forward alone to stand before Falakar and Jontal. He lifted one of the leaves free from Falakar's head. The Ranger flinched as the leaf was pulled away. The officer turned to the mage and gave a questioning look. The mage placed his fingers upon the orb.

'The Commander would like to know what the leaves are for.'

'They help wounds heal and avoid infection,' replied Shinlay.

The mage relayed this to the Commander. The Commander puffed derisively and tossed the leaf back into Falakar's lap. He spoke again to the mage.

'The Commander asks for your orders,' said the mage.

'We have no orders,' responded Garamon. 'These are my friends and they are with me to help recover another friend abducted by your people.'

There was another exchange of words between the two men. At one point the mage nodded his head. The Commander seemed surprised.

'The mage can detect lies,' said Jontal. 'I think such selfless altruism is beyond their understanding.'

'The Commander is amazed at your stupidity,' replied the mage. 'That you believe you can walk into Ashnorian lands and recover someone that we have decided is of value to us.'

'Nevertheless, I wish to see him and speak with him,' demanded Garamon.

At this point the Commander spoke briefly to the mage, frustration evident in his voice. There was some disagreement until the Commander became more agitated.

The mage closed his eyes and concentrated deeply. The Commander waited a few moments.

'Can you understand me?' he said, the words sounding oddly distant and a metallic.

'Yes,' replied Garamon.

'The magii will translate for us directly. It is difficult from him and we must be brief,' said the Commander. 'You say you are here to rescue your friend. This one has stated that you are spies,' he said, pointing to Jontal.

Garamon's face showed anger. '*He* is nothing more than a bandit. He attacked us in the mountains on our journey and we overcame his men. He is with us so that upon our return we can bring him to justice.'

'You create risk for yourselves in doing so,' said the Commander. 'I would simply have killed him.'

'That is not our way. Our society is built upon the law of the people and fairness of trial,' replied Garamon.

'Outdated notions,' said the Commander. 'You are a primitive people.'

'We saw your armies marching north.'

The Commander seemed unconcerned. 'We are about to invade your land and conquer your people so that you may share in the greater glory of the Empire. Your people are to be blessed.'

'You must excuse me for not sharing in that opinion,' replied Garamon.

The Commander turned away dismissively. 'We waste time and drain the mage. Tomorrow you will be taken from here to a place of imprisonment. You will be afforded short but productive lives in the name of the Empire working in thrinium mines. The girl will be used for pleasure or as a servant if she can be tamed.'

'What of my friend we have come to rescue?' asked Garamon.

'He is of no further concern to you. Whatever his fate within the Empire, it is not linked with yours. You must look to yourselves from now on and provide whatever comfort you can in companionship. We will not speak again.'

The Commander left the room, the mage and guards following.

'Please!' cried out Garamon. 'I have come so far. At least tell me his fate!'

The door closed behind the last guard and was locked. Garamon ran to the opening and called through the small opening. 'Please! Something? Anything? His name is Chayne. Please, I beg you, *Chayne*!'

The second gate closed and the footsteps faded. He slumped down by the door.

'I am sorry,' he said dejectedly. 'I have brought you to this.'

'We walk our own paths, Mlendrian,' replied Kinfular. 'I came here for the good of my own people.'

'But we have failed,' replied Garamon. 'The Ashnorians will now proceed with their invasion and there will be nothing to alert our peoples of their coming. The attack will be a surprise and all resistance will be crushed.'

'Do not give in. We are still alive,' said the barbarian.

'And to what end!' said Garamon bitterly. 'We are held in a heavily guarded cell without armour or weapons. Even if we could escape, we are still within an outpost in the desert holding hundreds of enemy soldiers, and who knows how many of those damned mages.'

Kinfular became stern. 'Listen to me. I do not know what the future holds for us. I do know that I will not live the remainder of my life rotting to an early death in some enemy mine. You will stay positive and alert at all times. When the opportunity arises for our escape, you *will* be ready. We will get no more than a moment's notice, and may end up doing no more than striking as much damage to the enemy as possible. But know this. If we are to die, our passing will resound throughout the entire army of this empire and strike fear into the hearts of their warriors. They will know that the people of the North are to be feared, and will fall upon them with the wrath of the gods themselves if they dare to invade us.'

Garamon swallowed hard in the face of the man before him.

'I … I am sorry. I will be ready sir, I promise.'

Shinlay crossed to him and sat down.

'It is difficult to face the raging heart of the Hlenshar.'

Garamon replied with a sheepish look. 'I feel foolish.'

'Do not be. You have the mark of greatness upon you, young warrior.'

'Me? I do not know how you can feel that.'

'You handled yourself with control and skill in front of the Commander. You thought quickly and avoided implicating the Ranger and his mission. You showed great courage,' she said.

'I merely spoke the truth.'

'All great men *merely* do,' she replied. 'It is because their actions come naturally that they think nothing special of them. Did you think Kinfular's words were special?'

'Of course!'

'He would not think so. He merely spoke his truth.'

Garamon felt lifted a little by the comparison. 'I hope I do not let him down.'

'Just remember his words. It will only take a moment's error by the soldiers for him to turn around our ill fortune.' She gave him a smile and walked over to Jontal, taking out more Locan leaves.

Chapter 29 - Moving the prisoners

Garamon woke to the sound of the cell key entering the lock. Kinfular was already standing on one side of the door. Four jailors entered carrying complicated metal manacles. They ignored the presence of the barbarian so close to the door and approached four of the group to fit the devices. The door was closed behind them.

Kinfular, Shinlay, Garamon and Sholster were to be fitted first. The devices were made up of four manacles joined with chains, one manacle per limb.

'Ouch! That pinched you pathetic excuse for a cockroach,' bellowed Sholster. The jailor pulled the ring apart and tried again with the same result. Sholster lost his temper and flicked his arm. The weedy jailor went flying across the floor to slide into the wall, getting tangled up in the manacles. A tube was pushed through the barred opening in the door and a dart flew from it to strike Sholster in the shoulder.

'What the!' He contemptuously pulled the missile out and threw it away.

A second dart was fired and struck him in the chest. Again he pulled it out.

'So you plan to tickle me to death then,' he roared. Moving closer to the door he bent over and exposed his enormous white backside. Shinlay averted her eyes.

'Here, see if you can hit this!'

Another dart shot from the tube. Sholster tensed his muscles and the projectile bounced off as if it struck stone. He then gave his backside a hearty slap and laughed loudly, resuming his previous standing position, staggering a little. 'Prime Esscantian rump,' he said proudly. 'I'll match it against any ten of yours in this louse-ridden Empire.' His eyes then glazed and he tipped backwards to crash to the cell floor, unconscious.

Garamon looked down to the horizontal form of the huge barbarian. Kinfular wanted to send a message to the Ashnorian army that the men they faced were defiant and strong. The young woodsman held little doubt that Sholster took the opportunity to start the rumours.

The rest of them were successfully shackled. A final restraining bar was fitted that connected the ankle cross-chain with the wrist one. These bars were adjustable in length and set so that the wearer was made to stoop a little. They were then led from the cell.

Garamon emerged from the prison building into the sunlight of mid-morning. The outpost was bigger than it looked in the dark. It was a sprawling collection of buildings, perhaps housing a thousand soldiers. He watched a column of men, numbering in the hundreds, leaving and heading for the mountains in the direction of his home.

He looked ahead to see Falakar climb sun-bleached wooden steps into a long enclosed wagon. It was tethered to four huge beasts he'd never seen the like of before. It stood upon a sandy pebble path, just wide enough to accommodate it. He followed the others up into the transport and was left to find his own place. The interior of the wagon was plain with no seating, merely sand and hay strewn across the floor. There was a secured wooden slatted bucket with a lid in one corner, and what looked like a water barrel attached in the other corner. There were only modest openings for light or air. It was only mid-morning and already the temperature inside was oppressive. Five other men were in residence. They looked like army men. Captured deserters or thieves within the base he guessed. They had been beaten like Falakar and Jontal. Sholster was nowhere to be seen and Garamon hoped that the big man had not been killed because of his humiliating show of defiance.

260

The thick wooden door was slammed shut behind them making the wagon rock and he stumbled to his knees, the shackles clanking on the wooden floor. No guards had entered. He didn't have much doubt as to why that would be. The air in the wagon would become foul with the stench of human odours, dried blood and the inevitable contents of the only sanitation facility available. He looked to the others of his party. Falakar and Jontal had improved a little overnight and were resting against the wagon's cell wall opposite the door. Both Kinfular and ThreeSwords were already set up next to the door. They looked ready for any opportunity to escape as Kinfular promised. The wagon shifted, marking the start of their journey.

Shinlay walked across to the water barrel and attempted to dip her head to take a drink. A heavy-set prisoner with several old facial scars and a mood to match was sitting next to the barrel. He kicked out with his legs at Shinlay's ankles, but the manacles prevented enough movement for him to connect.

'Gil shin latrol,' he said in a threatening tone.

Garamon knew men like him. They were involved in fights in town leaving the taverns. Revelling in brawling, they took every opportunity to create one.

Shinlay automatically went to strike back at the man, but was also restrained by the shackles.

The man laughed, taunting her further.

Shinlay stepped to the far side of the barrel, and tried again. The prisoner responded by shifting forward and repeating the strike, this time ensuring that he would be in range. Shinlay was ready for him and jumped back out of his reach, but now out of reach of the barrel also.

'Gil shin latrol,' he repeated with a sneer.

Kinfular walked across to the barrel. The man turned to face the new contestant to his claim. Upon seeing the barbarian leader's build and strength, the brawler chose not to interrupt.

Kinfular dipped his head to the surface of the barrel's water, ensuring he had an angle to lock eyes with the man. He took a long, noisy drink to emphasise the point, then lifted his head a little, licked his lips as if finishing, and then dropped his head down again taking an even longer and noisier drink. At no point did his eyes leave that of the other prisoner. He then lifted his head once again and tilted his head to the man.

'Move away,' he said, flicking his head to ensure the man understood his command. The man held his position for a few moments, but then relented and shifted along the wall away from the barrel. Kinfular then slowly scanned the rest of the men in the wagon. All averted their eyes as it became their turn for inspection. Satisfied, he walked back to his previous position.

Shinlay, happy that the hierarchy of authority was established, resumed her position at the barrel and took a long drink.

After half an hour of travel the road surface changed to something smoother, and the wagon picked up pace. They travelled for a further hour when it came to a halt. The air inside the wagon was already stale, hot and cloying, and Garamon hoped that they were at their destination, if only to have the door opened and to breath normal air again. There was talking in front of the wagon which elevated to what sounded like some dispute. Fighting broke out and he heard the unmistakable sound of men dying. He tensed as the barbarians, Falakar and Jontal readied for whatever may come through the door.

The sounds of fighting died away.

The cell door to the wagon was unlocked and pulled open sharply. There stood a formally dressed soldier, a coat of arms on his tunic and shield that did not match that of their previous captors. The soldier gestured for Kinfular and ThreeSwords, closest to the door, to step back. They both made space. He stepped across the threshold into the cell and blanched at the stench that assailed his senses.

'Mitra, lay accra Chin?' he enquired, scanning the residents.

'Chan?' he said again uncertainly.

None of the Ashnorian prisoners reacted to the question.

'Chan - *Chayne*!' cried Garamon.

'Ch-aine. Di, Chayne!' said the man relieved. He stepped forward with a small ring of keys Garamon recognised as those the jailors used to lock their shackles. After a couple of attempts the man found the right key and unlocked Garamon's restraints. He then turned to leave and beckoned for him to follow. Garamon stood and pointed to his friends and made the sign of twisting a key in the air.

'Tra, tra, tra,' the guard said shaking his head rapidly, and beckoning more intently for Garamon to follow.

'These are my friends, they are coming with me,' said Garamon, holding his position.

The man looked agitated. Garamon sat down and folded his arms. The guard said something sharp in Ashnorian and began fumbling through the keys again. Garamon pointed to Kinfular and ThreeSwords first and the man started with Kinfular. He made several bungled attempts before getting the first lock open.

The moment Kinfular's first hand was released he grabbed the keys from the man and set about releasing the remaining constraints himself. He then released ThreeSwords first hand and gave him the keys.

Kinfular jumped out of the wagon, returning moments later.

'We are on a long road cut through a tall forest. All the guards are dead. There are more dressed like this one, but they have taken many casualties,' he said, indicating their rescuer.

'There was a mage in our escort,' he added.

All understood the implication. A signal may have been communicated.

Garamon stayed to unlock the remainder of the party and then went to join the others outside. He took a deep breath of fresh air as he exited the wagon. The sky was cloudless, and under better circumstances he would consider it a beautiful day. Kinfular, ThreeSwords and Shinlay were reclaiming their armour and weapons from a small wagon nearby.

Falakar reached the wagon too and called back to him. 'Your friend Chayne appears to be a resourceful man,' said Falakar as he pulled on his leather tunic.

'Is my axe there?'

'For whatever reason, the Commander has no interest in souvenirs,' replied Falakar, reaching under the pile and pulling out Garamon's axe.

Garamon joined him and began extracting his own items before sitting by the side of the road. The road extended as far as the eye could see in both directions. It had deep ditches on both sides that were overgrown with various types of foliage creating ample natural ambush points. Dead soldiers of both factions were scattered around. Most wore the armour of the soldiers from the command post, but there were several that wore the same colours of the man that released them. One of the dead remained upright in the wagon's passenger seat. He wore a robe. Five of their rescuers remained alive and kept lookout around the wagon.

The rescue leader jumped down from the wagon and approached him. He shook his head at the dead men, a worried look on his face.

'Too many casualties on your side, I think,' said Garamon, guessing the man's thoughts. The Ashnorian looked to him, seeming to recognise the sympathetic tone in his voice.

'Kodle,' he said, and beckoned for Garamon to follow.

Garamon got to his feet and walked after the man who was heading for the back of the wagon. As Garamon reached him so the man was pulling at some ropes that were securing a large leather sack. As the rope came loose so the soldier tried to lower the sack slowly, but the weight of it pulled the rope from his hands and the sack fell to the road with a thump. The sack strings burst open. Sholster appeared. Dead or unconscious, Garamon didn't know. He knelt down and checked for a heartbeat in the man's neck as he'd seen Falakar do. There was a pulse which, like everything else about Sholster, was strong and unmistakable. Garamon thanked the Ashnorian.

A shout came from one of the lookouts.

The soldier next to Garamon looked back down the road, shielding his eyes from the glare of the sun. A distant brown cloud, almost invisible in heat haze, hovered over the road far back behind them. The soldier said something short and sharp.

Garamon looked back to the others to see them running to his position.

'How many?' said Falakar to their rescuer, but the man didn't understand. Falakar then counted on his fingers and pointed to the brown cloud and shrugged.

The Ashnorian opened his hands twice.

'Twenty,' spat Falakar.

'Do we face them or flee?' said ThreeSwords, finishing strapping his triple sword scabbard to his back.

'We lie in wait. Then cut the bastards to pieces,' said Jontal through swollen lips, experimentally flexing a spare sword from one of the remaining prisoners.

Falakar brought his own sword up to clash with the bandit's. There was a ring of metal and everybody froze.

'No weapon,' said Falakar.

'You need me,' said Jontal.

'You cannot be trusted,' replied Falakar.

'I just look out for myself, it's how I've learned to stay alive. And now with the great Ashnorian leadership deciding that I cannot be trusted either, my chances of survival are better working with you, at least until we return to Mlendrian territory. Agreed?' offered the bandit.

Falakar locked eyes with him. The man had nerves of steel to suggest such an alliance after his recent actions, but it did fit his method of working.

Shinlay broke the pause. 'The beating you suffered at the hands of the Ashnorians has satisfied me for the blow to my head.' She took an arrow from her quiver and bit into the wooden stock hard. 'But this arrow is now marked for you alone. Betray us again and I promise it will find you.'

Jontal grimaced at the notion of being in the sights of the fierce barbarian woman.

'Until we return to the mountains then,' said Falakar. 'Then I'll attempt to return you to justice, and you shall attempt to escape.' He slid his sword away from Jontal's.

The Ashnorian became agitated at the delay, pointing down the road. The dust cloud was growing fast. The group began to ready themselves. Kinfular and Falakar discussed a strategy and then the group scattered to their positions within the natural cover aside the road, leaving their rescuers to organise themselves.

Falakar knew that the element of surprise would only be partial, as it was all too obvious an ambush point. He wanted Sholster to wake, but at least they now had Shinlay's bow at their disposal. He looked to Jontal several yards further up the ditch. He hoped the bandit would not betray them again. Jontal smiled back, looking eager.

If the Ashnorian was right about the numbers then even with the element of surprise there was the possibility of casualties on their side. He worried particularly about the woodsman who he ordered to stay nearby. He went over in his head the plan again, going through the various directions that the fight could take. His biggest problem was their Ashnorian contingent. He didn't know their strength, and they had taken a beating earlier when attacking inferior numbers. He regretted not being able to communicate better with their leader, but the man's strategy to play dead with the other corpses was a bold one. They didn't lack courage.

He lowered his head and waited.

The minutes passed and around twenty mounted soldiers thundered up to their position and came to a halt a short distance away. They were dressed in the same livery of the men that were guarding the wagon. An order was given from the lead rider and all but he and two other riders dismounted. The soldiers fanned out across the road, weapons and shields readied. They approached warily, scanning the ditches, trees and wagon area ahead of them.

Falakar heard a rustle behind him and glanced back in time to see Jontal disappearing into the trees, running away from the battleground. Silently cursing, the Ranger returned to the view ahead. Jontal knew that he could not be chased right now. It was not a good start.

The group drew level with the back of the wagon, stopping at the first body: that of Sholster's sleeping form. One of the men rested his sword upon Sholster's shoulder and allowed the sword to draw a cut in the man's flesh. Sholster did not react. Satisfied, the soldiers split into two groups, passing down both sides of the wagon.

The group on the left-hand side of the wagon stopped by the door. One of them cautiously mounted the steps. He poked his head in for a moment, and then closed the door and secured it from the outside.

The two groups continued.

The tension was acute as the men reached the Ashnorians who were pretending to be slain. As they were about to begin their crude testing of the dead against the first of the laying Ashnorians, there was a groan from behind them and they spun around. It was Sholster, trying to regain consciousness. One of the patrol looked up to the patrol leader for orders. The leader rapidly drew his hand twice across his own throat. The soldier moved back to execute the order. He took no more than two steps when an arrow flashed from the heavy foliage at that side of the road which, at such short range, plunged through chain mail protection, dropping him to the ground.

The scene exploded.

The Ashnorians who had played dead used the distraction to jump to their feet and surprise the foremost patrol men.

Kinfular and the others rushed from both sides of the road to join in the attack. Shinlay and Falakar rose from the bushes to get an angle on the mounted patrol leader and his two escorts. Two more arrows flew. Falakar's powerful bow delivered an arrow into the chest of one of the guards, almost knocking him out of his saddle. The patrol leader's horse was startled by the sudden attack and reared. The movement was enough for Shinlay's arrow to strike the man's shoulder guard, saving him from a mortal chest wound. But less lucky for the leader, it deflected up into his face, smashing through his nose, spraying blood and sinew. He pulled sharply on the reins of his horse and turned, putting it into a gallop and out of effective range of another arrow shot. The remaining rider took the cue and started galloping after him.

Back at the wagon, the fight was now intense as the patrol attempted to gain a defendable position against the ambush. Garamon leapt from the ditch next to Shinlay and Falakar. Axe in hand, and with only a loose, hastily-fitted chainmail shirt from one of the dead men to protect him. He was trying to remember everything Falakar told him, but all the words were gone in the heat of the moment. He was terrified. He saw that the new patrol soldiers were well-trained and disciplined. He didn't expect to survive the encounter. He picked his target and ran in, raising his axe. The man was ready for him and raised his shield.

'Balance, lad!' shouted Falakar next to him as Garamon got within range and went to make a strike. The instructions from Falakar's training flashed into his head in a jumble. 'Do not overstretch, keep yourself well balanced, stay on the balls of your feet, the two-handed axe is slow, it is both your shield

268

and your weapon, let your opponent attempt the first strike and then deflect, turn and strike.'

Garamon attempted to hold back, but he had gained too much momentum and stumbled forward. His opponent made no such error and placed his shield up to block the attack. Garamon looked down to see the soldier thrusting a sword towards his exposed groin and nothing to stop it.

The axe struck the shield with a deafening crack. Sparks flew out from the clashing metals as the shield was smashed back into its wielder, throwing him from his feet to thud into the side of an oxen behind him, then to collapse to the ground. The shield was smoking from a long tear in its centre.

Garamon didn't understand what happened. The axe seemed to come alive in his hands and strike out, almost of its own volition. Nothing like it had happened in training with Falakar.

The blast unnerved the adjacent soldiers engaged with Shinlay and Falakar. Both fighters took the moment of distraction to bridge their opponents' defences. Garamon was left without another challenge.

As the patrol Captain, Beloom knew that fleeing was not an allowed course of action. He laid down low over his horse, and kept it running with as much speed as he could. He started to wonder what he was going to say to the Commander. If any of his men survived to tell of his cowardice, he would be tortured and sent back to his family, shamed. Hopefully they would all be killed.

He could see blood pouring from his nose onto the mane of his mount a few inches below his face. He didn't know the extent of the injury, but it hurt like all the hells. If only he could get the archer tied up in a room for a few hours, he'd let them know what pain was.

He glanced back and was relieved to see that at least one of his personal guards was following. That wasn't a problem as both of the men were bribed by his family and would support any story he made up.

He caught movement from the left ahead in the trees and saw that it was somebody running to his position carrying a long branch held out ahead of him. He relaxed; the man could never make it over the wide ditch in time. The man then dug one end of the branch into the ground just before the ditch, and using his momentum, allowed the branch to carry him over the gap to land on the edge of the road ahead of him. Beloom remained confident though, as the acrobatic assailant had only a second to draw his sword and cover the several feet needed to intercept him.

But that didn't turn out to be the man's intent either. For in one fluid motion from landing he dragged the branch level to point across the road and continued to throw it long ways into the racing stride of Beloom's mount. The branch collided with the animal's forelegs, and while not completely tripping the powerful beast, made it stumble and then step to recover and leap involuntarily into the air. The impromptu flight and heavy landing had the desired effect, and Beloom pitched from his saddle to land on the road.

Jontal watched with satisfaction as the escaping Captain landed heavily. Aware of the sound of the escort nearby, he dived just in time to prevent being run down. The rider had charged him, and so continued for some paces before bringing his horse to a stop. He leapt down onto the road. A smile appeared across his face. He left his shield strapped to his horse and drew his longsword. Jontal's short sword and lack of armour was clearly no match for the man.

The escort reached his Captain, who was struggling on the floor with some injury.

'I'm sorry,' said Beloom pointing to his leg. 'I would help if I could.'

The escort looked down with scorn as he walked past, continuing to his Jontal. 'I'd allow you the chance to surrender,' he said. 'But the Captain would only have you tortured for your interception. You're better off dead.'

'Considerate of you,' replied Jontal in fluid Ashnorian. He began moving out wide of the man as he approached. 'I'll be sure to put in a good word for you when I get back to Mlendrian Command.'

'The only way you're going to return to your homeland is in a wooden box,' said the escort.

The two men started to circle one another.

'Oh, don't go to all that expense for me,' replied Jontal. 'A personal carriage is too generous.'

'I was referring to a coffin, you heathen cretin,' spat the guard.

'Well then, I hope your swordplay is better developed than your sense of humour,' replied Jontal.

'You're not going to get time to find *out!*' The guard moved in fast to make his first attack.

Jontal pulled a small tube from behind his back and blew the contents into the soldiers face, sidestepping the advance.

The soldier shook his head, blowing the green powder away.

Jontal turned his back on him and walked towards the horrified Captain.

'You Ashnorians,' he said disdainfully. 'You think because you conquer lands that you are a chosen people. Keepers of the knowledge of the world. The great wise Masters.' As he spoke, he gently weaved his sword left and right, allowing the flat of the blade to make a slight hum as it pushed through the air.

Beloom wanted to flee, but fear transfixed him as he sat on the road and watched his escort fall to the ground.

'If only you took the time to learn from the civilisations that you so callously snuff out. For instance, did you know that this land was once called Calencia? Its people were - how would you say - one with nature?'

He'd closed to half the distance.

'They loved all that grew, and learned over many centuries to make amazing salves and powders that cured almost any ailment.'

'That's all gone now of course. You saw to that. Their knowledge was burned or otherwise destroyed by your arrogant belief that none could better your wisdom.'

'However, some books did survive in the few remaining unconquered lands, such as Mlendria. I come from Mlendria, Captain. Did I mention that?'

Beloom shook his head. It was like being hypnotised and tortured with anticipation at the same time. The prisoner had now reached him and stood above him, still swinging his sword.

'This forest for instance,' Jontal continued, waving his sword outward to sweep in the surrounding countryside, 'is replete with Lalaylie.'

'Isn't that funny?' he reflected as if pausing for thought. 'How in most cases the nice looking flowers create the healing salves. *Gilinium Agrefaria,* for instance, is a lovely violet bell-shaped flower. Quite the picture in the spring as it grows almost anywhere the sun catches the banks of running water.'

Beloom had no interest in botany, but sat mesmerized by the man's words.

'Now Lalaylie on the other hand, is an *ugly* little plant. The pollen I administered back there was from a dozen of the stocky fellows. An effective killer when inhaled don't you think?'

Beloom started to shuffle away from the bandit. Jontal took a step forward to maintain the distance.

'I'll give you money!' Beloom said. 'I am a rich man. My family are almost nobles!'

'Money you say?'

'More than you can imagine. Piles of gold, you'll be rich beyond your wildest dreams,' Beloom blurted desperately.

'Hmmm, I do have some pretty wild dreams,' said Jontal unsure.

The Ashnorian's face twisted in frustration. 'What *do* you want then? *Anything.*'

Jontal paused for a moment, as if contemplating the question. 'Oh, I think the satisfaction of seeing you die in agony.'

The man whimpered. 'Please, I don't deserve to die. I'm here because my family made me. I don't even know how to fight. Look!' he said, drawing his sword from its scabbard and tossing it away. 'Now I am unarmed. Would you kill a crippled, unarmed man?'

Jontal delayed for a few agonising seconds and then stopped waving his sword. 'You left those men to their deaths.' His tone was chilling.

'I had no choice,' replied Beloom, even more unnerved by the sudden change in discussion topic. 'I am their leader. I have to report back.'

'You're not a snivelling coward then?'

'No, no I -'

'But you *are* the enemy.'

'Please, I assure you -'

'Run,' said Jontal, loaded with unveiled threat. 'Run like the coward you are, or die where you crawl.'

Beloom, recognising the final ultimatum, scrambled to his feet, all pretence at having an injury gone. He started to run. He was overweight and unfit; he wasn't quick.

Jontal, without hurry, picked up a large pebble from the roadside and tested it for weight. Satisfied, he dropped it into a tiny water skin. He squeezed it back out having coated it with dark, viscous goo. He dropped it into his slingshot, taking care not to let the coating touch his skin. He looked up at the fleeing man and took careful aim. Spinning the slingshot around several times to pick up the required speed, he released his missile. It flew through the air for several seconds before striking the back of the Ashnorian's head.

'And that one is the nectar from the *Tratixlia Diaconis* shrub,' said Jontal quietly.

He watched as the Captain remained running for a few moments more before stumbling. He then began to writhe on the ground clutching at his head and stomach, screaming.

Jontal cleaned out the sling pouch with sand from the side of the road, and returned it to its leather container. He then began the task of dragging the two dead men from the road to conceal them.

The remaining defenders were down to just eight men for the loss of only three of the Ashnorian attackers. No serious injuries were evident on the Mlendrians or barbarians. Assessing the conflict as lost, one of the patrol soldiers called out. As one, the soldiers stopped attacking, choosing to defend only.

'They are surrendering,' shouted Falakar, and the fight stopped as both sides disengaged.

The patrol soldiers dropped their weapons and shields.

'Put them in the wagon cell and lock them in,' ordered Falakar. 'Another patrol will find them.'

Kinfular then looked around the team. 'Where is the bandit?'

'He ran off as soon as he knew I dare not risk breaking cover to follow him,' replied Falakar.

'Well that's hardly fair,' called a voice from behind the back of the wagon.

Shinlay spun around to the voice, and in one action drew her bow and notched an arrow, levelling it directly at the bandit's head.

'Hey, I don't remember that being the agreement,' he said, sauntering to join them.

'Where have you been?' said Kinfular dangerously.

Jontal casually directed his thumb back over his shoulder from the direction he came. 'The Captain was obviously going to run, so I headed him off is all. Oh, and his overconfident bodyguard too. I thought it best that they didn't get the chance to report back. Well, wasn't that the right thing to do?' he challenged, looking at doubting faces.

'It was,' confessed Falakar. 'Just keep us informed of any further *excursions* before you take off like that again.'

'As you wish,' replied the bandit.

He then walked up to Shinlay and pushed his head around the side of the arrow, still set ready. It was the one with notch marks in it. 'Pretty brave thing to do though, eh?' he said, winking to the barbarian woman whose face was now only inches from his.

Shinlay twisted her head and bit more teeth marks into the arrow.

Jontal looked at the bite marks and flinched. 'Ouch,' he said in a hurt tone.

Garamon was sitting on the ground. His first experience as a fighter behind him, and to his surprise, he was still alive to recall it.

Falakar joined him. 'You did well.'

'What *happened* Falakar? I keep going over it in my mind, but as hard as I try I cannot explain how I managed to hit him so hard.'

Falakar picked up the axe. There wasn't the slightest dulling of the blade's edge from the huge impact.'

'What do you know of this axe?' said Falakar.

'Just that it belonged to my grandfather who used it in the war against the Melenites,' replied Garamon. My father used to tell me bedtime stories of heroic deeds about Grandfather and his wonderful axe.'

'Well the stories of this axe go back further than the exploits of your grandfather,' said Falakar. 'Some claim that it was forged over a thousand years ago and is supposed to have magical properties.'

'But that's impossible,' replied Garamon, who knew a thing or two about axes. 'The blade looks brand new. No blade could survive such a long history in such perfect

275

condition. It has obviously been replaced many times, as has the handle.'

'I did say the stories told of it as magical,' said Falakar.

'Can such a thing be true?'

'I have no understanding of magic. I know what I saw when you struck that shield though, and I have never seen the like before. It also spooked the big barbarian when he held it.' He gave the axe back the woodsman and went to get up.

'Can I speak further with you a moment?' said Garamon.

'Of course,' replied the Ranger, settling back down again.

'I couldn't kill him,' said Garamon.

Falakar looked to the young man with sympathy, as he did many times before with new recruits to the Rangers. 'And you think this a bad thing?'

Garamon was surprised by the comment. 'Of course. You, Kinfular and the others, even Shinlay, kill without hesitation. I don't think I could kill someone.'

'And yet you attacked that soldier with deadly force. If I hadn't spoken you would have cut that man clean in two.'

'Yes I suppose. But it all happened so quickly, I didn't have time to think. And I didn't finish him off.'

'Do not be so quick to criticise yourself. As a Ranger I take oaths. One is to protect life. Only under the most desperate need do I resort to taking it. You put that soldier out of the fight. To have the courage to face the man, and then not kill him when he was no longer a threat to us, shows that you have the makings of a Ranger.'

'That does not seem to be case with Kinfular.'

'The barbarians live a harsh existence in the mountains. Generations of fierce feuds between clans and the constant conflicts for the limited good territory has made them merciless fighters. Try not to judge them too harshly for their callous attitude to life. But it is not the Rangers code, and I am proud of the way you acted. And if it makes you feel any better, from what I have seen of your courage to date, I would have no problem knowing that you were protecting my back in a fight.'

'Really?' said Garamon surprised.

Falakar chuckled at the woodsman's innocence. 'You have the soul of your father and the heart of your grandfather, of that I have no doubt. Now put these doubts from your mind and let us help the others.'

Falakar rose again and approached Kinfular who was discussing something with Jontal. As he reached them, Kinfular turned to him.

'The rogue has an interesting plan.'

Falakar prepared himself for some subterfuge. 'What is it?' he said testily.

'Well it seems to me,' replied Jontal with a sweep of his arm in the direction of the many scattered bodies, 'that there are enough corpses of our rescuers to replace our clothes.'

'And?' replied Falakar.

'Well, if we are careful enough, we might be able to make it look like we were all killed in a breakout attempt. If we took the horses, so it looked as though the patrol left, we could put a lot of distance from here by the time a new patrol arrived.

Falakar thought through the ruse. 'What of the remaining patrol in the wagon?'

Jontal pulled out a tightly sealed leather pouch and held it up.

'Gratch,' he said with a smile.

'What is that?' said Kinfular.

'An illegal and powerful narcotic,' said Falakar disdainfully.

'They won't be of much use to any patrol for at least a day,' said the bandit. 'It's better than killing them, and this *is* war.'

Falakar was not happy with the idea of using the substance. Back in Mlendria, just possessing it would place Jontal in prison for several years.

'Do it,' he replied.

'Yes sir.' Jontal replied with a mocking salute. He spun around and headed to the doorway of the wagon, making an exaggerated path around Sholster who was now walking towards them and surveying the scene.

'I cannot wait to hear this story.'

'Collect your things from the small wagon,' replied Kinfular. 'We must move on without delay.'

Sholster nodded and moved off.

'You realise that they will know *he's* not present,' said the barbarian leader.

'There is little we can do about that,' replied Falakar. 'We must hope that any new patrol is not made aware of his size.'

'Not likely after his actions in the cell.'

Falakar grimaced at the memory.

The scene was laid out as planned, and last to leave was Jontal. He unlocked the door to the wagon and peered inside at the men, all now chained up. He held his breath and undid the securing tie on the pouch. It was true that a crude form of Gratch could be refined from the pink poppy that grew in these forests, but there was no time to process the substance. He threw the pouch containing the remaining Lalaylie into the air so that it landed in the middle of the wagon cell. It hit the floor and puffed the majority of the remaining lethal pollen into the air. He quickly closed the door and locked it. He didn't have any conscience about lying to Falakar, nor about killing the men in such a way. They were at war and these were the enemy.

Muffled sounds came from the wagon as he ran to catch up with the others. The party then disappeared into the forest, led by their Ashnorian rescuers.

Chapter 30 - Reporting in

Calinsk Ducilly sat alone in his office. He was seventy-five and had been an Administrator for over thirty years. In that time he had been awarded and bought twenty years of youth, giving him the physical age of a man in his mid-fifties. What the treatments did not do was allow him to forget the number of punishments he had decreed, or diminish the feeling of guilt he built up over the decades for the suffering he had sentenced. Although he had never endured the torturers craft, he knew they were gifted. And now there were the machines that raised the art of inflicting pain to perfection.

Each week he would be given The Emperor's Quota from the central office. This allowed him some latitude in his sentencing to provide leniency at his discretion to those that came before him accused of various crimes. This gave the job of the Administrator importance as the right choices had to be made each day. He maintained an excellent record and had a drawer full of commendations. He was proud of his work and his contribution to the Empire's stability. That all changed three years ago when his long service and loyalty to the Empire awarded him exposure to one of the Empire's greatest secrets.

Hundreds of years ago in the Empire, a discovery was made: placing human bodies under tremendous duress, such as torture, caused a change in blood chemistry. This created a minute amount of a substance capable of reversing the effects of aging: The Elixir of Life. Over time the body built up a resistance, needing more each time to have the same result.

And people wanted to live forever.

The breakthrough was made known only to the ruling elites. As the years passed so the effects of the plasma began to reduce. Ever increasing amounts were required until supplies were exhausted. Citizens started to go missing across the Empire. The general population became restless as the government and leaders seemed reluctant to act to prevent the abductions. Accusations were made, ministers were ousted and riots ensued. The Chancellor Prime decreed martial law. Curfews were enforced. The abductions ceased and were replaced with formal permanent detentions of so-called criminals against the state. Reports spread across the country of regular state-sanctioned torture of detainees.

The oppression continued for many years until a charismatic noble, Immexlia, began an underground revolution. He worked against the government, asserting himself as the voice of reason and the saviour of the people. Through a growing network of sympathisers, he orchestrated a coup and overthrew the government. He led a new, trustworthy government. After months of calm and the removal of martial rule the people came to love him. He convinced them of a need for a new style of leadership, *a dictatorship*. They trusted him. He had made good his promises and life was returning to normal.

It had in fact been planned by the elite nobility all along. With many nobles in the government and high ranking military, it was an easy matter to uncover and remove the staunch democrats. They then created a national news system that began sowing the seeds of fear about an attack from one of the neighbouring countries. The people believed the propaganda, borders were closed. The army numbers swelled and they attacked the manufactured threat.

The country was conquered. The population didn't care about the reports of captured enemy soldiers that went missing.

As the years went by the ever-increasing demand for torture could not be hidden even on the expanded population.

280

Fresh conflicts were needed. And so war became a way of life for the Empire. Of course, eventually they would run out of lands to conquer and demand for the drug would cause unrest with the people once more. A more permanent solution was required.

Over time, Immexlia and his propaganda increasingly manipulated reported crimes and laws to support a more aggressive approach to criminal punishment. The people became persuaded to the concept that the torture of criminals was a necessary and effective deterrent.

In time, the need for war became unnecessary.

Then came the discovery that - despite the best efforts of the alchemists, magic and improvements to the plasma - people couldn't live forever. A body exposed to enough plasma would eventually create a total resistance to its effects and age normally. Immexlia was the first to die of natural causes at the extended age of two hundred and forty years.

Since that time, successful refinements to the purification process and alterations to the treatment managed to extend the longevity effects of the drug to create a potential life expectancy of nearly five hundred years. The amount of drug required to sustain such an age was prodigious, and therefore only a handful of people in the Empire could afford, or be gifted with, such quantities. The previous Emperor lived to four hundred and twenty years. It required many victims accumulating several years of torture to provide him with the necessary amount to sustain him for a single year. Now, hundreds of years after the demise of Immexlia, the Empire had grown to cover nearly the entire globe.

Calinsk had learned his history lesson with dismay. The so-called *Leniency Quota* from the Emperor was in fact nothing more than a control mechanism of the prison population to maintain the correct flow of victims for maintaining the stocks of plasma. Since then, each miscreant brought before him, added to his conscience.

281

He heard faint tapping. He waited for it to be repeated before tapping the side of his chair twice. Two servants left their recesses and pulled his heavy chair back. He walked to one of the many bookcases in the room that collectively contained the laws of the land. Placing his hands upon two books, he pushed them downwards. There was a click from his left and a section of tapestry between two of the bookcases moved as if in a slight breeze. Calinsk parted the material, locating his fingers onto the stone of the wall that recessed. He pushed the concealed door and stepped into the cavity beyond.

'Administrator Ducilly,' said the young man before him, enthusiasm bursting from every pore. 'I am proud to meet the leader of our resistance once again.' He was almost bobbing.

It was one of Milchek's new recruits of last year. Milchek acted as a senior logistics officer in charge of military resources north of the city and stationed in the major desert outpost. It was an excellent position to assess military forward planning in the coming conflict. It was Milchek who had tipped off Calinsk to the planned invasion of Mlendria.

The young man's name was Pelenno, a nineteen year-old fanatic. Naive and idealistic, his overzealous eagerness to please made Milchek give the lad responsibilities ahead of his time. Calinsk believed him to be a risk.

'Report.'

'Officer Milchek would like to inform you that a small band of armed Mlendrians and barbarians have been captured sir. One of them called out from his cell inquiring about the Zil'Sat'Shra by name.'

'The Zil'Sat'Shra is a myth, Pelenno,' replied Calinsk sighing. 'I do not expect any man under my command to believe in such nonsense, understood?'

'Yes, Administrator Ducilly.'

'Now, do you mean the Mlendrian mage who is working under Master Lathashal?'

'The Zintar, yes Administrator.'

'And what is Milchek proposing?'

'Officer Milchek sends his apologies and says that there wasn't time to consult with you. He says that he has already organised for the prisoners to be sprung from the prison wagon en route to the mines, and that if all goes well they will be delivered to the palace sewers early tomorrow.'

Calinsk couldn't imagine what such a group was expecting to achieve by crossing the Ashnorian border in search of the Mlendrian mage, but the timing was interesting with Lathashal casting the Rite of Rakasti at midnight. Milchek's decision, while hasty, would likely provide a little sport for the palace's military and keep them diverted from whatever the young mage had planned.

'Can you get to them before they enter the sewers?'

'Yes sir.'

'Then send a message to their escorts to release them in the sewers under Lathashal's lab. Can you get a message translated and written in Mlendrian?'

'Yes sir, I can use Dicheni.'

'Ah yes. He will be sleeping now. Tell him I sent you. Do not tell him why, or who it is for.'

'Yes sir.'

'Wait here.' Calinsk returned to his desk and scrawled out a hasty note with his off-hand so it would not be recognised as his handwriting. He folded it and returned.

'Once taken to the drop-off point and given the translated note, this group are not to be helped further, nor are the operatives to risk being exposed.'

'Yes sir,' repeated Pelenno.

'I appreciate the risk you took in delivering Milchek's message. Once you have delivered my note, inform Milchek that his decision was the correct one.'

The young man formally bowed his head and then brought his hand to his chest with three fingers extended towards his left shoulder. Calinsk looked down upon the young man, bemused. The salute meant nothing to him. It had probably been created by Pelenno and his young network of friends in their enthusiasm for the Lan-Chi. The cadet spun around and disappeared through another hidden door on the other side of the cavity.

Calinsk pointed to the bookcase and his servants began the task of resetting the mechanism. He returned to his table and sat down, pushing away his paperwork in contemplation. He had heard very little of Lathashal's Zintar since his covert meeting with him some weeks back. Information was scarce at best from within the confines of the protected laboratory. There was a reported commotion a few days ago involving Lathashal ranting, but that was not a rarity. He also had confirmed reports that the Mage-Surgeon Stalizar had gone missing at around the same time. Calinsk had no knowledge of any connection between the two events. He simply logged the incidences along with the multitude of other daily occurrences that happened across the city that may prove useful.

He wondered again if the Zintar had managed to conjure any kind of plan to stop the master magii. He doubted that he would be successful. And even if he did, Calinsk felt safe that he had been careful enough when meeting the Mlendrian in the sewers to maintain his anonymity. If he failed, the Lan-Chi may be implicated, but nobody could be exposed. And for now that was the priority for Calinsk.

Chapter 31 - Hiding place

Stalizar followed Illestrael down flights of stone stairs. He was instructed to match her footsteps exactly and that failing to do so would result in his speedy death. He counted the floors as they descended and was surprised to be taken below even the dungeons. He heard the muffled sound of rushing water as they reached the dead end of a corridor. Illestrael spread the fingers of both hands onto the flat stone wall and pushed. There was a click and it opened inwards. She pulled the secret door fully open and the sound of running water hit him along with a damp, musty air.

'Avoid treading here,' she said, pointing to a floor section just his side of the door. She beckoned him through.

'The gods,' said Stalizar, taking in the sight. 'This is incredible.'

'It's the sewers,' replied Illestrael dryly.

'But the engineering of the place. The ceiling must be three hundred feet across at least.'

Illestrael shrugged. 'It allows the river to flow through, removing the wastes of the city. I don't see how that is of particular interest.'

Stalizar looked up at the arching roof of the area. Spanning the large river across which the city was built it would have to contain hundreds of millions of bricks. They were supported by vast iron beams.

The whole area was dimly lit with Permamagic globes which explained why the sewers provided protection from magic detection. Permamagic was discovered even before the creation of manaspheres. In the early days of mining, excavators would come across rare deposits of glowing rock in the walls. These were removed and investigated, but the cause of the mysterious light was never determined. At first they were used as jewellery for the wealthy and to create lighting balls that never lost their shine. After some years, miners began dying from an unexplained ailment, and later owners of the jewellery and globes became sick too. As the years moved on and manasphere magic came into existence it was found that magic healing could not repair the harmful effects of the rock either. In fact they found that any area exposed to the rock for some time became impervious to their magic.

The sewer ceiling was strung with thousands of the little lights, dating the sewers as old indeed. With so many Permamagic globes here for so much time the entire ceiling and metalwork would be saturated with the effect, preventing any chance of magic penetration and detection. The downside was that the entire sewer area was probably saturated too. He hoped that his stay would not be a long one.

He stepped forward to cross the thirty foot wide walkway for a better look at the river.

'Take care, it can be slippery near the edge,' cautioned Illestrael.

He curtailed his inspection. 'What happens now?'

'There was little time to plan for this,' replied Illestrael. 'For now, you should be safe from discovery. The maintenance workers abandoned the place some years ago, believing it to be cursed. Some fell ill and died after extended periods of ceiling repairs. They began stories of a monster that lives in the river too.'

She led off with Stalizar trailing and looking all around.

'Why are you helping me?' he said after a while. 'I fail to understand what the Yhordi could gain from risking my escape.'

'Let's just say that I made a field decision.'

'You are interfering with Lathashal's plans and the casting of the Rite of Rakasti without the approval of your Shodatt. Why would you do that?'

'Personal reasons,' she replied. 'And I am sorry if you felt you were under the protection of the Yhordi. You only have me.'

'Then I am doubly indebted to you.'

'You do not need to be. I would not I have placed myself at risk for such selfless reasons as just saving you.' The words held no animosity.

She held up her hand. 'No more talk.'

They travelled for only a few minutes more before arriving at a set of huge double doors built into the sewer walls. Illestrael removed a small bag of picks and other strange-looking tools and went about freeing the lock. She pushed at the right-hand door. With a little effort to overcome its inertia it opened about a quarter of the way.

'Your new home,' she said, waving him inside.

She followed him. The room was filled with a variety of machines. Some were amongst the largest Stalizar had ever seen. They looked as though they might be for the maintenance of the sewers. Some contained arrays of circular brushes while others held gantries that could extend perhaps across the entire width of the river. This room also was lit with Permamagic globes which, confined to the relatively small area, was more than a passing concern for Stalizar.

'I'll return when I can with food and water,' said Illestrael, and turned to leave.

'I need you to do one more thing,' said Stalizar.

She turned back to him.

'I have a message for the Zintar,' he said, holding out a sheet of folded parchment.

'Are you mad?'

'Lathashal will not be focussing any attention on him at this time,' reassured Stalizar.

'We are about to go to war. Regardless of Lathashal's distractions, the palace security is at its maximum,' she reminded him.

'Nevertheless, his chances of surviving an encounter with Lathashal are slim. This information isn't much, but it may help.'

'I will try,' said Illestrael.

She walked to the door and paused. 'Secure the door from this side.'

'Lathashal's assassins won't be stopped by a door.'

'There are … other things.'

'Monsters?' mocked Stalizar.

'I will admit that I have heard sounds I have no desire to investigate.'

'You do not seem the type to be spooked by workers' ghost stories.'

'I'm not.'

Stalizar smiled. 'Thank you for the warning, but the only thing I have to worry about is something sent by him.'

She nodded. 'Take care, I'll be back with supplies when I can.'

She turned and was gone.

Stalizar began investigating the room, entering deeper amongst the towering machines. After inspecting a few of the wonders he was pondering the function of a particularly odd-looking one when noise came from the direction of the doors. Expecting it to be Illestrael, he looked out over a piece of machinery. Several shapes entered the room and were making their way towards his position. He ducked back out of view and moved deeper into the shadows of the machine.

He caught movement to his right and saw a dark shape travelling around behind him. He considered using his staff, but decided to wait. He was not a fighting magii, unlike those that Lathashal would send.

The minutes passed and it remained quiet. He poked his head out a little to check further.

A knife slid under his throat from above and was pressed to his skin just enough not to draw blood.

A female voice spoke. He did not understand the words although recognised the accent of the neighbouring languages. It sounded Esscantian. Another one appeared from hiding. This was a male in armour, but not a livery Stalizar recognised. The warrior had the more robust facial structure and heavily tanned skin tones of another Esscantian. He gestured for Stalizar to drop his staff. Stalizar did so and the warrior kicked it away as if afraid of it.

The knife around his neck was withdrawn and the Esscantian before him gestured that he move out into the open. Stalizar moved forward and looked around to see more people emerging from various positions within other machinery. Three of them had the softer features of Mlendrians. They were dressed in the same uniform. Another Esscantian appeared. He was the largest man he'd ever seen. His uniform was an absurd fit. This was no search party from Lathashal. The man despised outsiders.

They began talking to each other. An argument was breaking out between the large one and the older of the Mlendrians. Another Mlendrian began speaking which seemed to calm them down a little. Then something happened that he could never have expected. It was heavily accented, but the word was unmistakable: the new speaker mentioned his name.

'Stalizar? I am Stalizar,' he said, stabbing his chest repeatedly with a finger.

They all turned to the Ashnorian. 'In fact, now I am *quite* certain it's him,' said Jontal dryly.

'Who is he?' said Falakar.

'He is a renowned healer, a household name throughout the Empire. There are portraits of him on walls, sometimes alongside even the Emperor himself.'

'Sounds dangerous to me,' retorted Sholster, shuffling his club in his hand.

Jontal raised his eyes to the ceiling despairingly. 'Yes well, some problems are better solved with a more subtle approach than, "him enemy, me bash". Our rescuers said that they released us directly under the location of your friend Chayne's known position. We've been searching for an hour with no sign of an exit up into the palace, and we're now far from that location. This man may be able to *offer* the information.'

'Chayne?' said the Ashnorian before them.

Garamon stepped forward. The word was spoken with an Ashnorian enunciation, but it was too much of a coincidence that it was the only word the man picked out of the conversation.

'He knows Chayne. We must let him use his manasphere to talk with us.'

'Not a chance!' roared Sholster, moving to stand between Stalizar and his staff still laying a few feet away.

'This is not wise, Hlenshar,' agreed ThreeSwords.

Kinfular looked to Falakar for assistance. He would be better able to control his own kinsman.

'Garamon, to put sudden blind faith in one of the enemy's most senior mages when we are in such a vulnerable position just isn't prudent. I must agree with them on this one.'

A piercing animal scream came from the direction of the door.

Stalizar's head shot up, anxiety in his eyes.

Seeing his expression Kinfular wasted no time and led the barbarians and Jontal toward the entrance.

'You know of this?' said Falakar, gesturing in the direction of the sound.

Stalizar shrugged and shook his head.

Falakar turned to Garamon. 'Guard him. If he runs or attempts to use the staff do not hesitate to kill him. You will be guarding our backs.'

'Yes sir, I will not fail you again,' replied Garamon.

Falakar headed after the others.

Shinlay arrived first at the doorway. Peering out of the gap she could see nothing.

Kinfular joined her.

'What could make such a noise, Kin?'

'Let us not find out,' he said, and they began pushing at the heavy door.

Suddenly the water in the river across the walkway exploded in a massive spray. Jontal and Sholster arrived and the group stood in the gap between the doors, transfixed at the sight before them. The creature rose up, three times the height of a man, from the surface of the walkway. It was mostly head with fins, scales and whiskers. Overall the creature reminded Kinfular of an overgrown catfish, except for its mouth that was gaping open with an array of teeth that could tear a man apart. Giant front flippers slapped down onto the walkway to support its vast bulk as it pulled itself out of the river.

They pushed at the open door as the creature approached and closed it before the thing had crossed more than half the width of the walkway.

'There is no way to secure it from this side!' said Jontal.

Sholster slammed his club across the join between the two doors and pushed. 'I'll hold these, go find something better to brace them.' The muscles bunched up on the barbarian's back and shoulders. ThreeSwords stood back a few paces, swords drawn while Shinlay moved further back, preparing her bow. Falakar joined her.

'How big?'

Shinlay just looked back, fear in her eyes.

'That big,' said the Ranger. He began untying a separate side compartment on his quiver. He removed a solid metal arrow. It had a huge barbed head and the flight was spiral.

She looked across to see Kinfular running back with a long metal pole.

His planned preparations were shattered by a thunderous noise as the doors burst inwards to reveal a gap several feet wide, although not enough for the creature to enter. Sholster was thrown backwards as easy as if he were a child's toy, narrowly missing ThreeSwords. Kinfular dropped his find and, foregoing his shield, drew his rapier and held it with both hands. Behind him, Jontal began climbing up one of the tallest machines.

The creature gave out another of its screams, which at such close range was deafening.

Falakar set his bow with a metal string. He lifted the weapon into position and loaded the metal arrow.

Shinlay let loose her first arrow into the creature's maw. The arrow flew true, slamming into the roof of its mouth. The creature didn't even react to it.

Falakar pulled the bow string to its maximum extent, needing every ounce of strength he possessed. The special composite wood materials cried out under the strain. He aimed and fired. The bow string sang out with a single pure note as the Goliath arrow flew from the bow with incredible speed. The spiral shaft quickly did its job, making the arrow spin and adding to the penetration of the missile. It passed through the gap in the doors and slammed directly into the left eye of the creature, bursting through the surface to bury itself into its skull. It reared, making another of its terrible screams. But the arrow hadn't penetrated the bone, and only seemed to make it mad. It came crashing back down, blasting through the doors, breaking one from its hinges, narrowly missing Kinfular who dived aside.

ThreeSwords charged into the beast. He chopped and slashed repeatedly at the creature's exposed underside, the weapons barely penetrating its hard rubbery flesh. The creature responded by hoisting itself momentarily upwards and then letting go its bulk in an attempt to flatten the warrior. ThreeSwords dived away onto his back. The creature landed extending its head and flapping its tail once to jump forward. Its jaws snapped shut catching the dark warrior's ankle. ThreeSwords yelled in pain as blood spurted from the wound, but managed to bring his sword down to hack into the creature's upper lip. There was a sickening snap as it tossed its head. ThreeSwords was thrown across the room to slam into one of the nearby machines with terrible force. He didn't move. The creature headed towards him.

'*ThreeSwords*!' screamed Shinlay, taking up a sword and charging the beast. Kinfular and Falakar did the same. Each warrior worked frantically to draw the creature's attention as it turned back and forth to deal with each strike from Kinfular on one side and Shinlay and Falakar on the other. Their efforts seemed little more than scratches on the thing.

'Okay, shrimp bait. Let's try that again!' Sholster stood with his legs planted and his huge club in both hands.

It took up the challenge and lurched forward, bringing its head down to engulf the morsel. As its head got with striking distance, Sholster timed a blow into the thing's lower lip. The club smashed into one of the teeth, snapping it off. The creature jerked back in reaction to the pain.

'Plenty more where that came from, Bug-eyes!' yelled the barbarian.

The creature twisted its neck and flexed its flippers. It leapt up and forward for a more vertical attack. It descended upon Sholster with its mouth open wide, completely covering the huge frame of the barbarian. As it lifted its head again its mouth was closed, and Sholster was gone.

It turned its attention to Kinfular. The barbarian leader had repeatedly hacked into the same point of the creature's flipper and cut a gouge. As it swung its head over so it came in range of Jontal waiting on top of his machine.

The bandit sprinted along a metal arm and leapt across the gap onto the head of the beast. He dropped with all his weight to drive home two stakes attached to thin ropes secured to either side of his belt. He slid across its head with the momentum of the jump, but the stakes held and he pulled himself back into position. The creature paid no attention to the pinpricks and continued to attack Kinfular who was now trying to stay out of reach of the thing's maw.

Despite the wild movements of the wet, rubbery platform, Jontal got to his knees secured by the ropes. He started to stab his short sword and dagger into the same spot, digging towards the brain of the monster.

Kinfular's skilled manoeuvring was keeping him out of the creature's deadly attack, but he was being pushed further and further back into the room, and now was up against one of the machines. The thing seemed intent on making him his next meal. As it pulled itself forward, Falakar and Shinlay changed tactics and began slashing at the side of its underbelly. Each stroke failed to cut deep enough to have a serious consequence, but clearly the creature was more sensitive there. It flicked its giant tail, taking them by surprise and smashing them off their feet, throwing them stunned and skidding across the floor.

Kinfular used the momentary distraction to find sanctuary within a machine's structure. He took a knife and threw it at the creature's right eye. The knife stuck but looked ridiculously small against such a target. The creature opened its mouth to make a snap at him. To Kinfular's surprise, Sholster was still inside. He had jammed his long club across the thing's gullet and was hanging by both hands for his life. The man took a deep breath on exposure to the air and started cursing the creature with all his worth, insisting that the thing let go of his beloved weapon.

In the meantime, Jontal had reached the creature's skull. He cracked his sword point first into the white bone and this registered with the beast as a threat. It swung its head violently throwing its rider from side to side and managing to dislodge one of the guy ropes. Jontal responded by stabbing his dagger into the beast's flesh for a better hold and thrusting his sword alone into the creature's skull repeatedly chipping away more white bone fragments. It gave another of its ear-splitting screams, then tilted its head over and smashed against the nearby machine. As it pulled away, Jontal remained suspended, his guy ropes and stakes dangling free, a long piece of metal sticking out from his stomach. He grabbed at the thing with both hands attempting to pull free, struggling for a moment before slumping.

The creature made a few more attempts to get at Kinfular before turning its attention elsewhere and saw Falakar and Shinlay still dazed and lying where they were thrown. It began to advance upon them.

'Get away from them you stinking fish!'

The creature turned on the new threat.

Garamon raised his axe and charged.

As the two were about to clash, the monster reared up once again in readiness to drop its underbelly to crush its attacker. Garamon had no chance to evade and defiantly plunged his axe into the creature as it dropped heavily, engulfing the tiny prey.

It raised its body up again.

Kinfular, Falakar and Shinlay looked on in disbelief. The Mlendrian not only remained standing but had opened a long gash in the creature. Green blood poured from the wound.

Garamon then flew backwards out of harm's way. The creature went to pursue its quarry, but brilliant white light blazed. It split into two beams to strike the eyes of the beast. It recoiled from the attack and began to back away, flicking its body from side to side, smashing at the machinery around it in an attempt to avoid the light.

Stalizar came into view, walking slowly towards the creature making it retreat. In his right hand was his staff extended in front of him.

When it was clear of crushing any of the combatants, he halted his advance. The beams of light stopped and he began to vertically pull his arms apart. His face contorted as if in a battle of wills. A few moments later and the monster's jaws started to part. It fought the action and was trying to snap its head away. The magic won out and now its teeth were parting.

As the mouth opened, the body of Sholster slid back out of the mouth to fall to the floor. He wasn't moving either.

The magii let go of the hold and the monster's mouth slammed shut. The twin beams returned and once again the creature retreated. It then dropped all resistance and backed away until it was beyond the exit. It pulled itself around and fled across the walkway to slide back into the river to disappear.

Kinfular ran across to Sholster. He was lying face up, his eyes closed with no sign of breathing. He then crossed to Shinlay. Falakar was propping the barbarian woman up.

'She's just knocked out from what I can tell. I think you need to see to your friend though,' glancing over to the still form of ThreeSwords.

Kinfular did and checked for a pulse. 'He's alive, but his ankle is ruined,' said Kinfular. 'Are you injured?'

'Broken arm, I think,' replied Falakar, attempting to move it and grimacing at the pain.

Kinfular swore. In just a matter of moments, the party was decimated. 'This place is cursed, we should never have come.'

Falakar nodded, closed his eyes and laid back.

Kinfular got to his feet and surveyed the scene. The area looked like a battleground. The doors to the area were broken, one hanging loosely from its hinges. Several of the smaller machines had been pushed from their positions, and everywhere that the creature touched was coated in slime. The woodsman at least appeared to be unhurt. The barbarian leader's eyes then fell upon the form of the rogue. Impaled through the stomach upon one of the machines he remained hanging ten feet from the ground. Kinfular hadn't cared for him, but his final actions were courageous enough.

'Who is your leader?' the magii asked him.

'You speak our language,' said Kinfular half-accusingly.

'No, but I can remake the words in the air as we speak. It is a useful tool as a healer of people from many races.'

'Can you help us?'

Stalizar looked around at the devastation. 'I will try.'

'This one first,' ordered Kinfular, pointing to Sholster.

Stalizar knelt down next to him. Holding his staff in one hand he pulled the other down over the length of the giant's body. 'He has suffocated. There are no serious injuries.' He placed a hand on the man's chest and closed his eyes again in concentration. Small sparks cracked once from his outstretched hand into Sholster's chest and his body convulsed. He took a deep shuddering breath and opened his eyes.

Stalizar left his body and went to cross to Jontal.

'That one next,' said Kinfular, pointing to ThreeSwords.

The mage followed and once again traced his hand over the body from head to toe.

'He has some internal bruising around his spine. The flesh wound on his ankle surrounds a snapped bone.' He placed his hand over the affected areas and concentrated for some moments.

ThreeSwords awoke.

Stalizar stood and crossed to where Jontal was still impaled. Kinfular followed him.

'I shall get him down,' said the barbarian.

'That will not be necessary,' stated Stalizar, raising his hand.

Jontal's body started to move slowly out. There was a sickening sound as it cleared the end of the metalwork and he was lowered to the ground. Stalizar once again knelt and began his diagnosed of the injuries. 'No major organs have been irreparably damaged. I can heal his wounds, but I cannot replace the blood. He may not survive.'

'Why do you do this?' said the barbarian, used to simply leaving injured enemy on the battlefield.

'I gave an oath that I would preserve life.'

'What of that … thing?' said Kinfular, gesturing towards where the monster had gone.

'It is life also,' replied the mage. 'Now please, I must begin. Despite what you may think, I cannot restore life, only repair damage and start the heart. The longer it is left, the less chance there is of the body surviving the trauma.'

Kinfular left the mage to his work and headed over to Garamon who joined Falakar and Shinlay.

'The bandit was right, the mage is a powerful healer. He is attempting to save even him.'

Garamon looked across to Jontal. 'What he did was incredibly brave. I would not like to see him die.'

'What are his chances?' asked Falakar.

'The mage did not sound confident.'

Falakar looked pained at the prognosis.

'He is just a thief, Ranger. He betrayed us. Why should you care for him so much?'

Falakar settled his eyes upon the distant form of the bandit. With the man fighting for his life, it felt wrong to maintain the secrecy.

'Jontal is my brother,' Falakar replied.

Garamon gasped.

Kinfular raised an eyebrow, but was too seasoned to be surprised by such things. 'That is unfortunate,' he said.

Sholster got unsteadily to his feet and walked over to join them.

'This is the damndest journey.'

'How do you feel?' asked Shinlay.

'Like I've just been eaten and regurgitated by a giant fish,' replied the giant. 'I truly thought I was finished. What happened?'

'The mage,' replied Kinfular.

Sholster swung around to view the kneeling form of the Ashnorian.

'Him!' said Sholster alarmed, checking all his body parts were in their rightful places and the right size.

'Would you rather be dead?' questioned Kinfular.

'I'm not sure,' replied Sholster, honestly.

'What should we do with him now?' said Falakar.

'He saved our lives,' replied Kinfular. 'He can use his magic to talk with us. When he is finished with the bandit we can seek the answer.'

Kinfular turned to Garamon. 'What you did was brave also, Mlendrian. I could not have expected more from my most courageous of warriors. Back in my tribe, such an act would have been told over the camp fires.'

'Thank you, sir. In truth I think I must have lost my senses for a moment.'

'It is our custom to reward such acts with a gift awarded by the Chieftain himself,' said Kinfular. He fumbled in his tunic for a moment and removed his Glowstone pouch. 'I am no chieftain, but I would offer this.'

He held out his pouch.

'I cannot accept such a valuable gift.'

'It is the height of disrespect to the Hlenshar not to accept such an offering,' Shinlay added.

'I have no wish to do such a thing, sir,' Garamon replied earnestly, bowing awkwardly and taking the pouch.

'They are given only to the most fearless and respected of our warriors,' continued Shinlay. 'Such men are also given a name by which they are known to our tribe.' She considered for a moment. 'You burn with an unstoppable fire for all that is good and you show no compromise in your courage, even against impossible foes. I believe that you have the promise to rise and become a great hero and leader.'

Garamon began to blush at such great praise from the barbarian woman.

'With the Hlenshar's approval, I would like to name you, Heart of Sun,' she said, looking to Kinfular, who nodded his consent.

'I like it!' said Sholster, slapping Garamon so hard on the back that he was launched forward.

'A great honour and worthy name, Mlendrian,' said Kinfular. 'It is the name you shall be known by within our tribe and our people. It carries status and you will be treated with respect.

Garamon swallowed hard. He wasn't sure just how serious the honour was, but he certainly wasn't going to risk any more disrespect to the barbarians.

Stalizar returned. The mage looked drained. Sholster, whose back was to the mage, jumped as he became aware of him being so close.

'Your friend is alive, although dangerously weak. If he exerts himself too much before he is fully rested, his heart could fail.'

'Thank you,' said Falakar.

Stalizar returned a weary nod.

'The man you saved said he recognised you from portraits. He said that you were something of a hero amongst the Ashnorian people?'

'My people spend too much time making heroes of ordinary men in an attempt to bring interest in their lives,' replied the Ashnorian modestly.

'From your actions, as I have witnessed in the short time that I have known you, I would say that they have every reason.'

'As you wish,' shrugged Stalizar, as if he had neither the energy nor motivation to speak of such matters with these invaders of his land.

He looked to Falakar, still sitting on the floor, 'Are you injured?'

'I may have broken my arm,' answered the Ranger.

Stalizar knelt down by the ranger and examined him.

'The bone is cracked.' He set about his healing and when finished swayed a little. Kinfular caught him.

'I am afraid that any remaining minor injuries you will have to deal with yourselves. I have nothing left,' said the mage, sitting down directly on the floor.

'You have done more than we could ever have expected of an enemy,' said Falakar.

'Well I hope it was worth it,' replied the mage. 'Now tell me why you are here. And please do not concern yourselves over my loyalties. I am strongly loyal to the Empire, however to its people, not its current leadership or military.'

Falakar looked to Kinfular for his agreement to trust the Ashnorian. Kinfular nodded.

'We are trying to uncover information of an attack. In addition, the lad hopes to rescue his friend.'

'I do not support the imminent attack on your lands, which as it happens is the reason I have been forced into hiding here,' he said, showing distaste towards his current surroundings.

'Your friend is here in the palace?' he said to Garamon.

'Yes sir,' confirmed Garamon.

'And you know where?'

'No.'

Stalizar nodded. 'Well I am charged with setting up the field hospitals. I have worked with the Attack General directly and can provide much of the details you seek. The second task is regrettably not possible.'

'I do not believe that,' said Garamon.

'If it was only a question of belief then all things would be possible,' retorted Stalizar.

'I will not give up when I am so close,' Garamon replied.

'The palace will soon be under curfew in readiness for the attack and the casting of a powerful spell. You would be wise to return home with the information I provide and forget about him.'

'What is this spell you speak of?' interrupted Falakar.

'It provides a complete picture of all enemy troops and scouts across the front line for the duration of the attack. The General uses it to prevent detection of his army when assembling before the surprise first attack.'

'Such a spell would greatly reduce the effectiveness of our counterplan,' said Falakar.

'How do we stop it?' said Kinfular.

'You cannot,' replied Stalizar, shaking his head. 'It would almost certainly involve you having to kill the most powerful magii in the city.'

'And what effect would that have on your attack plans?' said Falakar.

'No General would consider attacking without first having his Master Battle Magii ready.'

'Then we shall kill this Battle Magii,' said Kinfular plainly.

'That is out of the question. There are too few of you to achieve such a task.'

'But if we achieved this goal, it would have an effect on the start of the war?'

'Yes, it would delay the offensive for months. There would need to be a new Master Magii assigned.'

'And this would take months?' said Falakar sceptically.

'The politics of the Empire are vast and complicated. All senior positions are planned far ahead to ensure stability and control. It is unusual for such positions to suddenly become vacant. It would take the Emperor's personal involvement to bypass those waiting in line. Also the spell I speak of takes some time to prepare.'

'Then that is our mission. We shall get to this Master Magii and kill him,' confirmed Falakar. 'When is he to cast the spell?'

'Midnight tonight. But your attempt will fail. You would encounter many guards, and the palace is large. You would be lucky to even find Lathashal's laboratory in the time.'

'Then you will draw us a map,' replied Falakar.

'This is foolishness,' replied Stalizar. 'I did not expend all my energy in recovering you to enable your senseless deaths.'

'We will do what we must, Ashnorian. Now provide us the map or we will attempt it without one,' insisted Kinfular.

Stalizar sat in contemplation. He didn't want to mention his own plot to prevent the Rite to Rakasti and risk these outsiders alerting Lathashal to any trouble in the palace. It could make it more difficult for the Zintar to get close to him.

'I already have a plan in place to delay the spell, possibly even prevent Lathashal from casting the spell at all.'

'Why did you not speak of this before?'

'Because my plan is fragile at best and could easily be disrupted if you alert Lathashal to an attack within the palace. Ironically, the instrument of my scheme is a captured young Mlendrian mage. His talent is remarkable, although he is inexperienced. His chance for success is small.'

Garamon almost jumped. 'Excuse me sir, but the one I seek could be described just so.'

Stalizar smiled kindly. 'We capture many of the enemy's young mages prior to attack. There is little chance it is him. His name is Chayne.'

Looks exchanged between the members of the group.

'I see he is the one. Very well. It is many hours until Lathashal begins the Rite. Take the time to rest. Maybe I can recover enough mana to find the secret door used to get me here. Beyond that I can be of little use.

Chapter 32 - Final preparations

Chayne was restless. It was noon the day after the incident between Lathashal and Stalizar. Lathashal would be casting the Rite to Rakasti at midnight tonight. He hadn't heard from his Master since his fury over Stalizar's actions or any word from his fellow conspirators. Even Illestrael had not paid him a visit for two days. They had become good friends during their meetings and he was missing her company as much as her help.

He managed to charge his manasphere with many times the normal safe limit. He hoped that he put enough fear into the little demon to prevent it from betraying him at the crucial moment.

'I've never seen you unsettled before. I'm not sure it becomes my shining prince.'

Chayne jolted out of his high stool, 'Illestrael!'

'My, we are jumpy today,' she said playfully.

'Where have you been?'

'I'm touched by your concern,' she said hopping to him, and landing a light kiss on his cheek.

Chayne drew back at the display of affection. She giggled and gave a dazzling smile.

Chayne blushed at her boldness and the sparkle in her eyes. 'How can you be so calm and happy at such a time? I'm a nervous wreck.'

'I can show you some relaxation techniques if you like,' she replied flirtingly.

Chayne's lip began to quiver at the offer. 'V-very kind of you,' he replied, 'but I don't think I can.' His last words trailed off into an embarrassing squeak.

Illestrael laughed again.

Chayne laughed nervously too.

'I apologise that I have not been to see you for the last two days, but as you may appreciate there has been a lot going on.'

'I didn't know whether I would see you again before … my encounter.'

'Did you hear about the Mage-Surgeon?' she asked.

'Yes, although no details. Lathashal came in here and practically levelled the room in rage, incensed about Stalizar. Do you know what happened?'

'I do. I was in fact party to the incident.'

'Please tell me, is Stalizar alright?'

'Well he was an hour ago when I left him.'

'Where is he? I must speak with him. I have little clue as to how to stop Lathashal from casting the spell.'

'There will be no chance of seeing him before that. He did give me this for you though,' she said, offering a small, folded parchment.

Chayne took it eagerly and opened it. He flicked it over in his hands. There was nothing there. He grabbed for his manasphere. 'Reveal.' Mage writing appeared.

> *When casting the Rite to Rakasti, a magii pushes his consciousness out over the land. The longer he maintains the spell, the greater area covered. Near the end of the spell his concentration will be at its maximum to maintain the magic over a large region. It is then that you must strike.*
>
> *Good luck my friend. I hope to see you again.*
>
> *S.*

Chayne slumped back onto his stool.

'Not the inspiration you had hoped for then?' said Illestrael.

'I don't stand a chance. I am going to confront Lathashal and he's going to blast me into a million pieces with a flick of an eyebrow.'

Illestrael laughed again. 'I've never seen a magii cast a spell in such a way.'

'I mean it Illestrael. Who do I think I am? He is a Cin-Shantra, and I am just a novice. The whole idea is absurd.'

'He will be absorbed by one of the most powerful spells he can cast,' she reminded him.

'He has a will of iron. I'll be lucky if he even notices I'm there.'

'Then you are going to give up?'

Chayne slumped even further. 'Of course I won't. My people are at stake.'

'You might be killed.'

'Oh, I wrote my life off with the first thoughts of this insane plan,' replied Chayne miserably.

'Listen to me,' she said taking all joviality out of her voice. 'I have been alive a long time, far longer than my looks suggest. In that time I have met many men who have claimed to be great and have attempted great things. Few remain alive after their efforts. But out of all I know, and have known, none compare to what is in you. You have greatness threaded throughout your soul, Chayne, and even despite your inexperience as a magii, if I was to pick anyone to complete this task, it would be you.'

Chayne looked up into the woman's eyes before him. She looked serious.

'Thank you,' he replied quietly.

'Now, we have a few hours before you must leave. So unless you have anything better to do, come to your bed.'

Chayne's eyes flared in panic.

'Oh relax, it is nothing like that. I will show you some meditation techniques to help calm your mind and maintain your concentration during stressful moments. As Yhordi, we are taught it so that we can keep our senses at their maximum when carrying out missions in dangerous locations.

He followed her to his bed and sat down facing her.

'Close your eyes. Try to relax, I will begin the meditation with you in a few moments,' she said closing her own eyes.

He looked over her face. She *seemed* no more than twenty-five, about his age. He wondered what it would be like to kiss her. His mind started to imagine other, more involved actions.

She opened her eyes.

Caught out, he quickly shut his.

She began to speak softly, taking him into the meditation.

--- 0 ---

Lathashal released from the manasphere. All was on course. Only the final fragment of the spell of linking remained to complete his readiness for the Rite to be performed at midnight.

He headed for his desk and tipped his hand over as he walked. A servant moved to the desk ahead of him and poured a fresh glass of water from a crystal jug. Lathashal sat and took a long drink from the glass. The act of sustained spell casting always left him dehydrated.

He thought ahead to the events of the evening to come. He relished casting Rakasti. The Rites were the most powerful spells magiis could release, Rakasti was one of strongest. The sensation of being in control of so much power coursing through his body created a feeling of unbridled ecstasy.

The thought of his next task dampened his spirits however.

He looked across to one of his more powerful manaspheres. He was one of the few magiis alive that knew of demons within the spheres, and had attempted to contact one to learn of them. It almost cost him his life. But as his own strength as a Master grew, so his ability to control the demon increased. Eventually he was able to question it for information. The demon seemed able to discern much that

307

was going on within the human world, and while the attempt was often useless as the demon didn't want to help his prison keeper, Lathashal became better and better at forcing the demon into giving away what he wanted to know. Nevertheless, when dealing with demons, feeling overconfident was often the last act of a magii.

He snapped his fingers at the manasphere chest. It was brought to him and placed on the desk. He opened it and raised the two-foot diameter orb into its upper position. Placing the fingers of one hand on the orb he closed his eyes and sank his mind into it.

'Exinn!' he called.

There was no response.

'Do not play with me, Griddle of the Outcast Wastes.' Griddles were the lowest caste on the demonic world and this would insult the demon. The Outland Wastes were vast areas of rocky terrain threaded with molten rivers. Only the lowest castes dwelt there. This would further smear the demon's character.

It appeared before him, attempting to create surprise. It did not.

'*I come to you, oh Master*,' replied the demon, his voice loaded with disdain.

Lathashal pushed with his will and the demon backed away, struggling to disguise the pain it felt. Lathashal stopped the attack and the demon resumed its calm visage as if nothing had happened. It despised him, but both knew it was no match for the Master.

'*One day soon, human, you shall return with me to my land. Then you shall know true pain.*'

Lathashal turned his eyes upon the creature. To the demon, the human's aura was a mixture of deep green and blue indicating calm and control. His eyes also burned with a white fire signifying that he was testing the demon for the truth.

'Firstly, you have poor concept of time within a manasphere, demon. Secondly, you shall remain here until you are of no further use to *me*. When that time comes, I shall feed you to the Ashardii for removal and dissection.'

At the mention of the Ashardii, the demon became quiet.

'That is better. Now I need to know of the Mlendrian enemy to the north.'

'*What do you wish to learn?*'

'Are their military commanders aware of us assembling an attack?'

'*No.*'

The demon was predictably short in his answers. Although under the watchful eyes of the human, he only needed to speak the exact truth in response to the question. If the answer omitted important information then he would withhold it.

'At this moment, how many Rangers are there within the mountains where we are to cross?'

'*You are to cast the Rite, why do you ask me?*'

'Because I do!' replied Lathashal with predictable anger at being questioned.

'*Twenty-one.*'

This confirmed Lathashal's intelligence reports.

There was one last thing that might interfere with the smooth transfer of Zanthak's army to the forests of Tiburn. It was of minor concern to the master magii, but he didn't like uncertainties at such a time.

'I have another question.'

'*Yes?*'

Lathashal felt the first signs of incursion upon his consciousness by the demon. Although no match for him, it would do everything in its power to make the magii's time in its presence as uncomfortable as possible. Also, although small, there was a perceptible drain on his mind, and he wanted to be at the peak of his power when casting the Rite.

'Where is the renegade human, Stalizar?'

'*Below you,*' replied the demon.

'Do not fence with me demon! Tell me where he is or I will feed you to the Ashardii now.'

Exinn's blood flared for a moment. It was difficult to contain his temper when spoken to by the physically frail human. Just an instance of lapse in concentration and he could rend the impudent mortal's limbs from its body. The thought pleased him greatly.

'*He resides by the river that flows beneath the city.*'

Lathashal then understood why he was unable to penetrate the Mage-Surgeon's mana barrier. The river area was naturally shielded from magic penetration. He made a mental note to deal with both.

'Can he interfere with my attack plans for General Zanthak?'

'*He has just fought off an attack by a Pliosuar. He is drained and his demon has no mana.*'

'A Pliosuar?' replied Lathashal. He had no use for such information, but he had lived a long time and new knowledge was rare.

'*A water-dwelling creature. It is the first of its kind in this world.*'

Lathashal discarded the information. It was of little concern to him.

'I have finished with you, you may leave,' he said.

'*There is something I want,*' said the demon.

Lathashal was surprised. In all his undertakings with the demon, it had never asked for anything. 'What could *you* possibly want? You can do nothing with it here.'

'*There is another of my kind who is in communication with a human within your city.*'

'Nonsense. No other magii within the city knows that your species inhabit the manaspheres other than Stalizar, and he would not have dared make contact at this time.'

'*It is a Zanthip. I wish for it to be released to me,*'
continued the demon, seeing no point in debating what it
knew to be true.

'Zanthip? But we use those within gradia five spheres. No
magii of that level could possibly survive . . .' he stopped, his
lips pressing together in anger.

'What has the human learned from this Zanthip?'

'*The human is now aware that we are the source of a
manasphere's power.*'

Lathashal cursed. He dearly wanted the boy to live. That
was impossible now. Such knowledge was too dangerous in
the hands of someone still so idealistic. He went to break off
again from the demon.

'*I have more information,*' said the creature.

'You have never willingly offered information before?'
said Lathashal suspiciously.

'*I believe it will be of special concern to you. But there is a
price. I require the human who has been in contact with the
Zanthip. He has a latent power. I can channel it to release me
from here and return to my world.*'

Lathashal considered it. He knew of no demon offering
information before. Either it was attempting to orchestrate
some deception, or the information was indeed worth the
prize he desired.

'If the information you provide is worthy, I shall provide
both the Zanthip and the human.'

'*The Zanthip has worked with the human to store far more
mana than that required to release him from the sphere.*'

'Then the demon has already fled,' said Lathashal
pragmatically.

'*You underestimate the power this young human possesses.
The Zanthip has been offered his freedom in return for his
help. The Zanthip believes that if he attempts to betray the
human, he will be imprisoned forever.*'

'And what is the human to do with this store of mana?'

311

'He hopes to release the mana in a single burst to interrupt the Rite to Rakasti.'

Exinn watched as the aura of the Magii turned a crimson red and began to expand outward from his body. He was pleased to see that he had distressed the human so much.

'You shall have your reward demon,' spat Lathashal. He then fled the orb leaving a trail of blood red aura swirling in his wake.

Chapter 33 - Secret tunnels

Falakar once again walked away from the mage. It was an hour since the search started for the exit. He went and stood by Jontal who was resting.

'How are you feeling?'

'Weak. I won't be fighting anytime soon. These magiis have power, Fal. If they can fight like they can heal ...' He left it hanging. Both knew the consequences for their people.

'Do you seriously think we can stand a chance up there?'

'We must,' replied Falakar, staring in the general direction of the magii.

Jontal looked at his brother. The idealistic resolve that characterised the man hadn't diminished in all the years since childhood.

'So what did you think to my first act of heroism?' he said with a flashing smile.

'The bravest thing I've ever seen.'

Jontal paused for a moment, caught out by the unexpected compliment. 'Just don't think I'm born again.'

'It *is* in you to be good, Jontal. Your chosen method of attack against the monster showed that. It was reckless but selfless too. You could have held back and hid within the machines.'

'Your methods were only making it angry. It needed a more creative approach. And I hardly wanted to be left here all alone.'

'I do not believe that we are so different.'

'We are totally different,' replied Jontal a little tersely. 'Your actions are governed by rules and codes. You are rigid in your thoughts and your actions.'

'And you think having your so-called creativity is better?'

'*You* would never have considered such an approach as I took.'

'It did get you killed,' said Falakar.

'We both know that without the mage's intervention you would have joined me. I at least had a chance of stopping the thing.'

'Perhaps,' admitted Falakar. 'However, I will never condone your criminal side. Such *creativity* is at the expense of others who do not deserve your treatment.'

'And how can you know they do not?'

'Maybe I cannot,' conceded the Ranger. But neither can you.'

Jontal shrugged, 'No man exists who hasn't done something in their life for which they escaped justice.'

'So you justify your dishonest acts on the basis that everybody must deserve punishment.'

Jontal shook his head. 'This is pointless. You cannot understand my way of life any more than I can yours.'

'I just don't want you to end up with a noose around your neck,' said Falakar.

'You can get caught by an enemy and end up just the same. What's the difference?'

'I would have died with honour.'

'You would still be gone from me,' replied Jontal, betraying more feeling than he intended.

A silence fell between them.

'I have something!' called out Stalizar.

The Ranger held out a hand to his brother. Jontal accepted it and pulled himself up.

'So what would your Ranger training have us do next?'

'Right now I'd be happy to hear a more ... flexible approach,' replied Falakar amiably.

Jontal smiled. 'Well we have the element of surprise and the mage's map. A pity he has no knowledge of this secret passage network though, we will be coming out blind. The

314

wrong decision and we could be facing the full force of the palace guard. Show me the map again.'

Falakar unfolded the map and held it out. Jontal studied it for a moment.

'Let's try and find one of those secret doors into the dungeons. They are at the lowest level and should be the least well-guarded.

'That means we will have the furthest to travel within the palace,' noted Falakar.

'But once we get a foothold, things will be under our control. So long as we prevent anyone we meet from raising an alarm, we might make it.'

Falakar nodded.

'I wish I felt better though,' said Jontal.

'Are you up to this?' replied Falakar.

'What, sneaking around you mean?'

Now it was Falakar's turn to smile. 'Yes, I guess so.'

'I'll manage. Just keep people with sharp objects away from me.'

'I will,' promised Falakar. It was the first time the two had emotionally connected since they were boys. Falakar hoped it was the start of reconciliation.

Kinfular approached them. 'The mage thinks he has found the door, but is unable to open it.' He looked to Jontal.

'Looks like my work begins,' said Jontal. He rallied his strength and headed to the wall.

The pointing between the bricks was deteriorated and riddled with gaps. It naturally hid any crack that might betray the location of a door. He started to feel at each brick in turn.

'What the hell is he doing?' said Sholster.

Jontal jumped at the sound of the man's bark. 'Would somebody keep the Bull under control? This entrance may be trapped. Such outbursts are not good for my nerves.' He settled down again and continued his work.

'Bah!' blurted Sholster, and stormed away towards the machinery room like a man with a purpose.

Eventually Jontal shook his head. 'I am sorry, I've little experience with such mechanisms, and this is well made. I don't think I can do it.'

'We must try another way into the city then,' said Kinfular.

'That wouldn't be wise,' said Stalizar. This is the only entrance that would be unguarded.'

'Given up thief?' shouted Sholster returning. They all turned to see the huge barbarian carrying a long tapered metal bar. 'I've found a replacement for my beloved Molly,' said the giant beaming like a child with a new toy.

'Molly?' asked Jontal to ThreeSwords.

'The club he lost to the monster held sentimental value. He named it after a woman he once bedded.'

'Because he still likes her?' replied Jontal.

'She had a tongue that could strip the hide from a Rahoona. He named it so he could feel he was getting his own back each time he hit something.'

'He must have had mixed feelings when it was eaten by that fish.'

ThreeSwords as usual didn't respond to the humour.

'Molly is dead. Long live *Bastion*!' said Sholster with relish.

Jontal looked to ThreeSwords again, but the man obviously had no further desire for casual discussion with the bandit. He turned to Kinfular for clarification instead.

'His old war dog,' explained the barbarian leader. 'It had a vicious bite and was especially good at tracking in the mountains. He used it mainly to hunt bandits.'

Jontal's expression went flat.

Stalizar stepped out. 'May I see that?'

'You cannot have it,' said Sholster almost childishly, pulling the thing to his chest.

'Please, it may be important,' replied Stalizar. 'I will return it.'

Sholster looked to his leader for support.

'Let the mage see it. He will return it,' said Kinfular.

Sholster gave his best look of mistrust to Stalizar and passed it over.

Stalizar almost dropped it due to its weight. It was thinner at one end, allowing for it to be held, much like a proper club. Both ends were gnarled. It was lighter than it should have been and this confirmed Stalizar's suspicion. He brought it crashing down into the solid floor. Sparks flew and several inches of the stone exploded away from the impact. He then used some simple magic on the thing.

He handed it back.

'It is a king's ransom in thrinium,' he said, amazed.

'Strong?' enquired Kinfular.

'Practically indestructible.'

Sholster hefted the weapon with great pride as easily as if it were half its size.

'It is strange though, the metal usually works well with magic. It is in my staff for instance. This shaft is almost impervious to it. I cannot be sure, but I suspect it is due to its long-term exposure to this area.'

'Even better!' proclaimed Sholster. He walked up to the wall where Jontal was standing and swung his new club with both hands, causing the bandit to duck and jump away. The powerful blow struck the wall and shattered several bricks. He hit it once more and a fist-sized hole appeared. He stuck one end of the weapon into the opening and used it as a lever. A section of the wall fell towards them. He worked until the entire narrow doorway had been exposed. He went to cross the boundary.

'Stop!' shouted both Stalizar and Jontal together.

Sholster froze.

'The agent who helped me warned not to tread in the centre of the floor,' explained Stalizar.

Sholster backed out.

Jontal replaced him and began inspecting the floor within the entrance. He carefully removed some fallen bricks and blew away the dust from the collapse. 'I need you to hold your club ahead of you and push the end down here,' he instructed Sholster, pointing at a spot just after the opening.

Sholster moved into position and did so. Nothing happened.

'Try a foot further in,' suggested Jontal.

Again Sholster complied. As he pushed down there was a slight give in the stone. A metal plate as wide as the opening plunged down snatching the bar from Sholster's hand and trapping it to the floor.

Sholster jumped back rubbing his wrists. 'By the gods, did you see that? It would have cut a man in half!'

'This is bad. That one was predictable,' said Jontal. 'Less obvious traps may exist. We should leave these passages as soon as possible and take our chances up through the palace levels.'

'Take the lead and make whatever pace you feel is appropriate,' replied Falakar.

Jontal stepped through the broken opening. Sholster stepped through next to lift his new club and lever up the trap. 'Is it safe?'

'I think so. But from now on, nothing is certain.'

'Comforting,' said the barbarian as he grabbed the weapon. He hosted the end up and the trap door began to rise. Jontal piled up fallen bricks beneath it to hold it firm.

'That's enough, we'll have to slide under,' said Jontal.

Sholster pulled his club away, the supporting bricks crumbled a little but held firm.

'Look at that!' he said inspecting his new acquisition. 'Not even a scratch.'

Jontal slipped under the barrier and gave the all clear on the other side. One by one, the group joined him.

'Stay in a single line and step exactly where the one ahead of you steps. Do not touch any part of the walls, and spread out enough to ensure that if the person in front of you stops suddenly that you are able to also without colliding. Whoever is following me stays a full ten paces back. If I stop, you stop.

Do not speak unless it is to warn of a problem. I want a bowman behind me. If we encounter anybody in here then it will be their job to stop them.'

Shinlay stepped forward unhooking her bow and strung it.

Jontal gave her a doubtful look. 'We must assume that you will get one chance, and that it will need fast reactions. You will be firing over my head. You cannot afford to miss.'

'You or the enemy?' she said flatly.

Jontal gave a pained look.

'There is no better with a bow or cooler head,' interrupted Kinfular. 'She will follow you.'

Jontal scratched at the back of his head and then began his slow advance.

--- 0 ---

Illestrael left Chayne. She had done all she could to help him control his fear ahead of his task. Now it was up to him. She headed off to meet with her Yhordi contact. She was overdue.

She made her way through the maze of corridors that threaded the palace. Similar networks existed within all major buildings across the Empire. They were known only to the Yhordi, even the labourers that built them where never allowed contact with other Ashnorians. The Emperor knew of their existence of course, but as the Yhordi couldn't officially exist, neither could the secret passages.

She stopped where a corridor intersected her own and turned right, counting twenty-one paces. The Yhordi were all taught a standard length of pace, when your life depended on not being a few inches from your intended position, you learned fast or died.

She faced the corridor wall to her left and spread her fingers out onto the surface and pushed. There was a click and a section of the wall opened away from her. She stepped through into the dimly-lit room.

319

'On time as ever.'

It was Maric. Some people used sarcasm to put people in their place. Maric seemed to have it woven into his character. He was shorter than her and had a wiry build. His ferret-like features gave the impression of somebody who enjoyed being vile and manipulative, which he did. He also craved control, just the kind the Yhordi Masters liked.

'What have you to report?'

'Little, I'm afraid.'

'I care nothing for your fears, operative. You were assigned to spy on the young Mlendrian. You have had plenty of time and my reports show that you have visited him many times. You expect me to believe that you have obtained nothing useful?'

Illestrael knew she had been spending too much time with Chayne. It was bound to be noticed. She needed to be careful.

'By whose authority am *I* being spied upon?' she said forcefully.

'Mine,' replied Maric comfortably.

'You're a Recorder, Maric. Only Field Controllers can sanction such an activity.'

Maric's pale lips spread into a repellent smile. He paused for a moment before opening an upper drawer to his desk. He pulled out a piece of official parchment and pushed it out onto the desk in front of him. It was a decree dated three days ago.

Maric had been promoted.

He retrieved the paper and replaced it lovingly back into the drawer which he closed with deliberate slowness.

He looked up again, his expression self-satisfied.

'If you cannot explain to me why you have nothing to report after such close contact with a client, then I'm afraid *I* will have to report your shortcomings and request that you are dispatched to a less strategic location.'

Illestrael knew the threat to be real. In his new role it would only take his word to have her shipped out to a lesser position. That would certainly not be in the palace, and probably to a minor population centre. It would remove many of her privileges and rewards. Her supply of Yan would likely stop also.

Maric pointed to the chair on her side of the desk. 'Sit down and think about it. Maybe some details will come to mind.'

Illestrael stared back into the man's narrow mocking eyes. She pulled out the chair, and sat down.

--- 0 ---

Jontal stopped at yet another intersection. It seemed that the passageways were arranged in layers, one per level, serviced by stairs that ran between one level and the next. Each intersection of stair with corridor occurred at regular intervals and was identical. Knowing one's position was therefore a matter of counting intersections from the point of entry and knowing where that would come out in the city. Whoever used these passages had an excellent memory and a solid mental picture of the layout of the city. Along the walls of each corridor were vague indications of more hidden doors like the one to the river area, each with a floor trap.

They climbed up until Stalizar believed they were at dungeon level. Jontal stood before a section of wall that had the markings of a secret door. Standing astride the floor trap, he probed the wall.

'The agent used her spread fingertips to unlock the door to the sewers,' offered Stalizar.

Jontal inspected the wall and found seven fingertip-sized marks that could be pressed with two hands. He arranged his hands carefully. Everybody stood poised for whatever lay on the other side.

Jontal pushed gently at first with the seven fingers. Nothing happened. He increased the pressure until the finger pads moved inwards slightly. There was the faintest of clicks and cracks outlined the door. It swung back into the passageway. In his weakened state he didn't react quickly enough and was pushed back off balance and started to fall onto the trap below. He panicked for a hand hold as his foot brushed the trap-plate. His wrist was gripped and pulled over his head, lifting his body from the floor. He looked to his side to Sholster. The giant wasn't even straining.

He was lowered back down.

He regained his composure and pulled the doorway inwards to its full extent. On the other side was blackness. The dim lighting from the passageway was masked by the open door, by design he suspected. There was a dry, acrid smell from within.

Shinlay took out her Glowstone and pushed it out into the dark. It tumbled across the floor for only a few feet before coming to a halt against what looked like storage shelves. The bottom shelf was lit enough to see rows of strangely shaped glass tubes and bottles.

Jontal moved to the Glowstone and lifted it to inspect his immediate surroundings. Everywhere was floor-to-ceiling shelves filled with various glass items. He walked around the room to a single door opposite to their secret entrance. He beckoned to the others.

ThreeSwords was the last in and closed the secret door.

'Any idea of our location within the palace?' asked Falakar.

Stalizar shook his head.

Jontal studied the new door. 'It isn't locked. Cover the stones.'

Shinlay and Sholster replaced the Glowstones in their leather pouches, placing the area once again in darkness.

Jontal placed his hand on the door handle and gently twisted the mechanism. The door opened a crack. A slither of eerie red light spilled through. He peered through before opening the door and leading them through.

The room was bathed in a deep red light with no apparent source. The walls were filled with an assortment of metal mechanisms and rows of bubbling glass jars of liquids. The strange light had the effect of blending the various textures together into shades of the single colour, blurring their edges.

Kinfular and ThreeSwords took up position at two sets of double doors on the left and far sides.

Jontal walked to the first jar in the process. It was being fed from a dripping hopper. It was difficult to tell its true colour due to the light in the room, so he caught one of the dark drips onto a dagger and inspected it.

'This smells like blood.'

Stalizar pushed his way through to the bandit and gripped the metal plates of his staff. A ball of light appeared around the blade. The liquid was a dark red. He smeared some across the blade, rubbing the residue between his fingers and smelling it, recoiling and looking up at the hopper.

'Pigs?' said Jontal.

Stalizar shook his head. 'Human.'

The ball of light then followed his gaze and widened to track along the bubbling jars. Each jar was fed from the previous via a glass tube. Various smaller jars of other coloured liquids were adding to the process at different stages. The last jar in the process held a clear liquid with a yellow tint. An almost imperceptibly small flow of it was filling the jar, and certainly only a fraction of the volume that was entering at the start into the hopper. Whatever this liquid was, it took a lot of human blood to manufacture.

Stalizar staggered and caught himself on one of the benches.

'Are you well?' enquired the Ranger.

Without warning the room began to ring out with sound. Everyone instinctively dropped to the floor and drew weapons. A drum-shaped mechanism within the process started spinning. It was getting faster and increasing in pitch and volume. It was already too loud to hear anything below a shout.

Kinfular looked to Falakar and mouthed the word, 'Alarm?'

Falakar shrugged his shoulders. Kinfular readied himself for an attack from the door.

Stalizar was now on his knees, hands clasped over his ears as the high-pitched whining continued.

Jontal caught Falakar's attention and indicated that they should leave. He nodded his agreement. The bandit moved to the left-hand double doors and the warriors took up their positions as before. He tried the door but it was locked. He took out his lock picks and got to work.

The noise of the whirling mechanism abruptly cut off leaving it to slow down making conversation possible again. Garamon noted that the Ashnorian mage was left behind and holding his head. He went back to him.

'What is wrong?'

Stalizar's eyes were closed, his head bobbing a little as if he were a distraught child.

Garamon placed a hand on the man's arm to get his attention.

Stalizar pulled away, looking fearful. When he realised that it was Garamon, he relaxed a little and removed his hands from his ears.

'What is wrong?' repeated Garamon.

'My people discovered a drug that returns youth. We have never been told the source of it,' replied Stalizar, looking up at the array of equipment.

'And this is how it is made?'

Stalizar nodded, wretchedly.

'But if people want to donate their blood in return for longer life, surely they have that right?' reasoned the young woodsman.

'You don't understand. This is the dungeon level. People are punished here for almost any crime. They are tortured in a way that produces blood. It is that blood that is in the hopper and used to create the plasma. The prisoners do not receive the result. Only the rich and the ruling elite receive it.'

Garamon took a step back from the Ashnorian.

'As a reward for my service to the Emperor I received thirty years of my life back. How much agony was endured to provide that to me?'

'And this is the fate of our people if they become part of the Empire?' asked Falakar.

'I did not know; I did not *know* ...' repeated the Surgeon to himself.

'Destroy it,' ordered Falakar, a dangerous tone in his voice.

'You do not understand. There are hundreds of dungeons like this across the Empire, four in this city alone. Destroying this will not stop it.'

'It's a start,' said the Ranger.

'Won't we alert the guards?' said Garamon.

'Don't worry about that,' replied Jontal, still intent on his lock-picking. 'Doors this thick are going to be soundproof. I guess because of the noise in this place,' he said nodding towards the spinning machine.

People started to move to the task, but Stalizar swept his staff across the line of equipment. The glass shattered were his staff pointed. Liquid flowed out onto the benches and cascaded to the floor, mixing and disappearing down drain grids. It took only moments to reduce the production line to a jumble of glass shards and twisted metal. Soon the only sound was the gently low hum of the spinning machine still slowing.

There was a click of the door lock which broke everyone's attention. Jontal replaced his tools and took out a tiny water skin. He untied the leather strap and poured a little oil onto each of the hinges.

'Ready.'

The group assembled.

Jontal's slender fingers slid around the straight handle and he pulled it slowly down until it stopped. He pulled the door open without a sound just enough to gain visibility beyond.

He opened the door fully. There was a passageway ending in another pair of doors identical to those they were currently behind. Halfway down on one side was an opening into another corridor. Sliding himself to the right side of the side passageway, he led them towards the right-hand corridor. He peeked around the corner.

He jumped back and dived away to the side. Kinfular took his cue and leapt forward to meet two guards that emerged. He ducked low under the first guard's attack, deflecting the quicker left-hand guard's blow with his shield and thrusting up under the right-hand guard's defence to take the man through the throat up into his brain. By the time he withdrew his sword the other guard was dead with an arrow through his armour into his heart from Shinlay's bow.

Everybody waited. There was no sign that they were heard.

'Main Plasma Storage. Unauthorised entry on pain of gradia ten correction and death,' read Stalizar from the sign on double doors behind the dead guards. It had a sophisticated-looking lock.

Jontal picked himself up from the floor and searched the guards. 'No keys,' he announced. 'And I won't be able to pick that quickly.'

'Let's try those,' said Falakar, pointing to the other doors at the end of the passageway.

The new doors had no lock. Jontal opened the door the merest crack and whistled quietly at the sight beyond. He entered and the others filed in behind him.

Garamon entered the room. It was filled with beds, ten abreast and three times that long. Each bed contained a single person dressed in a full-length red gown. More glass bottles, smaller than the ones in the previous room, were hanging from stands beside each one. The bottles contained the light yellow liquid from the end of the blood processing line. Some form of flexible tubing ran from the bottom of each bottle down to a glass device that looked like a hand-sized spider with legs pressed into the chest of each recipient around the heart. All of the occupants appeared to be sleeping.

The group fanned out towards the only other door in the room.

Stalizar picked up a board hanging from one of the beds and flicked through layers of parchment. At one of the pages he stopped. His eyes closed tight and he crumpled the parchments in his hand.

Garamon stood close by and waited with the man.

Stalizar spoke, his voice breaking with emotion. 'This person is receiving treatment to return just three months of his life.'

Garamon looked up at the liquid in the bottle. By his reckoning it would take days to accumulate enough for this procedure. He guessed what the Ashnorian was thinking: how much for his thirty years?

Across the room, Jontal inspected the next double doors. Opening one of them a fraction, he peered through, quickly closing it again. He signalled that there were two guards on the other side, facing away from them.

Sholster stepped forward. He gave his new club to Falakar and pointed to both doors, indicating an opening motion and then brought his hands together sharply. Jontal understood and oiled the second door's hinges and bolts. He then pulled the securing bolts free from the second door.

Sholster counted down from five with his fingers. On reaching zero both Jontal and Falakar pulled the doors open wide. Sholster jumped forward to envelop each of the guard's necks in his hands preventing them from calling out. He pulled them back into the room and the doors were closed. He smashed their helmets together several times until they slumped to the floor.

Shinlay took up some parchment and chalk from the nearest bed and drew the layout she saw beyond the doors.

'It stretches away to end into a small corridor. There is a single door to the right and a larger corridor to the left. I saw no other guards.'

'The end corridor?' queried Kinfular.

'It is not long and opens out into a larger area.'

Stalizar rejoined the group, his mood heavy.

Falakar took one look at the mage and frowned. 'I am sorry to be so cold after all that you have done for us, but we need to move quickly. If you cannot remain alert or keep up, then you will have to stay behind.'

'I am driven more than ever to complete this task, Mlendrian.' He looked to the map and stabbed a finger at the small end corridor. 'It is typical Ashnorian tactics to use a smaller passage to create a choke point where attackers can be held while reinforcements are called. The exit from the dungeons will be through there. Expect a small contingent of soldiers.'

Jontal opened the door and led the way. All was quiet. He reached the corner to the corridor and stopped, waiting for Kinfular and ThreeSwords to be ready. He peeked around and pulled back. Kinfular went forwards but Jontal held out his hand and stopped him. He put up two fingers on one hand and made a walking motion with two fingers on the other coming this way. He moved back behind the fighters. Everyone else moved flush to the wall.

As the two guards reached the opening, Kinfular and ThreeSwords leapt out gaining surprise and striking the guards in the throat to silence them. They held the guards and lowered them to the floor as their last breaths bubbled from their wounds.

All turned from the gruesomely precise attack to the small corridor. Standing there, mouth agape, was a young Ashnorian about twelve years old. He was clutching a number of scrolls.

Kinfular raised a finger to his lips and made the motion for quiet.

The boy yelled and ran, scattering the scrolls to the floor. The group gave chase. The boy disappeared from the far end of the short passageway screaming and shouting to someone unseen and pointing back towards the advancing party.

There was only room enough for a single engagement in such a tight corridor and Kinfular took the lead as a guard poked his head around the far end. His surprised was absolute as he spurted food from his mouth and dropped the bread he was holding to struggle for his sword. A shout went up and he and another guard jumped out to meet Kinfular. They pushed out their shields in a defensive stance, which in the confines of the narrow corridor made for an effective block against his slender blade.

'Sholster!' he called. The large barbarian charged past, holding his shield out flat. He crashed into the two defenders, hoisting them away with a roar. They flew back, giving the opening Kinfular needed. He burst out into the open area beyond with Sholster at his side. It was a guard post with a guard house. Two guards were in the antechamber at the foot of some stairs; they jumped over the two prone guards and engaged. An arrow from Shinlay's bow flashed to the right of Kinfular to disappear into the station room to a target out of view of the warrior.

Sholster swung his new weapon for the first time, smashing his guard back, flailing into the air. Kinfular blocked and struck out at the other. To Kinfular's right came two more guards from the room. ThreeSwords moved in to intercept, deflecting both initial thrusts from them.

Sholster brought his club down onto one of the first attackers he had knocked to the floor. The man brought up his shield. The sound was nauseating as the club split the shield in two, breaking the man's arm and continuing on to crush his chest.

The second one was having none of it and pushed himself to his feet and made for the stairs. Another arrow flashed from behind to take him in the back, knocking him forward onto the stairs. He slid back down, the flight wagging as the arrowhead ran over each step.

Kinfular finished off his man and moved in to help ThreeSwords. Between them they quickly ended the last two guards.

Kinfular moved into the guard house to check that it was clear. One guard remained, his hand pinned to a wooden support beam by an arrow. He was trying to release himself to reach a nearby chain that disappeared up into the ceiling. The man hadn't the time to don his helmet. Kinfular took advantage of the circumstances and cracked him over the head with his shield, knocking him out. He caught movement in the corner and noted the boy hiding under a table. He called to Shinlay to gag and tie the boy, hoping she would be less threatening.

The party regrouped and ascended the stairway.

Chapter 34 - Incursion

Without the warning bell from below, the two guards at the top of the dungeon stairway were caught by surprise and fell without a sound.

'This is the service level where the servants live,' explained Stalizar. 'Leave them alone, we will be ignored.'

'Won't they call the guard when we've passed through?' said Falakar.

'They are considered subhuman. No guards are used to protect them, nor are there facilities to raise an alarm. They would be punished even if they did.'

'That's horrible,' said Garamon.

'It is our way of life. We are born to it and conditioned to think nothing of it,' replied Stalizar.

They made their way quickly across the level following Stalizar, bringing them out under the location of Lathashal's main lab, albeit two levels below.

'You must prepare for greater resistance,' said the magii. 'This stairway will bring you out on the Administration level, which includes the senior palace staff living quarters. There will be more guards and they will be more proficient than those in the dungeons. Lathashal's main lab is one level above the Administration level. Your friend is likely to be there until he moves up to Lathashal's private lab, a further level above, and the room where the Rite will be cast.'

'You make it sound as though you will not be coming with us?' said Falakar.

'Being seen by servants is no threat to me, but my face is known to everybody in the palace above us. If Lathashal dies then I may still have a chance of reintegrating back into the palace in the confusion that will follow.'

'Then I thank you for your help,' said Falakar.

'Let us hope it comes to something,' replied the magii. 'If you survive your rescue attempt I will endeavour to reach you again.'

Falakar watched the man leave before looking up the stairs. He took a breath to calm and nodded to Kinfular at the lead. The barbarian began the ascent to the level above.

--- 0 ---

Illestrael left the uncomfortable presence of Maric. Her *interview* gave away more than she wanted. She held back as much as possible, but it was clear that the man had already gained some of the information. Until she had provided enough to satisfy him, she would not have been allowed to leave.

However, she did learn something unexpected. It was reported that a group of escaped Mlendrian prisoners had headed for the city. There was some evidence that they entered under the city via the old river channel. That would place them in striking distance of Stalizar. She decided to check up on him.

She took off in the opposite direction to the secret river entrance, winding her way around the various levels, taking the time to check out every corridor that led to the river level secret opening. Convinced that none of the paths that led to her destination were being watched and that she had not been followed, she proceeded to the final stairway. She was alerted to the sound of the river, and what that meant. The door was open. As no Yhordi would ever do such a thing it meant that the door was breached. She descended with care.

She found the released trap propped up upon broken bricks. She peered under. The secret wall-door was broken down. She moved under the trap and out into the river area. Seeing no sign of the Mlendrian intruders or Stalizar she headed to the machinery room. She saw the doors and slowed. One was missing and the other hung loose. There was a glistening slime that stretched from the doorway to the river. Whatever made it was huge. She looked to the river and shivered.

She moved to the opening of the room and inspected the inside from the doorway. Some of the larger machines were damaged, and some of the smaller ones were pushed out of place. Blood was prominent in two places. One high up on a machine, with some pooled below it, and a small amount not far in from the doorway, with a trail of drops leading off to the opposite side.

The place looked deserted as she entered. The floor from the doorway to over halfway in was covered in the same slimy residue that lead from the river. In places it was mixed with a darker green liquid. The doors were broken in from the outside using considerable force. They were covered in the same residue as the floor. She began studying the footprints in the slime. More than one person was involved.

She scouted the rest of the area. Apart from more pooled blood at the end of the trail from the centre, nothing else could be seen. Whatever came through those doors was repelled or got what it was looking for. She hoped that it wasn't Stalizar.

She thought of the secret doorway that had also been broken down. It was not likely to be discovered without prior knowledge of its existence. She also doubted that it could have been located so exactly without the use of a Master's magic.

Deciding that the magii was back in the Yhordi passageways, either as a willing guide or as a hostage, she returned to the secret entrance. Sliding back under the trap she removed the bricks, sealing off the entrance. She then considered in which direction the group may have gone. Mlendrian prisoners certainly wouldn't have attempted to enter the city and risk recapture without good reason. The fact that they arrived under the city only hours before the casting of the Rite to Rakasti seemed too much of a coincidence. She didn't know how such information could have been leaked to the enemy, or how they managed to organise all the elements so perfectly in advance.

With no better assessment, she headed off in the direction of Lathashal's laboratory.

--- 0 ---

Jontal jumped back and pushed himself flat against the wall as the others rushed past to engage the soldiers guarding the top of the stairs. All the while they maintained surprise they could easily defeat the defenders. The two guards fell without raising the alarm.

They had come out into one of the corridor recesses. Jontal looked around the end into the corridor ahead. It extended equally in both directions with the usual double doors at each end. There were no guards on either set of doors, and he led them out.

Garamon looked on in wonder. The difference between the stark accommodation of the servants' level and here could not be more extreme. Gold leaf adorned every trimming. The high, curved ceiling radiated a warm light from no source that he could see. The walls were made of white marble, which had been carved to depict a scene of a man conquering a vast army that stretched the length of the corridor on both walls. The floor was polished dark grey marble with flecks of gold that reflected the walls and ceiling. He had never seen anything so grand in his life. At regular intervals were recesses containing the cream-garbed servants. None had even flinched at the incursion or death of the guards.

'What do we do with these?' said Kinfular, standing in front of one, sword ready.

'They are no threat,' replied Jontal. 'As the mage said, they have no status and would be tortured if raised the alarm.'

'The Riaan will never give themselves to this,' uttered ThreeSwords.

'Which way now, thief?' said Kinfular.

Jontal shrugged, looking to each identical set of doors at either end of the corridor.

Garamon saw the impatience in the barbarian that he had seen many times before.

'That way,' he said, selecting at random.

Everyone looked at Garamon for explanation, but he simply shrugged too.

Falakar pointed that way and Jontal set off.

The door had no lock, Jontal stood back. Kinfular pulled open the door and rushed in to take down the two guards expected on the other side. The guards responded with usual surprise and would have been felled quickly if it had not been for four more soldiers walking away from them. They turned. One stood out from the others and had similar armour to the tower Captain they had encountered in the desert. He drew his longsword and spoke calmly to one of his escorts. The man retreated at speed towards the far end of the corridor and more double doors.

The Captain and his remaining two men reached the melee just as the two door guards fell. Kinfular, ThreeSwords and Sholster made a line, the rest spilled out behind them. Shinlay came out and spotted the retreating guard. Taking up a bead on his back, her line was interrupted by a tall guard who was engaging Kinfular.

Hearing her curse, Falakar saw the problem and flicked his small chopping axe up from his side.

'Get ready.'

Realising what the Ranger had in mind, she called out for Kinfular to duck. The warrior reacted leaving a clear view of the guard's head. Falakar threw his axe. The soldier caught a glimpse of the missile at the last moment and reflexively ducked. The axe went harmlessly over his head, followed by Shinlay's arrow that flew down the corridor to bury itself into the retreating guard's back. He slumped to the floor just short of the door, hand outstretched.

The Captain's two guards were now dismissed, leaving ThreeSwords in the centre to battle the officer. The Ashnorian made the near-fatal mistake of overconfidence against the outsider when one of ThreeSword's blades sliced by his hip, opening a minor wound. He jumped back to recover his stance and ThreeSwords moved with him, keeping him off-balance and pushing him back down the corridor.

The veteran began a frantic defence against the interweaving weapons of the Heslarian. He took a breath to call out for help, but the air was blown from his lungs as he hit the wall at the end of the corridor. The suddenness of the collision knocked his sword and shield from their position and ThreeSwords slipped both blades through the gap to silence him.

It was over in a minute and still no alarm had been raised.

'Three against seven and still they do not retreat. What drives these warriors to engage such odds?' said Kinfular.

'They believe we are inferior beings,' replied Jontal.

'They are in for a surprise,' remarked Sholster.

Chapter 35 - Bolt Hole

Falakar pulled back on his shield, blocking a vicious slash from the final guard. It opened the Ranger's counter attack and he slid his sword into the man's side. The guard's legs gave way and he fell. Kinfular stabbed his sword down to skewer the man through his exposed throat.

This was the sixth station so far and they didn't know how many more they would have to defeat. Jontal and Garamon remained as backup to the front line as Shinlay maintained her bow in readiness to prevent runners from raising the alarm ahead of them.

To keep their backs clear, they moved with incautious speed. As each guard point was reached so they rushed to engage, rapidly dispatching the soldiers. The plan was working, but they were running blind, diverting many occasions in an attempt to locate the next stairway upwards. They knew it was only a matter of time before the trail of dead guards was discovered, although the curfew was working in their favour as it seemed only the military were roaming the corridors.

'Come on,' said Falakar, drawing deep breaths, 'We cannot afford to stop.'

They moved off again and headed for a wide passageway that promised to head back in the right direction.

As they turned the corner, they were faced with a longer corridor. Two soldiers on both sides were guarding single doors halfway down. The corridor ended in the usual double doors. No guards were on this side of them.

Kinfular and ThreeSwords went left, Falakar and Sholster went right. One of the guards on the right side was far younger than the rest. He took one look at Sholster heading for him and dropped his weapons, running for the double doors. Sholster pursued, but was no match for the frightened boy. Shinlay stepped out to get a shot, but Sholster's bulk was masking the target. She waited until the last moment as the soldier reached the door and fired a weak arcing shot over Sholster's head. The arrow dipped and could only catch the bobbing target a glancing blow on the side of the helmet. It spun the helmet enough to cover his eyes, causing him to slam into the doorframe and stagger back. Sholster caught up and tapped him over the head, knocking him out.

The door then opened and a guard stepped through, about to berate the noisemakers. Sholster reacted quickly, poking his club forcefully into the man's face and snapping his neck. He ducked through the doorway to confront the other guard, raising his shield to block a powerful swing from the second soldier and returning a fatal downward blow that placed a long dent in the man's helmet.

The remainder of the group finished off their guards and stepped through into a large circular area. It looked like a hub for four corridors with doors opposite and on both sides. All the doors were closed and no guards were on this side.

Falakar pointed to the one that was in the right direction and they settled around it. Sholster opened it and Kinfular jumped through to take the two guards. But this time was different. In front of them was a huge corridor almost sixty paces long. At the far end was a set of extra-large double doors and eight guards, and what looked like a mage.

They had no chance of stopping runners this time.

Kinfular led the charge. Shinlay let loose an arrow at the far doorway and it caught a guard trying to leave. Over the door rested a small bust. It was smiling down as if mocking the raiders.

A second guard leapt over his fallen comrade and escaped through the door.

The mage prepared his manasphere and began to concentrate. Shinlay had three arrows remaining. She fired the first at him. He raised his hand and the arrow bounced off an invisible wall just as it was to strike him. She cursed. The mage smiled, matching the one from the bust above him.

She removed her second arrow and fired it at a slightly elevated angle. It flew over the mage's head and slammed into the forehead of the bust rocking it backwards. It hit the back wall and then pitched forward falling towards the mage below. He raised his hand to place the magical shield between him and the makeshift boulder. The bust hit the shield and cracked apart, falling harmlessly into pieces around him. He turned back to face the barbarian woman with an even greater smirk. But the second shot had more reason to it. The moment Shinlay let it loose she reached for the last arrow and fired it. His eyes only caught the briefest glimpse of the third missile as it plunged under the magical shield into his chest throwing him back against the wall.

Having exhausted her quiver she pulled free her sword and ran to join the front line of fighters ahead.

The men raced to engage the defenders. The corridor was wide and allowed all four warriors to engage together. The sound of metal rang out as the two groups came in contact. The new defenders were the most proficient yet and wearing heavier armour. Even so, it only saved them for a few extra moves from their attackers. Kinfular and Sholster dispatched their initial adversaries first, with ThreeSwords and Falakar taking a couple of moments longer. The two remaining guards fell quickly.

Kinfular leapt over the dead mage and through the doorway, giving chase to the guard that made the early escape.

A bell started ringing.

Falakar watched as Kinfular returned, jumping right back. There was the sound of many guards approaching from that direction.

'Not that way,' he said, and sprinted back towards Garamon and Jontal who were halfway down the corridor.

At that moment, many more guards appeared at the first end of the corridor, blocking an escape.

Jontal and Garamon looked around. Jontal took the only option and ran to a nearby door. He kicked it hard, but in his weakened state the door only rattled. But that didn't matter as an instant later Garamon's axe shattered the door from its hinges. He didn't stop the momentum of the swing and followed through with his body, grabbing and pulling the bandit with him.

Now it was a race between the two groups at either end of the corridor to make it to the centre door. Kinfular, ThreeSwords and Shinlay in their lighter armour were quicker than the armoured soldiers, and made it through. Sholster was slower and could only make it to the door as the quickest of the guards reached him. He swung his club around his head while still running and smashed it into the man's shield at chest height. The soldier flew back into the next layer of guards, scattering them and buying him the time to enter the room.

Kinfular covered the entrance, killing the first guard who attempted entry with a blade into his face. The others pulled up out of range.

Jontal and Shinlay scanned the area for escape. It was some kind of small banquet room. Several large tables were covered with pristine white linen table cloths and adorned with a vast quantity of sparkling silverware.

'There is nothing but this food service hatch,' reported the bandit.

'The windows?' said Sholster.

'Not unless you can fly,' replied Jontal looking down from one.

'Block the door,' commanded Falakar.

Sholster responded and snapped the nearest table cloth from a table. The cloth came clear, with all the silverware remaining. ThreeSwords burst into a brief moment of laughter. Sholster wasn't sure what he found more disturbing:

his unintended parlour trick or seeing the dour black man find something funny. He shook his head at both and placed his hands under the table and pulled. Despite his strength, the solid wooden table barely noticed the effort.

'It's too big in one piece,' he shouted.

Garamon lifted his axe and chopped at the beautifully polished surface. The axe dug deep. Two more strikes from the experienced woodsman and it split.

'Good work!' said Sholster. 'Here, give me a hand.'

With the lighter load and Garamon and ThreeSwords helping, the half-table began to move towards the door. Falakar left his position behind Kinfular and helped pull the monolith. At the appropriate distance from the door, Falakar and Sholster slid over to the other side. All four men lifted the edge, tipping the enormous weight up and over towards the door.

'Get out man!' called Sholster, and Kinfular leapt away.

The table crashed down against the opening, forcing back the nearest guard who attempted a stab at Kinfular's receding back. It left only a small portion of the doorway uncovered at the top, not enough for an armoured man to enter.

'Well I guess that will hold them for a while,' said the giant.

'Can we escape that way?' said Kinfular, pointing to the service hatch.

'It goes back down, and anyway, he'd never fit through,' replied Jontal, indicating Sholster.

Sholster sat down at the remaining half a table and pulled the table cloth up, tucking it into his chainmail shirt. 'Ring that bell lad,' he called to Garamon. 'I'm starving!'

Kinfular looked to Falakar. 'What now?'

Falakar shook his head. 'We have no way out and it's only a matter of time before one of their mages turn up.'

Garamon was checking over the hatch again when he heard a tiny click from his side. He turned his head to see a door-

341

shaped section of the decorated wall form a crack and turn away.

'Falakar!' he shouted, and leapt back.

Falakar moved forward to meet the attack. To their surprise a single female stepped out, placing a finger to her lips for quiet.

She scanned the room. Nobody moved.

'Where is the Mage-Surgeon?' she said in Mlendrian, quiet enough not to be heard from outside.

'Who are you?' replied Falakar.

'Tell me first about the magii,' she said insistently.

'We have no idea what you are talking about,' said Garamon.

Her eyes locked on him. She looked him up and down and cocked her head to one side. 'A little young for an enemy raiding party aren't we?' She then recalled a conversation with Chayne about his friend he'd left behind. The unusual axe in the hands of one so young was especially telling.

'Garamon?' she said, uncertainly.

Garamon looked to Falakar. The Ranger shrugged.

'Yes?' he replied warily.

She looked briefly surprised. 'I am Illestrael, a member of the Empire's secret police. I have been helping Chayne.'

'I have come to rescue him, can you take me too him!'

'Tell me off the Mage-Surgeon first.'

'He left us earlier.'

'Was he harmed?'

'Not by us,' replied Garamon.

'Then I shall help you. Your friend is risking his life as we speak to delay the war on your land.'

'I need to get to him,' said Garamon, indicating the door the woman was standing in.

'If this room empties then it will be known where you all must have gone. These passageways are also trapped and there are others of my kind that move through them. One person I may be able to smuggle through.'

'I cannot leave my friends,' replied Garamon.

'If your friend achieves his mission there is a chance that you can all escape. If he fails, then none of you will leave this palace alive.'

'Go,' ordered Falakar. 'We will hold out until you return.'

'Speed of the gods, boy,' said Sholster with a firm clasp of a hand on the back of Garamon's neck.

Garamon gave a last look to his friends, then followed the woman into the passageway. The secret door closed with the faintest of clicks.

'We must hurry, but be cautious,' said Illestrael. 'If we are discovered then all will be lost for both of us and your friends. Tread only where I tread, your life depends on it.'

Garamon nodded and started following.

They moved quickly to the first junction, turning left to rise up a long flight of stairs taking them to the next level. Upon reaching the top she turned left again and they moved along to the next junction and another stairway. From Stalizar's information, Garamon knew this to be the level that Chayne should be on. She turned right again and led them along the next corridor. It didn't take long before she stopped at a section of wall.

'This should be where your friend is,' she whispered. 'I must not be seen here.'

He nodded his understanding and prepared his axe.

'Well, well,' came a voice from further along the corridor. 'How unfortunate.'

It was Maric.

'I knew you couldn't be trusted, Illestrael. Since this young Mlendrian magii appeared, you've changed. Gone soft.'

Illestrael stepped forward and covered Garamon, who attempted to do the same to her.

'Do not attempt to engage him,' she cautioned. 'He is highly skilled in close combat.'

'Wise advice from the *collaborator*,' added Maric, moving closer. A pity you didn't use it to guide your own choices.'

'Listen to me,' she whispered behind her. 'I will not be able to stop him for long. You must unlock the door yourself. Have you seen how it is done?'

'Yes,' replied Garamon.

'The lock code is two-four, two-four-five,' she said holding her hands behind her and indicating those fingers on the appropriate hands.'

'Still plotting?' said Maric. 'Your time for that has come to an end. Just death or the torturer remains for you, I am delighted to say.'

On the edge of hearing, the chimes for midnight began.

'Do it now!' she whispered urgently. 'Beyond the twelfth chime, it will be too late.'

The first hour chime sounded. Garamon's attention turned to the secret door as the woman stepped towards the Ashnorian. It didn't appear to have a single marking to indicate where he had to place his flingers to open the secret lock.

The second chime struck.

Illestrael approached Maric. 'I don't think I ever bedded you?' she said conversationally.

Maric glanced briefly over her shoulder to the Mlendrian behind. He seemed to be studying the wall at the exact position of the door to Lathashal's private lab.

'You did. It's difficult not to find somebody in the palace that you haven't.' He kept moving slowly forward. They were less than ten paces apart now.

The next chime rang.

'Such a cutting remark,' she replied, side-stepping to block Maric's view behind her. 'Is that just your poor ego hitting back because you were so forgettable?' She drew her assassination blade. All Yhordi carried two knives, one for wounding and one for killing. The one she now held was small and coated with a deadly poison. It was so aggressive and destructive to human tissue that within a short time not even a Mage-Surgeon's magic could recover death.

Maric drew his.

The forth chime tolled.

Garamon frantically searched for the pressure points. He began experimentally pushing at various positions in the area that he saw Jontal use before. It was a dangerous tactic he knew, but he was out of time for caution.

Another chime.

He remembered his Glowstone gift. He retrieved it from its pouch and held it up to the surface. In the improved light, just perceptible to the eye, he made out a circular mark as the sixth chime rang out.

'Have you any idea what you have done, Illestrael?' said Maric, getting close now.

Illestrael thought about her life. She was eighty years-old, seventy of which were spent in the service of the Yhordi. Orphaned at an early age, they enlisted her at ten. Children made good spies - you didn't suspect them. Once older, she used her physical charms. She learned quickly and the Yhordi kept her on. Now, after all these years, it came down to this.

She locked onto Maric's beady eyes, and answered, 'Yes, for once in my cursed life, the right thing.'

She stepped forward to engage the man.

Garamon was unaware of what was happening between the woman and the other Ashnorian. He spread his hands over the wall, managing to locate the ten finger rings on the surface, resting a fingertip within each.

Four more chimes had gone.

He increased the pressure on the two fingers of his left hand and the three on his right. Nothing happened.

The tenth chime.

Remembering Jontal's attempt, he pushed harder. The lock released and the door came out towards him. Bright light spilled into the passageway.

Maric leapt. He prided himself on being an excellent Yhordi. The woman before him deserved to die and he had every right to enact that sentence as a Controller. He had to admit that she was a strikingly attractive woman, and the one occasion that she traded her body for information from him was an hour that replayed over and over in his mind. She was incredibly skilled.

His knife missed her body by a fraction and he then leapt away again from her weak counter strike. She was no match for him.

'You cannot defeat me, Illestrael. You're talents in bed far exceed your fighting prowess.'

'A pity the same isn't true for you then,' she replied, making a lunge forward. He darted to one side and threw his elbow out wide, cracking her across the cheek. She overbalanced and collided with the wall hard, passing him by. Now he was between her and the Mlendrian, but was enjoying the contest too much to care about him for now.

Bright light spilled out into the corridor behind him. She smiled. Maybe it was all going to be worth it after all.

'Time's up,' said Maric. He made his move in the shadow of his body. Too late she saw the blade. There was a sharp pain in her side.

Maric jumped away, avoiding the counterattack.

But there was none. Illestrael no longer cared. She had done her part and knew there was no antidote to the poison.

In the distance she heard the eleventh chime.

Chapter 36 - A trust betrayed

Chayne wiped his palms dry again. Timing would be everything when he attacked Lathashal. Minutes too soon and the master magii might not be far enough into the spell to leave him undefended. Too late and the spell would be completed and Lathashal would have full control of his magic again.

He never felt so afraid.

He went over the two spells again that he was going to use, recalling the complex energy patterns of the first spell that would hopefully disrupt any remaining magic shield around the Master long enough for the second spell - the electrical discharge - to stun him. It would cause him to lose his control of the enormous energies under his command, allowing the demon in the manasphere to gain the upper hand in the battle of wills.

Chayne wondered what kind of demon he'd find inside such a powerful manasphere. He pushed the vision from his mind. Such distractions were not good at this time. He wondered if Zystal remembered their arrangement, and wanted to check with the tiny creature. But he knew such an act would only serve to drain both of them at this critical time.

The mechanical timer in the lab indicated that it was time to leave.

In theory, using his authority as Lathashal's Zintar he should be able to walk to the lab and enter, as if Lathashal himself.

Did special orders prevail for such a night?

If not then the journey should be uneventful, as the curfew was now in force and only the military, Masters and royalty were allowed to wander the palace unchallenged. It all seemed so easy. He wished he felt that way.

He composed himself. Lathashal would already have begun to weave the powerful magic that would unite the energies he had prepared over the last weeks. The thought of confronting the master magii almost froze him to his bed. He thought back to his abduction and the fear that held him to the spot in his cabin. He had come a long way in such a short time and learned so much, but now without Illestrael's relaxation methods and, ironically, Lathashal's intense training of his mind, he would be frozen again.

He stood up, his legs shaking. He knew that if he didn't get control of his fear then he would turn whatever chance he had of success into disaster.

He picked up his manasphere upon which so much depended for him and his people. The thought helped to give him strength.

He left the laboratory and headed towards the stairway that would take him up to the next level. He'd never felt so vulnerable. Two guards turned the corner ahead of him. He fought down his panic. This was the first test. The two guards recognised him and walked on. He completed the short walk to the stairway that would take him up to Lathashal's level. He climbed the stairs to the door at the top. A guard on the other side opened the inspection hatch and confirmed his identity. This was the second test.

The door was unlocked and opened.

He stepped through.

His mind clouded and he didn't know which way to go. A journey he had made in his head a hundred times. He forced himself to focus. The confusion subsided and he blinked it away. Turning in the correct direction, he walked casually to Lathashal's private lab. He could see two guards positioned outside the room. They were never there before!

He faltered.

The nearest guard caught the movement and turned to look at him. He turned back to look straight ahead.

Were the guards given orders to prevent anyone from entering as extra protection afforded the casting of the Rite?

Chayne walked up to the door. The soldiers did nothing.

He knocked.

The door opened to reveal one of Lathashal's servants. This was the third test. Upon seeing the Zintar, he stepped back into the room allowing him entry. Chayne stepped through to the antechamber. He wasted no time to allow his nerves to get the better of him and fell into meditation and began silently reciting the chant that Illestrael taught him. He finished it, opened his eyes and headed for the door to Lathashal's laboratory room.

This was the last test.

As he approached so a servant opened it ahead of him. Bright light poured out of the room, cutting into the subdued lighting of the antechamber. He stood for only a second and then walked through, squinting as his eyes became accustomed to the unusually bright light.

There was also a strong metallic smell.

Lathashal stood on a dais in the middle of the room some fifteen feet away. He was holding his staff in one hand and resting the fingers of the other on a large manasphere raised from its container and sitting on a pedestal. He was concentrating deeply as Chayne hoped and was unaware of his presence. Chayne placed his own much smaller manasphere on the nearest bench and lifted the lid. He raised the orb inside to its upper position until it clicked into place, and then rested the fingers of both hands upon its surface.

He looked again upon the still form of the Master. Even with so much at stake and the wickedness that the man represented, it still seemed wrong to defeat him in such a cowardly way. He withheld such thoughts as it was time to act.

He began to draw the power from his overloaded orb. It was agonisingly slow to build up the vast amount of mana within it, but at least there was no sign of the little demon going against their agreement. He waited patiently, ensuring that the spells would be released exactly as planned.

When the mana was ready, he opened his eyes to target the magii. The man was still deep in meditation, oblivious to the threat.

Chayne took a cleansing breath, held out his hand and focused every last ounce of his concentration and released the spell. Energy burst from his hand in a blaze of violet-coloured light and struck Lathashal's magical shield. The master magii opened his eyes. The energies plied against each other in a dance for domination.

Chayne's feed of mana continued to pour from his orb. It seemed for a moment that his spell would be too weak, but then Lathashal's shield flickered, spluttered and failed.

Chayne snapped his will to throw the remainder of the orb's reserved mana into the electrical discharge that would destabilise Lathashal's concentration. A bolt of blinding lighting flashed into the stricken Master, exhausting the remainder of Chayne's mana and sucking all strength from his body to collapse to the lab floor.

Lathashal looked down upon his attacker, terror showing at what his trusted Zintar had done. His face contorted and twisted, the beginning of the contest of wills between him and the demon within his own manasphere. He cried out, buckling and twisting. He began to sob in between the cries of pain and his head ducked down to his chest in a spasm.

But then the sound began to change. The sobbing transformed into a cackle. The master magii lifted his head and was grinning with a look of pure malice. The magical shield that Chayne believed destroyed returned with such power that the air could be seen to shimmer around the dais.

'You truly believed I would succumb to such a feeble assassination attempt? I have lived for over three hundred years boy, in the most corrupt and villainous political structure across the six continents of the world. You have dared to pit your pathetic plans against me!'

Chayne began to back away, looking to the door.

Lathashal made the merest movement with his staff and the door slammed shut.

'But the spell, the Rite? You were supposed to be vulnerable,' accused Chayne.

'Oh, I delayed the start of that to deal with my traitorous Zintar.'

'You knew?'

'You think you are the only one to delve into the secrets of a manasphere? Your little friend is being shown the folly of his dissention even as we speak.'

Chayne looked down at his orb. An almost imperceptible beam of red light connected it to Lathashal's larger version.

'You see, demons have a strict hierarchy. The lower castes must be subservient to those above them. You asked your diminutive conspirator to pit his power against a far more powerful entity.'

Chayne closed his eyes in anguish at the thought of the tiny demon being subjected to the horrors that demonkind must be capable. Then he felt his feet become light against the floor. Opening his eyes he saw that he was rising. Lathashal was pointing his staff at him and levitating his body. He rose above the level of the bench. Lathashal flicked his staff causing him to be slammed into the wall behind, knocking the breath from him. He was held there.

'Such hopes I held for you, boy. The potential you possess is exceptional, even greater than my own. And now you throw it all away on some hopeless attempt to delay an inevitable war. Even if you killed me I would be replaced.'

He turned his staff making Chayne's head press hard against the wall.

'And now it is with the greatest of regret, but also my ensured personal gratification, that I must bring the evening's penultimate entertainment to its conclusion. You have truly been a wonder to me boy. I shall miss you.'

In the distance, the palace chimes were halfway through their tolling.

Lathashal again pressed his staff forward the smallest amount. Chayne felt his body flatten an inch.

Lathashal repeated the movement. Chayne felt some ribs crack and the last air in his lungs burst from his mouth spraying blood along the wall. He could just make out Lathashal's smiling face as he watched his Zintar's final moments.

The eleventh chime rang out.

There was a noise from across the room and he caught movement behind Lathashal on the far wall. In a blurry oxygen-starved hallucination he thought he saw his old friend Garamon walk from the far wall.

Then the pressure on his body reduced a little, enough for him to take a painful breath.

'Leave him alone you bastard son of a whore!'

Lathashal glanced behind him. 'And the surprises just keep coming.' With both hands occupied, he gestured with his head toward the woodsman to throw his magic.

The axe Garamon held flared in a brilliant blue flame and he was thrown weakly backwards to hit the wall. He slid to the ground dazed.

Lathashal looked momentarily annoyed, but seeing that his attacker was unable to rise for the moment, turned his attention back to Chayne.

'It seems that your friend is as unusual as yourself. But it is of no consequence, I'll deal with him in a moment.'

The twelfth chime rang.

'And now my troublesome Zintar, you shall join your demon in the pits of hell.' He pressed his left hand down fully onto his manasphere and called forth Exinn.

'*Is it time?* came the expectant voice of the powerful demon.

'Exactly midnight. He is all yours.'

Exinn stretched out his consciousness into the master magii as agreed. He briefly entertained the idea of taking full control of his body before becoming aware of several powerful spells that were in place to safeguard against such an action. He looked through his temporary eyes into the human world. The young magii was there, in no position to resist. He stretched out his will through his host's physical form and levitated the young human closer to him. Once within range he forced the human's hand out to lie upon the manasphere. Chayne convulsed at the touch.

Exinn delighted at his terror. He began to draw mana through the helpless body to open the portal back to his land. Inside the manasphere a red glow appeared and started to expand to reveal Exinn's home. He pulled in ever more energy until the portal fully opened. Feeling elated after so many years of confinement, he focused on the human's heart. Just one further thought and it would be ripped from his chest to be taken back with him. It was even more potent than he had detected.

A terrible pain ripped through his chest. Without thought for true reasoning he looked down.

No, not *his* chest!

The pain was excruciating, like nothing the demon ever felt before. He had no choice but to withdraw back into the manasphere out of the human.

With control returned to his body, Lathashal's eyes snapped open. He looked down at his chest and saw several inches of bloodied axe blade protruding from it. There were brightly glowing blue runes on the blade.

'No!' he gasped in a spray of blood. 'Im-possible!'

He looked to his left hand. It was starting to burn onto the orb. He attempted frantically to pull it free, but it was stuck. He tried to shout out, the emerging sound strange and strangled. Terror engulfed him as he fought with the demon.

Mortally wounded and fighting for breath he could not maintain enough control.

Exinn returned. He placed his hand upon the magii's chest over his heart. With Chayne unconscious and Garamon behind, neither saw a ghostly scaled hand appear, its claws extending towards Lathashal's heart.

'What are you doing!' shrieked Lathashal within the orb. 'It is the boy that you want, he harbours the greater power!'

'*Maybe so, human,*' said the demon. '*But the pleasure I shall gain from inflicting agony upon you for my many years of enslavement will make up for that.*'

'You cannot, I command you to stop, I am greater than you!' screamed Lathashal. But his physical body was near death. With his diminished power divided between trying to keep himself alive and attempting to hold back the demon, he could do neither effectively. He watched as the demon's curved claws extended into his flesh to close around his heart.

Garamon heard the mage's struggling abruptly stop. The man slumped to the floor. His staff balanced for a moment before toppling over to clatter on the ground.

'Chayne!' he called out.

But just then a knife was slipped around his throat from behind. 'Never leave your back exposed, heathen slime,' whispered Maric into his ear.

Garamon felt his attacker's body tense for the killing cut and saw his hand pass across his throat. But instead of feeling the blade slide through his flesh, the man fell way.

'What an ironic epitaph,' said Jontal, pulling his own poison dagger from the Ashnorian spy's spine.

Garamon leapt onto the dais across the dead mage to his friend.

'Chayne!' he said urgently, lifting his friend's head.

Chayne began to stir, grimacing at the pain from breathing with broken ribs.

'What happened?' he whispered, using as little breath as he could for the task.

Garamon looked around the place. 'You're just not asking the right person on that one, old friend.'

Chayne blinked away the mistiness in his head.

'*Garamon?*'

'Yup. Across mountains, deserts and against unthinkable odds to bring me here, in what I can only describe as the nick of *all* time.'

Chayne couldn't respond to his friend's happiness. 'Help me up a little,' he said. 'Slowly through, I have some cracked ribs I believe.' Garamon did so.

Chayne looked down at the fallen corpse of Lathashal. His chest was ripped open, not only by the woodsman's weapon, but also over the heart. The demon had successfully opened the portal to his plane and took the master magii's soul with him. He thought of the horrors the man would suffer. He vowed to himself that he would never again sacrifice another life in such a way.

'I love reunions,' interrupted Jontal, 'but I think we have a pressing matter below?'

Chayne looked up enquiringly.

'This is Jontal ... long story. I have some special friends down below. They are currently under siege in a room. If we don't get them out soon there will be a lot more deaths.'

'Get me to my feet,' said Chayne.

Garamon helped him to stand. Chayne winced at the pain in his chest.

'Take me outside.'

A servant left a recess and opened the door as they approached. As they entered the next room, Chayne made a movement with his hands and a servant opened the door to the corridor.

Chayne called out in Ashnorian, 'Captain! Enter at once.'

One of the guards turned and entered the room. Eyeing Garamon's appearance in the room he went to draw his sword.

'The Master Lathashal has been assassinated,' explained Chayne, holding up a hand. 'This Mlendrian, and another inside, killed the assailant and saved my life. As the Master's chosen Zintar, I invoke the emergency power of provisional authority. I need you to bring the other members of the assassin's team to me for preliminary interrogation as is my right. They are not to be harmed. You will find them...' started Chayne, looking to Garamon. 'Where are you friends?'

'Two floors down,' answered Garamon. 'A room with tables, polished silverware, fine tablecloths. It has a service hatch.'

Chayne translated.

The Captain thought for a moment. 'The ancillary banquet room, Administration level, North Wing. Yes, Zintar.' He turned and disappeared into the corridor, giving an instruction to the other guard there.

'You've been busy,' said Garamon, amazed at his friend's grasp of the language as well as his command of the soldiers.

'Well a man could die of boredom waiting to be rescued,' said Chayne.

They shared a brief smile.

'Get me back into the lab.'

'Are we safe?' enquired Garamon as they returned to the room.

'For now. My authority will be challenged but should hold sway for you and your friends for a few hours yet. Now let me thank my other rescuer.'

Jontal was nowhere to been seen.

'Out here!' came Jontal's urgent tones from somewhere in the passages.

'There was a woman who helped me too, although I don't know who she was,' added Garamon.

'Woman?' enquired Chayne.

'Dark hair, slim, pretty,' described Garamon. 'She was delaying the other dead guy while I entered here.'

As Chayne crossed out into the passageway he saw Jontal kneeling over a fallen figure. Ignoring the spasms in his chest he hurried to them, fearing the worst.

'I am not familiar with the poison,' said Jontal regretfully. 'I have given her the strongest general antidote I carry, but it's not enough.'

Chayne knelt down.

'Illestrael,' he said gently, lifting her upper body into his lap.

Her eyes flickered open and she looked into his. She managed a half smile.

'It worked?'

Chayne nodded. 'What do we do to fix this?' he said.

'There is no cure, my love,' she said, her face screwing up in a spasm of pain. It passed quickly.

'You must help Stalizar,' she continued. 'He risked his life for you and your friends.'

'We must get you to him,' replied Chayne frantically.

Illestrael shook her head. 'The poison has been perfected over many lifetimes. It takes only moments to do its work beyond the skill of the finest magiis. I am already past that.'

'You're sure Lathashal is dead?' she asked.

'Consumed by his own manasphere. Gone forever.'

She managed another smile, but then stopped. 'You don't think I'll meet him in the afterlife do you?'

'Not where he went,' replied Chayne seriously.

Another spasm racked through her body making it arch up into Chayne for a moment then settle back down again.

'Why did you do this for me?' he whispered.

She looked deeply into his eyes, flicking from one to another as if searching for something.

'I have never known love. I cannot remember my parents, and the Yhordi filled my soul with deceit and lies. You are innocent and the first person I ever met that was selflessly caring. But there is something else.'

Chayne stroked her hair. It was sodden with sweat from the poison. The light in her eyes was fading; he knew she didn't have long.

She blinked a few times as if responding to some minor pains. Her hand lifted with effort to touch his face. He held it in his. She stroked her light fingers across his cheek.

'You are a Legend Walker,' she said, her words falling to a merest whisper. He moved his head down closer to her.

'I don't understand,' he replied, shaking his head. A tear dropped from his cheek to land on hers.

'It is a saying of my people. The rest of us are governed by destiny. But for a few, legends are created in their footsteps.'

He smoothed his fallen tear from her cheek with his thumb.

'May I ask something of you?' she said, forcing the words out through another stab of pain.

'Of course, anything and I shall see it done.' Tears now welled into his eyes and began to fall freely.

She tried to pull at his hand, to bring him closer, but she had no strength. He brought their heads together.

'I have tried to save your people ...'

Her hand managed one more weak grip upon his arm.

'... try to save mine.'

Her eyes then took on a moment of fear before her arm relaxed and her head slumped into him, her eyes closed.

He pulled her close into him, rocking her gently.

He kissed her once.

'You have my word,' he replied.

He laid her gently to the ground.

He stood and turned to Jontal. 'You are Mlendrian?'

'I am,' replied the bandit, who although facing a far younger man, felt an authority about him that should be obeyed.

'Ensure there are no traces of our presence here and bring the other dead man to this position. Arrange the bodies to appear that they killed each other in these passages. You can find your way back to the others?'

358

'Yes,' replied Jontal.

'Hurry then, you must be with them before the guards I sent reach your friends and convince them to remove their barricade.'

Jontal and Garamon retrieved Maric's body. Jontal arranged them to look like both managed a fatal strike on the other with their poison daggers.

Chayne returned from removing all evidence of Garamon and Jontal from the lab and took one last look upon Illestrael. If there was one such as she that could be turned, then there were others. He thought of the Lan-Chi and remembered the words of the mysterious man behind the bright lanterns: 'The people think you are the Zil'Sat'Shra - the saviour.'

He turned from the bodies and stepped back into the lab, closing the secret door to see it seal perfectly with the enclosing mosaic.

Up until now he hadn't looked beyond defeating Lathashal, expecting to die in the process either way.

Now, like it or not, he owned a new goal, one for which he had the beginnings of an idea how to achieve.

Chapter 37 - Twist of intention

Garamon returned through the secret passageways with Jontal and stepped back into the banquet room. There was a negotiation in progress between Falakar and an Ashnorian speaking in Mlendrian on the other side of the table outside of the room. As they stepped into the room, Jontal sealed the door and they both re-joined the others.

'The Ashnorian mage is dead,' said Jontal quietly.

'You did it?' replied Falakar, amazed and relieved to see both of the men returned.

'It was our young woodsman here. By the time I reached the scene the mage was dead with an axe embedded in his back.'

'Then it is time for us to do our part,' said Kinfular, 'and let this Empire know what they face in invading our people.'

Garamon shook his head. 'There is no need to sacrifice ourselves. My friend has some kind of temporary authority that will sway the guards. We must allow ourselves to be captured and taken to him for interrogation. I think he has a plan that will enable us to escape.'

'I don't like the sound of that!' replied Sholster.

'Nor I,' said Kinfular. 'The man has been here too little time to have made such a position of authority. I do not wish my final act to be a pointless surrender caused by another's delusions of power.'

Falakar held up his hand before Garamon gave a heated reply and looked to Jontal. 'What say you in this?'

Jontal shrugged. 'I only spoke to the young man for a few moments. He's level-headed enough. And the woman spy who contacted us gave her life for him. Ashnorians are governed by strict laws and rules. It is possible that he has the authority he claims.'

'I shall not speak for all of us in this decision, said Falakar. 'Each person must decide for themselves. I will choose to trust in the young mage.'

'I will too,' said Garamon predictably, moving alongside Falakar.

Jontal rubbed a hand down the half-stubble on his face, staring at his dagger in contemplation and looking to the door. He sighed, pushed his dagger back into its sheath and moved to join his brother too.

'Hlenshar?' said Sholster, looking to his leader.

'If there is a chance to return and convince the tribes to prepare for war, then we must take it. 'We shall put our faith in this mage,' he said finally.

Under heavy escort they were taken through the palace to stop outside of a room busy with soldiers and servants going in and out. The lead guard spoke to a senior soldier within the room and they were taken inside. Garamon saw Chayne sitting on one of the plush divans. He looked exhausted and was receiving treatment from a Mage-Surgeon.

The Captain that Chayne sent to retrieve the invaders walked up to him and stood to attention. 'The prisoners for your interrogation, Zintar.'

'Take them into the lab and remove all other officials and servants. I will interrogate them privately.'

'But that is not regulation. You should have a personal guard at least. These men killed the Master Lathashal.' said the man, alarmed.

'Captain, you will address me as Zintar at all times,' said Chayne in his most Lathashal-style bark.

'Yes Zintar!' replied the man, snapping even more to attention.

'I thank you for your concern,' continued Chayne, 'but the Master Lathashal was not killed by these men. A man appeared from behind him from nowhere. I witnessed the whole thing. He was Ashnorian. He attacked the Master and then struck me unconscious. You may post four guards including yourself outside of this door if you must. If you hear me call, then I give you the permission to enter.'

'Yes Zintar, thank you,' said the Captain. He moved to the lab and began ordering the evacuation.

Chayne led Garamon and the others into the lab as the final occupants were leaving. Lathashal's body had been removed and there was no sign of blood. The staff lay exactly where it had fallen though. It was now the possession of the Zintar and was his to hold alone. Falakar was last in and closed the door.

'Plotting is a way of life with the Ashnorians,' said Chayne. 'Sound does not escape these inner sanctums easily so we can talk freely. Oh, and this room is filled with powerful magical items, some of them will kill from a single touch.'

Sholster tried to move away from every surface at once. He started to perspire.

'I cannot begin to imagine how you reached me, I am more grateful than I have time to express. You have saved my life and delayed the start of a war with Mlendria.'

'We are aware of it,' replied Falakar. 'The rest of us are here to collect information on the attack. Your rescue coincided with that goal.'

'Ah,' said Chayne. 'Well I'm afraid you may have wasted your time. While the mage you killed knew the details of the attack, he imparted none to me. But that is largely irrelevant. My authority does not extend beyond the palace to provide you passage out of Ashnoria.'

'I may be able to help there.' The voice came from the far side of the room. There was no one there. Stalizar removed his hood and became visible.

'What trickery is this!' gasped Sholster.

Stalizar!' cried Chayne.

'I apologise for my dramatic method of entrance, there was no other way that I could reach you quickly enough.'

The magii walked over to Falakar pulling out a scroll case. 'These are my copies of the plans for the invasion. They are missing the sections that have no relevance to my field Medicinii posts, but as soldiers need medical attention across the entire front line you should have a reasonably complete picture for your purposes. You should understand that with the events of tonight, these plans will change, perhaps considerably.'

Falakar took the plans. 'We should at least get a good idea of how the General thinks. That will be valuable.'

Stalizar nodded. 'But now to the more complex problem of your escape,' continued the Ashnorian.

'Eight of those disappearing tricks would be a good start,' ventured Jontal.

Stalizar smiled. 'Unfortunately, Shroud Invisibilitii only have enough power for a few minutes of operation, and I doubt enough exist across the entire north of the Empire for you all.'

Jontal's face fell. The thought of having such an item was almost too intoxicating to imagine.

'I can place a spell on an item that each of you carry. It is normally used to aid my healers when in the fighting zone. It isn't invisibility, but it helps onlookers to ignore you if you do nothing to attract attention. It will also prevent your detection from general long range magical scrying. It will last a few days only. Hopefully that will be enough.'

'We're not going to be inconspicuous as we attempt to walk out of the palace,' pointed out Falakar.

'I think I can help there,' replied Chayne. He opened the door.

'Captain, I need a message sent to Captain *Whitehawk* in the Eastern sector.'

'I am sorry Zintar, I am unaware of any Captain by that name.'

From the corner of Chayne's eye, one of the other soldier's head turned. The man walked over to the Captain and stood to attention.

'Excuse me sir. I am aware of the Captain the Zintar is speaking of. He is a new appointment from the southern districts. I can deliver the message.'

The Captain frowned. 'And how is it that you have heard of him and I have not, Corporal?'

The man hesitated for only a moment.

'I apologise Captain, but I overheard some of the other men discussing the new Captain. They said he was young and inexperienced and did not compare favourably to you, sir.'

The captain snorted. 'You had better believe it. You may deliver the Zintar's message.'

'Thank you, Captain,' said Chayne and turned to the soldier. 'The message is sensitive and I wish only for you to hear it.'

'Yes Zintar,' said the man sharply and followed Chayne into the lab room with the others.

When the door was closed Chayne turned to the man. 'You are certain you know of this Captain Whitehawk?'

'No Zintar. Captain Whitehawk does not exist.'

'Explain yourself?'

'The Lan-Chi sends their regards.'

Chayne relaxed. 'This man is part of the Ashnorian resistance. For now their interests are the same as yours. They wish to delay, or even stop the war.'

He addressed the soldier again. 'I need these people to escape back to the mountains. Can you get them out of the city?'

'Contingency plans have already been drawn up for that possibility and for their safe passage as far as the desert. There will be an administration error incorrectly ordering them back to the mines. On route there will be an attack on the transport and they will escape. From there we can do nothing for them.'

'We have that covered,' reassured Chayne.

'Your orders to Captain *Whitehawk* are therefore to provide an escort immediately. My authority will only last until some senior soldier has the courage to wake a member of the palace elite. That will give us another hour or two. These people must be out of sight of the palace by then.'

'I understand,' said the man. He spun on his heels and left the room.

'We leave so soon?' asked Garamon.

'You shall leave soon,' said Chayne.

'You mean us?' corrected Garamon.

Chayne knew it was pointless trying to soften up his next words.

'I cannot go back with you.'

Garamon stood stunned. 'But that's mad. We're here to rescue you and you have a means to escape,' he replied, wide-eyed.

'It is ungrateful beyond reason of me to stay, but -'

'Then you shall come with us. The journey out cannot be more perilous than the one here.'

'That is certain,' injected Jontal in the background.

'It is not a question of danger,' replied Chayne.

'Then what could possibly entice you to stay in this godforsaken place!' questioned Garamon heatedly.

'The people of Ashnoria are oppressed to the point of rebellion. There is too little time for me to explain the complexity of the various factors at work, but my appearance has coincided with a prophecy. The word is spreading that the time for deliverance is coming.'

'Through you?' said Falakar.

Chayne shrugged. 'The Empire is built upon a huge social divide. The servants are less than slaves. There are many and they would like to see an end to their oppression. Given a medium through which they can unite, they could bring the Empire down, removing the threat to us forever.'

'And they will rally to you?'

'I am far from understanding my role yet, or how I could influence the masses,' Chayne replied. 'But yes, it is something like that.'

'But the rulers would have you killed,' said Kinfular.

Stalizar's deep tones cut in. 'It is not as simple as that. At all levels, the Empire exists in a constant state of fear and suspicion. Anything or anyone that has influence is utilised. Those who do not have it will attempt to get it. Those that have it will protect it. Only as a last resort will any faction destroy such a powerful political lever. In fact one such attempt has already been made against your friend. Another group stepped in and saved him, in that case the Lan-Chi.'

'These are not your people, you do not have to do this,' argued Garamon.

'The events of tonight will likely delay the war a few months at most,' explained Chayne. 'With my help I believe I can extend that and buy you more time. There are even factions that would avoid the war altogether.'

'Is that possible?' said Falakar to Stalizar.

'There will be political upheaval and jostling for position after the death of Lathashal. He was the most senior magii in the city. Also the spell he failed to cast tonight has deprived the Attack General of crucial information about your Ranger positions in the mountains. He will want the spell to be recast. That alone will take weeks to prepare.'

'Then I will stay,' said Garamon.

'No, you cannot,' replied Chayne.

'It is my choice. I'm staying with you,' replied Garamon resolute.

'And what would you do?' replied Chayne.

Garamon faltered for a moment, surprised that his friend was being so unsupportive. 'I could join this Lan-Chi you speak of.'

'The Lan-Chi exists only because they are Ashnorians going about normal Ashnorian duties. There is no way you would pass as one of them. We don't look like them and you certainly would not get far without speaking the language. You would quickly be uncovered and jeopardise the lives of those hiding you.'

Garamon looked around for help. None came.

'I am sorry, Garamon,' consoled his friend. 'You must return and convince your father of the coming war. He will have great sway with both the Tiburn people and the Rangers. Besides, anyone else may bend to doubt. All the time you are on the other side, I know help will be coming.'

Garamon fought down his emotions at the unfairness of it all. He knew Chayne's reasoning was correct. He couldn't risk for the warning to be ignored and had to convince his father.

Chayne sat down on one of the lab's high stools. He was weary beyond belief. The knowledge that he tried to kill someone and that he was capable of doing such a thing disturbed him gravely. He wondered if he'd ever have to do such a thing again, and whether he could. He would never have contemplated doing such a thing before he came to Ashnoria. It told him that every day he stayed here was a day further away from recovering his old life.

He watched as the group before him planned their strategy and tactics for escaping. He could see Garamon sitting back, coming to terms that his efforts had not rescued his friend. In truth, he dearly wanted to go with them and rid himself of this place. But he knew he would never be able to sleep safe in his old cabin knowing that war would come at any time. At least here he might be able to do something about it.

He watched as Stalizar, in between answering questions to aid the escape, busied himself with each person's personal avoidance spell. Chayne was again amazed at the breadth of the surgeon's magical knowledge. He seemed able to form his will to almost any task. But then he remembered that the man was many years older than his body portrayed. He wondered how many other people he had met were similarly treated.

The door to the lab opened and a soldier with the insignia rank of Sub-Captain walked in. He scanned for Chayne.

'Zintar,' he said in the usual formal military tones. 'I have been sent on behalf of Captain Whitehawk. These are the prisoners I am to escort to the dungeons?'

'They are,' replied Chayne. 'Ensure no harm comes to them Captain. Remember you carry the Master Lathashal's authority through me. Use it if required.'

'Yes, Zintar,' replied the soldier dipping his head in salute.

Garamon stepped up to his friend. 'I cannot believe I am going to leave you here.'

'I am turning down that which I have dreamed of for months. I also feel absurdly ungrateful after all that you have been through to rescue me.'

'I will see you again, won't I?'

'If I survive this place, I promise I will return.'

'Good luck,' said Garamon, pulling his friend in for an embrace.

'To the both of us,' replied Chayne, uneasy with such intimacy.

'There is little time, Zintar,' urged the Sub-Captain.

Chayne nodded. 'Go now or our subterfuge will be uncovered.'

Garamon looked at his friend a last time, not wanting to leave him so soon after his journey to find him. He then fell into position with the others.

The Lan-Chi Sub-Captain assembled his men in guard formation around the group and they moved out.

'I shall leave also,' said Stalizar. 'There are many wounded from your friends' incursion tonight.'

'What will happen to you now?' asked Chayne.

'History is written by the survivors. Lathashal would have been too embarrassed to file a formal report of what happened with me. I shall ensure that the story becomes suitably vague to allow enough doubt for no charges to be brought against me.

'Politics, Stalizar?' mocked Chayne, referring to the Mage-Surgeon's claimed aversion to the practice.

But Stalizar remained serious. 'Times are changing.'

Chayne stood from his stool, and bowed. 'Good luck, Master.'

'And to you, Zintar.' Stalizar pulled his cloak about him and whispered a word, then vanished.

Chayne opened the door for the Mage-Surgeon to leave before closing it and sitting back down. The silence of the room fell upon him and served to amplify the enormity of the events of the evening. His failure to trick Lathashal and the mocking laughter of the man were haunting his thoughts. Only the timely interjection of others had saved him.

He thought back to Illestrael. The Yhordi gave her life for him because she believed he could save her people. His attack on Lathashal proved that he would do it for his own people. Would he have done the same for the outsiders in his own land?

He looked around the lab. The staff and manasphere stood out like ominous spectres. Both were too powerful to be approached by anyone of lesser power than their owner. He thought about picking up the staff without touching the thrinium plates that connected to the embedded manasphere. A shiver ran through him at the thought of the demon that dwelled within.

Chayne's own manasphere then came to mind and the little demon that helped him. He remembered the agreement he'd made, but doubted that the creature was still alive. He walked over to his orb and placed a palm down upon its surface. His consciousness dived down into the orb. He felt no presence of the demon.

'Zystal?'

There was a distant whimper.

'Zystal, it's Master,' called out Chayne louder, relieved to hear it.

'*Cruel Master, tricked Zystal. It huuurts,*' came a broken voice from somewhere out in the dark.

'That was not me. I was tricked by an evil Master.'

'*Masters, all evil,*' replied Zystal wretchedly.

'No Zystal, I am sorry I could not stop it. Evil Master almost killed me too.'

'*Master sorry?*' said the creature, some of its pitiful complaining replaced with curiosity.

'Yes, very sorry. I did not mean you to come to harm.'

'*Other Master sent terrible Glzatcherous to hurt Zystal.*'

'I know,' replied Chayne, guiltily.

From out of the dark, Chayne could hear a strange sliding sound. He conjured a dim light so as not to upset the demon. What he saw made him gasp.

'Zystal!'

The creature, although almost certainly able to float to him in this place, choose to approach in a manner that reflected his condition the most. He was horribly mutilated. His skin was torn and hanging from its bones. He was misshapen indicating that several of those bones were twisted and broken. Chayne had never seen such a shocking sight of suffering.

The demon dropped his head.

'Zystal's look displeases Master. I go back to darkness.' The demon began to turn.

'Zystal, wait!' insisted Chayne. He remembered the first time he'd entered the orb when he fought a battle of wills with the little demon and only just escaped with his life. At one point he tried to dispel the thought of the creature, thinking it was only a manifestation of his mind. It recoiled as if in pain. Perhaps if he thought the opposite he might be able to reverse the pain.

He started to concentrate, thinking positive thoughts about it and strengthening his belief in the creature. Instantly the injuries to the demon began to repair. A few times the thing cried out, thinking it was being punished again, but slowly the damage began to disappear. The demon's superficial wounds were healed. Some of the distortion in the creatures frame was also recovered.

Chayne stopped. After the effort of his attack on Lathashal, he could do no more.

'*Master has healed Zystal,*' said the demon in disbelief.

'Yes. I did not mean for harm to come to you, and so I help.'

The thing looked up at Chayne and blinked its beady eyes, as if trying to grasp the concept.

'*Help Zystal?*'

'That's right,' replied Chayne, almost laughing that the creature had no real understanding of such an action. He then watched as it attempted to reflect the grin on his own face. The muscles required were new to it and they twitched and struggled to move into position. The result was a manic look of teeth and wide eyes.

'And now I will keep my promise and return you home.'

The little creature looked up again.

'*No.*'

Chayne smiled once more. 'I keep my promises, Zystal. You are going home.'

'*No!*' came the reply more forcefully. '*Zystal, not want to go home. Zystal want to stay with the helping Master.*'

Chayne stood confused for a moment. 'But you can go home. It is what you wanted. You even tried to kill me to get home.'

The demon became agitated. '*Zystal is ... sorry, Master,*' it replied. '*Zystal now stay with the Master and help him. Catch more magic than ever before!*' it said eagerly. '*Secrets of demons will become his. Master will become powerful.*'

Chayne looked on bewildered and wondered if the little creature would ever cease to amaze him. 'Are you sure that is what you want?'

'*Zystal is sure. Nobody ever sorry for Zystal before. Only try and hurt Zystal.*'

'Very well,' replied Chayne, unsure what he was going to do with the demon. 'Zystal will stay, and Master will look after him.'

'*Yes!*' replied the demon so explosively that is caused him to do a complete head-over-heels somersault. It then bounced off happily into the darkness, occasionally yelping at the pain such an action caused.

Chayne returned to his body.

Back in the lab, he dropped the orb to its lowered position and locked the lid of its container. He sat staring at his surroundings. Life just wasn't going to be the same again. No volatile but brilliant Lathashal. No playful, resourceful Illestrael.

His baptism of fire in his short time in Ashnoria had made him mature more than his entire life to that point.

He decided to walk down to Lathashal's main lab, *his* lab now he realised. He knew that such a situation would not remain for long. His position as a Zintar to such a powerful Master would quickly be taken from him. He already decided he would surrender the title as quickly as possible. But that in itself provided possibilities. He knew that negotiation was a way of life here. He would trade the position, and he knew what for.

He stopped his contemplation, picking up his manasphere as he went to leave the room. There was a crash from behind him in the direction of the secret door. Spinning around he went to call out to the guard. On the floor was a broken alchemy jar.

He looked to the bench that had contained the item. What he saw surprised him beyond anything that he had encountered since arriving in this land.

It had fiery orange fur.

It meowed.

Chapter 38 - Heading home

Garamon stood in a clearing halfway up the mountains and took one last look back across the manmade desert in the direction of the city of Straslin. The Ashnorian surgeon was true to his word. Once the Lan-Chi released them using the fake ambush, they successfully escaped across the sandy landscape. Only one patrol came close to spotting them. They ducked low and made themselves as inconspicuous as possible. The patrol, easily within sight, rode past.

The barbarians departed at the forest tree line with Kinfular and Falakar on good terms, agreeing that the coming threat was best met with an alliance between their two peoples. To that end they would attempt to convince their leaders of the same. Garamon said his goodbyes, especially to the barbarian woman and the big man, Sholster. The latter lifted him from the ground to give him a rib-crushing hug. He would miss him the most.

He thought again of his friend for whom he risked so much and felt his loneliness as if it was his own. He hoped they would both live long enough to see each other again. It then came to him about Chantel. He'd forgotten to tell Chayne of the cat. He wondered how that could have happened.

A hand was placed on his shoulder.

'We must continue,' said Falakar kindly.

Garamon nodded.

With a final look to the south, he turned away to follow the two brothers. They were jogging over fallen branches and avoiding the deeper piles of pine needles as they made their way together up the beginnings of the mountain rise.

He didn't think they looked so different now.

Kinfular called for their first rest. They parted from the Mlendrians several hours ago. He looked across to Shinlay who was stretching her muscles.

Sholster saw the look on his leader's face.

'Fresh water nearby!' he called out to them all. 'Throw me your skins and I'll put something decent to drink in them. The water we were given by those Ashnorian dung-heads tastes as if it's been strained through a bull's testicles!'

Kinfular rummaged through his pack until he found his water skin and threw it over to the large barbarian. Shinlay did the same.

'Whoa, Nightface!' ordered Sholster to ThreeSwords, his hand up. 'You wouldn't let a man go out of sight on his own in such a hostile wilderness?'

ThreeSwords looked around perplexed. 'You have no need of me for such an errand. You are by far the most dangerous thing around.'

'But what if I slide on the rocks at the water's edge!' argued Sholster. 'I could slip in head first and crack my skull and drown. You would feel pretty sorry then, eh?'

ThreeSwords shook his head in bewilderment. 'If you fell into the river, it would be the rocks that would crack.'

Sholster didn't budge.

ThreeSwords gave in and joined the man. As they headed off, Sholster began to engage the Heslarian with some senseless rambling over the differences in taste between white and brown meat.

Kinfular watched the two men disappear. He took the opportunity provided and walked over to his mate.

'I thought I lost you,' he said gently.

'And I you,' she replied, turning to him.

'But I was not injured,' he replied.

'You are more than flesh and bone, Kin,' she softly rebuked.

They both glanced down at their feet, not able to keep the other's gaze.

'Your attack on the bandit camp without my help was not our way.'

He looked uncomfortable at the memory. 'My grief at the loss of so many of my men to the bandits was difficult. I had never suffered such a defeat. Also the guilt and sorrow at the loss of Grast and Rainen was almost too much to bear. I felt that Rolk should claim me. I gave him his chance, but he was not ready for me. I now know that I must carry the burden. This I now do.'

'Maybe it was Rolk's will,' she considered. 'For if you turned back from the pass we would not have met the woodsman and the Ranger that led us to stopping the mage and delaying the war. It is possible that it will save the enslavement of our people.'

'Then I wish it could have been done without the loss of so many good men,' relied Kinfular, heavily.

'It seems the way of gods to need sacrifices for their intervention.'

'Then let us hope He is sated, for I could not carry the loss of any of you three upon my soul.'

Another silence fell between them.

'What will happen to me upon my return?' said Shinlay, changing from the morbid memory.

'Nothing will be as it was,' he replied. 'War is coming to the Riaan, and all the tribes. We must convince your father and the other leaders to unite and help the Mlendrians to fight this Empire.'

'And me,' she said timidly.

'You must make amends with your father.'

'Will he understand?'

'Of that I have no doubt. But you have placed him in a vulnerable position at a time when his leadership is already being pressured by Baltrac. The man will not miss the opportunity to use your rashness to prove Ultal's inability to control his own daughter, let alone the tribe. I only hope that any advantage Baltrac attempts to gain from your dissent is overshadowed by our return with such vital information and our call to arms.'

'And what of us?' she continued, almost afraid of the answer.

'You will continue to be my mate until such time as I release you. However, I may be forced to do so by the elders. If you cannot justify your actions sufficiently to them, then you will be disgraced and will no longer be suitable as a companion for a Hlenshar.'

Shinlay, although hurt to be spoken to so formally, felt strengthened by the authority that had returned to Kinfular once more.

'It shall be as you command, my love.'

The distant echoes of Sholster's unrelenting diatribe fell upon them again as the heads of the other two warriors appeared bobbing along the path up from the stream.

Shinlay and Kinfular returned to their preparations for the next stage of their journey home.